# THE UNNAMED

## By

## Holly Campbell

This book is a work of fiction. All names, characters, places, and events are either the product of the author or used in a fictitious manner. Any resemblance to actual persons, living or dead is purely coincidental.

*For Jess and April*
*Thank you for helping me channel my insanity and create something*
*from the darkness within.*

Through the eyes of the innocent, he will be seen,

And through their fear, he will be made flesh.

When he walks amongst the living,

The children of Eve will weep,

For the blood of their purity will fall.

The sun was setting, painting the sky with shades of scarlet. A lone crow skimmed the treetops, the bare branches reaching up like skeletal arms. The trees thinned and gave way to a large clearing, a sea of green that turned to blue as the grass merged with the lake edge. A single gnarled trunk was balanced precariously at the waterside, leaning over the edge with roots protruding from the uneven ground. At the base of the tree, where the grass grew thickest, a splash of white broke the green.

The crow perched on a branch and cocked its head to the side, eyes fixing on the thing in the grass. After a moment of wary regard, the bird swooped down and landed about a foot from the object.

Disguised by the grass and splattered with thick mud, a passer-by could have been forgiven for not noticing or realising exactly what lay beneath the tree, but at closer inspection it became undeniable. A pale tangle of limbs, an emaciated frame, a mess of dark hair.

She was naked, her body a twisted misshapen thing, stunted in growth and dangerously thin. The body was curled into the foetal position, arms wrapped around herself. Her stomach and breasts were swollen, a gross distortion on her tiny frame. Her hair was matted and thick with mud, leaves, twigs and other debris, her nails ragged and encrusted with filth. Her skin was waxy and eerily pale, almost translucent, except for her veins which were pitch black like someone had spilt ink on her body. Streaks of blood and a tapestry of bruises were visible across her skin between the patches of mud, leaving barely a shred of her form unmarked in some way. Her feet were sliced to ribbons, the skin shredded to a bloody pulp by the rough ground she'd crossed. Her eyes were open, staring up vacantly at the darkening sky. There was a peculiar lifeless quality about her. She resembled a broken doll, discarded haphazardly, twisted and battered beyond repair.

The crow pecked at the girl and she let out a weak groan but made no move to defend herself. The crow hopped closer, probing with claws and beak, trying to determine if this girl represented foe or food.

The blood was thickest on her left leg; an open wound, still fresh, a mess of torn flesh and crimson liquid in various stages of coagulation. Each tiny movement the girl made agitated the injury and sent fresh rivulets of blood running down her leg, disappearing into the ground beneath her.

The crow pecked, more aggressively this time, at the injury. The girl whimpered, her leg jerking spasmodically. She was too weak to fight, but she shifted position slightly in an attempt to scare the bird away as best she could. When this didn't work, she settled for sheltering her fragile body, attempting to minimise the damage.

The crow let out an angry caw and jabbed at her leg persistently, snapping at the flesh. Its wings fluttered furiously as it scrabbled, hungry and eager. The girl's fingers clawed at the dirt, her glassy eyes staring up at the darkening sky. Unable to do anything but lay there as the scavenger began to feast, the girl longed for the numbness that had taken hold of her fingers and toes hours before to spread and spare her the pain.

A twig snapped and the sound of laughter floated across the clearing. Two figures pushed their way through the undergrowth and stumbled away from the treeline. The crow took off, startled by the sudden intrusion. The girl turned her head slightly, eyes coming to rest on the strangers. They were little more than silhouettes, barely visible in the dying light. Their voices carried on the air to the girl, light and completely at ease. They were dressed relatively lightly for the season and the taller of the two, a young man of eighteen, had a beer bottle in one hand. He took a gulp of the liquid and tossed the bottle into the water before turning to his companion, reaching over and pulling her in. She giggled softly and stepped back, skirting passed his fingertips. Her actions were playful, teasing. He laughed and wrapped his arms around her.

The girl on the ground let out a soft groan, the sight of people stirring something inside of her, a need to fight or flee.

The couple moved through the clearing, reaching the tree. The boy pushed her against the trunk and pressed himself against her, lowering his face to meet hers and locking her in a passionate kiss. Her arms wrapped him, merging their silhouettes into one.

The girl at the water stirred at the sounds. Her lips parted and she let out a strangled groan, body jerking slightly as she tried to sit up before slumping back into the dirt as her strength eluded her.

The couple by the tree continued, unaware of the voyeur to their tryst. The young man's hand slipped under her top and groped her roughly before beginning to descend down her sides.

12

"No... not here... it's freezing and muddy..."

"I'll keep you warm, I promise."

His hands continued their path, his lips moving to her throat. She made a noise and turned her head away from his searching lips, her own hands going to restrain his wrists. He ignored her, his other hand fiddling with the button of her jeans.

"No... Kaleb I don't want to..."

"Come on, Beth."

"No, quit it."

Reluctantly, the boy's hands returned to her waist, their voices fading as they locked lips once more.

Numb fingers grasped hold of the tree, the rough bark leaving little impression on the frost stricken digits. The weakened girl tried to drag herself upright, the proximity to the couple driving her to fight the gaping blackness that lingered at the edge of her mind, threatening to engulf her. The couple, wrapped up in their own activities, failed to notice the movement. Only the sound, the faint rustling of grass and leaves amongst the tree roots, registered to them but went disregarded.

Reaching out to pull herself forward, her fingers brushed against the exposed ankle of the standing girl. Both of them recoiled automatically at the contact, the standing girl stumbling back slightly in startled confusion.

"What is it?" the boy asked.

"Something... something touched my leg."

"Oh come on, don't be ridiculous."

Disregarding her concerns, the boy began to kiss and caress his girlfriend once more, as she shifted uncertainly. Despite being able to see no sign of anything around her, she couldn't help but feel uneasy, as though she was being watched. Her focus quickly diverted when his hands once again returned to her jeans.

"Kaleb..."

Her pleas started weakly and grew more insistent as his hands pursued their target, unfaltering.

"I said stop!"

She gave him a hard shove, pushing him away from her and distancing herself from the tree.

"Seriously? I'm just having a bit of fun."

He made as if to follow her. She took a few more steps, moving towards the water's edge. The girl beneath the tree twitched, as she tried to summon the will to lift her fading body and call out to the couple.

"Well it's not fun for me, okay? Let's just go back to the others."

"Fine, if you're going to be a bitch about it."

He rolled his eyes, reaching out and touched her hand, in an attempt to placate her. She jerked back, her shoe catching in the soft mud at the edge of the lake and sending her stumbling forward. She fell, landing inches from the figure in the grass. Her fingers collided with the cold flesh, a disturbing realisation settling on her as she registered the out of place texture. She let out a short cry and pulled back, scrabbling to her feet.

"What's wrong?"

"I... I don't know..." Her eyes searched the ground, her hand fumbling at her pocket for her phone. She pressed a button, illuminating the screen and casting the area in a muted light tinged with blue. The light seemed to reflect off the naked girl's skin, her body almost glowing and making her seem even more unnatural. She cringed backwards away from the light as if she had been burned and cowered against the trunk, whimpering softly.

"Holy shit..."

The young man moved to get a closer look and after a whimpered plea, his friend followed him. He knelt down and touched the girl's arm.

"Don't touch her... this is just... we can call the police and let them deal with it."

The young woman reached out to touch him, to tap him on the shoulder and try to draw him away from the girl in the grass. The girl let out a rasping sob and her hand clamped onto the young woman's leg, leaving behind a distinct imprint of bloody fingerprints. The girlfriend screamed and the man jerked back in surprise, getting to his feet and retreating from the body. The girl let out a low groan, her arm going limp once again, her eyes rolling back in her head as the pain, the blood loss and the exertion of her movements became too much for her.

"We need to call the police…"

The branches of the tree stirred although the air remained still. The sun had disappeared entirely and the darkness seemed to be gathering around them. The man looked around, his façade of relative nonchalance dropping and fear began to show on his face. He pulled his friend close to him, wrapping a protective and restraining arm around her. When he next spoke, his voice was hushed and unsteady as he tried to mask his growing nerves.

"We need to get out of here."

The boy grabbed his girlfriend's hand, attempting to pull her away.

"We can't leave her! She needs our help!"

"You know we're not meant to be out here. If we call the police, we'll get in deep shit for breaking curfew."

"She'll die if we don't!" His friend said, staring at him in disbelief at his callousness.

"We'll make an anonymous call, like they do in the movies, as soon as we get out of here but *we have to go*!" His tone was firm and left no room for negotiation.

He grabbed her wrist and pulled her away. She resisted weakly before conceding, unwilling to remain there alone, and she let him drag her away from the body. The girl watched them with vacant eyes and she let out a weak noise that, had she been able to form coherent words, would have been a cry of protest, pleading for them to return and help her.

The young woman bit her lip as she walked, conflicted between her desire to help and her mounting fear. She looked back, unable to see the unconscious girl in the darkness but knowing she was there, lost in the shadows. She felt terrible, wanting to turn back, to do something but she didn't, choosing instead to turn her head away once more and look

15

firmly ahead. They retreated into the trees, the image of the girl burned firmly into both of their minds.

The clearing was silent once again, the water still and mirror-smooth, reflecting the starless sky. After a moment, the crow returned, descending from the trees to perch beside the girl's head. Two more followed in quick succession, settling around her, then more. They hopped forward, gathering closer until they formed a loose ring around the girl.

For a moment, nothing moved. The girl lay, corpselike, before them as they regarded her. Her chest rose and fell erratically, stilling for minutes at a time before she would let out a single rasping breath.

When they moved, they moved as one, swarming over her body until they were indistinguishable from each other, forming a single heaving mass of endless black feathers.

# Police Report

**Case No**: 07-1-00036-8

**Date:** April 19th

**Reporting Officer:** Fraser, Jack

**Prepared by:** Fisher, Marisse

**Incident:** Missing child reported

## Details of Event:

At approximately 07:12 am I, Officer Jack Fraser, and Officer Peter Brennan responded to a call from Mrs Evelyn Knight reporting the disappearance of her eldest child. The child in question is female, four years of age.

When we arrived at 12 Ash Street, Mrs Knight showed me to the child's room while Officer Brennan recorded a statement from the father, Dr Richard Knight (attached). The child was last seen at 22:35 pm the previous evening when Dr Knight checked on them before retiring for the evening. The younger child, [female, two years of age] was undisturbed during the time and was still in the shared bedroom upon Mrs Knight entering the room at 06:30 am. After failing to locate the older child, Mrs Knight reported the absence. Between 22:35 pm and 06:30 am the couple reported hearing no sounds of a struggle or anything to cause alarm.

Further investigation found no sign of forced entry, however, the gate to the backyard was discovered to be unlocked and the family dog was found deceased in kennel. Veterinary reports to follow.

## Action Taken:

Officer Brennan and I approached residents of the street for possible witnesses. Statements from both parents were collected.

## Summary:

Preliminary investigation shows no clear signs of abduction, however, given the victim's age a runaway situation is unlikely. Further details needed.

# I

"In local news, citizens of Redwood have been petitioning against the release of a convicted felon, Russell Alexander. Alexander was an illegal trader of rare and exotic wildlife who came to the attention of law enforcement ten years ago after one of his snakes escaped, resulting in the death of his wife and two of his three children. Alexander is serving a twenty-five-year sentence however he is currently being considered for parole, outraging locals who have labelled him a menace to the community."

Jamie Harper flicked through the channels, pausing only briefly to take in the images on the screen before moving on. The room was dark, except for the glow of the television which illuminated the teenager. His hair was mussed, sticking up in an unwieldy manner from where he had raked his fingers through the strands. He was dressed in a vest top and faded pyjama bottoms, dark blue adorned with crudely drawn cartoon mice playing the guitar. The trousers were old, frayed at the ankles and several inches too short in the leg.

He rested his head against the back of the sofa, curling one leg around him. He settled on a program, watching the colours and movement on the screen with little interest. The dark circles under his eyes were deeply ingrained from countless sleepless nights, his body lethargic but somehow still possessing a tension to it that never truly disappeared. Despite the television, he had an iPod beside him, resting on the sofa arm, with one earbud in, filling his brain with strains of guitar music. A dog, a red and brown Akita, was nestled on the sofa beside him, head resting on his front paws.

The light turned on sharply and Jamie recoiled, shielding his eyes. His father, fully dressed in his work clothes, was in the doorway. He gave his son a sympathetic smile when he saw him sitting there.

"Can't sleep?" Jamie shook his head. "Nightmares again?"

His son's eyes flickered over to him for the briefest of seconds and he shrugged his shoulders ever so slightly, just enough to show an acknowledgement of the question.

"Jay…?"

"Yes. But… it's fine."

"If you're struggling again-"

"I'm fine," Jamie cut in. "Really. Just… one too many horror movies before bed."

He looked over at his dad once again, making an effort not to look away. They regarded one another, both aware of the lie but unwilling to acknowledge it. Eventually, his father nodded and headed over to the coat hook by the front door.

"Someone died?" Jamie asked as his dad shrugged on his jacket. His voice was light and teasing but there was a slight, barely detectable undercurrent to it.

"Too early to say. There was a call about something in the woods. Probably some kids playing pranks but I've got to go check it out. You didn't see anything while you were out there did you?"

"No… can't say I did."

"Alright…" As he spoke, his hand went to his belt and gun, running his fingers over it briefly as if to confirm its presence. Satisfied, he opened the front door but paused, looking back at Jamie as the cold night air swirled around them, dropping the temperature in the room instantly.

"Try and get some more sleep tonight, okay?"

"I'll do my best"

His dad nodded and headed out. Jamie watched from the corner of his eye, his fingers idly tracing patterns on the fabric of the sofa. Through the window, he could see the front drive and the police cruiser pulling away. He doubted he'd be gone long; nothing ever really happened in the town. Then again, the woods which surrounded Sarum Vale on all sides were a different story entirely. There were plenty of rumours flying around about things happening in the trees. Everyone had at least one story of a friend of a friend who had seen something or knew someone that had gone in and never come out. Jamie had always thought the stories were bullshit. He'd been in the woods plenty of times, hunting with his dad and uncle, and he'd never seen anything.

He closed his eyes, the light beginning to agitate them. He knew he should go to his room before his dad got back, that was the best way to avoid concerned questions, but he couldn't summon the energy to move.

His hand found his iPod and his fingers ran over the buttons, moving out of memory and practice, as he switched to a familiar track. He picked up the other earbud, which was dangling against his chest, and put it in. Soft piano filled his ears, the soothing rhythm one he knew by heart. His fingers twitched in time, striking invisible keys in an act that he had repeated so many times before that it required little to no thought at this point, it was more like instinct.

The dog whined softly, gently nudging Jamie's hand with his nose. The boy opened his eyes and looked down at the animal, who looked back at him with sad eyes. Jamie wasn't sure if his pet could actually sense his mood, but he certainly behaved like he could.

The TV had switched to a nature documentary. On-screen, a wasp was laying its egg on another insect while a calm narrator described the scene. Jamie switched it off, feeling nauseous. He tucked the iPod into his pocket, stretched and got to his feet, the dog immediately rising beside him. The two of them headed out of the living room, switching off the light on the way. The hall was dark and silent, only a few patches of light shining through the windows from the streetlamp outside. The stairs disappeared into the blackness of the floor above. Jamie continued up, footsteps almost silent on the steps although there was really no need. His mother was working the night shift and, with his father gone, that just left him and his sister in the house.

He paused outside her door, left ajar as always, and peeked in. He could just make out her form, curled up under the blankets in her narrow bed, a stuffed animal under each arm. He smiled slightly to himself and continued down the hall to his room.

The room was spacious and tidy, wooden floorboards with scattered mismatched rugs, the walls painted a light grey, spotted with a few scant movie posters and faded photographs. The furniture was minimal, a mixture of second-hand items made of natural and whitewashed oak. Everything seemed to have a worn quality to it, giving the room a homely, lived-in atmosphere. A frayed patchwork blanket was draped across the foot of the bed, a stack of tattered paperbacks on the bedside table and a lumpy, threadbare pet bed tucked in one corner.

The dog brushed against his leg, wandering in ahead of him, before making himself comfortable in his basket. Jamie left the main light off and went to his desk. It was messy, crumpled pieces of paper strewn around, pens and pencils overflowing from multiple mugs, the wood coated with a layer of glue, paint, and ink.

Jamie switched on the desk lamp and retrieved a bulging notebook from the desk drawer. It was old with paper and other items stuck in, the pages curling at the corners from age. He set it down on his desk and began to turn the pages slowly. The writing was neat and had a gentle curl to it. There were drawings, tiny black and white sketches as well as more elaborate watercolours. He sighed and ran his fingers lightly over the paper, feeling the imprint of the pen under his fingertips. He paused on a page with an intricate sketch of a lily, faded but still distinctive. He smiled slightly, his fingers faltering on the edge of the page, reluctant to turn it.

He felt a buzzing sensation in the back of his brain, like a lot of people talking all at once right in his ear. His other hand reached up to run his fingers through his hair, before moving his hand to his throat, gently tracing the shape of a thin scar that descended down the curve of his throat, across his shoulder and disappeared into his shirt. He let go of the book sharply, fishing the iPod from his pocket and turning the volume up until the music was at an almost painful level. He closed his eyes, focusing on his breathing. In his mind, he counted backwards from ten, taking his time with the numbers.

When he reached zero, he opened his eyes once more. The noise in his head had faded a little, to a level where it was bearable. He turned down the iPod volume once again and turned the page. It was blank. So was the next few. When the writing started up once again, the handwriting was different. The pictures were less refined, still talented but lacking the practised precision of the original artist. Jamie sighed softly and flicked through, ignoring the writing itself until he reached the most recent entry.

There was a short piece of writing, accompanied by a drawing. It depicted a pair of eyes, the irises painted a vivid green that seemed to leap off the page. On the next page, a scrap of fabric had been stapled in. It had once been yellow, patterned with tiny daisies, but now it was stained, ragged and muddy. Jamie brushed his fingers over it lightly, frowning to himself. One corner was stiff with a dried rust coloured substance that flaked when it was disturbed.

Outside, an ambulance sped down the road, the harsh flashing lights out of place in the peaceful nighttime surroundings. Jamie lifted his head slightly at the sound of the sirens, reaching over and pulling his curtain ever so slightly to the side so he could peek out. He watched the ambulance, the lights fading into the distance and disappearing from view entirely.

He released the curtain and looked back down at the piece of fabric. He'd found it during his last visit to the woods, on the annual hunting trip. He wasn't sure what exactly it was from or what it meant but he couldn't help but feel that it was something important. It reminded him of the dresses that his little sister wore in the summer, simple patterns and primary colours, but there was something unsettling about it, which he didn't fully understand.

He turned to the next blank page, picked up his pen and held it, poised over the page. He faltered, unable to find the words that he really wanted to write. He sighed and put the pen back down, closing the book. He switched off the desk lamp and went over to the bed. He positioned himself carefully, laying on top of the covers with his arms tight to his sides. The dog rose from his basket and jumped up, laying on his master's feet. Jamie took out his earbuds, carefully wrapping them around the device and tucking them into his bedside drawer. He closed his eyes, rubbing his thumbs back and forth against the bed covers.

He lay there in the cocoon of darkness, trying to switch off his brain and get some sleep. Without the distraction of his near-constant stream of music, he found the silence began to eat away at him. Every minuscule sound seemed amplified. The steady drip of a leaky tap, the noise of cars passing by on the road outside, the creak of floorboards as the house settled around him. It built into an endless assault on his ears, a cacophony of noises around him.

He dug his fingers into the bedding beneath him. His skin itched and burned with chills spreading through him all at once. Every spring in the mattress seemed to have uprooted itself for the sole purpose of driving itself into his back. He gritted his teeth, willing himself to sleep, knowing even as he did that it would not offer an escape but merely a different kind of torment.

Jamie sighed and opened his eyes. He glared at the ceiling, feeling momentarily envious and resentful of his younger sister, sleeping peacefully down the hall. The shadows danced overhead, the streetlamp outside casting enough light to form a playground for them to romp through. They crawled and crept like insects, expanding and shrinking, advancing and retreating all at once. Jamie watched the interplay of light and darkness with mild fascination. Gradually, the noises that had been drowning him seemed to fade into the background and were eventually replaced by silence. He let his body relax, his breathing slowing. The darkness in the room seemed to thicken, growing even blacker and imperceptible.

He accepted the embrace of the darkness willingly and slowly slipped into a state of oblivion. Had anyone been observing the boy, they would have seen the tension which usually graced Jamie's face fade away. He seemed to slip back in years, with the stress in his features gone he looked far younger and more vulnerable than he was. Above him, the shadows seemed to gather and a sound like many people whispering together all at once filled the room.

The sound grew louder before fading away almost entirely, then peaking once more. It was like the ebb and flow of water lapping at a shore, a sound that was somewhat soothing if a little eerie.

Half an hour passed with only the sound of the whispering. Jamie lay in his bed, barely moving save for the soft rise and fall of his chest. Through the window, the sound of the ambulance making its way back drifted in. The whispering stopped abruptly, as though the shadows themselves were listening to the noise. Jamie let out a quiet groan, the sound of the sirens filtering through his ears and into his unconscious mind. At first, nothing happened. He fell as still and as quiet as before.

Jamie's nose twitched. Whether real or imaginary, he wasn't sure but there, unmistakably, was the smell of bleach. The acrid smell pervaded his nostrils, accompanied by the far fainter, musty smell of damp sawdust.

He wrinkled his nose and clenched his fists, fingers tangling amongst the covers. He groaned again. His body seemed to stiffen, trembling with exertion as he tried to move but found himself locked in place. The whispering began again, louder and more insistent than before. The dog lifted his head and whimpered, ears twitching to catch the sounds and eyes tracking something unseen across the ceiling.

Jamie's body vaulted up sharply, his back arching off the bed. The dog yelped, sprinting to cower beneath his desk. The boy let out a strangled groan, thrashing wildly. Hot tears ran down his cheeks and mixed with a few beads of blood that had begun to flow from his right nostril. One of his hands released the duvet, reaching up to fend off an invisible attacker, the other went to his throat as a terrible choking noise wracked his body. His breathing was frantic, interrupted only by his cries of distress. He writhed on the bed, body jerking randomly, twisting into bizarre painful contortions. He clawed at his skin, nails repeatedly raking against flesh until it tore and began to bleed. He rolled over, squirming away from the monsters inside his head, and crashed to the floor.

His eyes opened and for a moment he lay there, halfway between asleep and awake. The cobwebs of his nightmare clung to the edge of his vision, mingling delirium and reality into a confusing haze. Gradually the phantoms faded and the world seemed to stabilise around him. He ran his fingers through his hair, matted and soaked through with sweat. He felt exhausted, like every scrap of energy had been sapped from his body.

He sat up slowly. The world swam around him as he stumbled to his feet, clasping the edge of the bed for support. He steadied himself, waiting for a moment while his bedroom stilled and he regained his balance. Once he was satisfied that he wasn't going to keel over, Jamie headed into his bathroom. He stood in front of the mirror, bracing himself against the sink. His skin was pale as bone, glistening with a sheen of sweat. Streaks of blood marked his arms and bruises had already begun to blossom where his body had collided with the bed frame. His hands, knuckles white with the strain of his grip on the porcelain, were trembling and no matter how hard he tried to still them, the shaking only seemed to intensify.

Jamie's eyes left his reflection and came to rest on a pot of pills, his name printed on the side. He felt the familiar temptation, the desire to sleep growing stronger with every moment that past. But despite the urge, the need to sleep, the fear of what would be waiting for him was stronger and he turned his head away. Instead, he picked up a washcloth, soaked it under the tap and proceeded to slowly and methodically scrub his arms free of blood.

When he had removed every speck, he rinsed out the cloth until the water ran clear. His parents were aware of his nightmares, but only Jamie knew the extent of their damage and the lengths he went to in order to keep it that way. He checked his clothes for anything that could give him away and wiped the sink clear of any trace of the watery pale pink residue that so often clung to the basin after his wash. Once he was satisfied, he returned to the bed and seated himself. He closed his eyes, not in an attempt to sleep but in an effort to isolate himself from the world for a moment or two.

He lightly skimmed his fingers along the length of his right arm, feeling the bumps and valleys, the crease of skin, the tiny ridges of his veins and the layers of faded scar tissue that congregated around his wrist. Touch. The one sense he could control, which couldn't lie or deceive. It ground him within himself and, just for a moment, there was nothing but his body and the mattress beneath him.

His phone buzzed on the bedside table. Jamie reached for it, eyes still closed as he attempted to prolong his moment of clarity. It was only when his fingers clasped hold of the device that he reluctantly opened them. A text from his dad lit up the screen. He sighed softly and tossed it onto the bed. He wondered what had happened to delay his dad's return home. He couldn't imagine it was anything serious, not in Sarum Vale.

He lay back, rolling onto his side so he was facing the desk. The journal lay open, the pages rustling slightly as though stirred by the breeze. Jamie frowned, eyes moving to the window. It was firmly closed, the latch in place. There wasn't even the slightest gap to allow a breeze through.

Jamie got up slowly and moved, somewhat apprehensively, over to the desk. The pages continued to rustle and sway in the non-existent wind until he reached out and placed his hand on the edge of the paper, stilling it. It lay open on a blank page, or what had once been blank at least. A large black mark had spread across the paper like someone had spilt ink onto the book. As he watched, the stain continued to seep across the page but when he skimmed his fingers over the mark, they came back dry.

He stared at the book in confusion, unsure of what to do with it. It couldn't be real, he told himself, it was a trick of the light. But as he stared at the page, he found himself feeling more and more uncomfortable. He wanted to close it but at the same time, he didn't like to touch it more than he had to. Despite the strange liquid not leaving any remnants on his fingers, he couldn't help but anticipate moisture. He hesitantly turned to the page before, curious to see if the mark had

25

soaked through but the paper on the other side was pristine. He felt deeply uncomfortable and was tempted to tear the page out. He knew the mark shouldn't upset him as much as it did, but just looking at it made his skin prickle.

The pages flipped suddenly, back and forth as though someone was aggressively flicking through them. The abrupt motion of the book caused the paper to slice across Jamie's hand. He recoiled, hissing slightly, lifting his hand to examine it in the moonlight. A thin cut ran across the centre of his hand, a single bead of blood bubbled up and ran down his little finger, dripping onto the journal. Despite how ridiculous he knew it was, he couldn't help but feel like the movement had been… intentional?

No. It wasn't real, it was just… his mind playing up from lack of sleep. Yes, that was it. He couldn't let it get to him.

He moved quickly, grabbing the book and closing it sharply. He carried it, clasping it in a way reminiscent of someone holding something disgusting, at arm's length and with as little contact as was possible over to his wardrobe. He knelt down and felt for the loose board, prising it up so he could slide the journal into the gap beneath. He released it gratefully and pushed the board down hard, sealing the journal away. Jamie closed the door and sat on the floor, resting his back against the wardrobe door. He ran his fingers through his hair and rubbed his wrist anxiously, feeling the rough scarred skin.

The dog came out from under the desk and nuzzled against Jamie lightly, whimpering softly. The boy lifted his head slightly and looked at the dog. He gently fondled his pet's ears.

"I'm not crazy," he said softly. "It's not like last time, it's just lack of sleep… it has to be. Right?"

He looked into his pet's eyes, like the animal would know what he was saying and be able to reassure him that everything was okay, but of course, he couldn't. Instead, Jamie sat in silence, stroking the dog's fur and staring numbly out of the window.

# REPORT OF INVESTIGATION BY COUNTY MEDICAL EXAMINER

DECEDENT: Lily Isabelle Alexander     RACE: Caucasian     SEX: Female     AGE: Sixteen

HOME ADDRESS: 12 Robin Way, Redwood     OCCUPATION: N/A

TYPE OF DEATH: Found Dead

COMMENT: Police called to the household by neighbour following a noise complaint. The decedent was found in the basement of the property along with a large number of reptiles. Mother and brother were found deceased in an upstairs bedroom. Younger brother found unconscious in a chest freezer in the basement.

IF MOTOR VEHICLE ACCIDENT INDICATE DRIVER/PASSENGER/PEDESTRIAN/UNKNOWN: N/A

NOTIFICATION BY: Margaret Lewisham     ADDRESS: 10 Robin Way, Redwood

INVESTIGATING AGENCY: Redwood Police Department

## DESCRIPTION OF BODY

CLOTHED/UNCLOTHED/PARTIAL: Clothed

EYES: Blue     HAIR: Blonde     MOUSTACHE: N/A     BEARD: N/A
WEIGHT: 122 IBs     LENGTH: 5ft. 4in     BODY TEMP: 65 degrees Fahrenheit

DATE AND TIME: January 9th, 15:31 pm

RIGOUR: Yes     LYSED: Yes

## MARKS AND WOUNDS

The decedent has notable bruises to left wrist and abdomen. Wound on the temple, minimal sign of healing. Scar noted on right shoulder. Dual puncture marks on ankle, inflammation and bruising around entry sites.

The decedent has no birthmarks or tattoos.

## ADDITIONAL NOTES

27

High levels of neurotoxin in bloodstream along with abnormal amounts of mycotoxins. Autopsy revealed decedent was in the early stages of pregnancy.

## PROBABLE CAUSE OF DEATH

Neurotoxin in bloodstream and puncture marks are consistent with a snake bite, as proposed by the police investigation. Head wound suggests blunt force trauma.

## MANNER OF DEATH

Unable to determine whether accidental or homicide. Blunt force trauma wound possible attempt to subdue decedent before snake was released but no way to confirm.

I hereby declare that the information contained herein regarding the death described is true and correct to the best of my knowledge.

Examination performed January 9th at Redwood Memorial Hospital by K. Mortimer

# II

The gurney was pushed down the corridor, the wheels squeaking on the tiled floor. A cluster of doctors pursued it, examining the girl as she was wheeled across the ward. They steered her into a vacant room and loaded her onto the empty bed. Her eyes were closed now, the congealed blood on her leg had split open and was flowing again. Her breathing was frantic, coming in short audible pants that shook her entire body. Her bare form seemed more grotesque under the harsh strip lighting. Her body seemed even paler, luminescent almost, and a number of faded scars could now be seen, dotted along her arms and torso before growing more numerous as they descended down her thighs. Her limbs were out of proportion; her distended, swollen stomach looked out of place on her fragile waif-like frame. She let out an incoherent groan, struggling to force her eyes open. Someone placed a hand on her arm, trying to calm her, as another doctor attached an IV drip. A mixture of sedatives and painkillers began to pump through her bloodstream, wrapping her in a blanket of numbness and separating her mind from the pain of her broken body.

She fought against the pull of the drugs, trying to cling to consciousness and remain aware of her surroundings. She found herself drifting in a peculiar state of limbo, not really present in the room but still somewhat aware of what was happening to her body as the doctors manipulated her frail form. She tried to resist their touch, wanting to pull away from their invasive hands but her limbs wouldn't cooperate, barely managing an uncoordinated jerk. Her eyelids were prised open and a bright light invaded her field of vision. Her gaze was vacant, her mind shying away from the intrusive noise and light in an effort to shelter her from the potential danger of the unknown. Something dark flickered across the edge of her sight and her body bucked sharply. The doctors struggled to restrain her as her body began to tremble and shake, pulling away from them and whatever unseen monsters plagued her mind. She was barely conscious but with every ounce of her remaining strength, she resisted. She thrashed and clawed at the air, screaming in pain and fear. Every touch sent her recoiling in terror and elicited a fresh flurry of strangled cries from her lips.

Finally, the drugs managed to take hold and, as quickly as it had started, the fight deserted her. She lay still on the bed, body going limp. Her arms fell to her sides and her cries were silenced. Someone spoke but the words they said made no sense to her. She vaguely recognised the sounds but there was no meaning to them. They might well have been speaking another language. The voices drifted in and out of focus, like a radio station being tuned. Through the haze, her eyes half opened, staring into space as the faces moved above her. She managed little more than the occasional twitch. What remained of her resistance was waning, the promise of sweet oblivion tugging at her, drawing her in. How she longed to surrender to it, to finally know some peace. The doctors worked on her, fading in her mind from many to a singular being. There was no longer a distinction between one person and another in her addled mind, they were all one endless entity.

As they worked, her breathing slowed and she fell completely still. The last shreds of her conscious mind slipped into the darkness and any meaning that her surroundings held to her faded away completely. She had no sense of the time that passed, lost in a haze where day and night, hours and minutes blurred into one.

Life continued on around her. The doctors finished their work, her wounds tended to as best they could. The cuts on her feet were cleaned, the bullet wound on her leg was stitched. Her injuries were bandaged and she was carefully tucked under a blanket before the doctors left her to rest and recover. She lay on the bed, lost in a warm cocoon of numbness and tranquillizers.

A young nurse entered the room to change the girl's IV. He paused, looking down at the girl. He'd not been on duty when she arrived but his colleagues had been talking about her arrival. Already word was spreading throughout the staff on the ward of the new patient. The town was small, so most patients brought with them some level of gossip; ordinarily, it was fairly mundane. This was… different. She was by far the most interesting patient that they'd seen in a long time, possibly ever. He'd seen the police officer in the hall, waiting for her to wake up so he could ask her questions (although when the nurse had seen him, the officer seemed more interested in the coffee machine than watching over the injured girl).

He scowled to himself. He'd known what he'd been getting into when he took the job but he did sometimes wish things were a bit more exciting. This would probably be the biggest thing to happen in the hospital for the next decade.

The girl was tucked neatly under her covers, now dotted with specks of dirt that had shaken loose from her body. Her face was peaceful, doll-like, despite the tiny cuts from where the birds had pecked at her. Arms rested at her sides, palms up. The nurse's eyes came to rest on the girl's exposed wrists. A thin scar ran across each wrist. They were pale silver and more delicate than the jagged marks that marked her lower limbs. There was a precision to them that was missing from the others, which held a frantic anger. There was a deliberateness to them. Someone had taken their time with these, ensuring that the damage was deep and efficient.

The nurse's gaze moved from the girl's wrists, drawn to the palm of her left hand. He frowned and reached out to examine it closer, his curiosity getting the better of him. He hesitated, his fingers an inch from the girl's skin. He bit his lip slightly and lifted her hand, bringing it close to his face. A symbol had been cut into the palm of her hand, a circle with a crescent moon shape positioned on top like a set of horns. His eyes widened slightly, his hand trembling a little. He wondered if anyone had noticed these yet. The marks were strange. Like the cuts on her wrist, they were precise and efficient but they were at various stages of healing like the symbol had been done and redone repeatedly as time passed.

As he examined the mark, the scars began to split. It was as though an invisible blade was slicing through the healed flesh. The skin tore and blood bubbled up inky black. He recoiled, dropping her hand hurriedly. The symbol on her hand was entirely ripped open by this point, her peculiar black blood running down her fingers accompanied by a stench of sulphur. There was an oily sheen to the liquid that clung to everything it touched, leaving a slick film on her skin.

The nurse backed away, hurriedly trying to settle on the best course of action. There was something very wrong here and he felt uncomfortable just being in the room. He was seized by an intense urge to get out of the room as fast as he could. He reached over and quickly flipped her hand over so that it was palm down. He looked around, feeling a little guilty. He left her room quickly, closing the door behind him and carefully schooling his features into a calm expression as he tried to rationalise what he'd seen. Scars didn't spontaneously split open... he had probably just aggravated the skin when he'd moved her hand. As

31

for the blood... it was probably the lighting that had made it seem so dark.

He busied himself on the ward, deciding that it was best to just forget what had happened and focus on his work. He moved from room to room trying to absorb himself with the tasks at hand. The nagging sense of wrongness continued to lurk at the back of his mind no matter how hard he tried to ignore it.

The hospital was rarely busy, too small to accommodate anything severe. It was rare for anything outside of the emergency room to be running at full occupancy. Everything was calm and he took his time with his work. He felt a little warm, beads of sweat beginning to form on his forehead. He paused by an open window, letting the afternoon breeze cool him. It was mid-autumn and there was a sharp chill in the air.

He mentally ran through what he had left to do today. He had another hour left of his shift and it was his brother's birthday so he needed to grab a card on his way over to his parent's house for dinner. The shops would probably be closed by the time he finished... He wondered if he could get someone else to cover him so he could slip out a little early. Maybe he could fake sickness and get out of the dinner? Family events were never fun...

He sighed and stepped away from the window, intending to head to the nurses' station. Maybe he could sweet-talk one of the young ladies into helping him out. He was sure he had a few favours he could call in...

He noticed a black mark on his hand. Some of her blood had stained his fingers and the edge of his sleeve. He wiped it absently, without much luck. He frowned and wiped his hand on his trousers more persistently. The blemish remained, clinging stubbornly to his skin.

He diverted from his route and headed to the bathroom to wash his hands. He wasn't sure why it bothered him so much. It wouldn't be the first time a patient had bled on him, it came with the job after all.

He skirted passed the girl's room, wanting to steer clear of her until he'd managed to sufficiently calm his nerves. There was no sign of the police officer that had been lurking before. Dr Knott was stood in her doorway, watching the girl with a peculiar expression. The nurse ducked his head, hoping to avoid any attention. Dr Knott had a reputation amongst the nursing staff that caused them to try and keep out of his way whenever possible.

As he passed by, the doctor lifted his head and fixed the nurse with his intense stare.

"Sam." The word was quiet but commanding and Sam grimaced before fixing a smile on his face and turning to face the doctor.

"Yes, Dr Knott?" He tried to keep his voice light and pleasant, attempting to hide his discomfort.

"You checked in on her, yes?"

"Yes…" He began to feel a nervous sensation forming in the pit of his stomach like it was clenched tight in a clamp that was slowly tightening.

"Did you notice anything… out of the ordinary?"

Sam felt his insides shrivelling up under the doctor's unflinching stare. He tucked his hands behind his back, hiding the mark on his skin. He wondered if he should mention what had happened… but he wasn't entirely convinced he hadn't been hallucinating.

"Sam?"

He realised he'd been staring into space and he blinked, sharply returning to reality.

"No. I… I didn't see anything… vitals were all normal…" He stumbled over the words, his stomach twisting anxiously. Dr Knott regarded him silently for a moment and Sam wasn't sure he'd convinced him. He clenched his fists tight behind his back, digging his nails into the palms of his hands.

"I feel like there's something you're not telling me, Sam."

Sam felt an intense urge to vomit and he bit his lip, trying to suppress it. He took a moment as he tried to work out just what he should say, how much he could reveal without sounding like he had lost his mind.

"Well… I did notice some lacerations on her hand…"

"That's to be expected given that she's been in the woods. Her feet had similar lacerations."

"No, it was like… something had been carved into it…"

"Like what exactly?"

"Like… a cult symbol? Maybe? I'm not sure…" It hadn't been a pentagram or anything like he'd seen in the detective, shows that he liked to watch but he couldn't think of any other reason for a person to cut a symbol into someone's hand. He wasn't sure, the whole situation just made him deeply uncomfortable.

Dr Knott frowned slightly and Sam felt the need to vomit increasing. The doctor laughed suddenly and Sam blinked, slightly shocked by the abrupt change in demeanour.

"A cult? In this town?"

Sam gave a nervous laugh. Now that he'd said it out loud it did sound a little ridiculous. He released his hands, relaxing a little. The nauseous sensation had faded and he felt a little more at ease now. It was like he had confirmation that he was overreacting. The things he'd seen couldn't have been real, his mind was just playing tricks on him.

The doctor turned his attention away from Sam and looked back into the room where the girl was resting. His expression became unreadable once more as he watched the sleeping figure.

"Thank you for mentioning your concerns to me. I'll have a look and if necessary discuss it with the authorities." He glanced at Sam, his gaze going down to Sam's hand which was hanging at his side. Sam quickly tucked it back behind him, looking down at the floor. "You should probably wash that."

Sam nodded hurriedly and went to the staff bathroom. That nervous feeling in his stomach was back. He began to wash his hands thoroughly, coating them with a thick layer of soap before scrubbing at the spot. The mark resisted, remaining where it was. Streaks of colour danced across the droplets as the oily residue mixed with the water. He rinsed his hands off and tried again.

It took three attempts before the spot faded sufficiently, leaving only a faint ring on his skin where it had once been. A drop of water, tinted grey, ran down his fingers and landed in the sink, leaving a slick of oil behind it on the porcelain.

Relieved, he dried off his hands and left the bathroom. He started to make his way towards the nurses' station. One of the patients was due to be discharged and he needed to check her file before he went to see her. He'd not gone more than a few steps when he was hit with a sudden wave of dizziness. He let out a soft groan and paused, steadying himself. He shook himself, cursing himself silently for not eating lunch. He brushed it off and continued on his way.

He grabbed the file and opened it, scanning the details. He was already aware of them but it was always good to get a refresher. The words blurred in front of his eyes, merging into one indistinctive mass. He shook his head and closed his eyes, taking a moment that he hoped would allow him to regain control of his vision and ensure the words made sense once more.

He opened them again and was relieved to see that words had cleared. Maybe he needed to get an eye test or something…

He looked around, hoping no one had seen his momentary lapse. The lights in the ward seemed brighter than usual, hurting his eyes a little whenever he looked towards them. He blinked, disorientated, shying away from the pain.

"Sam!"

Sam lifted his head to see one of the other nurses, one he'd become friends with. He gave her a half-hearted wave. A strange pressure settled on his head like something was pushing down on his brain. It didn't hurt, it just felt strange and uncomfortable, preventing him from thinking clearly.

"Hey Dominique," he managed a weak smile. She frowned, instantly noticing something was wrong with her friend.

"Are you feeling alright? You look a little… out of it?" she asked.

"I'm alright," he said, brushing off her concern.

She reached out to him and touched his cheek, testing his temperature with her hand. Her fingers felt icy to him and he flinched a little. She frowned.

"Sweetie, you're running a little hot. Are you sure you're okay?"

"I'm fine. I just need a little water or something."

Even as he spoke, he felt the pressure in his skull rising to the point where it felt like his brain was being squeezed in a vice.

"You really don't look well…"

Her voice sounded far away, echoing like she was calling to him down a long corridor. Her hand, which was still resting on his arm, went from ice to fire on his skin. He felt chills running down his spine and sweat dripping from his forehead. He pulled away from her sharply, giving her an apologetic grimace before hurrying down the ward and into one of his patient's rooms. He picked the room at random, not really caring which patient it was or if there was anything he needed to do there, he just wanted to get some distance from Dominique's concerned questioning.

He tried to focus and find a task in the room that would explain his presence. His hands were trembling. Everything seemed hazy like he was walking through fog. The patient in the bed said something but it sounded far off and the words made no sense to his befuddled mind.

Sam looked at the bed and blinked, as though only just registering the patient presence. She was looking at him with an expression of confusion and concern.

"Sorry… wrong room," he said.

What was going on?

In her hospital room, the unnamed girl stirred. A thick crust of her blood had formed over the mark on her hand, each small twitch cracking the shell and threatening to set a fresh stream of blood loss. She groaned weakly, her other hand moving unconsciously to rest on her swollen belly, cradling it.

A breeze stirred the curtains and toyed with the girl's bedraggled hair. She whimpered, goosebumps rising along the length of her neck. Her fingers curled and clenched into fists, gripping her covers. She tossed a little, turning her head to the side, away from the obtrusive sensation, and burying it in the pillow.

The breeze ran down her arm and she let out another whimper. Faint bruises began to appear on her skin, gathering around her wrist. They weren't particularly large, about the size of a fingertip, and were faded like they'd been there for a great length of time and had begun to heal.

The girl groaned and wrapped her arms tight around herself, curling up as small as she could under the covers. The heart rate monitor spiked a little, a nervous jump before settling out once more. A flurry of soft cries and sobs slipped from her lips.

The curtains stilled and, after a moment, the girl's body relaxed and she lapsed into silence once more.

Sam went back into the bathroom and gripped the sink. His entire body was trembling and his legs felt like rubber, barely supporting him. He looked into the mirror. His face looked washed out and pale, or was it the harsh strip lighting above that was doing that?

He rubbed his eyes. The dizziness hadn't subsided but it hadn't gotten any worse either. He clenched and unclenched his fists around the cold porcelain. He needed to go home, he knew that now. The phrase, be careful what you wish for, came to mind. He let out a quiet groan and rested his forehead against the mirror.

A good night's sleep. That would sort him out.

Even as he thought the words, he felt bile rising up in the back of his throat. He darted into a cubicle, spewing a mixture of vomit and acrid black slime. He groaned, supporting himself against the toilet as he continued to heave into the bowl. The room began to spin in front of him, the bright lights blinding him and causing spots to dance in front of his eyes.

He felt a sensation like ice spreading down his spine and across his back as he hugged the toilet. The walls felt like they were closing in on him, his skin felt too tight. He dry heaved, managing to eject a mouthful of phlegm. He looked down into the bowl and saw splashes of red.

Sam managed to pull away from the toilet, resting his head against the wall of the cubicle. The door had swung closed, enclosing him the tiny darkened space. He felt like the darkness was building around him, sealing him in like a tomb.

A disgusting smell reached his nose, stronger than the familiar smell of vomit and the faint scent of sulphur. It was an earthy smell like something was rotting nearby. He wrinkled his nose, looking around weakly in search of the source.

Every time he tried to move, another wave of nausea would hit him and he would be forced to return to his position hunched over the toilet. He retched so hard, a blood vessel in his eye burst. He grimaced in pain and slumped down, feeling exhausted. Every ounce of energy had been sapped from his body and all he could do was lay there, shaking and groaning into the stained porcelain.

His eyes fell on his hand, the one that had been stained by the girl's blood. The faint mark was still there but the skin around it looked different. It seemed to have taken on a purple-black hue like the whole thing was covered in one giant bruise. He wasn't entirely sure if it was because of the lighting. He examined his hand. The skin had a lifeless quality to it and the stench of rot grew stronger as he brought it closer to his nose.

*Dead meat.*

The strange bruise covered the side of his hand, up his thumb and index finger. The nail beds on those fingers had darkened and looked almost black. Looking at them, he didn't feel any fear, instead, he felt a peculiar numbness settling over him. His rational mind knew that he should be concerned by what he was seeing but his entire body felt vacant.

He scratched at the skin on his index finger lightly. His nail caught and the skin tore. Black fluid oozed out from the tear, viscous and heavy with the stench of decay. He probed lightly and felt the nail give under his finger, splitting from the bed and falling to the ground.

What remained of his strength deserted him at the sight and he curled up on the tiles, his head resting against the rim of the bowl. His entire body felt like it was choked with the black fluid, smothering his organs and suffocating him. He clawed weakly at his throat, trying to loosen the invisible bonds that were strangling him and threatening to drag him down.

What was happening? What was this?

He whimpered softly, the pathetic noise the only one he was capable of. The words echoed around his head in an endless loop.

*Dead meat.*

*This Book of Shadows is the property of Samyra Luis*

*February 12ᵗʰ*
*Waning Gibbous*

*Spell for banishing evil*

- ❖  *Birch*
- ❖  *Black Pepper*
- ❖  *Cayenne*
- ❖  *Curry Powder*
- ❖  *Yew*
- ❖  *Four black candles*
- ❖  *Three silver candles*
- ❖  *One item of obsidian jewellery*
- ❖  *A bowl*
- ❖  *Salt*

*Find a private place to perform the spell. Place the black candles at the points of the compass and circle the area with sea salt. Call the corners and build a fire in the centre using the birch and yew wood. Consecrate the silver candles and place on either side of the fire.*

*Light the first and speak the words: 'Under the eye of Syn I cast this spell and ask her to protect and guide my work.'*

*Light the second and speak the words: 'Under the eye of Bes I cast this spell and ask him to protect and guide my work.'*

*Kneel before the fire and place the third silver candle directly in front of you. Light it and invoke your personal deity in the same manner.*

*Cast the black pepper, cayenne and curry powder into the fire. Close your eyes and visualise yourself in a circle of silver light. Remain knelt until the fire burns out.*

*Gather the ashes in the bowl. Place a drop of wax from each of the silver candles onto the obsidian jewellery and place it in the bowl of ashes. This will protect the wearer from evil. Close the circle.*

*Take the ashes and scatter them to protect a space against dark forces.*

# III

Officer Harper let out a long sigh. He'd been in the hospital for a number of hours since he'd relieved his colleague. He'd drunk a few cups of coffee from the nearby vending machine and tried to get comfortable in one of the chairs that were dotted along the ward. The cushion was lumpy and the fabric cover of the seat was torn, leaking stuffing.

He looked through the notes he'd been provided with. Everything about this case was strange. When the call had come in about a naked bleeding teenager in the woods, most of the station had thought it was a prank, himself included. It wasn't unusual, kids got easily bored and the woods themselves were a source for most of the local stories. When they'd gone to investigate and had found her... that was an image he didn't think he'd ever get out of his head. Three days later and it was still all he could think about.

He checked his watch. It was early evening and he still had a few hours before he'd be relieved. He fished his phone from his pocket and dialled his son, Jamie. He picked up after a few rings.

"Hey, dad. What's up?"

"Hey kid, I just wanted to let you know –"

"You're not going to be home for dinner?" interrupted Jamie. Officer Harper ran his fingers through his hair, feeling guilty. It was becoming more and more common for him to need to work late.

"Yeah, sorry. I've got to stay at the hospital. Is your mother home?"

"No, she rang a little while ago. She's working late too."

That didn't surprise him. His wife worked at the hospital and often worked late when they were short-staffed. It was rare for them both to be home at the same time and, more often than not, they had to rely on Jamie to take care of himself and his sister.

"Are you alright to sort out dinner and put Callie to bed?" There was silence on the other end of the phone for a moment and Officer Harper could tell Jamie was upset.

"Yeah. That's fine dad."

"I think there are some leftovers in the fridge, or you can order pizza and I'll pay you back."

"Yeah, I know the deal dad. Homework, Callie in bed by 8:30, normal routine. See you later."

The line went dead. It was only after a moment of looking at the device's blank screen that Officer Harper remembered the promise he'd made to his son a few days before after he'd had to bail on their annual hunting trip. He'd promised to take Jamie to see a movie that night as a way of an apology. He sighed and tucked his phone back into his pocket. He settled back into his uncomfortable chair and stared up at the ceiling. It wasn't his fault, he tried to tell himself. He couldn't control what happened in the town. He knew Jamie understood that.

It didn't make him feel any better though.

"Her wound seems to be healing well. No signs of infection."

"That's good, considering the amount of dirt we had to clean out of it. Do you think she'll come round soon?"

"Let's hope so. Do the police have any idea who she is yet?"

The sound of voices, alien to her, faded and were gradually replaced with a steady beeping noise. The girl's fingers twitched, gripping the mattress beneath her before releasing. She continued, her fingers moving in coordination with the sound of the beeps from the monitor. The sensation of the sheets and the firm yet giving surface of the mattress felt strange to her and she groaned softly. Her eyelids flickered and opened slowly. She winced, the lights overhead dizzyingly bright and creating coloured dots which danced in front of her. She lifted her arm, reaching for the dots, and frowned when her fingers found nothing.

Her gaze moved to her arms and the wires that were attached to her body. She lifted her head, taking in the room for the first time. She searched for the familiar presence of dirt, leaves, and rocks but found nothing. Her heart began to race and her breathing hitched as panic set in. Her hand went to the wires and tubes on her arm and she clawed at them, desperate to free herself no matter the cost. Her fingers were clumsy and she struggled to get purchase. The machine began to beep more insistently and an alarm sounded somewhere nearby. The sounds seemed impossibly loud to her and she halted her assault on the tubes, clutching her head and curling up in a foetal position as she tried to block out the terrifying sounds.

A nurse came in and came over to the bed, fiddling with the machine until the sound cut off. The softer beeping of the heart rate monitor returned and slowly the girl lifted her head. The nurse gave her a pleasant smile.

"You need to be more careful sweetheart." She took hold of the girl's arm and checked the wires and the IV that was attached, making sure they were still in the right places. "These are very important, okay?"

The words made no sense to the girl but the tone in which they were spoken was soothing, the way someone might speak in an attempt to placate a distressed animal.

"It's okay… you're safe. You're in the hospital," the nurse continued, trying to soothe the girl.

The girl allowed herself to relax just a little, but her body remained tensed and she shifted into a crouched position on top of the mattress. Her eyes were fixed on the nurse who shuffled awkwardly from one foot to the other, feeling uncomfortable under the girl's unblinking gaze.

"I'll go get the doctors. They've been very worried."

The nurse left hurriedly, relieved to have an excuse to leave even if it was only for a short time. The girl remained where she was, watching the door intently. A moment later, the nurse returned with two men, a doctor, and a police officer.

"Now sweetheart, the officer is going to ask you a few questions so they can work out what happened to you, okay?" said the nurse.

The girl didn't reply, watching them with a peculiar expression on her face. The nurse waited before taking her silence as consent and nodding to the officer who approached the bed.

"Ma'am, can you tell me your name?"

Silence.

"How old are you?"

Silence. The officer glanced at the doctor, clearly unsure of the best way of proceeding. Perhaps the girl had been brain-damaged in whatever accident she'd been involved in?

"Maybe this should wait until she's had longer to recover? She's still quite weak," the nurse suggested. The police officer shook his head.

"The longer we wait, the less chance we have to find whoever was responsible for this," he said.

The nurse and the doctor exchanged glances but decided to let the officer continue. The girl had barely moved since the questions had started, her body rigid on top of the bed. Only her eyes were active, roaming over the three of them like a wild animal selecting its prey.

"Do you remember what happened to you?" he asked softly.

The girl opened her mouth and the officer's eyes lit up, thinking he'd finally got somewhere with her. She let out a strangled groan, a muted screech as though she was trying to speak but only noise came out. The cry was barely human, more animal in nature. The nurse flinched and both men stepped back a little at the sheer force of the sound.

Another doctor entered the room, perhaps drawn by the noise. He paused in the doorway before approaching his colleague and murmuring something in his ear.

The sound caught in the girl's throat and she gagged on the air, doubling over. She retched and a rancid black bile splattered on the sheets. It smelled bitter and stung the inside of a person's nostrils and throat with every inhalation. The nurse suppressed the urge to vomit herself as the stench reached her nose. The girl fell backwards onto the bed, her body shaking like a creature possessed. The second doctor rushed over to help her. As soon as his hands touched her skin, she vaulted upright and clamped her teeth on his throat. He yelled, pulling back sharply. She clung to him, surprisingly strong for her size, tearing at his flesh with her blunt teeth. She clawed at his face with her ragged nails, intent on inflicting as much damage as she could before she was separated.

The officer and the other doctor hurried over and managed to prise her off of her victim. The first doctor fell backwards, blood gushing from the wound in his throat and the scratches which ran the length of his face. The two men held her down on the bed as she thrashed wildly, screeching at the top of her lungs. Blood and bile ran down her chin, her eyes were wild as she tried to break free.

The nurse ran to a cupboard and fetched a set of restraints. The men held her as still as they could, allowing the nurse to secure her to the bed. The girl thrashed angrily against their hands and the straps, snapping at the air. The men stepped back, the doctor trying to determine whether further sedation was necessary. As they watched, she stilled and relaxed onto the sheets. Her face took on an expression of serenity, as though her violent attack had never happened. If it weren't for the blood and fluid on her chin, one would be forgiven for assuming she was a normal child.

The injured doctor and the nurse left to treat his wound while the first doctor and the police officer stepped away from the bed to talk.

"That was… something…" The officer seemed to be in a slight state of shock and the doctor gave him a sympathetic smile. It wasn't the first time he'd seen a patient act violently, although certainly not one so young.

"It happens. Not often but the mind can only take so much before it snaps."

The officer ran his fingers through his hair and grimaced slightly. He couldn't get the image of the girl with her teeth clamped on the doctor's throat out of his head.

"You administered her treatment?" he asked. He had to try and report something back to the station, he needed as much detail as he could get.

"I am the attending physician on this patient, yes. Dr Knott is also consulting on her case. He's the head of our paediatrics unit. And I'm sorry she wasn't more helpful. But you have to remember she has been through a tremendous ordeal."

"Do you have any idea what might have happened to her?"

"Well… it's hard to say for certain. She's pregnant, almost full-term, but she's also severely malnourished, she's deeply antisocial… it's not the correct term but I'd refer to her as almost feral based on the behaviour we've witnessed. I'm not one for guessing but based on the evidence, I'd say she's been away from people for a long time."

"Not that long given her condition." The officer gave a slight smile. The doctor gave him a stern look

"Now is hardly the time to be making jokes, officer." He sighed. "She shows signs of sexual assault. In addition to her bullet wound, she has severe deep tissue bruising localised around the legs and wrists as well as a number of cuts, some appear self-inflicted while others are more difficult to determine the cause of. To put it simply, she is in need of serious help. She needs multiple doctors; a surgeon, an OB/GYN, a psychiatrist."

"Can the hospital provide that?"

"She'd receive better treatment if we transfer her to another facility. She's still a child, the best place for her would be the children's hospital in Redwood. They're equipped to deal with child abuse cases."

"Is that necessary?"

Redwood was a fair distance from Sarum Vale and it would add complications to the investigation if the girl had to be moved.

"We have some of the resources here but they're stretched to capacity, particularly with psychiatric care, and it's certainly nothing compared to the care she'd receive in Redwood."

"How soon is she likely to be transferred?"

"By the end of the week at the soonest. She isn't in a stable enough condition at this moment. I also need to contact the hospital in Redwood and confirm they're in a position to take her, as well as warn them of what to expect."

The officer nodded and glanced over at the girl. She was staring up at the ceiling, seemingly unaware or unaffected by her restraints.

"Alright, we'll work with what we have to. If she says anything, let me know. In the meantime, we'll work on trying to locate her family."

"Are there any leads on her identity?"

"Not yet. We're reviewing missing person files and pooling others from the surrounding area but so far we've not found a match," he said, before turning to the door. He paused. "Good luck with her."

The officer left the room and the doctor turned his focus back to the patient. Her head was turned now, watching him. Her eyes were oddly vacant, appearing to look through him rather than at him. Her eyes moved, following something only she could see up the wall and across the ceiling. Her fingers clutched at the air and her lips twitched, whispering silently.

*What happened to you?*

He felt useless looking at her. He wanted to help her but he wasn't sure how; he'd never dealt with a girl this… damaged. He could treat her physical injuries but that was only a small part of the problem.

The girl's eyes flickered over to the doctor once again. She was aware of his presence in the room but he was a distant entity, separate from herself and her personal reality. She gave him no more thought than a person would give a fly on a far wall. Everything seemed heightened around her. The strip lighting above her head hummed incessantly, flickering off at intervals, leaving an impression burned into her retinas. She was aware of a faint mechanical churning sound somewhere above her head. The air felt wrong. It was too cold, unnaturally so, and it smelt peculiar to her, a chemical odour obliterating anything natural in the air. She whimpered softly and tried to roll onto her side, trying to curl up in a position that would provide her with some comfort. The restraints bit into her wrists and held her still, forcing her to remain on her back. The sensation was unpleasant and nauseatingly familiar. She let out a noise, like that of an injured animal and pressed her face against the covers that had become bunched down one side of the bed. It stifled the chemical scent a little. The dirt on her skin had rubbed off onto the sheets and if she closed her eyes she could almost pretend she was back in surroundings that, while not entirely comforting, were at least more homely to her than the sterile hospital room.

She lay there, her breathing slow and regular. Through the window, she could see the sun was starting to set. She half lifted her head, fascinated by the flurry of colours that had for so long been denied her. She watched silently as the sky was painted in shades of orange, red, purple. The sight of the night sky through the window both calmed and terrified

47

her, the threat of the blackness so close to her only held at bay by the ever-present strip lighting above her head.

She turned her head away from the window and instead looked up at the ceiling, letting the light burn into her retinas once more. Everything about this place felt wrong to her. It was too bright, too loud, and she found herself longing for the gloom and obscurity of what had become her home. She let out soft whimpers like an injured puppy, nuzzling her face against the dirty blankets. She rubbed her hands against the mattress, enjoying the rhythm of the act more than the sensation itself.

A shadow crossed the wall, just visible at the corner of her eye, and the girl lifted her head. She stiffened slightly as she watched. It seemed to flit from one wall to another before fading to nothing. The girl regarded the wall with suspicion. The shadows of the furniture seemed to thicken as she watched, spreading like ink across paper.

She began to move her arms, slowly at first but then with more vigour. She twisted and pulled, trying to work her arms free of the restraints. The straps ate at her wrists, blood bubbling up as the movement worked deep grooves into her skin. It hurt, but her body had long ago become accustomed to pain and she ignored it. The blood ran down her hand and across her fingers before dripping onto the sheets. She fell still, watching the crimson liquid shot through with tendrils of black.

Her eyes moved slowly back to the window. What remained of the light was dying, the colours of twilight now faded. Seeing it, the imminent embrace of icy shadow, she could no longer keep her fear at bay, even the electric lights failed to comfort her. Cold dread began to settle on her and she felt a sick, twisting sensation take root in her stomach. She began to pull at her restraints with renewed enthusiasm, desperate to free herself.

Down the hall, a bulb went out with a soft pop and a hiss. The shadows began to lengthen, creeping across the walls and the floors.

Still, the girl worked, her hands now slick with blood. She gritted her teeth and gave a sharp tug. The strap gave a little. She pulled again, letting out a short cry of pain as she did so, and her hand came free.

Above her, the light flickered, dimming for a moment before returning to normal. The shadows at the edge of the room continued to thicken, inching their way towards her, and a sound, like a hundred tiny whispers, drew her focus. Her heartbeat frantically in her chest, threatening to burst free. She tore at the strap on her other wrist, clawing at it and working her fingers into the restraint. She bit at the strap, hoping she could chew herself loose. Finally, sweet relief, her attempts yielded and she was able to break free.

She clambered off the bed, pulling the IV down with her as she crashed to the floor. She tried to stand but her legs wouldn't hold her. Instead, she crawled over to the door and peered out. Through the glass panel in the door, she could see the hallway darkening as one by one the lights went out. She whimpered and ducked back down. The gap under the door still allowed a small crack of light in but as she watched, the final hall light went out.

The girl retreated to the furthest corner of the room and curled up, cowering. Her light cut out again, momentarily surrounding her in darkness. She rested her head on her knees, rocking backwards and forwards. The light returned but it didn't give her any relief. The air in the room became icy, her breath frosting in front of her eyes.

Above her head, the light buzzed and flickered once more before going out entirely. For a moment there was a faint glow left behind by the strip lighting before that faded completely, plunging the room into near darkness, save for the sickly green glare from the hospital equipment.

A chill ran over her skin and sent a shiver throughout her entire body. In the darkness, something moved. The whispers grew louder and the girl clamped her hands over her ears in an effort to subdue them, but they persisted, burying themselves inside her very mind.

The shadows curled like smoke around her ankles, inching forward. A sensation of fingers brushing against her throat made her flinch. The feeling travelled down the curve of her neck, across her chest and down to lightly caress the curve of her swollen belly. Her breathing spiked, her heart racing in fear.

She wrapped her arms tighter around herself, pressing against the wall behind her as if hoping it would absorb her into it. She closed her eyes tight, trying to pretend that it wasn't real, that this wasn't happening.

In the staff office, the night staff were chatting away, enjoying the peace and quiet. A lone nurse sat at the nurse's station, doodling idly in a notepad. She hummed softly to herself, accompanied by the scratching of her pen.

Down the hall came the faint sound of whispering. The nurse lifted her head slightly, her pen pausing on the paper. She looked around, trying to pinpoint the source of the noise but couldn't see anything except the empty hallway. The whispers seemed to fade as quickly as she registered them and after a moment there was complete silence again. She made a face and returned her focus to the doodling, putting it down to the wind.

An alarm began to sound. Then another. And another. The nurse on duty leapt from her seat at the terrible crescendo of noise as one after the other, each patient on the ward flatlined. She shouted for assistance and rushed to the nearest room, the other staff bolting from their seats to help.

The patient lay on his bed, back to the door. At first, she couldn't see what was wrong but as she hurried to his side it became painfully clear. The sheets were tangled around his throat. One hand was stretched out, searching for something that would help him while the other gripped the sheets, attempting to claw himself free. All the colour had drained from his face, his veins were livid against his skin. His eyes were wide open and his face was contorted into an endless silent scream of terror.

**Name:** *Faith Knight*

**Period**: *5ᵗʰ*     **Subject**: *English*     **Assignment**: *Poetry*

**Task:** *Write a poem on the theme of 'sleep'*

Every night
I fight
A battle with myself.

I dress in armour
of cotton and cloth,
take up my post
on the battlefield.

My enemies
Are the warring shadows
Their weapons
Are my biting
thoughts.

Sometimes
I fight
Till the very end.
Till the rise of sun.
Yet in that fight
I lose.

And sometimes
I surrender
And lay
Lost
Entombed
in darkness
and blankets.

But sometimes
I cage my frantic mind
Drive the shadows
From my walls

And win.

# IV

The Harper house was ablaze with light. The kitchen was warm and homely, the fridge covered with childish drawings and post-it notes held in place by an assortment of magnets. Jamie stood at the fridge, staring at the shelves with a perplexed look on his face. He wore torn jeans and a frayed hoodie, the cuffs of which had been picked to pieces by nervous probing fingers. His iPod was tucked into his pocket, one earbud in while the other dangled free. His sister, Callie, was seated at the breakfast bar doodling on her homework while his dog nosed around them both, whining for treats.

Jamie reached in and picked up a container, sniffing the contents and giving them a dubious poke, as though hoping they might transform miraculously into something edible. Truthfully, he wasn't really focused on food. He'd spent the past few days on autopilot, too stressed and exhausted to really connect with anything around him.

Callie wrapped her knuckles against the counter, emitting a clear knocking sound, one short and three long. Jamie lifted his head and looked over. His sister was watching him intently.

"What?" He asked. Callie raised her hand to her chin and gave him a stern look.

*What's wrong?*

"Nothing. I'm fine." She scowled at her brother. Despite the difference in age, the two of them were exceptionally close and Callie was very in tune with Jamie's emotions, no matter how hard he tried to hide them.

"I am fine," he insisted, his hands automatically signing the words as he always did when he talked to her. He decided it would be better to change the subject rather than continue to deflect her questioning. "What would madam like for dinner tonight?" he asked, grabbing a tea towel and slinging it over his arm in a light imitation of a waiter.

After spending so many nights taking care of Callie, they had developed a routine and both of them were aware that Jamie's cheesy impression was an attempt to bring things back to normal, even if Callie wasn't entirely sure what was different.

"Tonight we have a choice of suspicious leftovers, macaroni and not quite mouldy cheese or, the chef's speciality, take out." Callie pulled a thoughtful face, pretending to consider.

"Take out!"

Jamie laughed and nodded.

"Good choice." He grabbed his mobile from the counter and hit the preprogrammed number for the local restaurant. He leaned against the cupboard and picked up the phone. As he waited for the call to connect, he suppressed a yawn and ran his fingers through his hair. It ran twice before there was a beep at the end of the phone and an automated message informing him that the line was busy. Jamie glanced at his watch, doing mental calculations. "Okay, I'm going to run out and get dinner. It'll be quicker than waiting to get through."

He pocketed his phone and turned to Callie.

"You know the rules?" Callie rolled her eyes and nodded. Jamie folded his arms. "Cal…"

He gave her a pointed look. She pouted and signed rapidly at him.

*Do I have to?*

"Yes."

His sister scowled and reluctantly took her hearing aid from her pocket, carefully placing it in her ear. She was supposed to wear it all day and at school she usually did, although not without some complaints. While Jamie was supposed to ensure she kept it in during the evenings, he often didn't. Given his predilection for having headphones on near constantly, both siblings found it easier and preferable to communicate non-verbally.

"Happy?" she asked, scowling at him.

"Yes." He slipped on his trainers. "I shouldn't be more than twenty minutes. Don't answer the door to anyone –"

"And don't play with the stove and if the phone rings, you're in the toilet," she said with the tone of someone who'd had the instructions drilled into her.

He nodded and headed out the front, locking the door behind him. Strictly speaking, he wasn't meant to leave Callie alone when he babysat her but sometimes he had to. Besides, she was smart enough to stay safe and what his parents didn't know wouldn't hurt them.

He popped his other earbud in and turned the volume up, timing his steps with the beat of the music. The sun was descending behind the mountains, staining the sky with dark blue and vibrant red. He hurried through the front garden onto the street that led to the town's only restaurant. Rather than follow the main road, he took a shortcut, slipping down a narrow alley between two houses and across a stretch of green with a sparse scattering of trees that bordered the main road and breached the gap between the houses and the town centre.

The cool night air woke him up a little but another yawn still slipped free. He rubbed his eyes as he trudged down the road. His sleep had never been great, frequently plagued with nightmares, but lately, it had been even worse than usual. Since the annual hunting trip with his uncle a few days before, his nightmares had taken a disturbing turn and after the night with his journal... he'd barely slept at all. He'd tried to rationalise what he'd seen that night but the idea that he was hallucinating wasn't especially comforting.

Thinking about the trip brought a scowl to his face as it reminded him of his father's broken promises. Their annual hunting trip wasn't something he'd ever particularly enjoyed but he liked getting a chance to spend time with his dad. They'd been going every year since he was nine years old. Even as his father had got busier at work and spent less time at home, he'd still made time for the hunt. This year though, the car had been loaded up when his dad had pulled out of the trip. He'd still gone with his uncle but it wasn't the same.

Although the trees in this area weren't nearly as dense as they were further in the forest, Jamie found himself straying into their trunks, grazing his skin. The sky was getting darker. A thick fog seemed to descend around him as the sun disappeared entirely, cold moisture settling onto his skin.

The trees gave way to a more open space with a wrought iron fence around the edges. An old brick structure loomed up in the distance, the roof slightly dilapidated. Gravestones were dotted around the overgrown grass, weeds clinging to the rough stones. He smiled slightly and paused, gripping the fence, gently rubbing his palms against the cold metal. Beyond the church, he could see the lights of the town centre. His eyes swept over the graves and his smile faltered. His hands trembled slightly and he felt the urge rising up in him to turn his head away.

*Jamie…*

He gripped the fence tighter. He held his gaze in place, his eyes watering.

*Jamie… you're not scared, are you? Be a brave boy…*

He released the fence and began to skirt around the edge of the graveyard. He'd only gone a few steps when a sudden burst of static shot through his earbuds. He cried out in pain and yanked them from his ears. Jamie fished the iPod from his pocket and prodded the buttons in confusion. It was dead.

A twig snapped nearby, close enough to be audible amongst the general sounds of the world around him and even distinct through the ringing sound lingering in Jamie's ears. He glanced over, more curious than startled by the sound. In the graveyard, something moved. A dark shape that separated itself from the gathering night. Jamie frowned slightly. He couldn't see why anyone would be there this late.

A low growl came from the shape and it seemed to unfold, growing larger and more distinctive. Jamie hesitated, unsure of what he was seeing and how to respond. He took a half step and the creature let out another growl. Its body rippled, like it was made of mist or water, and seemed to vanish in places. He stood, frozen to his spot, unable to move back and too afraid to move forward. He blinked rapidly, sure his eyes were playing tricks on him. The forest was home to many dangerous animals and it wasn't uncommon for them to wander into the town on occasion but what he was seeing didn't look like a bear or a wolf. People told wild tales of mountain lions with fangs as long as a man's arm, wolves the size of bears with red eyes and jet black fur. Jamie's father always insisted the stories were nonsense but his mother said that most stories had a little truth to them, however small. Now, seeing the gigantic shadowy form, Jamie couldn't help but wonder…

As he stared, he began to make out more details. It was hunched over and Jamie could see the shape of four limbs, but whether they were arms or legs he couldn't tell. Its head was indistinguishable from its body, just a dark mass. The shadows on the ground seemed to spread, slithering towards him and he heard a faint hissing, crackling sound like something was burning. He felt a strange sensation of something brushing against his ankle, followed by a faint stinging across his flesh. He flinched, his mind automatically conjuring the clammy sensation of scales that haunted his nightmares. He stumbled back a few steps, eyes leaving the creature to search the ground. While he knew the more immediate threat was the large lumbering beast in the graveyard, he couldn't help but focus on whatever was lurking by his feet.

He saw nothing in the grass, but his mind whispered to him that that meant nothing. Whatever it was could easily have hidden, disguised by the darkness. A rumbling growl that seemed to shake the surroundings emanated from the beast and his head shot up. It took a step towards him. Jamie felt the urge to run but it was like his entire body was frozen in place. Fight, freeze, flee, the options swirled around his head.

Even as he tried to remember what he was supposed to do when it came to wild animals, the thing turned and lolloped off into the night with a bounding motion.

Jamie stayed where he was for a moment, uncomfortable with the idea of moving and the creature returning. After he was sure it was gone, he took a slow breath, taking a moment to mentally stabilise himself, before continuing on his way. The image of… whatever he'd seen in the graveyard continued to linger in his mind. A bear, he told himself. That's what it was.

*Maybe not*, hissed his mind. *A bear, a trick of the light, how much longer can you keep pretending?*

He scowled to himself, wishing that he had his music to silence the whispers in his head. As he moved into the town and into the light of the streets, he felt a little more relaxed. It was slightly easier to pretend that the nightmarish fantasies that lurked in the recesses of his brain were just that, illusions that transformed the normal into something outlandish. It didn't comfort him to think that he was hallucinating but it wasn't unheard of for people to get freaked out by completely normal things at night. It didn't mean… it didn't mean anything was wrong with him…

As he neared the restaurant, he passed by a group of kids in his grade. One of them was talking loudly, with exaggerated hand gestures.

"She was completely naked and covered in dirt. And there was, like, this bloody hole in her leg, like she'd been shot."

Jamie frowned slightly and shook his head. Part of him wondered what they were talking about. A movie probably, maybe a video game.

He let himself into the restaurant, his body relaxing as warm air washed over him. He placed his order and took a seat to wait, fiddling with the cuff of his hoodie. He felt another yawn rising up in his throat and he closed his eyes. He slumped down in his seat, resisting the urge to sleep. He rubbed his eyes, the bright lights of the restaurant making them sting and burn. His fingers drummed lightly on the plush fabric of the chair, rubbing the material against his thumb.

The chime of glass and cutlery, the soft bubble of chatter that encased the room was soothing and he could feel the urge to sleep tugging at his eyelids more persistently. It wouldn't hurt to let them close, just for a bit…

He settled more comfortably into the chair and closed his eyes. He wasn't sleeping, not really, just resting his eyes for a moment, but he could already feel the threat of the monsters that lurked in his brain stirring. He groaned internally. Was he never to have a moment's peace?

Jamie decided to try and not let it get to him, instead, he called back an old trick he'd been taught when he was younger. He imagined himself in a green space, picturing trees around him and thick grass under his feet, the warm sun beating down on him. He focused on his breathing. Admittedly, he had tried doing this at night, to help him get to sleep without much success. Then again, things were always harder when you were alone in the dark with only your own thoughts for company.

*Help me…*

Eyes like two emeralds peered out at him from behind the trees in his mind. A figure, pale and lithe, visible between the branches.

*Help me…*

There was a sharp bang, a gunshot that ripped through his brain, and a terrified scream. Jamie vaulted upright, gasping. He looked around, frantically trying to realign his mind to where he was. The hostess peered over at him, a concerned look on her face. He gave her a small smile, before turning away, embarrassed. Fortunately, a waitress came over with a bag and he was spared the further awkwardness of sitting under the gaze of the hostess.

Jamie took the bag, his cheeks burning. He headed outside with his food, still wrapped up in his own thoughts. There were only a few people on the streets, the group of kids from his school had dispersed. He kicked a stone before stepping off the pavement. A second later, a motorbike sped up the road, sending Jamie leaping back to avoid it. The bike looped around and came to a stop in front of him. The rider hopped off, pulling her helmet off as she did so.

The girl was Jamie's age, with a cascade of dark hair, streaked with intermittent flashes of bright red and blue. Her eyes were dark, body short and slight but compensated for by boots which elevated her a decent amount.

"My delivery services not good enough for you anymore, Jay?" she asked, a small smile playing across her features.

"Sorry Sammy, but I keep getting this really horrible girl delivering my food," he teased. His body had instantly relaxed in the girl's presence. They'd been friends for a number of years, in fact, Jamie was the only person Sammy seemed to tolerate. They didn't spend much time together outside of their classes, due to Jamie taking care of Callie and Sammy being busy with her work, but they shared secrets with each other that no one else knew.

Sammy gave him a playful swat on the chest before reaching up to peck him on the cheek.

"How are you, loser?"

"Same old, same old. You got much longer left tonight?" he asked, inclining his head towards the bike.

"No, I'm just about to finish up."

"Want to join me and Callie for dinner?"

"I would... but I've got my shift at the radio station." She gave him an apologetic look.

"Oh yeah... how many places are you working at now? Seventeen?"

"Pretty much,"

"When do you sleep?"

"Between 1 am and 2 am," she responded sarcastically. "Which still gives me more sleep than you." She poked him lightly and gave him a stern look.

"Sleep is for the weak!" he protested. Jamie decided to divert the subject away from his sleep pattern. Despite his closeness with Sammy, he still felt a bit uncomfortable discussing it. "So, you ever get a night off?"

"I have the option, I just don't tend to take them. Why?"

"You know the Halloween dance? Were you planning on going to that?"

"I was considering it. I had a few invites, not accepted any of them yet.

"I was wondering if you might want to… ditch it and… spend the night watching horror movies with me instead?"

"Only if you're bringing the popcorn." She grinned and headed into the restaurant. Jamie watched her go before continuing on his way. He decided against going past the graveyard and instead took the main road, humming to himself in an attempt to replace his music.

The air had turned bitterly cold and seemed to nip at his skin like a wild animal. His breath clouded in front of him, hanging in the night sky for a moment before fading to nothing. Jamie picked up his pace, eager to get home to the warmth and uncomfortable with the thought of leaving Callie for any longer than necessary. He moved from each pool of sickly yellow light cast by the streetlamps, weaving his way through the darkness towards his house.

When he eventually reached his house, he was relieved to see it. Callie had laid out plates in the kitchen for their food and was curled up on the sofa, gently stroking the dog and watching the TV. She didn't look up as Jamie entered, intent on her programme, murmuring the words under her breath. The dog barked excitedly as he entered and raced over to greet him. Jamie reached out to pet him but the dog stopped sharply and let out a low whine, retreating rapidly.

"Echo? You okay?" Echo barked and fled up the stairs.

"What's wrong with him?" Callie asked.

"No idea," he said, frowning as he looked after the disappearing dog. He shook his head and headed into the kitchen to dish up.

He set down the bag on the counter. There were scraps of paper littered around, remains of some drawing Callie had done earlier. Jamie sighed softly and began gathering up the papers, pausing and shuffling through them. The first few were her standard drawings, bright colours, and misshapen animals, but on one page there was nothing but a black scribble that seemed to reach across the paper. He frowned for a moment before shrugging and tucking them away to make space.

Jamie began to plate up their dinner, evenly distributing the food and ensuring nothing green touched Callie's plate. Once he had finished loading up their plates and stashed the leftovers in the fridge, he went to retrieve glasses for their drinks. As he crossed the kitchen, he felt a strange pain in his ankle, almost a burning sensation. He frowned and balanced against the counter to roll up his pants leg to expose his ankle. At first, he saw nothing, but when he examined it closer he could make out a number of inch long marks. They were raised and seemed to have a silver hue when the light landed on them. Jamie skimmed his fingers over the marks. They didn't look fresh, in fact, it was almost like they were old and healed, leaving only a faint scar.

The sight unsettled the teen but he forced himself to rationalise it. After all, anything could have caused them. He frequently found bruises on his arms and legs that he couldn't remember causing, these marks could have been from him grazing his legs in the woods. Although, he couldn't quite make himself believe it.

Still, he pushed the thought from his head and hurriedly tugged down his pants leg. He grabbed the dinner plates and headed out to the living room.


The evening continued as many others had before. They finished their dinners and watched TV for a bit before Jamie put Callie to bed and headed to his bathroom for a shower. He switched on the water to let it heat up, before moving his towel over to the shower and undressing. Steam billowed from the shower, the glass walls around it turning foggy. Jamie stepped into the shower and rested his head against the wall, letting the water run over him. The soft lighting of the bathroom, the thickening steam and the warm spray cocooned him, working their way into his muscles and unwinding them slowly.

He stretched, relishing in the sensation, before grabbing the shampoo. He lathered up his hair and then moved to rinse it off, turning his head downwards as the soapy water dripped off his head and disappeared into the drain at his feet. As he watched the bubbles swirl into the darkness, a drop of red caught his eyes.

A small bead of blood ran down his ankle and mingled with the water. He frowned, peering at his leg. As he watched, the skin seemed to ripple, like something was crawling underneath it. Jamie's eyes widened and his breathing spiked. The marks on his ankle split and more rivulets of blood began to run into the base of the shower. The flesh bulged and darkened in the process as bruises appeared before his eyes.

Jamie let out a choking cry and fumbled for the shower door. Even as he did so, the tiny cuts grew, widening to allow whatever creature had found its way under his skin to claw free. Blood flowed down his leg and sharp pain ripped through the limb. A narrow head protruded from the cut, a flickering tongue darting out to taste the air. The creature slithered further from Jamie's leg, hanging in the air as its back half was still buried in his flesh. It resembled a snake but lacked details, there was a shimmer to it which gave the impression of scales but little else to identify it. Had Jamie been in enough of a condition to examine it, he would have been unable to make out any eyes, nostrils or even a distinct mouth.

The animal dropped from Jamie's leg and landed on the shower floor, circling its body around itself and turning to fix its eyeless gaze on the boy. He jerked backwards, the door swinging open as he did. He fell into the empty space, his head slamming against the sink as he went. He landed on the tiles, spasms racking his body as his eyes rolled into the back of his head.

In the shower, the snake-like creature watched the boy shaking on the cold floor. It made no move towards him, instead, its body seemed to dissolve, disintegrating into a thick oily substance that dripped down the drain, leaving no sign of its presence.

# DEPARTMENT OF HEALTH
## Certificate of Death

THIS IS TO CERTIFY, That out records show:

Name_____ Richard Anthony Knight

Died_____ October 12th _____at 17:51 PM at _____ 12 Ash Street, Sarum Vale

Age at death_____27_____Sex_____Male_____Ethnicity__Caucasian
Marital Status__Married

Immediate cause of death given was_____Suicide by hanging

Certified by__Adam Knott, MD__Address__Sarum Vale

Place of burial or removal__Sarum Vale Cemetery

Date of burial__October 19th__Funeral Director__William Carroll
Address__Sarum Vale

Record was filed__October 12th

# V

The girl sat in her corner, rocking back and forth slowly. She gnawed lightly at her hand, digging her teeth into her skin. In her mind, the hospital walls had faded away. The walls turned to stone and darkness engulfed her, footsteps in the hallway becoming the steady sound of dripping to her ears.

Her free arm was wrapped around her stomach, where a ravenous hunger had taken root. How long had it been since she'd last eaten? She wasn't sure. Time was meaningless in the darkness. It had blurred into one, only broken by brief moments of sensation that halted her general state of icy numbness. When she was tired, she slept. When she was thirsty, she would clamber through the rocks until she found a puddle of stagnant water to quench it. Hunger was a greater problem. It was like a monster trapped inside her chest, roaring into life to demand food. After a time, it would often quieten, only to awaken once more with renewed fury later on.

She ate whatever she could find. Usually, only insects strayed down to them, but occasionally she might find a rabbit or other such small creature who had wandered into tunnels. She was never sure if these occasions were an accident, or if He was responsible. Perhaps He was the cause, deciding to take pity on her and steer some food in her direction to prolong her miserable life a little longer.

He was always there, watching her. Even when she couldn't see him, He was there. He watched, He listened. No matter how far she tried to run or how well she hid, He always knew.

That was the fourth sensation, and indeed the fifth, although they had long ago merged into one. Pain. Fear. She knew no distinction between the two.

Sometimes, they didn't come for a long time, the times when the hunger and thirst grew so great that they consumed her entirely. She would curl up and begin to float away. That was the feeling she liked the most. Her skin tingled and she felt warm, safe. Sometimes she wished she could feel like that forever.

"How many did we lose?"

"Eleven. Almost the whole ward. We had two survivors. Jane Doe in room nine and Susan Amhurst in room four," the night nurse explained.

It was morning and the ward had ground to a halt. The doctors and nurses hovered uncertainly, waiting for instructions. No one was really sure what to do. The first of the day shift had arrived to find the chaos of the night before. The night shift were exhausted after hours spent slaving to see if they could do something for the patients. Patients died. It was a sad part of life. But never like this. Not so many at one time.

"Alright. Send the bodies down to the morgue. Full autopsies for all of them. I want to know what caused this. Notify the families, get started on the paperwork. We're going to have the two remaining patients moved to new wards while we investigate and I want them under extra supervision during that time, we cannot have a repeat of this. Check on them for the time being while I find somewhere for them to go."

The staff nodded and there was a general murmur of agreement. The remains of the night shift headed off to get some rest, a small group dispersed to take the bodies to the morgue while some went to start on the paperwork. Of those who remained, two hurried off to check on the patient in room four while the others reluctantly headed to room nine.

The girl was seated in the corner of the room. Her wrists were stained with dried blood, most from the cuts where she'd forced her arms free of the restraints but some came from fresh scratches which ran the length of her arms. She'd spent the night clawing at her skin, huddled in one spot.

One of the night nurses had checked in on her, but only briefly to ascertain she was still alive. When they'd tried to approach her, she'd growled and they'd quickly relented, deciding to leave her as a problem for someone else to deal with. Now she appeared far calmer. Her arms were limp at her sides and her eyes were closed.

Still, the staff approached her cautiously. She unsettled them and knowing what she'd done to their colleague didn't help matters. After a brief whispered discussion, one of the female doctors, Doctor Charlotte Tate, stepped forward. She knelt down in front of the girl, chewing her lip nervously. She didn't speak but the girl's eyes flickered open and fixed the woman with her stare. Her expression didn't seem angry or aggressive. If anything she seemed fearful, with a hint of curiosity. Her fingers began to scrabble at the floor, betraying the depths of her anxiety.

"It's okay," Doctor Tate said softly. "We just want to help you."

There was no recognition on the girl's face, no indication that she'd understood what was being said. The doctor offered her hand to the girl who, after regarding it suspiciously for a moment, took hold. Once on her feet, Doctor Tate carefully guided her to the bed and checked to make sure her IVs were still in place. Miraculously, they'd not been touched, as though the girl had deliberately avoided them when she'd clawed her skin.

"You must be starving," Doctor Tate said. "We'll get you something to eat and then we're going to move you to another room, okay?"

The girl regarded her silently before turning her head away, focusing on a spot on the wall. Doctor Tate glanced over but saw nothing out of the ordinary, just her shadow.

One of the group went and retrieved a tray with the patient's breakfast and deposited it before her. The girl sniffed at it, like a dog, trying to determine if it was safe. After a moment, she picked up a bread roll and began to eat, clutching it close to her as if fearful someone would take it away.

"Slowly, sweetheart. Your stomach isn't used to eating so much; you'll make yourself sick if you eat too quickly," Doctor Tate warned her.

The girl ignored her, tearing into her roll. The doctor decided to take advantage of her distracted state and instructed one of the nurses to fetch the materials to clean off the blood.

"Now sweetie, we need to get you cleaned up a bit. It might sting a little. Is that okay? Do you understand?"

The girl looked at her and nodded slowly. The doctor wasn't sure which part she was responding too but decided to take it as consent. Nurse Holland gently took hold of the girl's left arm and began to clean it carefully. Her hands shook a little, uncomfortable being so close to the strange teenager, whose face still bore traces of the doctor's blood from her attack the day before.

The girl paused mid-bite, regarding the nurse contemplatively. Her deep green eyes were unblinking, her intense unreadable stare unnerving to all present. She didn't seem distressed by the contact, just confused. If the antiseptic stung her cuts, she gave no indication. Doctor Tate found herself wondering how long it had been since the girl had felt positive human contact.

When the last of the blood was cleaned up, the cuts inspected and bandaged and the girl carefully wrapped in a hospital nightgown, Doctor Tate sent a nurse off to find out what the next step was. She perched on the edge of the bed to wait, silent but mentally taking notes. The girl had finished her breakfast and was regarding the nurses and doctor with an intense and curious gaze. The assembled group shifted uncomfortably. There was an uncanniness to the girl. No one could really identify what it was about her, but each was aware of it. Perhaps it was the way her body was put together, all the pieces were there but they didn't fit properly, creating a discomfort in the brain when it looked and registered human features presented in an abnormal way.

The nurse who had left returned, sticking her head around the door.

"Dr Knott says he's got space in paediatrics for her."

"Really? With all the other kids…? Is that a good idea?"

"The isolation room down there is available. I don't know if he plans to put her in there but… it's a room with space and it's either there or the maternity ward."

Doctor Tate got to her feet, cutting off the conversation. She looked at the girl, trying to work out the best way to move her. She still wasn't entirely sure if the girl understood when people were talking to her. In the end, she did her best, explaining to the girl in the same calm slow voice, before helping her out of the bed and guiding her towards the door. The girl stumbled, hunching over as she moved. If she felt any pain from her injuries, she didn't voice it.

When they reached the door, the girl froze. Her breathing turned to frantic pants. Her eyes went wide and she began to claw at her arms. It was fear of the unknown more than anything else which fuelled her panic. She'd identified the room as safe but beyond the door was unknown and presented new dangers.

As if in response to her fear, there was a stab of pain in her stomach and she doubled over. The group automatically moved forward, their medical training outweighing their discomfort as they reached out to help the girl as best they could.

She took a moment, before straightening up a little. The doctor hesitated before trying once more to lead the girl from the room. She spoke soft words of comfort as she did, encouraging the girl to follow her. Her tone reached through the fog of the girl's fear-addled brain and she allowed herself to be guided out of the room and down the halls. Her movements were slow, her eyes roving the surroundings in search of anything dangerous. The noise, the lights, the people. Her senses were assaulted with every step and she cringed against Dr Tate's side as unfamiliarity overwhelmed her. She was used to fear but in her mind, it was dark and silent. This was new and different and sent her brain into a spiral of confused terror.

The paediatric ward was quieter the others, only a handful of occupied beds, but the room held a buzz to it that was absent from the others. The walls were brightly decorated, stickers of princesses and cartoon characters clung to almost every available surface. Jamie was seated on a bed, scowling into space. Despite the touches meant to make the room seem more homely, he still felt uncomfortable. Hospitals set him on edge. He knew that the decorations were just a mask, that close by people lay dying and that a dancing sponge or a crime-solving dog wouldn't change that. He wanted to get out as quickly as he could.

"I told you, I feel fine."

"Jamie, you had a seizure. You need to stay here and let us take care of you."

Jamie let out an exaggerated huff and rested his head against the wall. He wondered if they'd be so insistent if they didn't know his mom. He'd been in the hospital a few hours since he'd been found on his bathroom floor still unconscious. The nurses had tried to find a reason for his collapse and, since he didn't think a snake emerging from his leg would be a suitable answer, he'd kept quiet. He knew it would only lead to trouble. Privately, he had slipped into a bathroom and examined his leg. There was no wound, just the same small scars he'd observed in the kitchen. But he was positive he hadn't imagined it… he couldn't have made up something that… vivid.

"Look, you know my mom, I'm going to be just as observed at home as I would be here. If not more."

The nurse sighed, seeing that he was going to continue to resist any help she offered. In truth, they'd not actually managed to find anything wrong with him despite running tests. Jamie bit his lip. He could see the nurse seemed almost convinced and decided to persevere.

"I promise, I am fine. I've just not been sleeping well. That's why I collapsed, that's all I swear."

"Okay, I'll ask Dr Knott. You can't go anywhere until he approves it."

The nurse got up but paused instead of leaving. A group of staff had entered the room. Jamie watched with mild curiosity as the nurse approached. A doctor at the head of the group murmured to her, heads bowed. The nurse seemed taken aback by whatever the doctor was saying and pulled back slightly.

"Really? In here?"

"Yes. Dr Knott – "

"Didn't say anything to me. I'll… go and find him and see what's going on."

Jamie's eyes skimmed over the group. They seemed on edge, shifting anxiously. Amongst them, a small figure almost obscured, caught his focus. He could only just make out her face but there was no mistaking her eyes. They were fixed on him, vibrant emerald eyes that he recognised instantly.

The girl, whose expression was usually occupied by wary confusion, seemed to light up as she looked at Jamie. She wriggled out of the group, her movements unnoticed by her escorts. She crossed the room as swiftly as she could with her damaged leg. Jamie cringed slightly as he took in the injury, feeling guilty. The girl reached his bed and seated herself. She looked at him for a moment before raising her hands to her face, covering all her features except for her eyes.

It took Jamie a moment to work out what she was doing, but then he realised she was recreating, as best she could, the view from their encounter.

"Yeah... that was me," he said softly. The girl lowered her hands and smiled slightly. Over by the doors, Dr Tate had noticed the girl at last and hurried over. She was taken aback by the girl's smile and her voluntary approachment of the teenage boy.

"Do you... know each other?" she asked hesitantly.

"I... not exactly..." he began. "I've seen her before... but we're not... friends or anything."

The encounter Jamie was referring to had taken place a few days before, the same day that the girl had been found. It had been early morning, the sun still low in the sky, on the last day of the annual Harper hunting trip. Jamie and his uncle had settled themselves near a deer path. Neither of them was in particularly high spirits. His uncle was disappointed by their catch and Jamie, exhausted from nightmares, the rough terrain and long hours hunched in cold, drizzly surroundings, was wishing he was somewhere else. He'd been picking at a twig, stripping the bark off for lack of anything else to do, when his eyes, which had been idly scanning the surroundings, landed on a pair of deep green eyes staring back at him from a bush.

The thick undergrowth obscured the features, allowing him only a glimpse of pale skin but nothing else to identify the owner of the eyes. He opened his mouth, not really sure what he was going to say, when his uncle fired his gun.

"You shot her?" Doctor Tate said as Jamie finished recounting his story.

"No!" he said defensively. "It was my uncle! And we didn't know it was a girl... and we didn't realise he'd actually hit it... her."

His cheeks flushed red and he ducked his head. He'd been thinking about the incident a lot, worrying about what had happened. The girl's eyes had haunted his nightmares, lurking in the shadows and weaving into the normal fabric of his dreams. He'd also not been entirely honest. He had known that they'd hit her. He'd seen the blood.

"Well, you'll probably have to give a statement to the police. Even if it was an accident, the details might help them pinpoint her movements a bit and work out where she came from."

The doctor turned away, her attention drawn to the door where Dr Knott had finally arrived. She went over to talk to him, leaving Jamie and the girl on the bed. The girl reached over and poked his cheek lightly as if trying to confirm that he was real. His face was burned into her mind, the first face she had seen in years. She knew that people existed. Somewhere, buried deep in her mind, were hazy recollections of a man, a woman and a girl but the images didn't really mean anything to her anymore. His face had triggered new feelings in her, feelings she didn't really understand. Hope.

"Hi..." said Jamie, feeling a little awkward and uncomfortable. "I'm sorry... about your leg. Does it hurt? Wait, that's a stupid question. Sorry." He bit his lip. "I'm Jamie. What's your name?"

The girl didn't speak, just looked at him sadly. He opened his mouth to say something but was cut off by Dr Knott who had approached the bed.

"So Jamie looks like you're feeling better but you're going to have to wait until we've got our little friend here comfortable before you can go home."

The two teenagers looked up sharply, both startled, as the doctor reached out and placed a hand on the girl's arm to guide her off the bed The girl's body went rigid and her hands began to tremble. She pulled back sharply, falling off the bed and onto the floor, scurrying backwards. Jamie blinked, watching with concern and confusion. Dr Knott sidestepped the bed, moving towards the girl. She pressed her back against the wall, shrinking away. She screwed her eyes shut and let out a piercing scream.

The sound was fuelled by rage and fear and seemed to echo around the ward. The room fell silent from the sheer force of it, children and staff alike turning to see what was happening. The scream sent chills rippling through the bodies of her captured audience, freezing them to the core. One of the lights overhead flickered and Jamie felt a pain like hundreds of red hot needles were being driven deep into his brain. He cringed, clamping his hands over his ears as the noise burrowed into his mind.

Dr Knott, frozen temporarily by the scream, moved towards her, grabbing hold of her arm. This prompted Dr Tate and nearby nurses also to move forward.

"Careful, you'll hurt her!" Dr Tate protested as Dr Knott tried to pull the girl to her feet.

"She's distressing the patients. We need to move her to the isolation room immediately." He gestured for his colleagues to assist him. The doctors exchanged glances, unsure of what to do. They didn't want to upset the other patients, but they were also reluctant to push the girl into potentially hurting herself or others.

The girl continued to scream, flailing and kicking out at the man. Blood had begun to run from her nose and her eyes seemed almost black as the light continued to flash overhead. There was a light thump at the window as a small bird hit the glass, leaving a smear of blood and a smattering of feathers.

Dr Knott, with the help of a nurse, had managed to lift the girl from her spot on the floor. His arms were wrapped around her chest, pinning her own arms to her side. He began to drag her away from the wall, across the ward as his colleagues watched in a state of shock at his actions. The girl tossed her head, her eyes meeting Jamie's and silently begging. He was on his feet before he really knew what he was doing, freezing as he registered his movements. The girl twisted sharply, her head flying backwards and slamming into the doctor's face. He let out a shout, releasing the girl who tumbled to the floor.

There was a bang, a cracking of glass. Jamie turned his head to look.

The window exploded. Shards of glass erupted, flung across the length of the ward, lacerating anyone who got in the way. Birds swarmed in through the hole, a swirling mass of winged fury. The patients and the doctors erupted into chaos, the air filled with screams of panic. Claws, wings, beaks, all blurred into one shrieking mass thick with feathers as an endless horde poured into the hospital. People dived for cover as the irate birds clawed and pecked angrily at anything they could reach. One collided with Jamie, it's talons slicing across his forehead. Blood dripped down into his eyes, clouding his vision. He couldn't think, he couldn't see, there was nothing but noise and blood and panic.

Jamie dropped to the ground, covering his face with one arm and flailing the other around in an attempt to ward off the birds. He crawled to a nearby bed and tucked himself into the space beneath. He wiped his face, squinting out into the destruction. In the fray, he caught sight of the girl. She was sprawled on the floor nearby, curled into a ball with her arms wrapped protectively around her stomach. He wriggled forward, stretching out to try and reach her. She was just a little too far. He grimaced and crawled out of his hiding place. Keeping his body low and an arm over his face to protect his eyes, he moved over to her. Jamie touched her arm, intending to draw her under the bed to safety. She lifted her head slightly, locking eyes with him. There was a moment where he wasn't sure if she was going to pull away but instead, she took his hand and let him lead her back to the safety of the bed.

The two of them lay in the narrow space beneath the bed as the sound of patients screaming and the cries of the birds filled the room. The girl lay rigid, eyes closed, whimpering softly. There was a strange childishness to her face that reminded Jamie of Callie in a way. He reached over hesitantly and took her hand in his, squeezing it gently. She flinched at first but, after a moment of tension, relaxed a little and pressed her face against his shoulder.

The birds, disorientated and angry, continued to hurl themselves at anything they could, crashing into the walls and furniture before dropping to the floor, dazed or dead from the impact. The screaming died and slowly the sound of wings faded. A few of the children were sobbing. Jamie peeked his head out from under the bed. The tiled floor was littered with bird bodies and now he could see just how many of them had swarmed the ward. Hawks, crows, pigeons, sparrows and others that Jamie didn't recognise lay there. A few were twitching, wings broken from the damage they'd sustained. One let out a weak caw.

"Okay everyone…" said Doctor Tate. "I think it's safe…"

The girl opened her eyes slowly and reached over, wiping a little of the blood from Jamie's cheek. He gave her a reassuring smile, before getting to his feet and helping her up. The pair of them stood, huddled together, in the wreckage of the ward.

"Who's injured?" Doctor Knott asked. There was a collective grumble from nearby patients and a handful of staff. Doctor Knott eyed them, assessing the damage."Right, any staff that are fit for work, I need you to start treating the injured. Patients first, then other staff." He turned to a nurse near the door that looked uninjured. "You. Go and find alternative accommodation –"

"Before you do that," cut in Doctor Tate. "The priority after treating them is to contact their parents. They need to know what happened. And they're going to need counselling, so contact the psychiatric ward and have them send someone down."

Dr Knott looked mildly annoyed by the interruption but didn't speak, choosing instead to usher the patients to the far end of the ward, near the door where there was less glass. Jamie, the girl close at his side, began to carefully make his way over, weaving between the bird corpses. His gaze lingered on an owl, wings twisted and broken, body matted with blood. It stared back at him with lifeless amber eyes, the image burning itself into his brain.

## HOW TO PREPARE THE OFFERINGS

*Begin the preparations a few days ahead of the dark moon. The offerings should fast and their bodies must be purged with a solution of saltwater and pokeweed. When they are cleansed internally, the offerings must be stripped and purified externally with ice, fire and salt.*

*Once the purification is complete, the offerings should be placed before the relic. They must renounce the ways of the heathens and open their hearts to the true lord. Once they have repented for their sins and the sins of their parents before them, they will be welcomed by the followers of the truth.*

*Take the athame and sanctify the blade with fire. Brand the offerings wth the lord's mark upon their left hand and bind their wrists.*

# VI

The injured were treated. The staff who were wounded left to rest while those fit for work remained to deal with the flood of anxious parents who had started to arrive. The girl had been escorted to a private room and Jamie, after his cut had been stitched up, slipped away down the corridor to look for her. The residents of the pediatric ward had been quarantined in one area while they were treated, assessed and reassigned to available beds or discharged. Because of the fray of people, children crying for their parents, mothers and fathers trying to reach their offspring or arguing with the staff, Jamie found it fairly easy to sneak off. He made his way down the halls, keeping his head down and peeking into the rooms he passed.

He eventually spotted her sitting on the floor beside her bed. She was tracing patterns on the tiles, seemingly unaware of the world around her. Jamie hesitated. He didn't know her, so why was he checking on her?

The girl lifted her head, locking eyes with him. He gave her a small friendly smile and let himself into the room. He seated himself on the floor, leaving a small distance between them.

"Hello again."

The girl stayed silent, her head lowered once more and her gaze flickering around the room anxiously.

"It's okay," Jamie said. "You don't have to talk. I get it. There are some things you just don't want to talk about… and if that's the only thing in your mind, it can be hard to know what else to say. To pretend you're okay."

He lapsed into silence, his hand fiddling with the pockets of his jeans. Something crinkled under his fingers and he smiled slightly. His mom had been the one to find him in the bathroom and had brought along some of his clothes for him to change into, knowing how much he despised hospital gowns. In his pocket was a packet of sweets, a habit left over from childhood. He fished them out of pocket.

"Want one?" he asked, offering the bag to her. She looked at him, seemingly confused by the gesture. He smiled slightly and shifted over, closing the space between them. He unwrapped one and placed it in her hand, before getting one for himself, popping it in his mouth. The girl hesitated but did the same. Jamie smiled a little more, crumpling the wrapper reflexively. He watched as she chewed the sweet, her eyes widening. "You... okay?"

She nodded enthusiastically, her hands trembling slightly as the sugar hit her. Jamie laughed softly, catching himself as he did so. He hadn't laughed in weeks and the sound felt strange to his ears. He looked down at the wrapper in his hand, the gold foil with two stripes of green. He smoothed it out carefully before twisting and folding it in an intricate manner. The girl watched him, her body jittering slightly as she did but her eyes were fixed on his hands.

"Tada!" He held up a tiny golden flower with a flourish. The girl smiled and clapped her hands. "My... someone I used to know showed me how to make them. They were better at it than I am though."

Jamie looked down at the flower in his hands. The girl reached over and touched his arm lightly. Her fingers gently skimmed up to his wrist, faltering on his scarred skin. She made a soft noise, something close to a whimper. Jamie gave a sad smile before carefully removing her hand.

"Here. You can have this." He reached up and carefully tucked the foil flower in her knotted hair. She touched it lightly and smiled at him.

"Am I interrupting?"

The teenagers lifted their heads. Officer Harper was stood in the doorway, watching them with an unreadable expression.

"Dad! What are you doing here?"

"I came to pick you up. The doctors said you were fit for discharge and... that the ward had been destroyed... by birds?"

"Yes, you did hear that correctly."

"Right... well... come on kiddo, let's get you home."

Jamie got to his feet but felt something tug on his jean leg. He glanced down. The girl was gripping his trouser hem, watching him with large eyes. Jamie reached down and carefully pried her fingers free.

"I'll come back," he said softly. He wasn't sure exactly why he said it but it felt right somehow. The girl looked down at the floor but didn't

76

make any further attempts to restrain him. Jamie let his dad usher him out of the room and down the corridor. Neither of them spoke but Jamie could tell something was on his dad's mind.

"I thought you'd be working?" Jamie asked as the pair exited the hospital and headed across the car park.

"I'm heading to the station once I drop you home." He glanced over at his son. "Unless you think you're going to collapse again?"

"No, I'm fine."

"Okay then."

They got in the car, lapsing into silence once again. Jamie rested his head against the window, staring out. The vibrant colours of fall had already begun to fade into the bleak grey of winter. The only break in the monotony was the flashes of orange as they passed by houses adorned with jack-o-lanterns and other Halloween trappings.

"So," his dad began. Jamie stiffened, something about the tone being used setting him on edge. "Your mom and I have been talking and she… we… think you should go back to counselling."

The words hit Jamie like a punch to the gut. He felt the breath leave his body and a sharp pain take root in the pit of his stomach.

"No."

His dad's eyes left the road and flickered over to him, his expression already set in a way that told the boy he was going to try to pacify him.

"Jay…"

"No, I'm not going back, I don't need it, I am fine," he said fiercely.

"You say that but we can see you're not. You're exhausted, you're not eating. The doctors told me your collapse was probably because of this. And, we know the nightmares are back, we hear you calling out at night."

"How can you hear me when you're never home?" he snapped.

"Look, this isn't a negotiation. We're doing what we feel is best." His dad paused. "Your mom found blood in your shower."

"It's not what you think," Jamie said immediately.

"Then what is it?"

The boy fell silent, glaring out of the window. He wanted to argue but there was nothing he could say that would help.

"We've booked you an appointment. If they say you're fine, you don't have to go back, okay?" his dad said, his tone softening slightly.

"Fine…"

They pulled up outside the house and Jamie got out, leaving his dad in the car. He went straight up to his room, slamming the door shut behind him and throwing himself on the bed. He curled up, burying his face in the pillow and letting out an enraged cry. He wasn't crazy, he didn't need help, he was fine, he was fine!

*Telling yourself it doesn't make it true.*

That voice, that nagging voice that wormed its way into his brain and filled his head with doubt. His hand reached out, fumbling blindly on his bedside table for his iPod. He had to drown it out, make it fade away until he couldn't hear it anymore. He felt for the smooth case, eventually finding it and sighing with relief.

*Can't block out the truth Jamie…*

He plugged the earbuds in, hitting the power button and turning the volume up high. The voices shrieked in his ears, overwhelming the lingering noise in his head. He sighed in relief, rolling onto his back and staring up at the ceiling. His cut, where the bird had slashed his face, stung and itched. He rubbed his cheek and sighed. He had to convince the doctor he was alright, he couldn't risk things ending up like before.

Jamie vaulted out of bed and went into his bathroom. His mom, or someone, had cleaned the shower as there was no sign of the blood. He grabbed the pots of pills from the sink and opened it, his hand trembling although he didn't know why. He tipped two into his palm and paused. He'd resisted till now, desperate not to be trapped in his nightmares but… he needed to convince them he was okay. He could endure a few nights if it meant they believed him.

He swallowed the pills dry. They tasted bitter on his tongue and stuck in the back of his throat, making him gag, but he forced them down.

He got changed into his pyjamas and stretched out. He could do this. It wasn't a big deal. He focused on his breathing as the pills began to sink in, drifting into oblivion.

"Jamie! Wake up!"

Jamie blinked and sat up. Brilliant sun streamed in through the window, the kind that only came on the most perfect of summer days, where you woke up with a sense of excitement at the promise of the day. He got out of bed slowly and headed down the stairs. Laughter and the clatter of pans from the kitchen, a smell of pancakes.

"Morning sleepy head!" His mom was at the stove, making pancakes. Callie was sitting at the breakfast bar next to his father who was reading the paper as Echo bounded around the room, barking excitedly.

"Morning..." Jamie frowned slightly, taking his seat.

"You okay champ?" his dad said.

"Umm... yeah..."

His mom placed a plate of pancakes in front of him, humming softly to herself. The tune was familiar and Jamie lifted his head, his frown growing. That song... his mom didn't know that, she couldn't...

"Mom, where did you hear that?" he asked.

"What are you talking about Jay? I've always known it."

The lights flickered and for a second Jamie caught sight of a different kitchen, a different family, but then it was gone and everything returned to normal. He looked down at his plate, the perfectly round pancakes dripping with syrup. They looked like something out of a movie... just too perfect. They were uniform in size, shape and colour. On the rare occasion that his mom made pancakes, they were an uneven lumpy affair that frequently verged on burnt.

"Dad... about going to the doctors..."

"You're not sick Jamie, you don't need a doctor."

"But you said..."

He trailed off, looking around the kitchen. The lights flickered again. Patched curtains, dirty dishes in the sink, counters slick with a sheen of grease. A woman, thin with a faint bruise on her temple, hair tied in a messy bun, humming a tune as she washed a pan. A teenage boy, dark-haired in a bedraggled hoodie and a pretty young girl in a white dress.

Jamie blinked and it disappeared like it was never there at all.

"Are you alright Jamie? You look pale."

"I'm... I'm fine..." He felt a peculiar nauseous sensation in the pit of his stomach and an overwhelming sense of wrongness. The lights began to flash more furiously, on and off with no sign of stopping. No one in the kitchen reacted, continuing with their breakfast as though nothing was wrong. Along with the flashing came a steady thudding of angry footsteps that grew more insistent as the blackouts grew more frequent. The surroundings fluctuated between the two kitchens, the world rippling around Jamie as they glitched back and forth. His head hurt, the constant throbbing of the light and the pounding of the footsteps making him dizzy and the nauseous feeling continued to build.

The blonde woman turned her head towards the door, her eyes fearful as the banging reached its peak. The light went out completely plunging Jamie into a pit of nothingness.

Darkness, engulfing darkness. The steady sound of dripping, a cavernous echoing quality to the noise. Faintly, somewhere in the distance, was another sound, a half-choked whimper. Crying?

Jamie found his legs moving of their own accord, pursuing the sound without any sense of where he was going. The ground underfoot was uneven and sloped up sharply. The crying grew louder and amongst the darkness, veins of light appeared, allowing Jamie to make out cracked stone walls around him. They looked natural, jagged rocks protruding haphazardly and with a damp sheen to them, forming a crude maze of tunnels.

Up ahead, the tunnel came to an abrupt end and from above, a shaft of light split the darkness in two. A hole in the roof, far above, allowing a sliver of night sky and the crescent moon to shine through. In the light lay a young girl, curled up in a tight ball. She was naked, her ribs and spine dangerously visible, and looked to be about twelve. Her skin seemed to glow in the moonlight, black veins standing out lividly. A smell like copper reached Jamie's nose, mingled with the stench of damp and rot that pervaded the cave.

Jamie looked down at the girl, crying and groaning on the floor. She shifted position, turning to look in his direction. She seemed to look through him rather than at him, wrapping her arms around herself in an attempt to keep from falling apart. Now Jamie could see more of her, see what he hadn't before. Blood, staining the girl's legs, deep gouges across her waist and chest like a vicious animal had tried to tear her apart. One of her legs was bent awkwardly, sticking out at an impossible angle, accompanied by a seemingly endless array of bruises which culminated around her thigh. A dark ring of finger marks adorned her throat like a horrific necklace. Every time she moved, even slightly, she winced and clenched her fists.

The sound of whispering filtered into the cave, growing louder until it sounded like Jamie was stood in the middle of a crowded room. A dark mist rose up from the ground, a peculiar smoke that seemed to clamber over the girl's feet and ankles, crawling up her broken body and slowly engulfing her in shadows. The whispering grew even louder and more numerous, the creeping crawling shadows multiplying into a dark swarm that completely swallowed her up.

Jamie stumbled backwards; his foot connected with something in the darkness and he fell to the floor. His hand collided with something hard and cold. He squinted, trying to make it out.

An eyeless face stared back at him, a body half-decayed, the neck twisted to an unnatural degree. Bones littered the area, belonging to animals of different sizes, and amongst them, a child's skull, staring at Jamie in an accusatory way.

He scrambled to his feet but something seized hold of him. Putrid fingers, the skin rotted away in places exposing the bone beneath, grasping his ankle, digging nails into his skin. The corpse vaulted forward, mouth twisting into a parody of a smile as its eyeless sockets fixed on the boy.

"Jamie…" The voice that came from its mouth was one that Jamie knew and he felt like his heart was being stabbed with hundreds of needles. It was soft and melodic, seeming all the more disturbing when it came from such a creature.

A snake, deep green, slithered from the corpse's eye socket, winding down and around its throat like a scarf. Fangs glimmered, a bead of venom visible. The snake turned its gaze on Jamie, eyeing him hungrily, its body still half-buried in the depths of the eye socket.

"Jamie..." the corpse whimpered. As Jamie stared, the decay seemed to repair, allowing him to see the face more clearly. Blonde hair, a soft blush surfaced on the dead flesh and a serene blue eye peered at him.

"Help me, Jamie... it hurts..."

The snake slithered free, descending to the ground and disappearing into the shadows.

"Lily... I..."

"Jamie..."

The body, somewhere between corpse and girl, began to retch. Its hand released his leg as bile and thick foam-like saliva began to spew from its mouth. It reached out to him, tears tinged with blood streaming down · its cheeks.

"Jamie!" It screamed, voice filled with pain and fear. The snake emerged from the shadows, entwining tightly around his ankles. There was a sensation of red hot agony. He recoiled, the sudden movement sending him tumbling into the darkness.


Jamie's eyes flew open. He was in bed. He had no idea how long he'd been asleep for but the room was in darkness. His covers were wrapped around his ankles, the rest of him left exposed. A cold sweat clung to his skin, his pyjamas soaked through.

He tried to sit up but his limbs refused to respond, trapping him in place. His skin seemed to prickle and he felt something brush against his arm, sending chills through him. He became aware of the sound of soft breathing somewhere near his head and the kiss of exhaled air followed, an unpleasant warmth with a faint smell to it that lingered about his nostrils.

Jamie slowly swivelled his eyes, the one body part still under his control, in the direction of the breathing. He wasn't entirely sure he wanted to see what was causing it but the not knowing was worse. On the edge of his field of vision he could make out a dark blur of something stood just out of sight. He was hyperaware of the presence looming over him, the feeling of something dark and hungry watching him with ravenous, lustful eyes.

He felt something sharp and cold graze against the curve of his neck, sliding slowly over his pulse point. He trembled, wanting to flinch away but unable to. The shadow moved further out of his line of sight and the breath on his skin intensified as though whatever it was had drawn closer.

The world seemed to still, an electric current of tension flowing between Jamie and the entity. His breathing was ragged as fear gripped his body, waiting to see what would happen, if it would make a move. He felt like a child once again, trapped at the mercy of an unforgiving monster.

The cold dragging across his skin continued. Jamie tried once more to move his limbs, not sure what he would do if he was able to but unwilling to remain at the mercy of whatever malevolent creature was watching him.

*You're not scared are you, Jamie?*

He wasn't sure if the voice was real or something conjured from his imagination and memory but it filled his ears. Something stirred his hair, an impossible breeze that brushed it away from his ear and rough finger caressed his face. Tears burned Jamie's eyes and they ran down his cheeks, seeping into his pillow.

*Don't cry, be a brave boy for me…*

He closed his eyes, blinking away the tears as best he could. Don't let them see you cry, pretend to be okay like always. He screwed his eyes tightly shut, praying for relief. It wasn't real, he told himself. It was a dream, just a dream, that was all.

But you're not asleep…

Jamie whimpered quietly, trying to force himself out of the horrific waking nightmare he found himself lost in. The touch on his skin of fingers and breath continued for a moment before pulling backwards. He waited for a minute, fearing a trick and that any movement would prompt a renewed assault, then tentatively opened his eyes, peeking out.

The room was as it had always been. There was no sign of the shadow, the hungry gaze he had sensed roaming over him was gone. His body relaxed, limbs released of whatever paralysis had held them trapped and he was able to sit up slowly. There was nothing. No monsters, no illusions to torment him.

Just an empty room, a mess of bedsheets and a tear-streaked pillow.

*This Book of Shadows is the property of Samyra Luis*

*October 5th*
*Full moon*

*Spell to ward off nightmares and aid restful sleep.*

- ❖ *Ylang Ylang incense*
- ❖ *Betony*
- ❖ *Valerian*
- ❖ *Thyme*
- ❖ *Tarragon*
- ❖ *St. John's Wort*
- ❖ *Spearmint*
- ❖ *Rosemary*
- ❖ *Poppy Seeds*
- ❖ *Two squares of white cloth*
- ❖ *Red thread*
- ❖ *Stuffing*
- ❖ *Mortar and pestle*
- ❖ *One small piece of quartz*
- ❖ *A length of green ribbon*
- ❖ *One blue candle*
- ❖ *Salt*
- ❖ *Water*

*Take your herbs and grind them together into a fine powder. Place the quartz into the middle of the bowl of powder and place the bowl on a window ledge under the light of the moon for one lunar month. You should start this on a full moon.*

*When the month is over, cast your circle. Using the cloth, stitch a pillow, leaving a small hole to allow you to put the stuffing in. Stuff the pillow and pour in the powder. As you do this, state 'I promise the recipient of this pillow peace and serenity, good dreams and happy days.' Sew it shut.*

*Cut the green ribbon into two and tie around the pillow, one horizontal and one vertical. Light the blue candle and the incense. Drip the wax on the spot where the ribbons cross.*

*Add a drop of water and say 'I seal this promise by water.'*

*Add a sprinkle of salt and say 'I seal this promise by earth.'*

*Place the quartz on top of the wax and add more wax from the candle until the quartz is sealed inside. Say 'I seal this promise by fire.'*

*Smudge the pillow with the incense and say 'I seal this promise by air'.*

*Place the pillow in a bedroom to grant the sleeper pleasant dreams.*

# VII

Kane Mortimer was working late. This wasn't especially unusual, however, the array of corpses lined up on the morgue tables was. In addition to the standard bodies, the deaths that were an unfortunate part of the hospital, he had had to abruptly accommodate the dead from Ward B.

He leaned against the wall, eyeing the bodies as he tried to work out what he was missing. Eleven deaths, all at the same time but all different ages and physical conditions. He'd spent the day trying to identify what might possibly have caused this bizarre situation. There didn't appear to be any clear link between them, nothing matched up.

People didn't just die. There was always a cause, no matter how obscure.

He sighed and returned to the table, the body of a middle-aged woman, face contorted into a permanent scream. That was the one thing they all shared. That look of absolute terror, the horrific screams that contorted their features into a mask of pain and fear.

Kane peered at the woman's face, searching for a clue. Unlike the others, who seemed largely unharmed on the outside, this woman's throat was covered in a number of lacerations like something had viciously clawed at her. His eyes skimmed over her and landed on her hands. The nails on her fingers were chipped and a thin layer of red powder coated the tips, clinging to the nail beds. Had she clawed her own throat open? He frowned and leaned closer to get a better look.

The door to the morgue swung open and Sammy strolled in. Kane straightened up immediately and pulled a sheet over the body.

"Samyra. What are you doing down here?" His voice was a strange mix of accents that made it difficult to place where exactly he was from.

Sammy grimaced at the use of her full name and produced a container from her messenger bag.

"I know you forget to eat when you're working late. Voila, pesto pasta and prawns."

"Thanks… but you know you're not meant to be in here." He frowned. "How did you even get down here? The lift needs a key card."

Sammy grinned and perched on a nearby table, fishing a key card from her pocket. The name on it read Dr Albright. Kane's eyes narrowed.

"Do I want to know how you got that?"

"My mom had a dinner date with the good doctor. And I found this carelessly lying around afterwards."

"Uh-huh. You stole it."

"Yes. Yes, I did."

She looked at Kane, eyebrow quirking slightly as though daring him to do something about it. He rolled his eyes and came over to sit beside her, taking the container from her. Samy grinned and handed him a fork from her bag.

"You really need to stop hanging out with me. It's not healthy," Kane said as he began to eat. "Normal girls do not lurk in morgues."

"Normality is overrated."

Kane gave a slight smile, a rarity from him, before returning his focus to his food. The pair of them sat in companionable silence as he ate, comfortable in each other's company without the need to fill the silence.

"Did you walk the dogs?" he asked after a while.

"Your hellhounds? Yes, I did."

"They like you."

"I'm good with animals." She smiled and pinched a prawn from his pot. "Maybe I should add dog walking to my lists of jobs?"

"Now you're being greedy. You need to leave some work for the rest of the town."

Sammy laughed softly but it sounded distracted and Kane could tell there was something on her mind. She swung her legs and fiddled with a lock of her inky black hair. The coloured streaks had started to fade and her expression made the rest of her seem faded out too.

"You alright?" Kane asked hesitantly. He knew Sammy liked her privacy, she was much like him in that respect, and if he questioned her too much it might send her running.

"Yeah… just worried about a friend of mine."

She looked down, her hair falling around her face like a curtain. The shoulder of her jacket slipped down, exposing the strap of her vest top, the ridge of her shoulder blade and a small tattoo of a black and purple butterfly just visible. He often forgot how young she was. These rare moments of vulnerability reminded him not only of her youth but the fact that, if he were a decent man, he'd send her away and not see her again.

"How's the pasta?" Sammy asked suddenly, straightening up and tucking her hair behind her ears.

"Too much garlic," he said, taking a large mouthful.

"Just trying to protect you from vampires."

"Of course, always top of my priorities," he said dryly. Sammy smiled and shuffled closer to him.

"So…."

"No."

"I didn't ask you anything yet!"

"I know but I can predict exactly what you're going to ask. You're going to ask me for details about my work and how each of these people died and I'm not going to answer."

"Oh come on Kane!"

"It's bad enough that you're down here at all, I'm not budging on this."

Sammy's expression hardened and she folded her arms, her resolve clear in every line of her body.

"Look, I can tell that you want to talk about whatever it is you've got going on. It's rattling around in your brain and it'll bug you until you talk about it. Besides, if anyone comes down here I'll hide in one of the drawers and play dead." She gave a mischevious smirk. "I mean, we both know I can fit…"

They locked eyes with one another, a standoff they'd had many times before. And just like always, Kane broke first.

"Fine. But you tell no one."

"Of course. So? Spill."

Kane got up and headed to the nearest examination table, gesturing for her to follow. Sammy hopped up and went after him. He folded back the sheet that covered one of the women that had been brought in, exposing her head, neck and shoulders.

"You're a bit busier than normal. What happened?" she asked, running her eyes over the tables.

"Well, that's what I'm trying to figure out. Last night... something happened."

"Descriptive."

"Eleven patients died. On the same ward. At the same time."

"That... that is something alright..." Sammy said, struggling to find something better to say. "What was the cause of death?"

"That's where it gets stranger."

"That's possible?" Sammy was beginning to regret asking for details but her natural curiosity got the better of her and she couldn't help but want to know more.

"Apparently so. The male patients all died of heart failure. And before you ask, only one of them had any history of heart problems."

"And the women...?" she asked, looking down at the body in front of them.

"Theirs varied. Cerebral haemorrhage, asphyxiation... one of them appears to have clawed their own throat open." He nodded to the covered form on the next table.

Sammy opened her mouth to speak but quickly closed it again, realising that there was nothing she could say that would accurately sum up how she felt. The pair of them stood together in silence, looking down at the body, neatly arranged on the table, empty unseeing eyes staring up at the ceiling.

Kane went to cover her up once again but Sammy touched his wrist, halting him. She moved closer and lightly touched the woman's cheek. She frowned, crouching down slightly.

"What are these?"

Kane followed her gaze and saw something that had escaped his eyes during the initial examination. Across her collarbone and up the curve of her neck were several small cuts, slender and about the length of a pin. They looked to be fresh and were clustered in groups of four like a small animal had clambered across her skin, digging in tiny claws.

"I... don't know."

He peered at the marks. Nestled at the hollow of the neck, over the blue of an artery, was a raised spot like a mosquito bite with a tiny dot of blood in the centre. It was darker than the rest of the skin around it and was surrounded by bruising and a web of thin black veins.

"Insect bite?" Sammy asked, leaning over his shoulder to get a better look. Kane shook his head.

"Too much bruising. More likely a needle mark."

"It's a hospital, that's not that unusual." Sammy stepped back and lifted the sheet on the next table, peeking at the body beneath while Kane continued to stare at the neck of the woman in front of him, trying to figure out what he was missing.

"It's not in the right place for an IV feed and I don't recall seeing anything on her chart to support her receiving an injection in that area."

"Foul play then?" Sammy looked over at him, tucking the sheet down once more.

"Maybe..." Kane closed his eyes, leaning back and pinching the bridge of his nose. "How did I not see this?"

"You're getting old man. Time to retire."

He opened his eyes and glanced at her, mildly irritated. He knew she was joking but he was in no mood for her humour right now.

"Shut up and go home Sammy," he snapped. "And while you're at it, leave that stolen pass here."

Sammy met his eye for a moment, hurt by his sharp tone but trying not to show it.

"Alright." She grabbed her bag and headed to the door. She pushed it open but paused, looking back at him. "Oh, by the way, that other body over there has the same marks. Just so you know."

She swept out, letting the door slam behind her. Kane blinked, staring after her, then turned sharply to the table where Sammy had been fiddling. He lifted the sheet, revealing the man underneath. Carefully, he pushed up the corpse's head, exposing the waxy skin of the neck. Just as Sammy had said, the man's throat was dotted with the same tiny scratches and a single raised puncture wound.

The sight set something off in Kane and he began to move from table to table in a frenzy, examining the necks of his patients. The same scratches along the neck, not completely identical in location just in the same general area, and each bore a small puncture over their carotid artery.

He gripped the edge of the examination table, his hands trembling slightly. It wasn't a coincidence, it couldn't be. It meant something, but it was like looking at part of a jigsaw. He didn't have all the pieces yet and he couldn't make sense of what was happening. The needle marks indicated an intentional act but Kane couldn't think of anything that would cause such a variety of reactions or any reason for someone to target that particular assortment of patients.

From the nose of one of the nearby corpses, black fluid began to ooze. At the sight of it, Kane stiffened and a terrible sense of recognition settled over him. He'd seen this before.

He went to his storage cupboard and retrieved a beaker and a syringe before returning to the tables. One by one he moved between the bodies, prying open their eyelids and examining the vacant glassy eyes underneath. He carefully searched for something hidden within their depths, moving on when he had determined it wasn't there.

Eventually, he spotted it, a black fleck like a tiny worm had burrowed its way into the eyeball. He carefully positioned the syringe at the base of the eye and slowly inserted it. As he pulled back the plunger, the vial filled with black fluid. He emptied the syringe into the beaker and held it up to the light. It was dotted with specks of white and grey, like a layer of scum on top of a pond, and had an oily sheen to it. It smelled like putrid flesh, mould and dirt.

As he watched, it seemed to bubble and writhe under the harsh strip lighting. He grabbed a pair of gloves and slipped one on before dipping the tip of his finger into the ooze. It clung to him, a steady hissing sound emanating from the glove as the fluid began to eat is way through the latex, searching for skin.

Kane quickly stripped off the glove and tossed it into the bio waste bin. He sighed softly, his worst fears confirmed. He went over to his sheet of notes and crumpled it up, before dumping the vile black liquid down the sink.

On a floor high above, the girl was sitting cross-legged on the floor of her hospital room, toying with the golden flower Jamie had given her. She was captivated by the way the light danced across the foil. An orange glow from the street lights outside shone through the window, intersecting the darkness of the room and it was here that the girl had seated herself, the light pooling around her.

Her ears, attuned to detecting the faintest of sounds, picked up a light scratching outside the door, like some kind of wild animal was prowling around, trying to claw its way in. The girl bit her lip and moved to lie on her side, curling up with her arms wrapped around herself like she had since she was small. The noise stopped and she allowed herself to relax just for a moment.

The crack under the door allowed her to see when anyone passed by, the momentary lapse of light as they crossed in front of her room. As she watched, the sliver disappeared entirely, something moving in front and staying there. The clawing sound started up again. The girl pressed her hands over her ears, trying to block it out. She began to lightly bang her head against the floor, wishing it would stop, but like countless times before it didn't.

Her eyes moved away from the door and rested on the flower. She removed one hand slowly, wincing as the scratching noise reached her ears again, and picked up the flower, holding it close to her. A sharp twisting pain in her stomach started up and she felt tears burning her eyes. The pain was one she knew well and had come to dread. If she was capable of speaking, she might have prayed. Prayed for it not to happen again, not to suffer through it again. The girl fisted her hospital gown, tugging at the fabric as though she could rip the agony away from her body.

Why did this always happen? Every time she felt her body begin to swell and change, the pain would come and then the blood would flow, the shadows would gather and multiply and He would come to start it all again.

She pressed the flower against her chest and closed her eyes. The pain seemed to dull slightly and she smiled slightly, thinking of the boy. She hoped he would come back. There was something kindred about him, a sense she didn't understand. Her memories of her family were distorted and faded but the feeling that came to her when she thought of them was the same feeling that stirred in her around Jamie.

As she lay there, allowing herself to slowly drift to sleep, she felt a strange sensation like fingers brushing across her shoulder and up her cheek. She whimpered softly but didn't stir, not quite asleep but not really awake either.

Eventually, the feeling stopped, the fingers retreating once more into the shadows.

# Mental Status Exam

CLIENT NAME: *J. Alexander*          DATE: *February 1ˢᵗ*

## OBSERVATIONS

APPEARANCE: *Dishevelled*

SPEECH: *Pressured*

EYE CONTACT: *Avoidant*

MOTOR ACTIVITY: *Restless*

AFFECT: *Constricted*

## MOOD

*Patient appears anxious and highly fearful.*

## COGNITION

ORIENTATION IMPAIRMENT: *None. Patient appears fully aware.*

MEMORY IMPAIRMENT: *Short-term memory impairment. Patient has no memory of events surrounding hospitalisation on January 8ᵗʰ*

ATTENTION: *Distracted. Patient appears unfocused and has difficulty maintain focus.*

## PERCEPTION

HALLUCINATIONS: *None indicated*

OTHER: *Patient shows some signs of derealisation.*

## THOUGHTS

SUICIDALITY: *None indicated*

HOMICIDALITY: *None indicated*

DELUSIONS: *None indicated*

## BEHAVIOUR

*Extremely guarded and withdrawn*

| INSIGHT | JUDGEMENT |
|---------|-----------|
| Fair | Fair |

Assessment conducted by *Dr Lois Stein*, at *Redwood Memorial Hospital*

# VIII

Jamie stumbled down to breakfast, groggy and disorientated. His hair was mussed, stuck to his skin by a coating of sweat, his face ashen with the dark circles under his eyes more livid than ever. The stitches on his face where the birds had cut him were surrounded by a light crust of blood. His headphones dangled around his neck, tangling as he struggled to do up the last few buttons of his shirt.

"Jamie, you got mail," said his mother.

He jumped, so used to his parents not being there in the mornings that in his preoccupied state he'd failed to notice both of them sitting at the breakfast bar.

"Huh?"

"Mail." She held out two letters for him. He took them and looked them over. The first was typed with a 'Private and Confidential' stamp emblazoned on one side. He shuffled it to the back to examine the next one. It was handwritten, a familiar spikey scrawl. He stared at it for a moment before shoving them both into his pocket, unopened. Even without looking at the return address, he knew who they were from and he didn't want to deal with either of them yet.

"Thanks. See you later," he said stiffly. He made for the door, popping his headphones in as he did so.

"Aren't you going to have some breakfast?" asked his dad.

"No time. I'm late." He catapulted out of the door, snagging his hoodie on the way. His parents watched him go, faces bearing a mixture of sadness, concern and disappointment.

"He's getting worse," said Officer Harper softly. "You were right."

"I heard him screaming in the night... it breaks my heart..." she paused. "Do you think we let him come home too soon? Maybe... maybe he should have stayed there..."

"The doctors said he was okay Ruth. We all knew there was a possibility of a relapse but it was a risk we had to take. He can't live his whole life behind protective glass."

97

"I know, I just… you saw his face when he saw the letter…"

"We will look after him. That monster won't get near him. We'll go through the courts if we have to, get a protection order or something."

The couple embraced, Mrs Harper burying her face in her husband's chest.

"I don't want to lose him again," she whispered.

"I know sweetie. It won't come to that, I promise you."

Sarum Vale High wasn't too far from Jamie's house and he managed to make it to his homeroom before the bell rang. He slid into his desk and pulled his hood up, keeping his head down. The rest of his class were chattering happily, their voices loud and obnoxious.

Jamie turned up the volume on his iPod, drowning them out as best he could before retrieving the handwritten letter from his pocket and set it on the desk in front of him. He regarded it warily, like a dangerous animal that might bite at any moment. He dared himself to open it, knowing that he never would. No, this letter, like the ones before it, would be hidden under the floorboards in his bedroom with all the other things he found too painful to look at.

He tucked the letter away once again and got out his notebook. The other letter he knew that he didn't even need to open. It was a confirmation of his psychiatric appointment, he'd seen enough of them to recognise it.

His teacher had begun to drone on but he barely heard her, letting his pen graze the paper in slow spirals. His cuts itched and he grimaced, resisting the urge to rub them.

Therapy. It wasn't that he hadn't known he'd eventually end back up there. His parents' obliviousness could only go so far, a fact he was well aware of, but he'd been hoping that his respite might last a little longer. There was nothing particularly wrong with the doctor that Jamie's parents had selected for him, he just disliked people prying into his private thoughts, particularly ones whose concern was entirely false and only motivated by money.

On paper, Dr Lilith Knott was perfect. Her credentials, her experience and specialities all lined up with his needs. And Jamie knew should be grateful his parents could afford to send him to a private practice rather than being placed on the bottom of the list at the hospital. But he couldn't help but feel a little resentful. Why wasn't he good enough the way he was? He'd endured his nightmares as best he could without complaint. He'd taken every pill offered to him. Why wasn't that enough? Ignoring the recent hallucinations, which he had put down to lack of sleep and an overactive imagination, he was fine. Absolutely fine.

Homeroom came to an end and Jamie headed into the crowded corridor. He moved in almost a dazed state, his mind occupied with everything but where he was at that second. His first class was biology and, while he usually preferred the more artistic classes over the analytical or scientific, he didn't mind biology. Usually, they were working from their dog-eared textbooks and it was easy for him to zone out in the back row.

Jamie took his usual seat and set up his books in a way that resembled a makeshift wall. If he kept his head down, he was almost completely obscured from view. The teacher, Mr White, was fairly new to the school and couldn't always manage to keep control of everyone, which made it easy for Jamie to go unnoticed.

The door opened and Mr White entered, pushing a large rattling trolley in front of him that contained several covered trays. The class slowly quietened, their curiosity peaked.

"Morning everyone. As part of our study on anatomy, today we're going to be performing dissections. You can do this in groups or individually, it's up to you. Get ready, come up to the front and collect your equipment."

He turned and began to copy a diagram onto the board as the class erupted into chaotic chatter. Jamie grimaced and reluctantly filed up to collect his specimen and equipment. He would work alone, he did in most classes except for those he shared with Sammy.

As he reached the front of the line, he could see that the trays were filled with birds. Large ones, with their wings bent awkwardly. Jamie felt bile rise up in the back of his throat at the sight of them.

"Umm… Mr White… could I be excused from this class?" he asked quietly, stepping to the side. The teacher glanced over at him, gave him a sympathetic look and shook his head.

"Sorry Jamie, but if I let people be excused just because they don't feel like it, no one would ever show up."

Jamie ducked his head and tried to suppress his growing nausea. He gathered his equipment and returned to his desk. The people around him had already started and were engrossed in their task, letting out the occasional exclamation of horror, shock or delight. Jamie grimaced and positioned his bird in front of him. The feathers were cold and rigid, its yellow eyes stared up at him accusingly.

Gritting his teeth, he picked up the scalpel, placing the tip against the creature's belly. His hand was trembling and he bit into his lip, hard enough to break the skin. Pressing down slowly, the blade of the scalpel pierced the bird's flesh. At first, there was resistance, then the layers of fat and muscle yielded. Blood bubbled up to fill the wound, running down its side and staining the cream coloured plumage a rust toned brown.

*It's your fault.*

The voice came from nowhere and everywhere, filling Jamie's brain.

*You did this. You're to blame. You need to make it right.*

He stared down at the hapless animal, with a horrified fascination. The slowly spreading blood amongst the soft, almost blonde tone of the feathers reminded him of something, the edge of a memory locked away at the back of his mind.

*Fix it.*

His hands came to rest on the bird's body. Actions uncertain, he just knew he had to do something. The amber eyes seemed to plead with him and for a moment, Jamie swore it let out a baleful croak, but he was quickly distracted by the sight of his hands. Painted in shades of scarlet and crimson, there was barely an inch of unstained skin left, and as he looked a new memory surfaced, more vivid than the last.

The classroom faded away and he was back in his bedroom. The scalpel in his hand became a penknife with a deep green handle, the blade out.

A towel, crumpled and stained, lay beside him. And the blood, endless, coating his hands, his wrists, dripping down onto the floorboards.

*This is what you deserve.*

The room spun before him and he saw his desk, paint-splattered and familiar. In the centre was the specimen tray, the bird spread out ontop. Its chest cavity had been pulled open, exposing its tiny, still-beating heart. As he watched, the feathers began to fall away and the flesh underneath seemed to melt, peeling off the muscles. The skin stripped back, the form beneath was not that of back but of a twisted half-formed infant, the limbs limp and crooked, contorted into abnormal positions.

It let out a weak cry, a pained wail, red tears running down its deformed skin. Jamie recoiled, stumbling backwards. He collided with something solid, sharply reverting back to reality. The classroom was silent, the other students staring at Jamie. He was clutching the scalpel, eyes wide and terrified like that of a cornered animal.

"Jamie…?" asked Mr White tentatively.

He looked at them, saw the judgement and the concern. His muscles tensed, adrenaline surging through him, like a deer in the headlights of an approaching car. Fight or flight.

Flight won out. He sprinted off, dropping the scalpel to the ground as he ran, careening around desks before throwing himself through the door. He kept running, his only focus on getting as far away as possible.

Out of the school gates, down the road, Jamie's feet carrying him on through the town. He didn't know where he was going but when he eventually came to a stop outside the church, it was like there was no other place he could possibly have gone to. He held onto the fence for support, his legs buckling, gasping for breath.

The church was silent, the front door closed. Jamie closed his eyes, taking a moment to collect himself, before entering the churchyard and heading around the side of the building. There was a smaller door at the base of the bell tower, overgrown with ivy, the metal fittings rusted. He crouched down by the base of the door to where a cluster of weeds grew thickest and brushed them aside to expose a large hole, the wood splintered and uneven. He wriggled through and into the dark recess behind it, where the crumbling stone steps of the bell tower curved up into the shadows above his head. It had been several months since he'd last been there but there was a time when the church tower had been his sanctuary. And now, as he sought refuge within the decaying stones once again, it was like no time had passed at all.

He took to the stairs, walking slowly. The stairs were badly in need of repair, several worn away while the rest were often slick with rainwater that had made its way through the leaking tower roof. Jamie made his way up, one hand pressed against the wall to guide him in the darkness. He could hear the skittering scratching sound of rats moving nearby and he grimaced slightly. Halfway up, the steps widened briefly into a ledge with a small door set into the wall. The rest of the steps continued, spiralling upwards to the bell, but Jamie paused by the door. It led to the gallery that overlooked the main area of the church and was seldom used, except during the occasional Christmas service when the choir would stand up there. He knew from experience that he would be undisturbed there.

He let himself into the gallery, a large curtain hanging loosely in front of the door. He settled himself in the corner, half-hidden behind the curtain, looking down at the pews below him. He rested his head against the railing, lightly rubbing his cheek against the smooth wood.

The light filtered through the stained glass windows, casting the altar in a multicoloured glow. Jamie sat there, watching as the light slowly moved across the room, tracking the progression of the day. His phone vibrated in his pocket a few times but he ignored it, content to be alone. The images he'd seen lingered in his mind, the half-formed child and the broken bird. The accusations echoed in his ears. He lay down on the gallery, putting his headphones in and closing his eyes.

The light in the hall faded away, replaced by the sound of steady rain lashing against the windows. Jamie found himself beginning to doze off, a sense of peace settling over him that he hadn't felt in a long time. He wasn't trying to fall asleep but the exhaustion that permanently clawed at him began to win out, drawing him in with the promise of warm oblivion.

There was a soft creak and the curtain was brushed aside. Jamie lay, unaware until he felt some brush up beside him and a cool hand touched his. He opened his eyes to see Sammy, hair soaked through and stuck against her skin.

"Hey," Jamie said sleepily, struggling up into a half-sitting position and pulling his headphones out.

102

"Hey yourself… budge up will you?"

He shifted over to make space and Sammy settled down next to him. Neither of them looked at the other, staring up at the vaulted ceiling.

"Did my parents send you?"

"No. I don't think they know yet."

"That's a relief."

"Mr White called your home though. You'll have to get back before them if you want to erase the message."

"That shouldn't be a problem." He turned his head slightly to meet Sammy's eye. "So, if they didn't send you, why are you here?"

"Because you're my friend, idiot. I wanted to make sure you were okay. I figured you'd be up here." She bit her lip. "So… you want to tell me exactly what happened or do I have to go with what I heard?"

"What did you hear?"

"A couple of things. Someone said that you went crazy and attacked Mr White with a scalpel?"

"That one's not true."

"Damn. How about that you had a mental breakdown and ran off?"

"That was true." He sighed softly and ran his fingers through his hair. "I heard her voice… she was talking to me… it was like that night all over again. I was back there… I felt it all again, the guilt, the fear…" He clenched his fists. "The blood was everywhere. It won't come off my hands…"

He looked down. Sammy reached out and gently took his hands in hers, turning them over so they were palms up.

"I don't see anything. Just you."

Jamie looked down. There was no blood, just two bare hands, trembling in Sammy's grasp.

"But I saw it…" he whispered incredulously. He flexed his fingers, unable to believe what he was seeing. Sammy stroked his fingers and carefully enclosed her hands around them.

"There's nothing there…" She paused. "Are… are things getting bad for you again Jamie…?"

"No! I mean… not… not really… I mean…"

He pulled his hands free and chewed his bottom lip anxiously. Sammy's gaze was unflinching and Jamie faltered, unable to lie to her.

"Yes."

"Have you spoken to anyone about it?"

"No. I just… I can't go through all of it again. People treating me like I'm insane… it just makes it all feel… I can deal with the nightmares… and the hallucinations… kind of… I'm used to it but when other people get involved it just makes it… worse." He paused. "Do you think there such a thing as being born evil? Like the whole bad seed thing?"

Sammy looked away, casting her eyes back up to the ceiling as she contemplated his words.

"I believe that there are people who are born with minds that work differently and that these can make them capable of evil things. But I don't think that someone can be born as a complete monster. And anyone who says their child is a bad seed or born evil is just trying to compensate for their own shitty parenting. Why?"

Jamie didn't respond and closed his eyes again. He knew he couldn't stay there much longer, if he wanted to keep what had happened at school from his parents he'd have to get home before they finished work for the day, but he just wanted to pretend everything was okay for a little bit longer. Sammy didn't push the subject, instead lapsing back into silence, trusting that her friend would talk to her when he was ready.

Below, the main entrance to the church had opened and the choir had gathered to practice. The soft chorus of voices rose up to the teens. Jamie found Sammy's hand and squeezed it lightly. He removed the crumpled letter from his pocket and held it out to her. She frowned and took it, scanning the return address and grimacing.

"You're not going to read it?"

"No."

"How many has he sent?"

"This is the sixth. That I know of. I wouldn't put it past my parents to have thrown some away."

"Did you read any of them?"

"No."

"Maybe he's sorry?"

"Sorry doesn't change anything."

Sammy rested her head on Jamie's shoulder and handed him back the letter. He tucked it away and pulled her close. Her top was damp, her wet hair soaking the fabric. She shivered in his arms.

"You're shivering."

"I'm wet and it's cold in here."

"Oh, yeah, shit sorry. Here." Jamie wriggled out of his hoodie and wrapped it around her. She smiled shyly and lay contentedly beside him.

"Why do you come here?" she asked quietly.

"I needed somewhere safe."

"I get that, but why specifically this place? You never explained it to me. And I know it's not a religious thing because I'm fairly sure breaking into churches is a sin."

"Yes, right up there with adultery and murder. Sneaking into churches," he snarked. She nudged him.

"Spill Harper."

He was silent for a moment and Sammy was uncertain if he was going to give her an answer at all. He ran his fingers across the faded carpet of the gallery, plucking at a loose thread. How many times had he lain in this exact position? Too many to count. And yet, he'd never really thought about why he constantly sort out the church as his refuge. He wasn't religious, in fact, he wasn't sure he believed in anything at all but he couldn't deny that he felt safe there.

"I guess… I feel close to people when I'm here… Lily used to sing here… and my mom did too."

"You never told me that."

"Yeah. Every Sunday and at all the Christmas services." He sighed softly and sat up. "I should get home."

Sammy nodded, getting to her feet. Jamie glanced down at the choir, pausing for a moment, before leading the way out of the side door, into the darkness of the stairway. The rain filtered in through the holes in the roof, soaking into their skin as they descended. The pair wriggled out of the broken door and headed down the street, huddled together with Jamie's hoodie over their head in an attempt to stay as dry as possible.

Their feet splashed through puddles and despite the rain, they found themselves laughing although they weren't entirely sure why. The streets were largely empty, a scattering of people, clutching umbrellas. As the pair passed under a street lamp, a man dressed in a long black coat came round the corner. A rottweiler was at his side and the animal pulled towards Sammy.

"Not now," the man said softly. He headed down the rain-soaked streets to a house, larger than the rest around it. He knocked at the door, head down, rain-slicked hair falling in front of his eyes. After a moment, the door opened and a tall man with thick brown hair, dressed in a suit was stood there.

"You're late," the man said, stepping aside to let his guest in.

"Apologies," the guest said cooly, his expression a mask of indifference. The pair headed through to a study. The walls were lined with bookshelves and two large german shepherds, one black and one white, were stretched out in front of an ornate fireplace which cast the room in a warm glow. The suited man seated himself in an armchair beside the fire, indicating his guest should sit. He took the chair, his rottweiler curling up beside him.

"Can I get you a drink?" asked the suited man. His guest pulled a pocket watch from the breast of his coat, considering it for a moment, pulling a face as he did.

"No, I don't think I have the time. I have another appointment shortly." The suited man inclined his head slightly.

"To business then."

"Yes." The guest tucked his pocket watch away once more and turned his focus back to his companion. "It is as we feared. All the signs point to him awakening once more."

The suited man sighed and pinched the bridge of his nose, closing his eyes and inhaling deeply as he tried to keep his emotions in check. When he opened them once more, there was a cold steel to them that hadn't been there before.

"How much time do we have?"

"His reach is already spreading, maybe two months at most? But of course, that doesn't take the girl into account."

"Indeed... if they get hold of her, then the situation will be unsalvagable."

"Can we offer some help?"

"Perhaps... of course we cannot be seen to be interfering but perhaps we can bend the rules a little."

"It wouldn't be the first time..."

"Those were extenuating circumstances."

"They always are." The guest smiled slightly. "What would you suggest? Any direct measures would make our help too obvious."

"Well, we'll work indirectly then, just pull a few strings in the right places, push her in the right direction."

"We both know that you're very good at that Isaac."

Isaac smirked a little and dipped his head.

"I trust you to watch over them. You'll keep me posted?"

"Of course." The guest got to his feet, his dog rising beside him. "Until next time."

He turned and headed out off the study, across the hall and out into the rain once more.

# SARUM VALE HOSPITAL ADMITTANCE FORM

*FORM TO BE COMPLETED BY RESIDENTIAL STAFF PRIOR TO BRINGING THE INDIVIDUAL TO THE EMERGENCY ROOM*

## ADMISSION STATUS

Severe lacerations to wrists. Impact injuries to knuckles.

Initial Prognosis:

Attempted suicide

## PATIENT DETAILS

Name: Jamie Anthony Harper

Age: 15          Sex: Male

Race: Caucasian

Birthplace: Redwood Memorial Hospital

Height: 5'5"     Weight: 120ibs

## ADMISSION DETAILS

Date: January 19th

Time: 03:27am

Mode of Transportation: Ambulance

## DETAILS OF INCIDENT

Patient was found by his mother in the bedroom. Patient was admitted at 03:27 am on January 19th with severe lacerations to the wrists. Patient also had a number of smaller lacerations to his knuckles, most likely from repeated impact trauma. Patient was unconscious when he arrived.

## NOTES

Medical records indicate the patient was receiving treatment for depression as well as auditory and visual hallucinations at the time of the incident.

# IX

When Jamie got home, he found three voicemails on the home phone waiting for him. The first was from Mr White, expressing his concern about the incident in biology class and the next two were from his parents both giving their reasons for being late home. He stabbed the delete button aggressively and went into the living room. Callie had after school clubs and would be dropped home by the mom of one of her friends later in the evening, leaving Jamie home alone for another few hours.

As he sat on the sofa in the darkened house, he wished Sammy had stayed with him. Echo whined softly, watching him from his bed. The clarity that had settled over him in the church was fading and he felt like the shadows were watching him, judging him. His fingers drummed anxiously against the arm of the sofa. Stirring in the pit of his stomach was the familiar itch. Whenever the hallucinations got bad, the voices got too loud that even his music couldn't drown them out, he turned to pain as his distraction. It was easier to ignore his mind if he had something physical to cling onto.

"Don't do it," he whispered to himself, closing his eyes. "Don't do it… it's not worth it…"

His fingers flexed reflexively and found their way to his other wrist, skimming over the scars there. A prickling sensation ran up the back of his neck followed by an icy numbness that spread down his arms. He got to his feet and went over to the hall mirror. Something seemed off.

Jamie locked eyes with his reflection, unable to fully identify just what was different. He cracked his neck to the side and back, the movement smooth and almost serpent-like. In the depths of his eyes, a dark speck seemed to linger, too small for him to focus on. The numbness inched its way along his fingers and for a moment his reflection appeared to glitch, like two images being laid over one another without quite matching up, flickering off and on abruptly before they merged completely. The prickling feeling surged along his skin, building into an intense burning. Jamie grimaced, letting out an almost animalistic yowl. A dark shadow seemed to pass over his eyes, clouding the irises an inky black. He closed them, arching his neck and back as the burning surged through him.

When he opened them, all traces of colour had vanished, there was nothing but an impenetrable void in his mask-like face. He cocked his head to the side, his expression perplexed. Nothing had actually changed about his face but the longer he looked, the less he recognised it and the more alien it became to his eyes. He lifted a hand and tented his fingers against his reflection's. The chill of the glass was distant, more like the memory of touch rather than the actual sensation of it.

"This isn't mine…" he said softly. His voice felt strange on his tongue, the movements of his mouth heavy and unnatural. His eyes ran down the length of his body, registering the form. A small smile spread across his lips. "Ahh… well, it has been a while."

He stepped back, stretching his arms above his head, watching his reflection's actions. He rolled his head in circles, relishing in the sensation of movement, flexing his fingers like he was playing piano in the air. Everything part of him felt hypersensitive, the lightest caress of the air like an electrical current on his skin. It had been so long…

"Hmm… this is usable." He ran his tongue over his teeth, his eyes coming to rest on his wrist. He scowled. "Damaged… but still usable."

Echo rose from his bed and growled softly, eyes fixed on the teen who's head turned sharply to look back at him. The boy bared his teeth and the dog cowered back, whimpering softly. Jamie smirked slightly, turning his focus back to the mirror, running his fingers down his cheek and across his chin.

"Very nice indeed…"

The sound of the front door opening attracted his attention. He blinked and the shadow faded, his eyes returning to normal once more. Jamie frowned, momentarily confused and disorientated. He looked around, getting a sense of his surroundings.

Callie came in, dropping her bag. She waved to Jamie, her expression clouding a little as she registered his confusion.

*'Are you okay?'* She signed.

*'I'm fine. How was school?'*

She shrugged, heading into the kitchen to make herself a snack. Jamie bit his lip and glanced back at the mirror. His reflection seemed to smirk back at him. He shook his head and followed after Callie, deciding to put it out of his mind.

It was surprisingly easy to slip into their standard evening routine and pretend like the day's events hadn't happened. With Callie to focus on, Jamie could put his mind on autopilot and ignore the lingering stresses that clawed at his nerves. They ate their dinner in front of the television, watching bad movies before Callie headed upstairs to get ready for bed. Jamie was usually fairly lax about bedtimes, especially on Fridays, letting her muddle around in her room until she felt tired.

Callie switched off the main light and turned on her night light, a small lantern style thing that turned slowly and cast decorative shadows across the walls. She clambered into her bed, putting her hearing aid on the bedside table and picking up her reading book. She settled down against her pillows, opening the book to a marked page. The light swirled around the room, patterns of stars and small woodland animals scampering over the walls and up the ceiling.

The rain outside had grown heavier and lightning began to flash. Callie hummed tunelessly to herself, undisturbed by the crashing thunder outside, turning the pages slowly. She easily slipped into the imaginary world, wondering at the brightly coloured pictures of bizarre abstract creatures that danced across the pages. Her fingers lightly traced the drawings, smiling to herself. Tonight she was reading *Alice in Wonderland*. It was one of her favourites and although she had her own copy, the one in her hands was from Jamie's room. The pictures were far better, beautiful watercolours that were a hundred times more intricate than the small printed ones in her own version, and it also contained *Through the Looking Glass* as well.

The lightning illuminated the room, the silhouette of a man's form momentarily visible on the far wall. The faintest sound of whispering spread through the room, soft murmuring that travelled from the furthest end of the room to the bed where Callie was hunched. She rubbed her ears, a tinny high pitched whine reverberating through them. She winced as it grew in pitch to an almost painful level. The voices grew louder for a moment before cutting off entirely, the silence consuming the room once more. The whining sound faded away with it and Callie relaxed.

The pages rustled, stirred by an unseen breeze. The night light let out a hum and a crackle before the bulb went out and plunged the room into darkness. She lifted her head and reached over to the nightlight, flicking the switch back and forth. When nothing happened, she got up slowly and moved towards the main light switch. The mirror over her dresser reflected the light from the street, allowing her a little to see by. As she passed by, she caught sight of her image in the glass. For a moment, out of the corner of her eye, she saw a second shape silhouetted behind her.

She frowned and turned her head, searching for the cause, but saw nothing. Her hand ran along the wall and found the light switch, flicking it up. The room stayed resolutely dark. Callie grimaced, moving towards the door, intending to call to Jamie for his help. She wasn't afraid of the dark but it made her a little uncomfortable, being without two of her senses.

A step away from the door, her nightlight turned back on, whirring faster than normal so the shadowy images danced dizzyingly around her head. She blinked and stepped back a few paces, watching the patterns with mild confusion.

The book on her bed flipped open, the pages beginning to turn, slowly at first and then growing faster. Callie went over to the bed and reached out to pick up the book. The second her hand came close to it, the movement stopped and it lay open in front of her. The light shone across the paper, illuminating the words clearly.

*Children yet, the tale to hear,*
*Eager eye and willing ear,*
*Lovingly shall nestle near.*

*In a Wonderland they lie,*
*Dreaming as the days go by,*
*Dreaming as the summers die*

She frowned and went to close the book. The pages flicked once more to a drawing of the white rabbit. As she looked, the images began to warp and change. The rabbit scampered across the paper, the pictures blurring and distorting into monstrosities of their formal soft selves. The pages turned to one of the Cheshire Cat, it's grin sadistic and threatening as it leered at Callie from the book. She let out a small shriek, pressing herself back against the wall.

The lid of a music box on her bedside table flipped open and began to play, the tiny figure inside twirling around. The light from the nightlight reflected off the tiny mirror inside, a bright stab of light-catching Callie in the eye. Once again she got a glimpse of a shape, something standing next to her, but when she looked there was nothing there.

The whispering started up once more, the high pitched sound that had accompanied it earlier piercing her ears. She winced, clamping her hands over her ears, the swirling nightlight growing faster and making her stomach turn, her head growing lighter, the world tilting sickeningly around her. On the bed, the paper bulged and rippled like something large was trying to claw its way free from the confines of the book. Callie chewed her lip nervously, unsure of what to do. She took a faltering step forward, pausing as a hideous furred claw emerged from the page, swatting at the air before retreating back once more. She squealed, hands trembling. Tears stung her eyes, her heart beating erratically.

Callie took a deep breath and darted forward, grabbing the book and tossing it across the room. It landed with a thump, face down. The music box fell silent, the whispering stopped and the nightlight turned off abruptly. She stood stock-still, her breathing rapid and eyes darting around the room. The lightning outside flashed brightly burning the image of the figure, seated on the end of her bed, into her retinas. Callie's breathing spiked and she screwed her eyes shut.

*It's not real, it's not real...* she told herself. Her mom had always said when things scared her and her mind played tricks on her to close her eyes and count to ten.

*1...2...3...*

The room was silent, even the rain seemed to die down like the world was holding its breath and waiting to see what would happen. The music box began to play once again, slower this time, each note dragged out, the silence between them hanging in the air.

*4...5...6...*

Callie felt something cold on her skin and she screwed her eyes shut even tighter. Her hands clenched into tiny fists, digging her nails into the palms of her hands.

*7...8...9...*

Something creaked nearby, like the afterthought of a footstep and her tension grew.

"Ten." She spoke the last aloud and opened her eyes slowly. Everything seemed as it should. The room was peaceful. A hand clamped down onto Callie's shoulder and she shrieked, turning sharply. Jamie was stood there, looking down at her with concern. He flicked on the light, his frown growing as he saw her dishevelled, tear-streaked face.

*What happened?* He signed hurriedly. Callie glanced once more round the room and then threw her arms around him, burying her face against his chest. He stroked her hair lightly, waiting for her to calm down before questioning her further. She took a few shaky breaths and looked up at him.

*I'm okay*

*Do you want to talk about it?*

*No.*

*Do you want to stay in with me tonight?*

Callie hesitated, her hands faltering. She bit her lip before shaking her head slowly and looking back up at him. He gave her a kind smile and picked her up, carefully setting her back down in her bed and tucking the covers up around her. Jamie headed to the door and went to turn out the light. He paused, finger hovering over the switch, and looked back at Callie.

*If you need me, I'll be down the hall.*

*Okay... night Jamie.*

*Night Callie*

He switched off the light and left the room, pulling the door closed behind him. Callie wrapped her duvet tight around her, curling up into a ball and closing her eyes. The storm was still raging outside, illuminating her prone figure with lightning, the wind seeping in through any crack it could find to send the house creaking and rustling around the occupants.

In his room, Jamie was changing for bed. He took the crumpled letter from the pocket of his jeans and went over to the wardrobe, kneeling down to pry up the loose floorboard. He removed his journal from the space, hesitating a little as he did so, remember what had happened last time he'd held it.

No. Not real.

He set the journal down beside him and slipped the letter through the gap instead. His hand brushed against paper, soft fabric with stiffened patches, and something thin, smooth and hard. He grimaced and pulled his hand back quickly, like the hidden objects had bitten him, before slotting the floorboard back into place. He climbed into bed and flicked through the journal, pausing at the page where the scrap of fabric was still attached. He brushed it lightly with the side of his hand, looking at it contemplatively. The girl had come from the woods, he knew that, but this piece of fabric didn't look like it would belong to a teenager. Did that mean another girl was roaming the woods in a similar state to the one at the hospital? A child? And if so, why?

Thinking about it made his head hurt. He closed the journal and tucked it away, rolling onto his side. The soft ticking of the hall clock, the drum of the rain, it formed a cocoon of sound around him and he relaxed, just a little. His nap at the church had helped a little but he felt like his exhaustion had become engrained into his psyche at this point. He desperately needed to get some decent sleep, especially if he wanted any chance of keeping his hallucinations (which he was convinced were a result of his lack of sleep) at bay. However, a lingering sense of unease was lurking in the back of his mind about... whatever he had experienced the night before and he couldn't quite manage to switch off. His ears strained, listening for any sign that Callie was still distressed. He wasn't completely convinced that she was alright, no matter what she had said.

Jamie heard nothing but across the hall, Callie was fidgeting in her bed, trying to get comfortable. Like her brother, her thoughts were consumed with anxiety. She whispered to herself, telling a story as a way to provide a tiny bit of comfort. Jamie had his music and she had her imagination, the playground she slipped into whenever she felt alone at school or when her parents would argue or when she heard Jamie's distressed murmurs during the times he didn't realise she was there.

She wound a loop of her duvet around her finger, reciting her story to herself, the same one she always told. The repetition of the words made her feel safe and secure in a way that nothing else did and she retreated into the private world that lingered in her head, a world that no one was allowed in or even knew about, not even Jamie.

Her legs uncurled as she relaxed and her feet kicked out, colliding with something solid at the foot of the bed. It took a moment for her to register the unfamiliar presence and when she did, she didn't scream or run. She stretched slowly, probing with her foot to get a sense of the... thing that resided there. Keeping her breathing steady, she lifted her head slowly, moving as if she was simply adjusting in the bed. Her keen eyes made out once more that silhouette, the shape of another person lingering in the room. This time, when she blinked it didn't disappear and, although she couldn't make out any details she got the distinct impression that the... person was looking directly back at her.

It wasn't fear that Callie felt as she looked at it, which surprised her. It was a strange kind of curiosity, a feeling of something unnatural and unsettling lingering in places it shouldn't. One of her hands snaked out to the bedside table, searching for her hearing aids. As her fingers came into contact with them, the thing at the end of the bed moved. She didn't see the movement and nothing seemed to change but she felt an awareness of it. Her hand stilled and something touched her skin. It wasn't like the touch of anything human or even an animal, instead, the touch was light as the soft kiss of icy mist accompanied by a brief needle-like pain where the contact was made.

The touch brushed against the back of her hand once, twice, three times before stilling. Her eyes rested on her skin, the shadow of fingers passing over her own. She lifted her eyes slowly, withdrawing her hand. Callie moved into a sitting position, pulling back slightly, not quite fearful but far from at ease. She wanted to call for Jamie but when she opened her mouth, the words died in her throat. She felt vulnerable, stripped uncomfortably bare under the watch of whatever had come to rest before her. The shadows caressed the trinkets on her bedside table, skirting over the music box, the nightlight, but the feeling of eyes on Callie's face never passed.

Slowly, she inched towards the edge of the bed, her intentions uncertain even to her. Maybe she would run or cry or scream, but as she reached the point where mattress dissolved into the sea of carpet, she felt like her limbs had seized up. The feeling of being watched seemed to build in intensity, locking in on her and skewering her with a power that left her breathless and terrified. Nothing was said, no words exchanged between the two of them but a type of message seemed to pass between them.

No.

She crouched there, half on and half off the bed, paralysed by the gaze. She waited and for a moment feared that she would never be freed, that she would be trapped frozen in place forever, but after a time, minutes or hours she didn't know, the shadows faded and the sensation with it. Her body was once again her own but she didn't move right away, instead, she hunched there, feeling like something important had been stolen from her.

She got to her feet, wrapping her arms around herself, feeling like every shadow was watching her. Callie tiptoed to the door and out onto the hall, where the chill bit at her toes and curled around her ankles. She crept over to Jamie's door and quietly pushed it open. He didn't stir on his bed at the small creak that signalled her entrance although his eyes were open. She moved swiftly to him and climbed up beside him, slipping under the covers and resting her head on his chest.

His arm came and wrapped around her, cradling her close. The pair of them lay there, staring into opposite directions, Callie at the shadows on the wall and Jamie at the mirror where his own distorted reflection stared back at him.

## SARUM VALE VETERINARY CLINIC     PATIENT INTAKE FORM

Owner Information

First Name: Evelyn            Last Name: Knight

Mailing Address: 12 Ash Street, Sarum Vale

Patient Information

Pet's Name: Lucky            Species: Canine/~~Feline/Other~~

Breed: Golden Retriever       Sex: Male/~~Female~~      Age: Six years

Patient Notes

Patient was admitted deceased for further examination. Autopsy found glass in the patient's stomach resulting in internal lacerations.

Examination performed by: *Miles Carter*

# X

It had been raining solidly for almost two days. In her hospital room, the girl sat by the window. She was unaware of the time passing, knowing only the good time when the light chased away the encroaching shadows and the bad time when those shadows thickened and gathered around her with nothing to fear. During the good times, she would sit at the window and watch the rain with fascination, tracing the slow progression of the droplets that lingered on the glass with her fingertips. The thunder and lightning, which came irregularly did nothing to disturb her, only making her fascination grow.

People came and went. Largely she ignored them, only lifting her head if they came too close to her. The staff's fear had faded and they'd come to understand that as long as they kept a respectful distance, she would remain calm and unconfrontational. This was fine when it came to changing her IVs but when her bandages needed replacing, she would only allow Doctor Tate to approach her. These regular intervals meant nothing to the girl, an unwelcome interruption to her study of the raindrops that she bore only because it was better than the alternative of the straps and the intrusion of unfamiliar hands.

On that day there had been far fewer interruptions and a noticeable tension around the staff who entered the room. The girl wasn't to know but they had been busily preparing for her transfer to the hospital in Redwood, only to have been informed that the storm had knocked down a number of trees on the main road that connected the town to the rest of the world, blocking access. Thus the hospital was left with a patient that they didn't fully understand what to do with or how best to treat in their limited facilities.

Because of this, the order had come that the ward where she had first been placed needed to be reopened and the girl moved. Isolation, they had deemed, was the best method of caring for the girl. Without knowing how long her good behaviour might last, it was best to seclude her and try to arrange some form of permanent staff to watch her rather than the constant string of nurses, forever changing. This way, she might begin to trust and allow them to do their jobs without the need to constantly call for Doctor Tate's assistance.

Around late afternoon, the door to her room opened and Dr Knott entered. His movements were silent and as he crossed the room it was with an almost predatory stride. Despite the silence, when he came within a foot of the girl, her head turned and she skewered him under her intense green eyes.

For a moment he paused, and the two regarded one another. He wasn't stopped by fear, as he looked down at her and she knew that. Slowly, he knelt down so his face was level with hers and reached out to touch her. She recoiled sharply and opened her mouth, preparing to let out a furious screech.

"Do not scream," he said, his hand pausing. "It would not be in your best interest."

Her mouth closed instantly, whether it was the words or something in his tone, he wasn't entirely sure. After a moment, to make sure she wasn't going to make a sound, he lightly touched her cheek, brushing her hair from her face. Her entire body stiffened at the contact and her glare grew fiercer. He continued to gently stroke her cheek, his other hand taking hold of her arm. He ran his fingers down the length of her arm, over the small bandage that covered where her cannula had been, down to her wrist. He raised it slowly so that he could examine the slim scars on the palm.

"So much trouble for such a little thing…" he murmured. "The fascination with you is something I do not quite understand…" He released her hand and instead moved his focus to her stomach, gently caressing the swell and curve of it. "Now this is something far more interesting…" She grabbed hold of his wrist, halting his actions. Her ragged nails dug into his skin, hard enough to draw blood. It bubbled up from the tiny cuts and ran down his wrist. Dr Knott didn't flinch, instead, he watched the girl with a peculiar expression.

Slowly, he unfastened her fingers from around his wrist and lifted his arm to examine it. He adjusted his sleeve to cover the worst of the cuts before bringing his fingers up to his lips. The movement was slow and deliberate, his tongue running along the length of his bloodstained finger. As he lowered his hand, he licked his lips, a small smile forming. His eyes never left hers.

"Now… that wasn't very nice… was it?" His voice was soft, with an almost seductive quality to it that made the girl tremble fearfully and want to retreat. His hand on her face, which hadn't faltered once, stilled on her chin, somewhere between touching and restraining. His thumb continued to sweep against her cheek, firm but not painful.

The anger in her eyes had faded and now there was only fear, fear of this strange man who's touch was familiar in a way she didn't understand. His expression had clouded and become unreadable to her.

"And she was mine, she was mine, the key was in my fist, my fist was in my pocket, she was mine…" he murmured under his breath before releasing her entirely and rising to his feet. He turned, posture suddenly rigid and firm, before striding out of the room. It was only once the door had closed behind him with a soft click that the girl felt her breathing return to normal and her body relax a little.

She looked down at her hands, the fingers bearing a light smattering of the doctor's blood. Despite all she had encountered in her life, her fears had been very much rooted in one thing. Now she was confronted with something different, something she didn't understand. It was clear that this place, that she had hoped would be a shelter to her, was just as dangerous as the one she had left.

The girl got to her feet and moved away from the window, stationing herself near the door. She could hear the sounds from the hallway, footsteps and the squeak of a trolley rolling passed. Two nurses walked by, heading up the corridor to the empty ward with arms full of supplies. They were talking in low voices, gossiping happily.

The pair turned off the hall and through the ward doors, heading for the supply closet to deposit their load. The younger of the two looked around anxiously as they stood by the cupboard in the darkened hall.

"Can we hurry up? I don't like it here."

"Why? It's just like anywhere else in the hospital."

"It feels creepy without anyone else in here, especially after what happened. Have they figured out what did it yet?"

"No. They cleaned up all the rooms and couldn't find anything. Maybe it was just a weird coincidence?"

"That seems really unlikely." She sighed. "How long is that girl going to be around?"

"No idea. There's snow forecast and once that comes down there'll be no getting her transferred until it thaws." The nurse wrinkled her nose, sniffing as a strange smell wafted up her nostrils. "Can you smell something?"

"Nope." The younger one leaned up against a wall. "Are you going to volunteer to be part of her care team?"

"I'm not sure. I heard that they're paying extra, that'd be good for Christmas."

"They'd have to. That girl is weird."

"That's not fair. She's just a messed up kid. You would be too if you'd been through the same things as her."

"Been through what? No one has any idea what she's been through. For all, we know she got pregnant, ran away from home and got lost in the woods. You can't just assume she's traumatised."

The older nurse rolled her eyes at her young colleague's scepticism and closed the cupboard door. The strange smell was still there, persistently burrowing up her nose.

"Are you sure you can't smell anything?" She turned away before her friend could answer, sniffing like a bloodhound and following the stench to what she hoped was its origin. Her colleague gave an aggravated huff but followed behind her, unwilling to be left alone in the darkened ward. As they moved, the smell grew stronger, almost nauseatingly so. It was a deep, earthy smell, like damp leaves but with a bitter acrid undertone.

They reached the door to the staff bathroom where the smell seemed strongest and paused outside. The younger nurse made a face as the older one slowly started to push the door open and grabbed her arm to stop her.

"Come on, it's just a toilet. Toilets smell."

"Not like this. And besides, they're supposed to have cleaned up the whole ward. If they missed the bathroom, there could still be an infection risk."

She shrugged off her colleague and pushed the door open fully, heading inside. The lights flickered on automatically as they entered, the harsh

122

white glow unnaturally bright. The smell was unbearably strong and the nurses gagged as they breathed in.

"Eurgh… smelled like something died in here…"

The older nurse said nothing, frowning as she cast her eyes around the room. There were three cubicles, all unlocked but the doors were pulled shut. At a cursory glance, everything seemed to be as it should. The sinks were clean, apart from a small black smudge on one of the rims, nothing to suggest that the smell was coming from them. The nurse hesitantly pushed open the nearest door, peeking inside the empty toilet.

"Can we go? Please?" the younger one asked, her voice rising in pitch as she grew more anxious.

"In a minute, I just want to check this out."

"Let's just call security. They can look into it!"

She went ignored, the older nurse moving onto the second stall, pushing open the door to check inside. It was empty like the first but on the floor was a faded black stain that disappeared into the final stall, like a puddle of ink had seeped across the tiles. The nurse began to regret her curiosity, wishing she'd listened to her friend and called someone else to investigate the odour, but she didn't leave the bathroom. Instead, she went to the final stall, knowing that whatever was behind the door was most likely the cause of the smell. She pushed it lightly. The door slowly swung open with a creak that seemed to echo around the room. The nurses screamed.

Huddled in the corner of the stall, between the toilet and the wall was the body of a man. The floor around him was thick with a mixture of blood, vomit and faeces along with a strange dark ooze that was unrecognisable as anything belonging to a human. His skin was taut over his bones, rotten and putrifying in places, and his fingertips were worn down to bloody stumps, nails gone to leave behind deep sores in their place. His eyes bulged wildly, glazed over with a milky film. His blood vessels had ruptured and black tears had run down his cheeks, streaking the waxy skin. He was dressed in a nurse's uniform, stiff with rancid vomit and bile, thick as sewage and dark like liquid night. A name tag was fastened to his chest, the words still readable despite the foul remnants.

Suddenly it slumped, the body falling forward onto the tiles. The back of the man's skull was caved in, his brain exposed. Thick leech-like creatures squirmed and crawled over the organ, a writhing mass that ate away at the brain beneath them.

The nurses fled, their cries for help echoing around the wards.

In her room, the girl heard the commotion and she dared to peek around the door, watching as staff ran to the aid of their colleagues, uncertain of what was happening. Their voices faded away, the corridor left vacant. The girl got to her feet slowly, taking a few shuffling steps into the hall. Her leg was healing well and she could move despite the pain it caused her, but not with any great speed. She moved down the hallway, heading towards the door she knew to be the exit.

Despite her silence and her lack of response to the nurses in her room, she wasn't stupid and she had been watching everything from the corner of her eyes. She'd be relatively unconcerned about the needles poking into her skin or the mysterious bags of fluid that the nurses replaced with regularity. They were just something on the edge of her periphery, not to be fussed with. Instead, her focus was the many doors around the ward. During the nights, she would move from the window over to the door and huddle in the slim patch of light to watch the night staff. She had noted the door where they would enter and exit wearing coats, clutching bags.

It was this door she headed out of. She moved as swiftly as her injured leg would allow, keeping her head down and her arms wrapped around herself as she went. The wards were quiet, a few members of staff dotted around but most of them were occupied with other things. The girl headed to the main entrance, her silent footsteps enabling her to pass by unseen. The ER was busier than the other wards but still, no one noticed her, too involved in their work. A pause, a quick look around and then she scurried out of the automatic doors, into the cold night's air.


Jamie lay in his bed, counting the passing minutes. He'd been lying awake for hours. His first therapy session was the next day and the thought of it was making his stomach twist sickeningly. He'd managed to slip into a half dozing state for a bit but had been disturbed by the sound of his dad getting a call and heading out to work. Now he was stuck lying awake, staring at the patterns on the ceiling.

He focused on the sounds around him. Even without his parents around and Callie asleep in her room, the house was far from silent. The steady tick tick tick of the hall clock, the groan and growl of the boiler and the faint sound of a long creak followed by a clatter of the back door as it swung back and forth in the wind.

Jamie sat up, the sound finally registering. He got up slowly and headed into the hallway, sure that he was hearing things. From downstairs, came the same creak and clatter, followed by a bark. That sound relaxed him slightly. They didn't tend to lock the back door at night, their latch was faulty and the dog could easily have knocked it open if it wasn't shut properly.

Feeling more confident, Jamie headed down the stairs, through the living room towards the kitchen. The living room was dark but the kitchen was lit by a strange cold lighting.

"Echo," Jamie called softly. He listened for the pad of his dog's paws but instead heard a bang, as something metallic hit the floor. He frowned and crept closer, curious. "Hello?"

A shadow was visible through the door, cast on the far wall, a shape hunched over. Jamie bit his lip and entered the kitchen. Echo was stood nearby, tail wagging happily, bathed in light from the open fridge. Huddled in front of it was the girl, dressed in a soaking wet hospital gown, feet bare and bleeding. She was holding a tub from the fridge, eating ravenously, her fingers red and cracked from the bitter wind. Jamie blinked, momentarily stunned. He was almost convinced that it was another of his hallucinations. How could she be here? How long had she walked to get there?

The girl lifted her head and looked at him, a small smile forming.

"Err... hi..." He approached her, somewhat hesitant. The girl straightened up as best she could and closed the gap between them. Her feet left small stains on the tiles, water dripping from her soaked clothes. Jamie bit his lip. "We better get you some dry clothes. You'll freeze to death... and I'll need to bandage your feet."

He took her hand and led her carefully to the living room, seating her on the sofa.

"Wait here, I'll find you some clothes."

Jamie headed upstairs and went into his room, grabbing the first few things he found in his drawers for her. He was about to leave the room but he hesitated and went over to his bed, kneeling down to pull an old suitcase from underneath. Inside were folded clothes, moth-eaten and at least a decade old. He grabbed one of the items on top before leaving the room, going into the master bathroom. His mom kept a first aid kit in the cupboard there and he had a decent knowledge of treating small cuts. Once that was done and the girl was warm, he could deal with the more serious problem at hand, namely getting her back to the hospital.

He returned to the living room, clutching his bundle of clothing, the first aid kit and a towel. The girl was curled up, the dog at her feet, arms around her stomach. The tiny foil flower Jamie had given her was clutched in her fingers.

"Umm so… first, you should dry off. Here." He held out the towel to her. She stared at it, expression blank. Jamie's hands trembled, chewing his lip to shreds. "Okay then… umm… do you… do you mind if I touch you?"

The girl said nothing. Jamie took her hands, steering her to her feet. He reached down and lifted up the hospital gown, making sure that his fingers didn't touch her skin. The girl shivered but didn't resist, letting Jamie undress her. He kept his eyes averted, looking at anything except the girl in front of him. When the damp clothes were removed, he wrapped the towel around her, rubbing her shoulders awkwardly in an attempt to dry her off. The girl's hand slowly inched out, touching Jamie's wrist lightly. He turned his head slightly, looking at her for the first time. She didn't seem afraid to be naked in front of him. The look in her eyes was strange, almost reluctantly expectant.

There was a creak on the staircase and he turned sharply. Callie was halfway down, peering through the bannisters at them.

"Callie! Go back to bed!" In his startled state, he forgot to sign, his hands shaking furiously.

*Who is she?*

"It doesn't matter, just go back to bed, please!"

Callie ignored him. She descended the last few steps and approached the pair, head cocked slightly to the side. The girl watched her closely,

126

shifting position slightly to see around Jamie. Callie stopped a few feet away from them, regarding them both before beginning to sign to her brother. The girl frowned, confused by the hand gestures. She didn't understand the words being said to her normally but she usually got a sense of what was going on by tone. These strange hand movements meant nothing to her.

"She says you have nice eyes…" Jamie mumbled. He turned away from his sister, knowing that no matter what he said she wouldn't go anywhere unless she wanted to. He continued drying the girl, before beginning to redress her. Callie seated herself on the sofa, watching the two of them with curious eyes.

With Jamie's help, the girl was clothed in the dress he had dug up, a lightweight garment with a twenties feel to it, more like a costume than an actual outfit. He also gave her one of his hoodies to keep her warm and several pairs of thick socks for after he had bandaged her feet. Once she was dressed, they both sat down and Jamie lifted her feet up so that he could clean the cuts.

"You are crazy, you know that? Walking here from the hospital?" He made a face and began to dab at the cuts. "You're lucky I'm good with things like this."

The girl winced as the antiseptic stung the cuts and she pulled back.

"It's okay," Jamie said softly. "I know it hurts but I promise I'll look after you. Just try to relax, okay?"

Callie reached over and began to gently play with the girl's hair, running her fingers through the strands. The action seemed to calm the girl and she relaxed against the cushions as Jamie resumed tending to her feet. Callie fetched a brush and started to slowly work it through the tangle of hair, her actions slow and relaxed. Echo curled up beside the sofa, wagging his tail occasionally as he watched the three of them. Jamie finished cleaning the cuts and bandaged the girl's feet, slipping some thick socks on over the top to help alleviate the pain she'd feel when walking.

The girl was almost asleep by this point, clearly exhausted by her long walk. Callie looked over at Jamie questioningly.

*What now?*

*I have to call dad. He'll take her back to the hospital.*

*But she doesn't want to be there…*

*Well, she needs them. She's not very well.*

He got up, being careful not to disturb her and grabbed his phone, gesturing for Callie to follow him. The girl let out a soft sigh, stretching out on the sofa and wrapping her arms around a cushion. She looked younger when she was asleep, the nearly constant tension that controlled her body disappearing as she relaxed. He paused, smiling slightly to himself, before heading into the kitchen. Callie seated herself at the breakfast bar, watching him with a disapproving look as he dialled their father.

"Jamie now isn't really a great time," his dad said as he picked up. "I'm kind of busy right now."

"Let me guess, your Jane Doe has done a vanishing act?"

"How… did you know that?"

"Because I found her in our kitchen."

"What?"

"Yeah. She's asleep on the sofa now, she was exhausted. Umm… what do you want me to do?"

There was a pause and when his father next spoke, Jamie could hear the exhaustion and exasperation in his voice.

"Just… keep her there, keep an eye on her. And keep Callie away from her."

"Why…? She's not dangerous."

"I would still prefer if your sister was kept at a distance. I'll send someone to pick her up."

The line went dead. Jamie leant against the counter, resting his chin on the top of the phone. He closed his eyes but he could still feel Callie's eyes on him. It was strange. He barely knew this girl and he already felt so responsible for her. Initially, he'd put it down to the fact that he'd contributed to her getting hurt but it seemed like more than that. Out of all the places she could have gone, she'd looked for him. He didn't know how but she had and she'd put her trust in him. Callie was right, she'd left the hospital for a reason. Even though he knew it was for her own good and that it was the best thing to do, he felt like he was betraying her somehow by sending her back.

"Callie go to bed," he said softly. Her glare was making his guilt feel worse and he didn't want to deal with it. He kept his eyes closed, listening for the scrape of her chair on the tiles. As she retreated, he opened his eyes slowly, watching her leave. He didn't move, not until he heard the creak of the floorboards overhead.

Jamie returned to the living room and stood beside the sofa, looking at the girl. She stirred and shifted position, her arm reaching out like she knew he was there and taking hold of his hand. At first, he didn't respond, but slowly his fingers closed around hers and he felt a kind of peace settle over him. Her skin was cool, her fingers felt tiny and breakable against his. This girl, she wasn't the wild feral creature his dad had told him about. She was something else, something exquisitely broken, something like him.

*Tash has signed in.*

**Adam wants to chat**

*Tash:* Hey Adam!

**Adam:** Hi. What you up to?

*Tash:* Stuck babysitting. You?

**Adam:** Homework. Algebra.

*Tash:* I'm supposed to be doing mine too.

**Adam:** lol bad girl

*Tash:* That's me. Bad to the bone.

*Tash:* You looking forward to winter break?

**Adam:** Can't wait!

**Adam:** I was going to ask you. You know the winter fayre?

*Tash:* Course.

**Adam:** Well, I was wondering if you'd meet me there? I love chatting with you, but I'd like to actually meet you.

*Tash:* I'd be up for that. I'm going anyway with my sister, on Xmas eve.

**Adam:** I can do that. I'll see you there!

*Tash:* I g2g. Mom's home.

**Adam**: Okay. Talk soon!

*Tash*: xoxo

*Tash has signed out*

## XI

Waiting rooms had to be the bleakest places in existence, Jamie thought to himself. It didn't matter how much effort was put into making it look homely, they always felt stilted and false. This one was on the third floor of an office block, above a recruitment agency and below the town radio station. Admittedly, they had tried hard but it wasn't quite enough to get rid of the discomfort in the air. Cream walls, four uniform doors each bearing a name of a doctor, a collection of rigid leather chairs around a pale wooden coffee table, a curved reception desk and a large fish tank. He'd spent hours in this room, waiting for appointments over the years. The only thing that changed were the magazines on the coffee table. And the fish.

Jamie yawned and rubbed his eyes. The events of the night before kept playing over and over in his mind. He'd sat beside the girl for almost an hour while she slept, holding her hand the entire time. When a squad car had pulled up outside, she'd finally woken up. An officer and a doctor had come in to collect her. She hadn't fought or screamed but the look on her face as they had led her away was emblazoned into his brain.

He hung his head, wishing he could play on his phone or something to distract him. They had a strict no electronics rule in the office and, while he usually broke that rule, his dad had driven him to the office and confiscated his phone and iPod, promising to return them when his session was over.

The door to one of the offices opened and a tall woman with a tight bun emerged.

"Jamie? Come on in."

Jamie grimaced to himself and headed over. Dr Lilith Knott had been his therapist for years and in that time, Jamie's impression of her had remained exactly the same. There was something severe about her, an underlying hardness beneath the image she presented like she was made of ice. Permanently dressed in shades of white, grey and silver, her hair was white blonde and her eyes a steely grey that only added to Jamie's glacial view of her.

He seated himself on the sofa, eyes sweeping around the room. The office hadn't changed much, the same toy box with a disorganised collection of dolls in the corner, the same books on the shelves, and the same knick-knacks on the desk. Exactly as it always had been. Then again, the doctor herself hadn't changed either. It had been nearly a year since his last session and she hadn't aged a day.

"So Jamie, it's been a while," she said, seating herself in the armchair opposite the teen. She crossed her legs, balancing a slim notebook on her knee.

"Ten months, three weeks and two days." He let his eyes continue to roam the space, eventually coming to rest on something he hadn't noticed before. A small birdcage in the corner of the room, a drab looking brown bird perched inside. It seemed to stare directly at him.

"I wasn't aware you'd been counting." Her voice distracted him from the bird and he switched his focus back to her.

"I didn't really want to come back here… no offence."

"None taken. I understand that no one comes here for pleasant reasons." She tented her fingers, her eyes fixed on him. "Is there anything you particularly want to discuss? Or shall we start by running through previous issues and catch up on that?"

"Run through is fine."

"Alright." She smiled and opened her notebook, positioning the pen nib on the paper. "I'll start with the most pressing issue. Last time we met was obviously following your suicide attempt. At the time you thought you were fit to return home… do you still agree with that assessment?"

"Yes."

"Any further thoughts of hurting yourself?"

Jamie hesitated, considering his words carefully. He knew from experience that Dr Lilith was slippery and had a way of worming information out of him that he wasn't entirely sure he wanted her to know.

"Thoughts… yes. Actions… no."

*Liar…*

He twisted his hands in his lap. It didn't count. She was asking about the big stuff, cutting himself again, not the small stuff that he was doing.

"And your thoughts about suicide?"

"I still think about it. But more... theoretically? Suicidal... ideation? Is that what it's called?"

"It is, well remembered." She paused, scribbling something down on the notebook. "Do you think you'd ever act upon these thoughts again?"

"No... well, I wouldn't like to think so. But then again I didn't think I'd act on them the first time..." His voice trailed off and he looked down at his hands, pulling at the sleeves of his shirt to make sure his wrists were entirely obscured.

"Have you thought any further about what exactly drove you to go through with it?"

Jamie paused, looking back at the bird. It fluttered its wings a little, its movements listless.

"What kind of bird is that?"

Dr Lilith followed his gaze, glancing over at the creature without much interest.

"It's a nightingale. You're evading the question."

"I guess... I felt like I deserved it... I don't know really... can we move off of this?" He shifted uncomfortably in his seat, quietly wishing he was still young enough to be given toys to play with and have that count as counselling.

"Of course. But understanding why is an important part of preventing it from reoccurring."

"I know that. I just don't want to think about it right now."

Dr Lilith pursed her lips slightly and turned the page on her notepad. She didn't speak for a moment, considering her next question carefully. It was important to strike the right balance between respectful and prying.

"Has there been any reoccurrence of your previous hallucinations?" she said finally.

"No," he answered quickly. She peered at him, expression one of disbelief. He grimaced; he'd never been a good liar.

"Jamie, as we've discussed before, these sessions are only of use if you tell the truth. I understand that it's not your choice to be here but since you are, you might as well make the most of it. Now, let me ask you again–"

"I don't know," Jamie cut in.

"Has reality and fantasy become that blurred?"

"No, that's not it. I wish reality was a bit more like fantasy."

"I'm not sure I understand."

"Yes, I have been seeing things but I assumed it was just because I've not been sleeping well. It's not like it was before."

"Lack of sleep can be a factor, however, given your history I think it's important to flag all hallucinations, no matter how minor. Are they strictly visual hallucinations or have the auditory ones continued?"

"The voices are still there. But they're not the same either."

"Can you elaborate on this?"

"Before it was like people talking to me. They were real. But now it's less like actual voices and more like intrusive thoughts. I know they're not real, they're just in my head."

"How do you deal with them?"

"I play music."

"Does that work?"

"It drowns them out. For a while anyway. Then I have to turn it off and they come back."

"Do you find that they interfere with your day to day life? School, for example?"

"It does a bit I suppose… it's okay at home but school can be…" he trailed off, trying to pick the right word. Horrific? Nauseating? Nightmarish? "Challenging."

"Do you enjoy school?"

"Sometimes. I like bits of it. Same as most of the people my age I guess." Another lie. He hated school with a passion and at times the mere thought of it had been enough to make him throw up.

"Have you given any thought to your plans moving forward? College? Career?"

"Not really…" He'd thought about the future but it was always in an abstract way. When he pictured it in his head, he saw Callie grown-up, Sammy, his parents, but never himself. His personal future was just a blank in his mind. "When I was younger, I always assumed I'd get a job in the family business… everything was planned out for us."

"And now that you don't have that plan, you don't know what to do?"

"I just don't think I'm good at anything."

*Useless. Waste of space. Pathetic piece of shit.* The words were engrained in his brain so deeply he wasn't sure he'd ever get rid of them.

"You're a bright, talented young man Jamie. You have a promising future ahead of you, I'm sure of it." For the first time since their session had begun, Jamie thought he could detect genuine emotion in her voice. He met her eye and she gave him a slight smile before returning her gaze to her notebook. "How are your relationships? I know you were having some interpersonal issues last time we spoke."

"You mean the fact that everyone at school thinks I'm a freak? No, that's not got any better."

"Kids can be cruel."

"They're right."

"Don't say that."

"I don't care. I know I'm weird. It doesn't matter though. If people are going to use it as an excuse to hate me, that's their choice. The people who like me are the ones that matter."

"That's a very mature way of looking at things Jamie." He gave her a slight smile, pleased. "Do you have a lot of friends?"

"Just the one. Sammy. And…" He cut off, thinking about the girl. Could he really consider her a friend? They barely knew each other after all. "I've got Callie as well. She's kind of a friend I guess."

"Things at home are good then?"

"Same old, same old."

"It was mentioned to me that you'd received some contact from-"

"I don't want to talk about that," Jamie said sharply. "Anything to do with that stuff is my business only."

"Understood." Looking at her, Jamie could see the hardness in her eyes, the façade of warmth slipping. She didn't like being restricted in any way. "But generally speaking you're happy with the Harpers?"

"Yes. I have no wish to change things there."

"Okay then." She wrote something down. Jamie squinted, trying to read her writing upside down. The doctor narrowed her eyes and slanted the notebook away, blocking his view. "You mentioned your sleep is still disturbed. Are these the same nightmares as before?"

"I didn't say I was having nightmares."

"Sorry, I assumed." She fixed him with her cold stare. "What is keeping you awake then? You're looking downright exhausted if I'm honest with you."

"I'm not… I'm tired today because of something else."

"And what would that be?"

"I had a… unexpected visitor last night."

"Oh?" Dr Lilith quirked her eyebrow.

"I don't know if you heard about the pregnant girl that was found in the woods?"

"I think most of the town has heard about her by now."

"Well, anyway, she showed up at my house last night. I had to look after her for a bit. Didn't get to bed till late."

"Did you like taking care of her?"

"I... liked being needed," he admitted softly.

"But I'm assuming incidents like last night aren't the norm... so what is it that normally keeps you from sleeping?"

Jamie looked away. The nightmares hadn't gone away, he'd just stopped letting himself sleep whenever possible. He kept himself awake because he was scared of his own mind.

"You were right. Nightmares, like before," he lied.

"Are they exactly as they were?"

"Not always. There's been new stuff mixed in recently."

"But primarily... your father... snakes... your sister?"

"Yes."

"And your ophidiophobia? Any progress?" Dr Lilith asked, sensing that her current line of questioning wasn't going to get her anywhere.

"Nope."

"Have you considered exposure therapy?"

"It's fine. It's not really an issue on a day to day basis."

"If you're sure."

The pair of them lapsed into silence, both waiting for the other to speak. Jamie subtly glanced at his watch, trying to see how much more of this agony he had left to endure. As he was looking, something dawned on him and he lifted his head to meet her gaze.

"So, doctor, how many sessions did my parents actually book me in for?"

"What do you mean?"

"Well, they told me it was just this one and then, if you said I was okay, I wouldn't have to come back... but I know that you only book sessions in batches. So... how many?"

"One a week for the next two months."

"Oh joy."

"Jamie… I understand that you don't want to be here. These are unpleasant circumstances and I appreciate that. But your parents are doing this out of love. They want what's best for you. You know your own mind but they want to help." She paused and smiled slightly. "Let me speak candidly. They prepaid so it doesn't affect me if you don't show up. But I think that you should. I'm not saying come to all of them, but at least try. It helped you before didn't it?"

"I guess…" She was right. It had, a little anyway. The nightmares had gotten worse when he'd talked about it but saying the words out loud, after a while, they hadn't hurt so badly. "Okay. I'm not promising I'll show up to all of them but… I'll come next week."

"That's all I ask." She glanced at her watch and closed the notebook. "That brings us to the end of our session."

"Seemed shorter than normal," Jamie murmured as he got up.

"It was just an initial review. If you have something you want to discuss now we can?"

"No, it's fine. See you next week." He headed out of the office and into the waiting room. The receptionist looked up and smiled as he passed her, but it was a smile of sympathy more than anything else. A nutcase, a weirdo. Someone to be pitied. He hated that.

Jamie left the office block and went to sit on a wall outside, waiting for his dad to come pick him up. The air was cold and the rain was a distant memory. Next would come the snow. There were always a few small flurries first before a heavier fall that all but sealed the town off until January at the earliest. The thought of those bleak months, grey days that stretched on endlessly, made him shudder. Even Christmas offered little respite for him; the visits from extended family serving only as a reminder of how much of an outsider he was. Always not quite fitting in.

He let out a long sigh, watching his breath mist in front of his eyes, and hopped off the wall. One place, one place he could go where he was welcome.

*****

138

"Harper! You busy?" called the chief. Officer Harper looked at the pile of paperwork on his desk, which never seemed to shrink no matter how much he tried.

"Err…"

"I want you to go out to the bridge. One of the park rangers called in about some kind of disturbance up there."

With an almost longing look at his papers and the knowledge that it would have mysteriously grown in size by the time he returned, Officer Harper nodded reluctantly. He grabbed his jacket and headed out to his cruiser.

His mind was far from work. As it had been so often recently, he was thinking about Jamie. He'd been improving, or at least it seemed like that. When he'd first been released after the incident, he'd seemed calmer. He'd started working out at the nearby ranch with the dog trainer who lived there. The work had clearly agreed with him, transforming his son from the pale, reclusive individual he'd been to a more social and happier person. Now everything seemed to be coming undone… and that was only what Jamie allowed his parents to see. Who knew what was going on underneath?

He reached the bridge. It stretched out across one of the widest and deepest portions of the river, connecting the town and the main (only) road out to the rest of the world. Patrick, one of the rangers, was perched on the railings nearby with a look of bemusement on his face. In the middle of the bridge was a handful of deer, mainly bucks. Officer Harper frowned and pulled his car over a few feet from the bridge.

It wasn't unheard of for deer to wander into the road. What was strange was to see so many males gathered out of the trees. It was their mating season and while that was when they were more likely to run into the road, they didn't tend to gather in such a way. The bucks should have been sparring and chasing does. Instead, they just stood there.

Officer Harper got out of his car and went slowly over to Patrick. The deer turned their heads, following his movements.

"Morning Michael," Patrick greeted.

"Patrick. Please tell me you didn't call just because there are some deer in the road?"

"You don't think this is odd?"

"Odd, yes. A police matter, no."

Patrick was silent for a minute, trying to work out how best to phrase his next sentence.

"You need to close the bridge," he said finally.

Officer Harper scoffed.

"Are you kidding? On what grounds?" Given the bridge provided the only route in and out of town, closures were a serious matter. Usually, it only got closed in winter, when the heavy snows made the roads impassable anyway. Apart from those occasions, Officer Harper had only seen one other closure.

"Unsafe conditions."

"Patrick, you've got to be joking. The dee are clearly visible to drivers. There's plenty of time for people to stop. And if someone drives through, the noise should be enough to scare the animals off."

"Do they look scared?"

"No... but I'm confident a car coming towards them will do the trick. I can't close the bridge for this and I'm hardly going to take a herd of deer into custody for 'odd' behaviour. The most I can do is get a sign put up warning people to travel slowly."

"If you're so confident, go ahead." It was clear he wanted to prove a point, one that Officer Harper didn't really understand. But since it was clear Patrick wasn't going to let the matter drop, and if someone did actually end up in an accident because of the animals he could be held responsible, Officer Harper nodded and returned to his car.

He started the engine and revved it, hoping the sound might be enough. The deer watched with mild disinterest. Scowling, he inched forward. The deer flicked their ears and stared at him. Patrick watched with a look that might have been mistaken for smugness. Putting on a burst of speed, Officer Harper sent the car shooting forward a few feet, thinking that the abruptness of the action might prompt the response he wanted. As his front wheels crested over the slight ridge where the road met the bridge, something seemed to pass over the animals. They pawed at the ground and tossed their heads. A few of the larger bucks lowered them, antlers aimed straight ahead.

It was only when his back wheels crossed onto the bridge as well that the officer realised something was happening. The herd surged forward, a furious wave of fur, hooves and antlers that drove itself into the police cruiser. Officer Harper let out a yell, hitting the reverse as quickly as he could. The deer swarmed the car, smashing themselves against the metal and glass. The windows splintered, cracks spiderwebbing across the surface, streaks of blood smeared wildly as they continued their assault on the vehicle with no regard for their own wellbeing.

Officer Harper weighed up his options. In the car, he had a modicum of protection and if he could wait out the animals he'd be okay. But one window was already entirely destroyed and they showed no sign of stopping. If he left the car, that is if he was even able to get out, he'd be directly in the line of fire. He knew how dangerous deer could be in the right circumstances. He'd seen a man gored by antlers before. But if he could get clear then he could run and his options for escape were greater.

Another window smashed. The passenger door was caved in.

He braced himself and threw open his door with as much force as he could manage. The motion had the desired effect, temporarily knocking back one of the animals and giving him the smallest gap to break through. He leapt from the car and ran. It took a moment for the deer to register, ceasing their assault on the car and instead charging after him. In normal circumstances, they would have reached him easily but whatever rage had seized their minds made their movements clumsy and uncoordinated. He reached the edge of the bridge and sprinted over to where Patrick stood, watching everything unfold. The ranger grabbed hold of him, stopping his escape. He turned the other man, pointing back at the bridge.

Officer Harper watched as the deer diverted from their path towards him and instead began to hurl themselves over the side of the bridge. The mass of bodies tumbled to the churning waters and rock below.

Patrick looked at Officer Harper and raised an eyebrow.

"Problem solved." The sarcasm was heavy in his voice. All Officer Harper could do was glare as he tried to catch his breath. "If you want your car back, you've got about ten minutes before they regroup." He started towards the dented pile of metal that had once been a car.

"You... you couldn't have just told me?" Officer Harper demanded, furious. Patrick glanced back at him.

"Would you have believed me?"

Admittedly, no he wouldn't but the officer didn't say that. He was still angry about being deceived and having his life put at risk, so instead, he stalked over to the car in silence. With considerable effort, the pair of them managed to guide the vehicle off the bridge. Once it was clear, Patrick turned to the Officer with an expectant expression. Officer Harper scowled and snatched up his radio, hitting the call button.

"This is Officer Harper. We need to close off the bridge."

"Harper, this is Fisher. Can you repeat that?" came the crackling response.

"We need to close the bridge," he repeated, glancing down at the water. Usually a murky grey it now flowed a deep red from the mangled heap of carcasses dumped at the edges. "And while you're at it, call disposal and have their roadkill team head up this way."

"Why are we closing the bridge?"

Officer Harper looked at Patrick and back at the bridge where a handful of deer had already gathered. He wasn't sure if they were the same ones or a new collection but the sight of them, staring at him, sent shivers down his spine. "Unsafe conditions."

# Police Report

**Case No**: 07-2-00052-6

**Reporting Officer:** Brennan, Peter

**Incident:** Missing person's report

**Date:** August 2nd

**Prepared by:** Fisher, Marisse

---

## Details of Event:

Officers were called to 12 Ash Street and spoke to Dr Richard Knight. He stated that, following an argument with his wife, Evelyn, she had left the house. This took place 48 hours before his call to the station. Attempts to contact her had been unsuccessful.

## Action Taken:

Following the conversation with Dr Knight, officers managed to locate Evelyn's car at the eastern forest entrance. Her keys and purse were located inside the vehicle. Further exploration into the woodland area found her coat and shoes left beside the river.

## Summary:

Signs indicate a suicide by drowning. Commencing with searches of the river.

# XII

The girl was dreaming. Her blood flowed with a cocktail of sedatives that had drawn her into their warm embrace. After she had been brought back to the hospital, her attitude had changed from timid and compliant to that of a wild beast. She had released her fear and frustration, not anger, on anyone who came within range and when there was no one to vent at, she turned her pain onto herself and clawed at her flesh until her arms were bloody. Dr Knott, approaching with caution upon hearing the commotion, had managed to subdue her momentarily and administer the sedatives.

Now she slept. And dreamt.

She was sat in a garden. Beautiful flowers bloomed around her, the lush grass tickled her bare feet, and the air was warm and heady with a thousand perfumes. A weeping willow bowed its branches overhead, the trailing fronds forming a serene curtain around her that stirred gently with the faintest strands of flute and wind chimes. The music was barely audible over the sounds of a babbling brook and childish laughter which drifted to her ears.

*Eden.*

She rose to her feet, marvelling at the ease of movement. For once, there was no pain. Her body was her own again, limbs no longer frail. She felt stronger than she ever had.

Calmly, the girl left the shelter of the tree and walked to the water. Two boys were playing there, splashing each other happily. They were unfamiliar to her and looked to be about ten years of age, dressed in loose clothes of a faded grey cotton.

As she approached, the taller of the two turned slightly and waved to her. His build was strong, face angular and defined. His hair was black and spiked up in disarray. As he moved, the girl swore she saw an undercurrent of red, like magma bubbling just below the surface.

She turned her focus to the other boy. He seemed softer in a way. His face was rounder and lacked the rigidity of his companion. He was pale, while the other had a light tan to his skin, he appeared almost as sun-deprived as she was. His hair was floppy and a deep earthy brown, but it was his eyes that were the most striking. One was a calm blue and the other a vivid green, an exhilarating electric colour that stole her breath away at a glance.

The shorter boy gestured for her to join them and, with a smile, she headed over to the water's edge, dipping her toes in. She was wearing a white dress that hung around her ankles. As she moved the hem brushed the surface but it remained dry. The tall one gave her a mischievous grin and kicked his leg out, sending a wave of water crashing into her. She recoiled, laughing loudly, and fell backwards.

The girl didn't sit up, just lay there, letting it lap against her skin. She closed her eyes. The sun was hot, the water beautifully cool and everything felt perfect in the way that only a dream could. Her hair fanned out around her, twisting and wafting like seaweed around her head. Slowly she dragged her arms back and forth, feeling the gentle resistance of the liquid.

Around her, the air seemed to grow colder and the sound of the children's laughing grew distant. She opened her eyes, sitting up. The sky was dark and stained a deep crimson, the trees were stripped of leaves, their branches battered by wind. Thick brambles and vines had grown and tangled around the plants, choking their fragile stems. The boys were gone, leaving her alone, her dress soaked and stuck to her skin.

She glanced down at the water, a wisp of red distorting the crystal clarity. She got to her feet and looked around, taking slow steps back to the bank. Her eyes spotted a figure stood on the other side of the brook, their back to her. The girl frowned, something familiar about the person despite her limited view. They appeared to be male, paler even than her, with black hair that stood up like he had been struck by lightning. Tall and lean, his body seemed almost like it had been stretched. His hands were stained, blood running down his fingers, head cast downwards as though examining something on the ground.

As she watched, the man turned to look at her. His eyes, two onyx orbs without white or iris, fixed on her, the gaze intense and familiar. Her hands began to tremble and she tried to retreat but her legs refused to obey, fixing her to the spot. The man's mouth twisted into a deformed smile and he began to stride towards her. Each step left a square of frost and when he made contact with the water, it froze beneath him.

He crossed to the bank, reaching out and brushing his fingers along her cheek. The touch burned with an arctic fire, sharp as glass and electrified on her skin.

"Hello princess…" he said softly, in a voice that was both melodic and cavernous to her ears. He moved to brush some hair from her cheek and she grabbed hold of his wrist, stilling him. She stared up at him, her body seized up with a peculiar combination of terror and comfort that she didn't fully understand. Seeing him, she wanted to run but at the same time, she wanted to hold onto him.

"No more running… it's time to come home."

Around his ankles, the shadows were gathering. They crept snakelike up his legs. Her vision seemed to be fading, the world reducing to darkness. She shook her head, pulling back. The world tilted sickeningly and the feeling of the ground under her feet disappeared. A thick smoke had begun to cluster around her, obliterating the surroundings and sending her tumbling into a black void.

When things settled back into place, she found herself in a deep cavern. She was tucked away in the entrance to a tunnel, almost hidden from view. A few shafts of moonlight filtered through narrow gaps in the rock ceiling, granting her enough light to see by.

The girl looked around, confused and afraid at her abrupt return to this hell she'd inhabited for so long. Had everything else been a dream? Her freedom? The hospital? Jamie? Just a figment of her mind…

She looked around. The man had gone, she was alone. Her body had degraded once more, trapped in her stunted adolescent body like a plant grown without enough light. Her skin was pale and fragile, her hair a limp shadow. Her body was naked once more, diminutive, short and dangerously skinny. The pain in her stomach that never quite faded, the hunger that never disappeared. The darkness ate time and her appetite was lost somewhere in the swirl of hours. She grew so used to the gnawing emptiness inside her that sometimes she would forget to eat and only realise when her body weakened, succumbing in the darkness. She thought she could hear the faintest whispers of crying in the tunnels around her. There used to be other children, she thought. Maybe there still were, hidden somewhere in the maze of tunnels. She had found bones in the tunnels before. She used to scurry past as the eyes of the skulls watched her, but as she grew braver she would linger near them and sometimes wish to join them.

A small pile of assorted items lay beside her in a tiny alcove, smooth pebbles with mirror-like surfaces, stray fragments of cloth found scattered in the tunnels, a small flower with faded petals and a bedraggled teddy bear prised free from cold fingers. Objects of little consequence that she had found and gathered as gifts for Him. It was strange how things had shifted. She still feared him but now she sought to appease him rather than flee from him as she first had. She picked up the flower, brushing her fingers over the petals. The soft texture felt abhorrent to her and she found herself longing for the crisp foil of Jamie's tiny gift to her.

A breeze drifted to her and she lifted her head. He was back, his skin almost luminescent. He didn't notice her, or if he did he didn't signify his recognition. She did nothing to draw his attention, knowing how fearsome his mood swings could be, but she was oddly comforted by his presence. It was better than being alone.

Why was she back here? It had felt so real... she was trapped, helpless once again.

As her thoughts had wandered, he had stalked through the cavern to stand before her, feet silent as a ghost. He knelt before her and idly trailed his fingers over her cheek.

"This is where you belong..."

His eyes roamed her body hungrily, coming to rest on the flower clasped in her fingers. He cocked his head, reaching out and gently prising it from her grasp. He turned it over, his actions slow and almost tender but his expression made her tense up. There was nothing explicitly unpleasant about it just something that unsettled her.

No flowers grew this far down, she must have gone near the entrance to retrieve it. Once or twice he'd seen her hesitating near the entrance to his underground kingdom, watching the sunlight with wonder. It was rare for her to stumble that far, the endless maze of tunnels keeping her permanently lost and disorientated. On the occasions she made it to the exit, usually she'd retreat quickly, the rays robbing her of her sight and forcing her back to the comfort of the darkness until it returned. If she lingered too long he'd chase her back, send her running until she was lost deep below.

"Such a pretty little thing. Is it for me?"

She nodded tentatively, the behaviours engrained into her by the years quickly returning. The memories… no, the dreams, of the outside were lingering, more persistently than any she'd had before.

From the blackness, slithered one of his Scáthanna, the darkness that creeped and crawled. It wriggled up his legs and along his arm before curling around his hand. At the sight of it, she stiffened, knowing what was to come. He knew the signs, knew how to play on her fears. The trembling of the parted lips, the ragged irregular breathing, the wide frantic doe eyes. He relished the taste, the smell that rose from every pore of her skin as he looked into her soul and drew out the darkest parts of it.

He laughed softly and gently ran one long finger across her cheek, drawing a shudder from her. His touch was both there and at the same time not. Just one of the shadows. But then, they were an extension of him, his eyes when he was away.

His hand drew down to her neck, tracing the bluish veins that lingered there. She looked up at him and he thought for a minute he saw something of himself deep inside her eyes.

"What are we going to do with you? You keep misbehaving, princess…" His voice was soft but no less menacing, sending shivers down her spine and causing goosebumps to rise across her skin. He leaned in closer. The girl pressed herself against the stone wall as if hoping it would absorb her into it.

The Scáthanna spread like ink, flowing towards her. She pulled her legs up so they were pressed tight against her as he continued to gently caress her face and neck.

A soft stinging sensation spread through her skin as the Scáthanna began to creep up her legs. She bit her lip hard, a single drop of blood blossoming on the reddened kiss, refusing to give even the slightest whimper of discomfort to him. He ran his thumb across her lower lip before licking it up.

He knew she wouldn't scream, although he did deeply enjoy trying. Over the years, their games had evolved as she grew braver. There was a kind of repetition to them, a slow progression of deliberate acts. She knew what would come next.

The first time. So long ago now. She had screamed and struggled and fought and he had loved every second of it. The more he played, the quieter she got. He reached a point where he settled for a gasp, a whimper, an expression, anything that would prove to him he had won, he had ownership over this girl, complete control. He could caress or he could break, hold or destroy. It was all down to him. But she had grown colder each time, hard and resistant and he would lose interest, abandoning her for fresh prey.

But he always came back.

The Scáthanna spread over her lower body, a single pulsating being almost. They wriggled into every crevice, every pore of her skin. The girl felt her legs go limp and they slipped down to lay in front of her. She tried to pull them back but they were held by the dark bonds and every movement of hers forced a crushing pressure on her fragile limbs, relenting only when she fell still and beginning again the second tension entered her frame. His hand ghosted down her cheek, her neck, to rest lightly on her chest.

This familiar dance reminded her, reminded him, reminded them both of that first time. He had looked at her and wondered how it would be to hold her, to really hold her and feel her, the way he never could. He felt the warmth radiating off of her but not her skin beneath his fingertips. He was a man, or he had been once, and seeing her made him hunger in a way he'd forgotten. He wished that he could touch, fully explore her soft flesh. For him, the delicious violation that had come as he'd felt her body breaking apart under his touch was something he desperately tried to recapture.

His hand skimmed downwards, brushing her waist, the curve of her hip, before reaching the Scáthanna. As he approached, they receded once again, fearful of their master. She let out a soft exhalation of relief, her legs already aching from the force they had endured, however brief.

He paused and pulled back. Ordinarily, this was where these games would end. Her surrender, her relief, they were signs that he was in control and he allowed whatever relief she experienced, she was dependant on him. He kept himself in check to make the moments when he did act that much sweeter, her fear all the more intoxicating.

He noticed a look of hope in her eyes, almost expectant. She'd learned back when he sought only to elicit a reaction that he would stop when he had achieved that. That look ignited a fire in him, unlike anything he'd ever felt.

He stood up, distancing himself from her. The Scáthanna seemed to amass at his feet, like faithful hounds waiting instructions. He rubbed his finger softly against the pad of his thumb for a moment, watching the girl. The hope was beginning to die in her eyes as she saw the change in mood and it was replaced by slowly rising fear, fear of the unknown. She had never encountered him like this and had no idea what to expect, no way to prepare herself for whatever onslaught he would unleash.

At a click of his fingers, the Scáthanna rushed forward, spreading and winding quickly over her limbs, twisting around her as she thrashed and clawed at the darkness, the walls, and her own flesh in a desperate attempt to be free of it. First, her legs, then her torso and then her arms fell prey. All were held still by the invading pressure and the sharp pains of the roaming shadows. But still, the Scáthanna continued, seeking out an entrance, a home that was equally as dark as them.

They rose up, wanting to consume her soul and take over body. They wrapped around her throat, shortening her breath as they tightened, then released. She realised their destination a second ahead of time and clamped her lips shut along with her eyes so that she wouldn't be scared by whatever fantasy he created to elicit a silent scream from her. The invading tendrils tried to pry it open but quickly changed their target, working their way up her nostrils. Her eyes flew open as the air was cut off. Her nose burned, like acid eating into her flesh and flowing through her veins. Her lungs ached for oxygen, but still, she fought on. Her eyes met his, pleading with him to stop this but he was impassive.

This couldn't be a dream, her doubt was gone. This pain, it was too real, too vivid to deny.

She felt warm liquid seeping from her nostrils. Everything was building. The pressure, the pain, the need for air. She wanted to surrender, her survival instincts were screaming at her to do so, but she struggled against them. Her vision blurred and faded, bright dots of light flashing in front of her eyes. She heard a sharp crack as her body moved and the darkness tightened its grasp, snapping a bone. She didn't know where, everything hurt too much to tell. But it was the final straw. Her mouth opened in a frenzied gasp. The shadows lunged, flowing down her throat and into her body. She choked, unable to scream even if she wanted to. All that came out was a stifled, gurgled sob. She felt like her heart was being squeezed in a vice. Her body couldn't handle it anymore. It was too much. She went limp, praying that it would be enough to convince him to stop.

"Enough."

In a second they were gone but she received no relief. Instead, she felt his weight on her, the familiar pressure and the sharp burning pain. Through the haze in her eyes, she saw his face. It faded in and out, distorting and twisting before her eyes into different people, different face.

Dr Knott, laughing as he looked at her.

The dark-haired boy, older now, smirking down at her.

The second boy, also older, his vivid eye burning into the back of her mind.

Jamie...

His face peered down at her, a soft smile on his lips. A hand came up to touch her cheek, fingers tender, but the pain continued.

"I'll always look after you..." His voice was distant, echoing like he was talking to her from far away. "I promise..."

She screwed her eyes shut, hating seeing him there, thinking of Jamie in that light. Try as she might she couldn't block out the feel of his hands, stroking her cheeks.

Stop, stop, stop...

Her mouth moved, shaping the words but no sound came out.

Stop. Stop. Stop.


The girl opened her eyes and Jamie looked down at her with concern, surrounded by a halo of white light. Tears were running down her cheeks and she struggled against him, too disorientated to register the change in her surroundings. No cave, no shadows, just a hospital room.

"You're safe, it's fine. It's not real," Jamie told her, trying his best to comfort her and calm her nerves. He knew the signs well when the line

151

between reality and nightmare faded it became difficult to distinguish between the two.

Slowly, the girl's wild movements slowed and her breathing settled. The surroundings became more real to her, the nightmare slipping away into the back of her mind. Her hand found Jamie's and gripped it, establishing the truth of the moment. She looked at him, trying to recapture that sense of safety that she had felt with him before. It was there but the fear still lingered like a bad taste in her mouth.

At the doorway to the room, Dr Knott watched Jamie and the girl curled up on the bed. Her head turned a little, her eyes resting on him for a moment, before burying her face in the teen's chest, letting him wrap his arms tight around her.

# Mental Status Exam

CLIENT NAME: *J. Harper*          DATE: *January 31st*

## OBSERVATIONS

APPEARANCE: *Dishevelled*

SPEECH: *Tangential*

EYE CONTACT: *Avoidant*

MOTOR ACTIVITY: *Restless*

AFFECT: *Flat*

## MOOD

*Mood moves between depressed and anxious, occasionally displays irritable behaviour.*

## COGNITION

ORIENTATION IMPAIRMENT: *Person and Time*

MEMORY IMPAIRMENT: *None*

ATTENTION: *Distracted*

## PERCEPTION

HALLUCINATIONS: *Auditory and Visual*

OTHER: *Derealisation*

## THOUGHTS

SUICIDALITY: *Self-Harm and Intent*

HOMICIDALITY: *None*

DELUSIONS: *Paranoid*

## BEHAVIOUR

*Guarded, withdrawn, agitated and paranoid*

| INSIGHT | JUDGEMENT |
|---|---|
| *Good* | *Poor* |

Assessment conducted by *Dr Lilith Knott*

# XIII

Jamie lay with her for hours. It had taken a while for him to find her again in the hospital; she'd been moved during her sedation to the new room. The ward smelt intensely of bleach, a declaration to the efforts of the staff to remove the stench left by the body they'd found. The rumours were already flying around the hospital, despite the police attempting to quiet things, and Jamie had easily found out what had happened. He was honestly a little surprised that the ward had been reopened so quickly but he guessed they were very keen to seal the girl away from the rest of the patients.

He'd expected to run into issues actually getting in the ward, particularly after the girl's bid for freedom the night before, but the officer on the door had recognised him and admitted him without too much grief.

Now he was stretched out on the narrow bed beside her, staring up at the ceiling. It felt nice not to have to talk, to just be. The girl was quiet as always, nestled in his arms, tracing patterns in the air with her fingers. She seemed different somehow, almost uneasy. Then again, he couldn't really blame her. This room was bleak, no windows, and no decorations. Anything that might have given the room any charm had been stripped away, leaving only the bed.

"I'm sorry," he said, breaking the silence at last. "I didn't want to send you back but… I knew that they'd look after you. And you're safe here. Safer than out there."

She glanced at him and then at the door, open onto the hall. The nurses' station was visible, the handful of doctors and nurses who'd volunteered or been selected gathered there, talking in hushed voices. She looked back at Jamie and shook her head slightly. He frowned and opened his mouth to speak, but was cut off by Dr Knott entering the room with his colleagues. The girl tensed up instantly, her body freezing and her eyes locking onto the doctor.

"Well sleeping beauty is awake so I think it's time for introductions…" he paused, looking at Jamie. "Jamie, right? Why are you in here?"

"I… she came to my house last night. I wanted to make sure she was okay."

"Right... well you really shouldn't be here but I'm guessing that short of an armed patrol there's nothing we can do to stop you?"

"That would be correct doctor."

"Fine. Anyway, Miss, until we are able to have you transferred to Redwood Memorial, this team will be responsible for your care. We've met but I'll reintroduce myself, I'm Dr Adam Knott and I'm from the paediatric ward. This is Dr Matting, he'll be in charge when I'm unavailable, and Dr Cantrell. They're joining us from the isolation ward and the emergency room respectively. We also have some skilled nurses with us. Mark and Lorelai from maternity, Tamsin and Bella from paediatrics and Toby and Jasper from the ER. We'll be alternating shifts but there will always be at least one doctor and two nurses available, minimum."

"Shouldn't she be getting some kind of... psychiatric care?" Jamie asked. He may not enjoy therapy but he could see that the girl needed someone to help unpick the trauma in her mind. Dr Knott glared at him for a moment before restraining his expression.

"As I was about to say, the psychiatric ward has a staff shortage at the moment so they were unable to donate any of their staff. Fortunately, my wife Lilith works in that field and both she and one of her colleagues, Dr Wilde, have agreed to make themselves available." He looked at the boy as if daring him to challenge him further.

"Good. Glad to hear it," Jamie snapped back.

Dr Knott eyed him with barely disguised contempt, before turning and leading the group from the room. The moment he exited, Jamie felt the girl's body relax beside him. He gave her a reassuring smile, glancing out the door at the doctor.

"It's okay," he said softly. "I get it, I don't like doctors either. What kind of person would want to spend their life fiddling with people's bodies for a living? I get the whole helping people thing but I feel that anyone who does this kind of thing has to have a bit of a god complex."

Jamie paused. He'd not chatted this openly with anyone for a long time. Only Callie and Sammy got to see this side of him, the side that hid most of the time. He looked at the girl. She was looking at him with a serene expression on her face. There was no indication she actually understood him but she seemed to be enjoying listening to him.

"You know," he continued. "I really need something to call you. I mean, I know you have a name... I assume so anyway... but since you can't tell me, maybe we should come up with something else until we figure out a way for you to communicate?"

Silence. Of course. Jamie couldn't tell if her lack of response was agreement or refusal. He took it as agreement, guessing that she'd make some form of noise if she was unhappy.

"Umm... Kelly? Leah? No... how about Emilie? One of my favourite singers is called that. You might like her music actually. It's kind of depressing at times and she can get a bit angry but it's... kind of beautiful. She sings about pain and old stories. Here you can..." His hands went to his pocket to retrieve his iPod, felt the empty denim and he remembered. "Oh... my dad has it... and is probably wondering where I am about now..."

Saying the words, he knew he should go home, yet he made no attempt to move. His hand found the girl's and squeezed lightly.

"Maybe next time I see you, I can bring you something? To make this place a bit less miserable? Music, maybe some paper and pens? You... you like to draw? Read? I could bring you some books, tell you stories? I mean... if you want."

She looked at him with a peculiar expression like she wasn't quite sure what to make of his kind words and gentle actions. There was something oddly intense about the look that held him captive while simultaneously compelling him to turn away.

"I... I should go..." he croaked out, his voice sticking in his throat.

Jamie carefully extracted himself from the bed. His eyes lingered on the girl, still wearing the clothes he'd given her. The sleeves were rolled up, her arms wrapped in bandages to cover her most recent injuries.

"Please don't do it again," he said softly. "Hurting yourself won't make things better... trust me, I know..."

The girl went still for a moment, then sat up. She reached out and took Jamie's hand, stretching his arms out to expose his wrist to her. Silently, she extended her own arm beside his. Side by side, the scars were almost identical, a thin stripe of raised skin, inconsequential on its own.

157

The girl lightly skimmed her fingers along the scar on Jamie's wrist, raising goosebumps up the length of his arm and sending a shiver down his spine. She traced his scar up to the hollow of his wrist and pulled back. Jamie frowned, confused by what she was trying to communicate. He settled for giving her a brief reassuring smile, feigning understanding, before leaving the room.

Dr Knott was talking with the officer on duty, voices low. Jamie paused, straining his ears to catch what they were saying. Fragments of speech drifted over to him, broken and confusing.

"-a closer eye on her. If she decides to-"

"-hardly our fault. I thought her leg was busted-"

"-missed the muscle, just grazed the tissue. Largely superficial damage, might slow her down a bit but not for very long-"

"-vigilant. It won't happen again-"

The doctor began to speak but stopped abruptly as he caught sight of Jamie lingering nearby.

"Your father should have raised you to know it's rude to eavesdrop on people."

"If you've got nothing to hide, you shouldn't worry about being heard," Jamie said coolly, shrugging his shoulders slightly.

"Are you going to leave?" Dr Knott asked impatiently.

"Considering it."

Jamie wasn't sure where the bravado was coming from. Ordinarily, he avoided conflict, ducking his head and moving on when someone tried to challenge him.

"You should go, Jamie," said the officer. "Your dad is calling round looking for you. He sounded pretty worried."

*Crap.*

"I'm going…" he muttered. "I'll be back tomorrow to see her."

"Can't wait…"

He stalked out, silently wishing the doctor had been sliced up by the birds that day on the kids' ward. Thinking of the incident distracted him a little, his mind drifting off on a tangent wondering how long it would take to repair the windows and whether any of the birds had survived.

*Well... some of them definitely didn't...*

The image of biology class, the bird sliced open in front of him, surfaced at the front of his mind, accompanied by rising nausea. He gagged, forcing down the bile which burned the back of his throat.

He quickened his pace, pushing onward and trying to drive the intrusive thoughts from his mind. He kept walking, through the streets, head down. It was quiet, a few hours left of the work and school days. That was something else he was going to have to face soon. He'd been allowed the day off school for his appointment, but he'd have to face everyone... everyone who'd seen him lose it in class.

He focused on his footsteps and breathing as a way to ignore the thoughts until he reached his house. He began to open the door but a split second it was wrenched away from his hand. Jamie's father stood in front of him, expression one of anger.

"Where have you been?" he shouted. The sudden wave of rage and concern sent Jamie recoiling, startled and fearful. "I've been worried sick!"

"I went to the hospital... that's all..." Jamie mumbled, sidestepping his father to enter the living room.

"I gave you one instruction. Wait for me after your appointment!"

"It finished early! I'm sorry! You had my phone so I couldn't call you!"

"You could have borrowed one?"

"You're overreacting."

"Don't tell me I am overreacting. I am your father, I was worried. I don't care how old you are, you live under my roof, you obey my rules!"

"Dad, I-"

"No! One thing! I told you to do one thing!"

Jamie was hyperaware of every tiny movement his father made, the slight clench of his fists, the throb of his temple. Each twitch made him flinch and his breathing spike.

"Go to your room. Right now."

The boy fled up the stairs and into his room. His heart was pounding so furiously he could hear it inside his head, deafeningly loud. Every breath was painful, his throat clenching. He hurried to the bathroom and leant against the sink, gripping the porcelain. He tried to ground himself, tensing and relaxing his grasp in an effort to establish himself in reality. His father's words reverberated in his ears, the voice distorted, wavering one moment and clear as day the next.

*One thing! I told you to do one thing!*

"Stop it..." One hand left the sink, fisting in his hair and pulling hard until it threatened to tear from the roots.

*Useless! You're fucking useless Jamie!*

"Stop it."

*You're worthless! Nothing! A mistake! You should never have been born!*

"STOP IT!"

His eyes landed on the penknife, the one with the green handle, resting on the edge of the sink. He grabbed it, moving with only one clear thought. Make it stop, make it all stop. He began to stab the blade furiously, not caring what it hit, striking the sink and his arm wildly. He desperately wanted to drive the voices from his head, to overwhelm his entire mind with pain so that was all he could focus on. The voice screamed in his head, the words refusing to die down. From Jamie's mouth came a stream of agonised grunts and wails as he continued to mutilate his flesh, arms and hands becoming slick with blood. Frustrated tears bubbled up in the corner of his eyes before streaming down his cheeks.

Not enough. Not enough.

He screwed his eyes shut and hurled the knife at the mirror. The sound of metal on glass never came, instead, there was a soft moist thud in its place. Slowly, Jamie opened his eyes. There was a smear across the mirror, a mangled bar of soap in the sink. No knife. He looked down at his hands, his arms. No blood, no cuts, just chunks of soap clinging to his skin.

"Is this how you want life to be?" The voice wasn't his own and didn't seem to come from any specific place. It was soft and almost seductive, the words tenderly caressing his ears as he listened. "You're worth so much more than this."

"Wh... what?"

"You let people push you around and break you down. You deserve better..."

For a moment, he saw a shape of a figure standing behind him in the mirror but when he looked there was no one there. He frowned, turning back.

"I'm losing my mind..." he murmured, staring at his distorted reflection. The greyish streak of soap cut across his face, blurring one of his eyes into a dark haze with no distinction between white, iris and pupil. There was something disturbing about it, despite knowing that it was just a trick of the reflection. Jamie reached up and wiped away the soap. The deformity seemed to linger for a moment, resistant even as the mirror came clean, but when he blinked it vanished, his eyes completely normal once again.

He stared, frowning to himself. There was a light tap on the bathroom door, one short and three long. Callie's knock.

Jamie went over and opened the bathroom door. His sister was stood there with his phone in her hand.

*'It keeps ringing'*

"Thanks," he said, taking it from her. When she didn't leave, he looked at her expectantly. "What?"

*'You look strange'*

"Well... I'm fine... go on..."

Callie looked reluctant but nodded slowly and retreated. Jamie went to the bed and sat down, unlocking his phone. The screen lit up, with an alert that stated he had six missed calls and ten text messages. They were all from Sammy and, as he went through the voicemails, he could

161

hear her voice getting steadily more and more stressed. Jamie sighed and dialled her number, laying back on the bed as he did so.

Sammy picked up on the second ring.

"Jamie! About fucking time!"

"Jeeze, Sammy, chill. What's wrong?"

"What's wrong? What's wrong is you had a mental breakdown on Friday and then didn't come back to school!"

"Yeah, I had a doctor's appointment…"

"Jamie, you disappeared and didn't answer your phone. I thought this was like before…"

Sammy's voice trailed away. Jamie opened his mouth to speak but no words came out.

"I'm sorry…" he said finally. "I didn't mean to worry you."

"Well, you did."

The line went dead. Jamie sighed and put the phone on his bedside table, closing his eyes. He felt rotten, intensely guilty for worrying his friend even accidentally.

***Piece of shit.***

Outside Jamie's bedroom door, Callie lingered anxiously. Through the slim gap she'd left, her brother was visible, stretched out in his bed with a tense look on his face. Watching him, she tried to remember a time when he'd actually looked happy. Her mind was blank. Although she'd seen him smile before, there was always a slight… strangeness to it. It seemed forced and wrong on his face, something off about the presentation of the features.

"Callie! Bath time!" her mom called from the master bathroom. The young girl scampered off down the hall, shedding her clothes as she went.

Inside the bathroom, the surfaces were already thick with condensation, the bath piled high with bubbles. Her mother was knelt beside the tub, testing the water with her hand. Callie took out her hearing aids and placed them on a shelf over the sink before clambering into the tub, submerging herself. Her mom smiled fondly and splashed the girl playfully.

"I'm going to fetch some clean pyjamas, shout if you need anything, okay?" she said, straightening up.

Callie didn't respond, distracted by the warm water and the bubbles, focused on cultivating them into a beard. Her mom headed out of the room, humming contentedly to herself as she went. Callie continued to splash around, grabbing two rubber ducks that were balanced on the edge of the tub and dunking them merrily into the water.

There was a soft creak and one of the taps at the sink began to twist slowly. Water trickled into the basin, building speed as the tap was turned further. The second tap also began to turn, the flow of water building. Callie remained oblivious, playing with her ducks.

The door creaked and swung shut with a light click. The lock, an old rusted thing that was never used, gave a pained squeak as the bolt was forced from its housing, sealing the door. Perhaps it was the movement that drew her attention, but Callie lifted her head from her toys and glanced over. She wondered to herself why it had been closed, failing to notice the lock, why should she when it had never moved in her lifetime?

Under the mist that had clouded every surface, the faintest of silhouettes could be seen, a figure lurking in the furthest corner of the room, captured by the reflections and only visible from the corner of the eye.

The bath taps twisted, not slowly like the others but sharply so that water began to pour into the tub. Callie noticed the sudden rise in water and moved over to the taps, trying to turn them off. They remained rigidly in place no matter how hard she tried to turn them.

Callie quickly gave up on trying and began to climb out of the bath, intending to get someone to help. Before even one of her feet had cleared the edge of the tub, something grasped hold of her ankle, pulling sharply. She fell backwards, disappearing under the rapidly rising water. Callie thrashed wildly, trying to right herself but was held in place by something unseen. The water consumed her and despite the limited size of the bathtub, it felt like a bottomless lake to her as she tried desperately to snatch a mouthful of air. Something sharp as razor blades dug into her wrists, clawing at her and pulling her back.

Water ran over the sides of the bath, spilling onto the floor and continuing to spread. Callie bucked furiously, finally managing to force her head up, gulping down air greedily. Abruptly, the force dragging her down vanished. The taps turned off, the door clicked and swung open. Her mother entered, stopping in shock when she saw the flooded floor.

"Callie! Look at the mess you've made!"

Callie blinked, dazed, still gasping. She started to protest, her hands shaking frantically as she signed. Her mother shook her head and held out her towel.

"Come on out you get. I expect better from you,"

After getting helped out of the tub, the girl was left alone once more, standing in the damp room. She began to dress, pulling on her nightie. Across her wrists were four large red scratches, livid on her fair skin. Callie gulped and hurriedly adjusted her sleeves to cover the cuts. Her eyes darted around for some clue as to what had happened, some sign of the creature that had marked her.

Out of the corner of her eye, she caught sight of the mirror, the condensation fading. There, still visible, were large letters, disappearing rapidly. M-I-N-E.

**Name:** *Faith Knight*

**Period**: *5ᵗʰ*    **Subject**: *English*    **Assignment**: *Creative Writing*

**Task:** *Write a short story from the point of view of an inanimate object.*

## What the Teddy Bear Saw

She was two when I met her. She was small, in a yellow dress like sunshine, wearing bright red wellington boots. Her brown hair was tied into two neat plaits. She looked like a doll brought to life. Her eyes were bright and when she saw me, her whole face lit up. She hugged me tight and I knew I would love her forever.

Over the years, I was always at her side. She was mine and I was hers. I was the first thing she saw each morning and the last thing she saw at night. When she slept she would hold my hand tight in hers and I would watch her fondly. She cried the first night she slept in a proper bed and I tried to comfort her as much as I could.

When she was five, she left for school. She wanted me to go too but her mother said no, said this was something she had to do alone. She cried. I wanted to cry too. I didn't, I knew I had to stay strong for her. I watched her go and I held myself together but I couldn't help feeling that she was slipping away from me.

That night when she came home, she babbled excitedly about everything she'd done, everything she'd seen and I knew that things had changed. But it was good. I knew she would always love me.

The next year her parents split up. I was there when her mother told her, saw the confusion in my sweet girl's eyes. I wanted to tell her it wasn't her fault, whisper comfort in her ears until everything was alright. But all I could do was watch.

After that, every weekend she would dutifully pack her little ladybird suitcase, face sombre, and wheel it out to the car that idled in the driveway. She would always hold my hand, for support. I was a little piece of home and the first few visits, she clutched me tight at night as her eyes searched the walls for the shadowy shapes of monsters.

Her father didn't like me. He tried to buy her affection with toys, books, trips out. She ignored his gifts, spurned the books and sat through the trips out with sad apathy. At home, she seated herself in the corner with me. He nagged her to play with them but all she did was hold me tighter, looking up at her father with large hurt eyes as she wondered why it had happened, what she had done wrong.

Over time she adjusted. She bore the visits with strength, faking a smile and putting on a mask of happiness for her father. It was too little too late. Her father had moved on, his eyes occupied with another woman. She was mean, she bullied my girl, but only when her father couldn't see. At home, things were no different. Her mother had met a man. He was nice to my girl, He was friendly and let her play computer games. They were all happy but Alisa was not.

The day her father sat her down and told her that he was marrying again, she cried herself to sleep. She kept up her mask of happiness as she watched the wedding preparations with dead eyes. Even I almost believed she was happy.

Nothing prepared me for that night.

She was nine. The wedding was still months away. The Woman had taken Alisa to get fitted for her bridesmaid dress. It was gold with an ivory sash. She looked adorable, like a tiny princess.

We came home late. Her mother was out with friends. He let Alisa in, sent her up to get ready for bed. I was glad to be home and she tucked me up in the corner of her bed. She went back downstairs to say goodnight but she didn't come back for a long time. I waited. And waited. And waited.

Eventually, she came back up. Her eyes were filled with tears, her nightie was askew. She climbed into bed and lay in the dark, but she didn't sleep. Her eyes were open, reflecting the glow from the hallway. The door opened, He came in. They spoke, voices hushed. The sheets rustled and she fidgeted as he pressed closer to her. I wished I could look away or close my eyes. People might have compared her to a weak animal and Him a predator. But this was no hunt. This was a slaughter. He caged her in with her arms and devoured her, leaving nothing behind but tears and bruises.

*I won't tell if you don't.* The whispered words that told her she had done something wrong, that she had something to hide and that he was guarding her secret.

When he was gone, her hand crept out from under the cover and held me close to her. Once it was over, she didn't cry again. It was as if he'd

166

stolen her tears. She quietly pulled down her nightie and held me against her chest. I could feel her heart, beating irregularly. It was broken.

# XIV

The next day Jamie was back at school. Standing outside the building, he felt strangely numb. He'd spent the morning in silence. No one in the family had spoken to him or even looked at him really, they'd just gone about their business like he wasn't there. Even Callie seemed oddly subdued. As he headed up to the school entrance, he wondered if he'd receive the same treatment from his classmates.

Something hard hit him in the back of the head, followed by the sensation of something moist and sticky running down his neck. He reached round to touch his hair, fingers coming back stained with translucent fluid and fragments of shell. He turned his head slightly, just in time for another egg to strike his cheek.

Jamie didn't yell or even flinch, barely registering the sting of the projectile. His eyes quickly landed on the culprit, Tucker Snow, and his cronies. Tucker was being handed another egg, preparing for a third assault.

***Fight back! Stand up for yourself! Be a man!***

Jamie felt his fists clenching, images of pounding Tucker's head into the cement surfacing. A small smile played across his lips at the thought.

"What are you grinning at, freak?" Tucker shouted, starting to cross the carpark. Jamie's smile vanished and he retreated hurriedly. His foot caught on the steps leading to the entrance, sending him sprawling. Before he could get back up, a foot came down heavily on his back.

"Hey psycho, I'm talking to you. What were you grinning at?"

"Nothing Tucker..." Jamie mumbled against the ground. The boy pressed down harder against Jamie's back, before reaching down and slamming a third egg against his skull. Yolk dripped down into his eyes. Tucker said something but it was indistinct, a wave of static seemed to have descended on Jamie's ears, obliterating the world around him.

The weight on his back disappeared but he didn't move, wary of a renewed assault. After a moment, Jamie felt soft hands on his arm, gently guiding him to his feet. He looked up to see a girl from his year,

Ashlyn. She didn't speak, just steered Jamie into the building and down the corridor to the toilets.

He went to enter the boys but Ashlyn stopped him, glancing around.

"They'll ambush you in there. Or wait till you come back out. You can use the girls; I'll keep it clear while you wash up."

Jamie was sceptical but figured she was probably right and obediently ducked into the girl's toilets, Ashlyn close behind him. He went over to the sink while she positioned herself by the door, ready to stop anyone who tried to enter.

"Why are you helping me?" Jamie asked quietly as he began to shrug off his damp and sticky clothes.

"Us outcasts need to stick together," Ashlyn murmured. She turned her head and looked over at him. "Do you remember the condom incident?"

"Vaguely…"

That was a lie. Jamie did remember, vividly. The incident Ashlyn was referring to had come about a year before, after someone in their year had allegedly spotted her coming out of Planned Parenthood. For the next month, she was ridiculed and degraded, called countless names of various levels of creativity and vulgarity. But one day, her accusers decided to step things up. When Ashlyn had gone to her locker that morning, she'd found the door had been damaged, like someone had pried it open and then forced it shut again. She'd expected that when she opened it, she'd find some of her things vandalised or missing.

Instead, when she opened the door, hundreds of condoms had fallen out. The locker had been stuffed fall of them. They were splattered with red, blood or something very similar. Underneath the condoms, tucked at the very back of the locker was a small lump of bloody, mangled flesh. It had half-formed limbs, the beginning of features developing on the translucent skin. One of the science teachers identified it as a deer foetus but no one could work out how the culprits had got it.

"After that happened, everyone was either horrible to me or acted like I didn't exist. But you didn't. You picked up my books when someone knocked them out of my arms. You let me sit on your table when no one else did. You were kind to me."

Ashlyn gave him a small smile. Jamie returned it with a shy one of his own before continuing to strip off the clothes on his upper half. His jacket was badly stained but only a minimal amount seemed to have seeped through to his top underneath. He scrubbed out the worst of it with damp paper towels, conscious of Ashlyn's eyes on his bare chest. He shifted uncomfortably, moving his focus to his hair which was thick with slime. He crouched over the tiny sink, letting the water flow down onto his head. He fingered a few strands as he tried to work the egg yolk out under the spray of the tap, pulling a face at the feel of the viscous fluid against his skin.

It took almost ten minutes for Jamie to completely clean himself up and even then he wasn't entirely sure he'd rid himself of every trace of the egg. He pulled his top back on and Ashlyn, who had been watching him with mild interest, headed to the door. She peeked out, checking for any sign of Tucker or his friends, before gesturing for him to go. After double-checking the coast was, in fact, clear, Jamie scurried off down the corridor. First period was already halfway through and he had Phys Ed second, a class he shared with Tucker. He decided it might be better to avoid school for a bit, at least until everyone had found something new to focus on.

He'd cut school a few times before in the past, particularly when he'd been at his lowest, so he knew the best route to get out unseen. In his head, he ran through all the places he could hide out for a bit. The church was tempting but they had community meetings on Tuesday, increasing his chances of being seen. He couldn't go into town, it would be too easy for his dad to spot him there, and he couldn't go visit the girl at the hospital because either his mom or the officer on duty would spot him.

Instead, he decided to go for a walk in the woods. He wouldn't go far, he rationalised, and he'd come back after lunch. This was just a preventative measure to keep him from getting his head bashed in.

Jamie slipped out of a side door and briskly crossed the carpark to the treeline, letting himself get swallowed up into the woodland. Most of the trees had lost their leaves but a decent canopy still remained, a medley of reds, yellows and browns over his head.

He sighed happily, weaving his way through the gnarled trunks that were as familiar to him as his own home. His mom had taught him the

170

names of the plants that grew around the town and he recited them in his head as he passed them. Up a gentle slope to an area where the packed dirt gave way to soft grass, great conifers loomed over him but they didn't make him feel trapped or claustrophobic as some might. He felt safer here than he did anywhere else.

From nearby came the sound of water, a merry babble from the stream that filtered through the rocks and undergrowth to his favourite spot. He followed the stream although he knew the way, ingrained in his memory. Up ahead a log, the remains of a tree that had been struck by lightning and now lay dead on the ground, crossed the water at the point where the stream widened and joined up with the river. He clambered up onto the tree and seated himself, legs dangling precariously over the flowing water. The teenagers preferred to hang out at one of the lakes in the wood where they could swim in the summer and skate in the winter, the hikers and hunters took the deep forest to the south of the town. This glade was his, a secret place that was undisturbed. He hadn't shown it to anyone, it was private and his alone.

He watched the ripples of the water, the pattern of the tiny stones scattered across the riverbed and the soft movement of the weeds, like hair draped across the surface. Everything was quiet. Even the constant murmur of the voices in the back of his head seemed to have fallen silent.

The weak sunlight drifted lazily through the branches overhead, making the water sparkle. In the depths, almost hidden between two pebbles, something metallic glinted, catching Jamie's eye. He frowned, his curiosity rising, and shifted position on the log so he could hang down and try to free the object. Jamie's fingers brushed the surface of the water, icy cold against this skin. He strained his arm to reach, curiosity growing with every moment that passed. His head began to spin and he could feel his tenuous grasp on the log slipping. Part of Jamie's mind warned that he should give up. The river flowed fast and if he fell in, he might not be able to get back out again. But something pushed him forward, insistent. He had no idea what the object was but he felt like it was something important, something he needed to have.

He finally managed to reach far enough, his fingers brushing something slim and hard. He hooked his index finger around it, tugging until it came free. He was breathing hard and simply lay there for a moment, his heart pounding in his head and his prize clasped tight in his fist. Moving slowly, he righted himself so that he was sitting straddling the log. Damp brown sludge oozed out between his fingers, a thin silver chain just about visible in his clenched fist.

Jamie relaxed his hand, opening his palm to examine his find. Amongst the silt pooled in his hand was a tangle of chain attached to a flat silver rectangle, heavily tarnished and coated in grime. Jamie rubbed his thumb lightly against it, clearing away the worst of the dirt. Lettering was dimly visible beneath, but he couldn't make them out clearly. Instead, Jamie tucked it into his pocket and inched his way off the log and back down onto the grassy bank. He moved downstream, away from the river to a patch of grass that was large enough to accommodate him. He stretched out on the dirt, shifting until he found the most comfortable spot and position. He balled his jacket into a makeshift pillow and tucked it under his head before closing his eyes. The air around him seemed to have warmed up a little, the impending frost holding off for a bit longer.

As he lay there, Dr Lilith's words drifted through his mind. The future. It was something he'd have to consider eventually but he didn't know where to start. College, careers, family – they were things that concerned other people and, while he knew they should concern him too, they felt like things that were permanently out of reach. He wasn't particularly good at anything, certainly not enough to make a successful career out of. Maybe he'd skip college, get a menial job and just… exist. *Besides*, he thought cynically to himself, *none of it really matters. Whatever I do won't make a difference to anyone else. I'm not important. I won't do anything important. I don't matter.*

Jamie stared up at the web of interlocking branches above his head. The sky had turned a muted grey. He didn't matter. If he didn't come home, who would really care? A handful of people at most…

They'd move on in time. Maybe they'd even understand… that's if they cared at all.

In his mind's eye, he saw an image of the girl, sitting on her hospital bed, waiting for him to come back. She wouldn't know. She wouldn't understand where he'd gone.

Another person he'd let down. That was all he was good at.

He let out a long exhale, wishing briefly that he had a cigarette. He'd gone through an experimental phase, trying anything he could. Cigarettes, weed, pills, alcohol, anything that might allow him a brief period of relief. It worked, for a while at least, before he found himself crashing back down to earth. Even so, sometimes when his mind got too much, he found himself tempted.

Jamie closed his eyes, pushing his tainted thoughts to the back of his brain. Instead, he focused on his breathing, trying to remember the techniques his mom had taught him. Inhale through the nose, tense his muscles, exhale through the mouth and relax his body. Inhale, exhale. Tense, relax.

The quiet sounds of nature around the boy, the brush of the air and the caress of the few rays of sunlight formed a warm cocoon that made every part of Jamie's body slowly relax. He raised an arm, moving his fingers slowly and deliberately like he was playing an invisible piano. He heard the sounds in his head, the music that he longed to create but was so often overwhelmed by everything else. A sense of calm settled over him, the worries of the day fading into the background.

Jamie lay there for a time. He read for a while but soon lapsed into simply staring upwards, watching the clouds gather overhead and the shadows lengthening around him. It was nice to take time to just breathe, a luxury he couldn't often afford, but the darkening sky was a reminder of his impending return to reality. It was difficult to tell the exact time, the late month drawing in the night far sooner, but as the limited sunlight began to fade, Jamie knew he needed to head home. He'd already stayed far longer than originally planned, missing almost the entire day at school rather than just a few hours. The next day would be even harder. He couldn't keep hiding, he'd have to face them all eventually.

He got to his feet, collecting his possessions before slowly making his way back through the trees to the town. As he passed by the school, he ducked his head. Even if classes had finished for the day, there were always afterschool clubs and no guarantee that he wouldn't receive unwelcome attention. He kept his eyes on his feet and moved swiftly through the town.

Jamie crossed the road and made to turn the corner. A small black and white cat darted out from a bush and scampered over, entwining itself around his legs. The movement was so sudden, he almost fell and had to stop sharply. The cat moved to stand in front of him, mewing loudly.

"Hey… cat…"

It looked up at him, eyes expectant. Jamie blinked and went to sidestep it. The animal quickly moved in front of him once more, tangling him up. The boy frowned and tried to swerve around the cat, but no matter which way he turned it kept getting in the way. He stopped and folded his arm.

"Look, I like cats but I need to get home. Please move."

The cat mewed, turned its head as though listening to something, before turning, trotting down the path and disappearing around the corner. Jamie rolled his eyes and continued on his way. The cat was waiting around the corner and gave him a smug look, before turning his head, as though gesturing for the boy to look. Jamie followed the animal's gaze. They were on the edge of the town square, tucked between two buildings. There were people scattered around, a group of teens on the far edge of the square, heading away. Tucker was amongst them. Jamie looked down at the cat. If it hadn't tripped him up and delayed him, most likely he would have run straight into them.

"Wow... lucky break... thanks, cat."

The cat seemed to nod before wandering off into the shadows. Jamie watched it go, smiling slightly to himself, before moving on in the direction of his house.

When he got home, he let himself in, kicking off his shoes as he entered. The house was mercifully empty, Echo was asleep in the kitchen and didn't stir as he approached. Jamie stripped off his shirt and tossed it in the wash with his jacket. Like with most things, it was better not to let his mom and dad know what was going on. They'd only get concerned and try to help which would inevitably make things worse.

Shirtless, he padded across the living room and up the stairs to his bedroom. The necklace felt strangely heavy in his pocket, weighing him down unnaturally. He fetched a flannel from his bathroom and perched on his bed, extracting the necklace from his jeans. He turned it over in his palm, letting the tarnished metal catch the light. It didn't look like it would take much time to clean it up. He wrapped the flannel around the pendant and with slow deliberate movements began to work away the dirt. Gradually more of the silver surface was exposed, the dirt flaking away in chunks. Two letters and a four-digit number became visible beneath the filth.

"E... K..." he murmured to himself. Initials? Or something else he didn't understand?

Confused, he flopped back onto the bed, letting the necklace fall onto the duvet beside him. He closed his eyes, wishing the world made more sense.

# REDWOOD MEMORIAL HOSPITAL ADMITTANCE FORM

*FORM TO BE COMPLETED BY RESIDENTIAL STAFF PRIOR TO BRINGING THE INDIVIDUAL TO THE EMERGENCY ROOM*

ADMISSION STATUS

Suffering from oxygen deprivation, frostbite to extremities and severe bruising. Right arm dislocated at the shoulder.

Initial Prognosis:

Injuries most likely sustained by abuse.

PATIENT DETAILS

Name: Jamie Anthony Alexander

Age: 6          Sex: Male          Race: Caucasian

Birthplace: Redwood Memorial Hospital

Height: 4'1"          Weight: 45ibs

ADMISSION DETAILS

Date: January 8th          Time: 23:31 am

Mode of Transportation: Ambulance

DETAILS OF INCIDENT

Patient was found unconscious in a chest freezer in the basement of home following an investigation by police. Bodies of mother and siblings were found in the house. Patient was taken to the hospital and revived.

NOTES

Medical records suggest a pattern of abuse at home. Injuries along with police reports and the injuries recorded on the other family members support this.

# XV

It was mid-afternoon. The sky was thick with clouds, a stormy grey. In the hospital, the girl was stretched out on her bed, arms at her sides. They were fastened with thick leather cuffs, but her expression was still. It wasn't quite peaceful, there was a slight glare to her eyes, but she seemed to possess a certain level of acceptance of her situation.

Doctor Knott and Doctor Matting were lingering near the door, watching the girl, arms folded with near-identical looks on their faces.

"When's the sonographer due?" Dr Matting asked.

"Half-past. But you know how they are, probably running behind as always."

"We can't keep her restrained much longer, it's not good for her."

The girl turned her head, resting her eyes on the two men. Her look was venomous and both men felt that if looks could kill they would be lying dead before her in a second. Her gaze locked with Dr Knott and seemed to communicate silently, something passing between the two of them that made a small smile curl on his lip and made her tremble in response.

His attention was diverted by a clattering sound from the hall. A young woman came in, wheeling a large machine with her.

"Sorry for the delay," she said with a cheery smile. She approached the bed, her smile faltering as she took in the restraints. "Are those really necessary?"

Dr Matting pulled his hand from his pocket, a layer of Band-Aids running from the base of his little finger down to his wrist.

"Trust me. They're necessary."

Dr Knott gave his colleague a stern look before focusing on the sonographer.

"We felt it might be safer this way. She can be a tad unpredictable at times and while an ultrasound is hardly invasive, this is a security measure."

"Unpredictable? I feel like a vet rather than a doctor," murmured Dr Matting.

The sonographer made a face but chose not to comment, instead, she turned her attention to the machine, switching it on and setting it up. The girl let out a soft whimper, unsettled by the strange device. The sonographer gave her a reassuring smile.

"Don't worry, it's perfectly fine. I just need to expose your stomach and then we can get started." The sonographer reached over to roll up the girl's dress but hesitated. She looked over to the doctors. "I feel a little uncomfortable doing this without her consent."

"She's not biting you, that's as much of a consent as you're going to get."

The sonographer sighed but reluctantly continued pulling up the girl's dress until her belly was uncovered. She tried to ignore the two doctors and act as she would with any other patient. She grabbed the bottle of gel and flipped open the cap.

"This will be a little cold," she warned before squeezing a small amount of gel onto the girl's stomach. She flinched, trembling slightly and attempted to squirm away from the intrusive presence. The sonographer gently squeezed her hand and picked up the ultrasound probe. "We're going to have a quick look and make sure your little one is okay."

At first, there was nothing but static and then slowly the sound of a steady heartbeat became audible. A shape formed on the screen. The girl, who had been fidgeting uncomfortably and trying to steer her body as far away as possible, stilled. Her eyes came to rest on the screen, her body relaxing as she did. Her expression seemed to sadden as she took in the shape of her child.

"Everything looking good?" Dr Knott asked.

"Seems to be. I'd say the baby is in better condition than she is." She moved the probe slowly, searching for any abnormalities. "Everything seems normal. Maybe a little small, but since we don't know how far along she actually is, it's hard to tell."

"Can you tell the sex?"

"One moment… looks like… it's a boy." The sonographer smiled and looked at the girl. She turned her head away, screwing her eyes shut and her face taking on a pained quality. The sonographer bit her lip and looked from the girl to the doctors, waiting for instructions.

"Any idea when she's likely to give birth?"

"I'd say mid to late December based on the measurements. Hard to say exactly." The sonographer switched off the machine and got up. She glanced once at the girl, feeling strangely uncomfortable with the situation she found herself in although she didn't quite understand why. She chewed her lip but said nothing, instead she simply wheeled the machine out of the room.

"Well that's all good news," said Dr Matting. "I suppose we'll need to remove her restraints."

"She'll be okay for a little bit. Unless you're feeling particularly keen to get a matching bite on your other hand?"

Dr Matting was silent for a moment, then nodded.

"Yeah, she'll be fine for a bit."

The two doctors left the room, leaving the girl alone on her bed. She curled up as much as she could, burrowing her face into her pillow. Her arms ached from their rigid placement and she felt tears sting her eyes. The blurred image on the screen had reached into her addled mind and connected with some part of her that understood the world and what she was seeing, drawing forward memories she'd desperately tried to suppress.

That tiny heartbeat. She could hear it in her head, mixed with others, the ones she'd never got to hear but for some reason still haunted her. She felt completely lost, this new world foreign and inhospitable to her. Despite the fear and pain that had so often possessed her over the years, she almost found herself longing for the familiar darkness, the cold and the damp of the below. Here she had nothing and nobody who cared because no one wanted to care. Down there she had no one because there was no one.

Clenching her fists and digging her nails into the mattress, she let out a strangled cry that faded into her pillow. A bitter taste rose up from the back of her throat, tainting her tongue, and the twisting pain that had taken root in her stomach since she had been brought to the hospital seemed to build, making her insides feel like they were caught in a vice. She coughed, a small amount of black bile splattering onto the pristine

180

sheets. The oily texture caught in her throat, making her retch. She spluttered, her throat clenching and making it difficult to breathe. The girl buried her face deeper into the pillow, silencing her raking, hacking coughs.

She wanted to wrap her arm around her stomach, to turn herself into a little ball and draw what comfort she could. The storm clouds outside the window were growing thicker, the room darkening around her. The shadows seemed to flit around her, scampering across the sheets and over her bare skin. For once she didn't cringe or move away, instead, she let them entwine around her fingers. Their touch was like she had plunged her limbs into a bucket of ice, a numbness that radiated out across her skin accompanied by a burning sensation.

The girl closed her eyes, trying to remove herself from the world around her. Everything was just too much… too bright, too loud, too… wrong.

One of the nurses came in, switching on the lights and sending the shadows fleeing. The girl stayed still, eyes closed, as the nurse approached her and freed her wrists before departing once more. She waited until the sound of footsteps had faded and sat up. Deep red marks circled both wrists, a reminder that even here she wasn't free, bound by invisible shackles even when her actual restraints were removed.

The girl got out of the bed, moving slowly. She still struggled to walk properly, her muscles atrophied and barely able to support her. The window was her target, now lashed with rain. She stumbled but made it without falling, resting her hands against the glass. The rain was falling heavily, thunder growled in the distance with the promise of an oncoming storm. The girl watched the sky with fascination, flashes of lightning illuminating the town. Her hand went to the window latch, fiddling with it for a minute as she struggled to work out how to open it. Eventually, the latch gave and the panel of glass swung open. The girl pushed it as far as it would go, allowing the rain to strike her bare feet and the wind to send her dress billowing around her.

She stepped up onto the ledge, balancing precariously on the slim strip of raised metal. Her legs trembled, the air sharp and bitterly cold on her exposed flesh. The furious rain quickly soaked into the fabric of her dress, glueing it to her body as she stood there. A peal of thunder echoed around her, making her ears ring. Keeping one hand on the window frame for balance, she stretched her other arm out and closed her eyes. The wind rushed around her making her feel like she was flying. She smiled slightly, moving onto her tiptoes and removing her hand from the window. She swayed hazardously, perilously close to falling. Her entire body felt like tiny needles were being stabbed into her skin under the icy bite of the wind.

Freedom. To fly through the sky, without limits or restraints. The girl lifted her foot, hesitating with it in mid-air. Total freedom, it was close and would be so easy. Death had never been something that troubled her, then again it wasn't a concept she really understood. She knew that people and animals could stop, she'd seen it happen before but she didn't fully know why. Still, the idea of not being anymore had appealed at times if only to give a reprieve from the pain.

But now… she wanted to fly. She wanted to feel the air whip around her as she tumbled into oblivion.

A hand grabbed her arm, pulling her backwards. She tumbled to the floor but landed on something soft instead of the hard floor. Two arms encircled her, holding her tight but she didn't fight against him. Instead, she lay there and began to sob.

"What the hell were you thinking?" Dr Knott snapped. He struggled to his feet, straining as he heaved her up with him. He turned her in his arms to face him, expression furious. "If you ever try to do anything like that, I will tie every part of your body to that bed and leave you there!"

The girl looked down, snivelling like a child who had been scolded by a parent. Tears ran down her cheeks mingling with the rainwater clinging to her skin. Dr Knott sighed and placed his finger under her chin, raising her head to look at him.

"Don't cry. Please don't cry." He stroked her cheek, wiping away a few stray tears. "You need to be more careful. If not for you, then for that child you're carrying."

He released his hold on her, going to the window and closing it, checking that it was secured before heading to the door. The doctor shut it with a quiet click and turned the lock. The girl stood in the middle of the room, shivering as her dress dripped on the floor around her. He looked at her and sighed, shaking his head in bemusement. He crossed the room in three quick strides and took hold of the sodden fabric of her dress, lifting it over her head. She stood obediently still as he stripped her naked.

The doctor's eyes ran over her bare body, drinking in each small detail. His fatherly behaviour had gone and instead, there was an animalistic quality to the way he looked at her.

"I think I'm starting to understand your appeal... you really are quite beautiful in a unique way." He took a strand of her wet hair and ran it between his fingers, coiling it around the digit like a small dark snake. His other hand came to rest lightly on her hip, one finger brushing back and forth against her skin. His nail grazed the sensitive flesh over her hip bone. The girl trembled and cringed away, disturbed by the sudden uncomfortable proximity between them. "I think we better get you into some dry clothes and then back in bed, don't you?"

Despite his words, he made no move to get her a fresh set of clothes. The girl looked down, her hair dangling in front of her face. Any fight she might have held had disappeared, vulnerable in front of him. He took her hands in his, rubbing his thumbs against the indents from the restraints still left on her skin.

"I don't know what it is but there is something... about the way your skin looks..." He trailed off, leaving the thought unfinished. His thumb made small circles over the inside of her wrist, his eyes locked with hers.

A sudden breeze stirred her hair and there was a sound like a cat hissing. Dr Knott released her hand sharply and cleared his throat, taking a step back.

"I'll get those clothes."

The girl watched him leave, the spell that had held her in place breaking. She went to the bed, climbing on top and wrapping the sheets around her like she was building a nest. The girl curled back into a foetal position, her eyes sweeping across the wall and the shadow that lurked in the furthest corner, watching her.

# Sarum Vale Gazette

*Wednesday, April 19th*

## MAYOR CONSIDERING CURFEW AFTER THIRD CHILD SNATCHED

Parents around Sarum Vale were left terrified after a child was stolen from the park. This marks the third such abduction, all occurring during the daylight and all involving children aged under five.

The abductions began a little over a week ago, with the disappearance of two-year-old Jenny Burns on April 10th. This was followed by four-year-old Ben Taylor on April 14th and now three-year-old Adelyn Kingsley on April 18th.

While no one has been able to identify a clear culprit, witnesses have described a woman with brown hair as being seen nearby during at least two of these incidents.

In response to the abductions, Mayor Hart is reportedly considering instituting a curfew and is coordinating with local forces to monitor all parks and recreation areas to ensure that a fourth such incident does not occur.

In the meantime, police are advising parents to pay close attention to anyone interacting with their children in public areas, even those that they know, however many parents are taking this a step further and keeping their children inside. Only time will tell if these measures are effective in keeping the children of Sarum Vale safe.

# XVI

Rain fell heavily, turning the ground into a thick soup. A fierce wind battered at the trees, the branches bowing and swaying. The town was silent, the late hour and bad weather having driven the residents from the streets.

In the woods, the river, swollen by the rain and stirred by the furious wind, split its banks. Water crashed over the sides into a makeshift valley that ran parallel to it. The sudden wave washed down the slope and careened into a figure who was crouched there. Knocked off his feet, he landed on his face in the mud.

The taste of metal and earth on his lips and tongue caused him to retch. He dug his fingers into the dirt and sat up, looking around in dazed confusion, mentally trying to retrace his steps. Images danced before his eyes, a hazy blur of incoherent memories that straddled the line between fact and fiction.

Almost two hours beforehand, the back door to 13 Willow Street had swung open and Jamie had exited, dressed in pyjamas and feet bare, eyes open but vacant and unfocused. Crossing the garden, Echo lifted his head and let out a nervous whine before retreating into the shelter of its kennel.

The neatly mown grass of the garden gave way to trees and matted undergrowth of the woodland that bordered the town. As Jamie continued through the trees, the ground grew uneven with protruding tree roots and stray twigs that snared and bit. The rain lashed at his body, soaking his pyjamas until they stuck like a second skin and his hair was slick against his forehead.

A flash of lightning illuminated the sky and the forest below in monochrome as Jamie moved around the outskirts of the houses, heading south and further into the woodland. Mud collected around the hems of his trousers, building up and thickening with every step.

The boy continued onwards moving seemingly without any sense of direction, turning at a whim before stopping abruptly, the rain striking and thunder echoing through the trees. On occasions, the trees began to thin and give way to the few buildings that were dotted on the edge of the town. At these times he would pause, as though contemplating the sight in front of him, before retreating once more into the safety of the shadows.

His face remained entirely blank, a passive mask, as he continued onwards with a single-minded purpose to his movements.

Jamie's rambling path came to the main road, the trees thinning out to allow for the single stretch of tarmac that cut the forest in half and provided the only connection between the town and the rest of the world. He paused, staring into space for a moment, before taking half a step forward, foot faltering on the line where dirt and tarmac merged.

After a second he continued, crossing in a few brief steps before stopping once more on the other side. Small stones clung to his feet, the mud glueing them to his skin. The trees across the road seemed darker somehow, taller, looming like a great wall. There was a moment of hesitation and for the first time, Jamie's face flickered with something akin to emotion.

He continued into the depths of the forest, leaving the safety of the road far behind. The trees became denser, the undergrowth thicker. Pine trees crowded together, branches whispered secrets and the trunks turned against him, blocking him out. Nearby, the sound of running water could be heard, the river which fed into the lake where the girl had been found.

Jamie persevered, pushing his way through the trees following the familiar hunter's trail to where it split, one path heading towards the lake, the other heading up towards the mountains. Leaving the trail, following the path of the river over the untamed terrain towards a thicket. The densely packed trees and mess of brambles surrounded a pile of stones with a narrow opening at the base.

The stony ground dipped and gave way to a steep valley. Jamie scrambled down the bank, his foot slipping on the mud. He fell to his knees and began to claw at the side of the bank, scraping out handfuls of dirt.

There was a flash of lightning and a loud cracking noise as it struck the nearby weeping willow tree, severing the trunk and sending it careening into the water.

He continued to scrabble at the ground, the craters he formed immediately becoming filled with sludge as the rain grew heavier and the ground continued to melt. Thunder echoed around the forest, a terrible grumble that seemed to shake the trees to their roots. Water began to pour over the river banks and down the sides of the valley to where Jamie was crouched, slowly at first and then with a fury.

His hands burrowed into the dirt bank and grasped hold of something smooth in the mud a second before a wave crashed down onto him, knocking him from his feet.

Jamie remembered very little of his journey and even less of the act that had consumed him prior to the abrupt disturbance by the water. The images that danced across his mind were vague, faded pictures with only the smallest hint of meaning. His hand automatically went to his waist, searching for his phone. He felt the smooth fabric of his pyjama pants and his confusion grew. He looked around, trying to make sense of his surroundings.

The water was continuing to flow down into the valley, faster than it could disperse, and was beginning to pool around his ankles. He stumbled to the side of the bank and tried to clamber upwards, moving instinctively. The ground collapsed under his weight, sending him tumbling backwards.

Within the dirt, the corner of something hard and wooden had become visible. Jamie, damp hair hanging in his eyes and rain clouding his vision, barely noticed the new protrusion. He scrabbled at the steep slope, trying desperately to find something to grab onto. His feet couldn't find purchase, slipping down every time he tried to place any weight on the bank, arms flailing wildly, clutching at anything he could no matter how futile.

His body was coated in the thick rust coloured sludge that was pouring every crevice and tears of frustration were running down his cheeks. Digging his fingers into the mud, other hand searching the surface for a rock, a root, anything. His fingertips brushed against a hard lump and he grasped hold. He heaved himself up, dragging his weight up the ridge. The ground continued to crumble, eaten away by the water.

There was a creak, a crack and Jamie found himself falling. The wooden item he had been grasping, dislodged by the extra weight, fell and splintered as it hit the ground. Jamie groaned, dazed, and turned his head.

A box, the sides smooth but decaying and fractured by age, lay on the ground next to him. Jamie got to his knees, wincing, his eyes falling on the box. A large crack, running the length of the lid, was visible. He frowned, his confusion returning accompanied by a nagging sense of curiosity. He reached over and dug his fingers into the crack, grasping hold of the wood as much as was possible. He pulled up sharply, the rotten wood breaking easily and the force of the movement sending him sprawling backwards.

The inside of the box was filled with the same thick rust colour ooze that Jamie was covered in. Amidst the fluid were the bodies of two children. Their naked bodies were curled up, hunched and twisted around one another grotesquely to fit in the small space. Thick rope was tied around their ankles and wrists, binding them tightly. The rope around their wrists held a few lingering remains of dried blood not obliterated by the slime. A gash ran across each wrist, largely hidden by the ropes. The fingers on one were worn down from endless clawing, the skin was a fetid mess, thick with maggots and eaten away in patches, exposing corroded muscle and bleached bone. Tufts of hair still clung to the scalp, strips of which were hanging from its skull. Their faces were contorted into a desperate scream, although whether from fear or a dire need to air was impossible to tell. Empty sockets, crawling with insects, stared up at the sky.

Jamie saw very little of this. He peered over at the box and saw the face of one of the children. He recoiled instantly, letting out a yell, and began to clamber up the bank, renewed by sheer panic as he determined to put as much distance between himself and the box.

He slipped a few times but managed to reach the top. He stood there for a moment, catching his breath. Around him, the dirt was still being worn away and he could see more boxes, identical to the first, being uncovered.

He sprinted away, his feet slipping on the mud. He searched for anything familiar that might lead him to people but the woods seemed to transform from a place of comfort to a hostile territory that stretched out without end.

His foot caught on a protruding tree root and he tumbled forward. The ground gave way to a slight slope and he rolled down, landing in a painful heap at the bottom. His ankle twisted sharply accompanied by a stab of pain. He cried out. There was a faint stinging sensation on his forehead and when he probed the location gently with his fingers, they came back damp and stained. It was hard to tell in the limited light but it seemed tinged with red and the sight of it sent panic racing through Jamie's body.

Everything his father had ever said in the woods flooded his brain and he tried to sift through the information for something that would help him. He grabbed hold of a nearby tree, using it for support and balance as he forced himself to his feet. He had to get out of here, he had to find someone and tell them what he'd seen.

He limped on, clinging to the trees. His ankle buckled underneath him and every step sent fresh jolts of pain through the injured limb. Blood was running down his forehead. Every part of him was soaked in mud and the wind whipped against him, biting into his flesh. He'd moved past cold and the icy wind seemed to burn instead. His fingers were numb and stiff, struggling to respond to him.

The ground began to even out and the trees thinned out slightly to reveal a small clearing with some fallen logs dotted around. Jamie let out a small noise of relief, recognising it as the place where he usually camped with his father and uncle. He picked up the pace as best he could, following the trail that he knew would lead to the main road and the ranger's station. His legs were crying out to stop, his body was battered and bruised.

The trail sloped down and the trees separated to reveal tarmac. The car park. He couldn't help a small cry of relief as he staggered down the slope to the car park. His ankle was screaming at him and with every step, it threatened to give way entirely.

He threw himself at the door to the ranger's station, collapsing against it. He slammed his fist onto the door.

"Hello! Hello!" he cried out. His voice was weak and exhausted, barely audible under the howl of the wind. He banged frantically, praying someone would be there and would hear him.

The door opened and he fell inside the building, relieved for some shelter from the elements.

"What the hell?"

"Jesus Christ, Jamie?" He looked up to see two concerned faces looking down at him, one of which he recognised.

"Patrick..." He was half-dazed, the bright lights of the station almost blinding him after stumbling around in the dark for so long.

"You know this kid?" asked the other ranger.

"Yeah, I'm friends with his dad. He's Michael Harper's kid. What are you doing out here Jamie? It's hardly a good night for a stroll!"

Patrick lifted him up, helping him to a chair. He fetched a towel for the boy who wrapped it around himself, his hands trembling. Jamie tried to conjure up the words to explain but his body wouldn't cooperate, his tongue felt thick and heavy and his lips were numb. He clutched at the towel, trying to draw some element of comfort.

"What were you thinking?" demanded the other ranger.

Jamie was rocking slightly, mouthing words incoherently and staring into space. Patrick waved his hand at the other ranger, signalling him to be quiet. He knelt down in front of the teenager.

"Jamie."

The boy's head shot up.

"B...bodies... th... there are b... bodies in the woods..." he managed to say. The two men exchanged glances.

"Come on kid, it's not a good night for pranks," protested the other man. Patrick gave him an annoyed look before returning his focus back to the younger boy.

"That's a very serious claim Jamie. Are you sure?"

Jamie couldn't manage the words but he nodded. Patrick grimaced slightly and straightened up. He retreated with his colleague and the pair began to talk softly.

"I am not going out in a thunderstorm because a kid thinks he saw a dead body!"

"I know him, he wouldn't make it up."

"He probably just saw a log or something and his mind is playing tricks on him. He doesn't look all there as it is."

"Look, whether you believe it or not, we actually do have to check it out. It could be that someone is injured out there. If you want to stay here that's fine, but I am going to investigate." Patrick turned back to Jamie. "Do you remember where you saw them, Jamie?"

"It was near the river... where it curves... there was a mud bank..."

"Hang on." Patrick grabbed a large map of the forest, accompanied by aerial pictures of the area, and followed the path of the river with his finger to the curve. Jamie peered at the map, searching for something familiar.

"Here," he said. "I think... there's a large stack of stones... in a thicket area. The ground near it slopes down... the river was on the other side of the slope."

"Alright... I'll see what I can find." Patrick put on a raincoat and grabbed a radio, flashlight and a small lantern. "I'll radio in if I find anything. Oscar, can you try and find him something dry to wear so he doesn't freeze to death while I'm gone?"

Patrick headed out into the rain and Oscar, grumbling, grabbed a spare shirt for Jamie. He ignored the clothing, his mind wandering away from reality and back towards what he had seen. He rocked slowly back and forth, the image of the children screaming up at the sky emblazoned into his mind.


After what felt like an age, the radio crackled and Patrick's voice came through.

"Oscar. Call the police. Right now."

Jamie lifted his head. Oscar, who had been playing on his phone, jerked upright instantly and grabbed the radio.

"Are you serious? You actually found something?"

"Yes. Call the police."

Oscar, his demeanour instantly changed, went to the phone and dialled. Jamie watched, feeling numb inside and out. In a way, it would have been better if Patrick hadn't managed to find anything, if he'd just imagined things. He barely heard Oscar as he explained the situation to the police, staring out of the window at the rain.

It didn't take long for the police to arrive. There were four, Jamie's father among them. When he saw his son, huddled up on a desk chair in his filthy pyjamas he did a double-take.

"Jamie!"

"H…hey dad…"

Officer Harper looked like he was going to say something but he gritted his teeth knowing that, despite his desire to ensure his son was okay, the priority was to investigate the bodies. The police chief, after speaking briefly with Oscar, turned to his men.

"Harper, Larkin, go with the ranger and investigate the bodies. The medical examiner is on his way. Daniels, take statements. Start with the boy."

"Sir, my son is bleeding. He needs medical attention," Officer Harper protested.

"And he'll get it, but for the time being, Daniels can take his statement."

Officer Daniels came over and took a seat next to Jamie. He knew the boy; most of the officers were friendly and knew each other's families. He gave his colleague a reassuring smile. Officer Harper scowled but followed Oscar and Officer Larkin out into the woods.

The two officers and the ranger headed into the trees. Oscar knew the forest well and went ahead, shining his flashlight onto the ground to watch for trip hazards. Patrick was waiting near the site and had strung the lantern on a tree branch. He called out as he saw them approach.

"Watch out. The ground's unstable."

The three men joined him at the top of the bank and watched as he shone his light down. The beam landed on the open box, the two children inside it. Something metallic glinted in the torchlight.

"Did you touch it?" Officer Larkin asked. Patrick shook his head.

"No, I've not gone any closer than this… but that's just the start of it." He turned the beam slowly, guiding it along the edge of the bank to reveal the edges of other boxes, exposed by the rain. "I don't know for certain but they look pretty similar to the one down there."

Officer Larkin grabbed his radio and called through to the chief. Officer Harper felt nausea rising inside of him. He'd dealt with a lot of cases but only two murders before. Seeing the box with the bodies inside, his first thought was of his own children. Jamie… he'd seen this…

He looked over at his colleague.

"What does the chief say to do?"

"Mark the area, put on our gloves and get digging. He's calling in the others to help and he'll be along with the medical examiner shortly. Hopefully, they'll bring some proper equipment too."

"Is my son okay?" he asked. Officer Larkin nodded.

"As well as can be expected. Daniels called your wife and there's a paramedic coming with the coroner to check him over."

Slightly relieved, Officer Harper pulled on a pair of rubber gloves and reluctantly descended into the valley. The rangers went to help escort everyone to the site while the two officers began to carefully uncover the boxes.

One after another, they scraped away the dirt around them, revealing more and more. They didn't move them or even open them but as the number increased, both officers felt a sense of anxiety settling over them.

By the time the rest of the officers arrived, Officer Harper and Larkin had already uncovered eight new boxes, and as the night progressed even more revealed. By the time the sun rose, the rain had stopped and the officers were standing beside twenty-nine boxes buried in neat rows. They were in various states of deterioration but each of the boxes were the same size and made of the same smooth dark wood. The lids were attached by hinges on one side, rusted by the elements. A latch and padlock on the other side held them shut.

"Holy shit…" muttered one of the officers.

"We don't know for certain that they have bodies in them," said another.

"Yeah, someone just decided to bury thirty boxes in the woods for fun and put two dead children in one of them."

The chief glared at his staff but didn't speak. None of them moved. None of them wanted to open the boxes and confirm their suspicions. Kane, the medical examiner, had finished with the first pair of bodies and climbed up the slope to join the officers.

"If no one is going to open the boxes, am I done? I've got bodies at the hospital to deal with."

"You work at the hospital too Kane?" Officer Larkin asked.

"Yes. Medical examiner for you guys, mortician for them. If there's a dead body in this town, chances are I'll deal with it at some point," he said, heading over to the closest box and kneeling down.

"I can't imagine you're kept very busy."

Kane glanced over at the officer and a small smile played across his lips. He took hold of the padlock and gave it a sharp tug. The lock snapped easily.

"Oh you'd be surprised how quickly the bodies can stack up in a place like this," he said. He lifted the lid and stepped back. A collective ripple spread through the assembled officers as they took in another pair of bodies.

These ones were less decomposed than the pair Jamie had found. The bodies were largely intact, their arms wrapped around each other. Both were naked and the officers could see it was one boy and one girl. The girl's eyes were glassy, staring up at the sky. The boy's eyes had been cut out, leaving two gaping empty holes, the flesh around them jagged. A metal cord with two small dog tags was clasped in the girl's hand.

"These can't be more than a month old," Kane said softly.

No one else seemed to be able to speak. They'd seen violence before. Some of them had dealt with homicides before. But violence against children… that shook them all to the core. Many of them had children of their own at home and seeing the tiny broken bodies in the box, they couldn't help but see their own children lying there. They felt sick to their stomachs. What kind of person could do this to children?

The chief broke the silence, clearing his throat.

"Get the rest of those boxes open. Kane, do what examinations you can and then we'll have the bodies taken to the morgue," he instructed.

The officers hesitated before slowly heading over to the boxes. Two of them continued to search to see if there were any more boxes buried while the rest began to open them, breaking the padlocks where they could and prying open the rest. Each box contained two bodies, a pair of dog tags, rusted and thick with grime, tucked away between the bare forms. Each set was in a different state of decomposition. Some appeared to be decades old, reduced to bones and bundles of rope. As the body count grew, the officers grew quieter and more sombre.

The bodies were given a brief examination by Kane, before being tagged and sealed in their body bags for transportation.

Officer Harper watched as his colleagues began to carry the bodies to the car park. Kane was kneeling nearby, examining one of the boxes with interest. He beckoned to no one in particular and Officer Harper came over to join him. Kane looked at him expectantly and then back at the box. Officer Harper followed his gaze.

"Do you see it?"

"I see a box with a skeleton in it."

"Yes. One skeleton. All the other boxes have two children in them. This box only has one."

"So they only killed one child that day instead of two?"

"Well, maybe, except…" he reached down and picked up a two loops of rope that lay discarded in the box. "It looks like there were two people in here when it was buried."

Officer Harper took the rope and from Kane and examined it. It was frayed and the remains of the knots still lingered but appeared to have been cut in places.

It seemed that Kane was right. It did look like someone had been placed in this box, tied up like the other children. He frowned and knelt down. There was no visible damage to the box, the padlock rested in the dirt beside it.

"Then where is the other one now?"

# Morningwood Sanatorium Incident Report

**Date of Incident:** *August 25th*

**Time of Incident:** *06:32am*
**Incident Type:** *Suicide*

**Patient Name:** *Andrew Tarrant*

**Patient type:** *Non-violent*

---

**Details of Incident**:

*Andrew was placed in isolation following a peculiar burst of anger in which he attempted to assault a nurse. Once restrained, it was decided he would remain in the isolation room for twenty-four hours, until suitably calm and able to explain his reasoning behind the attack. Patient's file described him as lucid and intelligent, with no tendency towards violence, making this attack rather out of character.*

*When a nurse went to check on him, he was found to have fashioned the bedding into a noose and hung himself.*

---

**Response:**

*No attempts to resuscitate were made as the patient appeared to have been dead for several hours. His body was incinerated.*

---

**Signed:** *A. Morningwood*

# XVII

The morgue was unnaturally crowded. The wooden boxes were piled on every surface, two of the bodies stretched out on a table in the centre of the room. The police chief, Officer Harper, Officer Larkin and Kane were gathered around the bodies, faces grave. The officers were exhausted, their clothes damp and muddy. After a fraction of the bodies had been removed they were transported to the morgue for a closer examination and Kane had left with them. The officers had remained at the site, working to uncover more boxes. None of them had slept or even had a chance to clean up. Officer Harper couldn't get his mind off Jamie, desperate to make sure his son was okay.

"So Kane, what do we know here?" the chief asked.

"Well, most of the bodies were too badly damaged to be much use however the more recent ones were able to give me some insight. With the exception of one box, they're all paired up, a boy and a girl. They all look to be under ten years but their exact age varies wildly. It seems that they were not... dead... when they went into the boxes. From what I can tell, the injuries are consistent across all the victims. All of them had their wrists cut, as well as a symbol carved into their hand. The male victims also had their eyes removed however it appears that that was done quite a bit prior to their placement in the boxes. The marks are...technical. Precise. Almost like surgery." Kane turned away from the bodies and picked up one of the dog tags. "The rope is pretty standard, the kind you could get from any hardware store. The tags are custom made I'd guess, and I'd also assume that they give the initials of the victims as well as the year they were buried."

"Okay, this is a good place to start," said the chief.

"There is one more thing," said Kane. "While not all the boxes have been removed yet, currently, based on the tags, it looks like you have two bodies every year... for about one hundred and fifty years."

No one spoke. The sheer magnitude of the situation weighed heavily on all of them. One hundred and fifty years. Three hundred bodies. However many still to dig up.

"Harper, Larkin, gather all the missing children files you can. Contact the Redwood department and get what they have too. Larkin, I want you to start working through the tags and compile a list of the years and the corresponding initials. Harper, go through the files and isolate all the children under ten. When Larkin has done the list, the pair of you need to start trying to match files to initials. If we can identify some of these kids, maybe we can find a common link between them. And if not… we might be able to give some parents a bit of closure. I'm going to call everyone else in, brief them on the situation."

The two officers nodded and headed out of the morgue. The chief glanced at the bodies and shook his head. It took a special kind of evil to harm a child. He sighed to himself and followed his colleagues. Kane watched them go. He was in for a long night processing and labelling the bodies.

As Officer Harper headed out of the building, he fished his phone from his pocket and dialled his wife's number. He had no idea if Jamie was at the hospital or if he'd gone home and he wanted to make sure he was alright. Luckily, the call was picked up on the second ring.

"Hey sweetie," he said. "How's Jay?"

"In shock. Hardly surprising. His cuts have been cleaned up and treated. His ankle isn't broken luckily, he just needs to rest up for a while… other than that… well, physically he's fine. The hospital couldn't do much for him, so I brought him home. I've washed him off and put him to bed, gave him some sleeping pills… I'm worried about what this might do to him though. He's suffered enough as it is, what if this pushes him back over?"

"We'll take care of him, we'll help him. Do what you can, for now, I promise I'll be home soon."

"Okay…" she paused. "How bad is it?"

"Pretty bad… too early to say just how bad… I don't understand how something like this can be happening…"

"I believe in you Michael, you'll figure this out."

The pair said their goodbyes and ended the call. Officer Harper headed across the parking lot to his car, mentally preparing himself for the mountainous task ahead of him. As he approached, Dr Knott came into view, unlocking the car beside the officer's.

"Evening Michael," the doctor greeted.

"Adam. Good shift?"

"Can't complain. I was watching over our Jane Doe. She's fairly low maintenance... once you get passed the biting." He gave Officer Harper a slight smile, which faded as he took in the other man's expression. "What's wrong?"

"Just... worried about Jamie."

"Oh yeah? He alright?"

"I honestly don't know. Do you think Lilith will be free for an emergency appointment tomorrow?"

"I'm sure she can squeeze him in. I'll get her to call you."

"Thanks."

"It's nothing... serious, right? Not like before?"

"No. Not yet anyway... but I'm worried he might go back that way..." Dr Knott looked at him expectantly, waiting for clarification. Officer Harper sighed. "He ended up in the woods tonight. I don't know how, but he saw... things. Things he shouldn't be exposed to and I'm worried how it'll affect him."

"I'm sure he'll be okay. He's resilient. And I'll make sure Lilith finds a way to squeeze him in."

The two men gave each other brief smiles before getting into their respective vehicles. Officer Harper sat there for a moment, staring out of the windshield. He hoped the doctor was right but he couldn't get rid of the nagging feeling that something bad was on the horizon.

He drove out of the parking lot and slowly down the road in the direction of the station, barely able to focus on his surroundings as everything swirled around in his mind. It felt like a bad dream, the most horrific one he'd ever experienced.

In the Harper house, Ruth Harper put down the phone and paced across the living room. Callie crouched on the staircase, watching her mother with anxious eyes. In her arms was one of her favourite teddy bears, worn from years of affection. Echo was sat beside her, head resting on her lap. She toyed with his ears, chewing her lip as her mother patrolled across the floor downstairs. Jamie was up in his bed and although Callie didn't know what had happened exactly to her brother, she knew it was something bad.

The girl left the staircase, tiptoeing up to the hall and over to Jamie's room. She peeked through the gap in his door, straining her eyes in the dark to make him out. He was stretched out on the bed, asleep or awake she couldn't tell, near motionless. Every so often he would let out a small groan or whimper as the images of what he'd seen flashed across his mind. Callie pushed open the door and crept over to the bed. She could see now that he was awake, eyes staring up blankly at the ceiling.

"Jamie...?" she said softly. He didn't respond, didn't even react to her presence. Callie watched him sadly for a moment before gently placing her teddy beside him, hoping that the simple gesture would do a little something to comfort him. She turned and left quietly, head down.

Jamie remained still, the events of the evening playing over and over in his mind. He couldn't get the image of the mangled skeletons, bare empty eye sockets staring back at him. He felt sick, an intense gnawing feeling in the pit of his stomach to accompany his aching limbs. It was still raining outside, the lightning still flashing and illuminating the space around him. He rolled onto his side, hands in front of his face. He ran his thumb over the curve of his palm, tracing the lines on his skin. Calmly, he dug his nail into the soft flesh, pressing down harder and harder until it split and blood bubbled up. He watched the bead swell and begin to trickle down his wrist. He felt no pain, it was like his body had been shut down by what he had seen.

He ran his finger along the line of blood, smearing it across his skin. It glistened in the lightning like a bracelet of rubies, the sight of it strangely fascinating to him. He sat up, his movements stiff and absent. His fingers stroked across the cover, the feel of the soft fabric had always served to comfort him in the past but now it seemed coarse and any sense of familiarity had gone.

Jamie rose from the bed and went over to the window. Every step felt like a metal clamp tightening around his ankle but he ignored it, balancing against the sill. The cat was perched on the ledge outside. When it saw Jamie, it began to scrabble against the glass, mewing pitifully. Jamie sighed and opened the window, reaching out to pull the small damp creature inside. It curled up in his arms, purring softly.

As Jamie pulled the window shut once more, his eyes swept across the rain-lashed street. A figure was visible under the amber pool cast by the streetlamp. The lighting transformed the person into a black silhouette, features indistinguishable. There was no way of knowing which way the person was facing, but Jamie got the sense that they were looking up at him. The cat mewed and leapt out of his arm, retreating to the bed. Jamie ignored it, placing his hand on the window, trying to determine if he was dreaming. The glass was cool to the touch and the light chill convinced him that he was awake.

The figure moved out of the light, approaching the garden fence. They stood there for a moment, head bowed, and then turned and walked away. Jamie knew he should feel concerned or at least mildly curious but he just felt numb. He stood by the window for a while, watching the street. Just remaining standing was a tremendous effort, every inch of his body had been sapped of energy. Jamie knew he should go to bed but the thought of movement was exhausting, never mind the actual act. Instead, he slumped against the window, staring out bleakly.


By the time Officer Harper reached the station, everyone else was already there, gathered loosely around the desk, mumbling amongst themselves. Someone had dragged out one of the display boards from the meeting room and pinned a few grainy pictures from the burial site up. No one really knew what to do or how to act, the situation was completely alien to them.

The police chief spotted Officer Harper lingering at the back of the group and cleared his throat.

"Alright, now we're all here, let's get this underway. Some of you are already aware of the situation but for the benefit of the rest of you, this is what's happening." He paused, looking at the tense faces in front of him. "At twelve minutes past midnight, we received a call from the ranger station regarding a body in the woods. Upon responding, the situation was found to be a great deal worse. We still don't know the full extent exactly but currently, over one hundred boxes have been recovered from the area where the initial body was found. Each box contains two victims and all the victims were under the age of ten. Each victim was found in possession of one of these." The chief pointed at a picture of one of the tags. "We believe that these identify the initials and the year of death of each victim. The most recent box appears to be little over a month old and, while we've yet to determine exactly how far back these murders span, they appear to cover at least one hundred and fifty years."

As he spoke, the murmuring began again. Even those who already knew the extent of the damage couldn't help themselves.

"Given the magnitude of these killings," the chief continued. "It seems incredibly unlikely that we are searching for just one person. It may even be a group. Now I understand this… situation is concerning to all of you. Many of you have children of your own. However, I would ask that for now, you refrain from discussing this matter with anyone outside this building. We don't want to cause a panic. Is that understood?"

There was a general noise of agreement. The chief nodded and stepped down, signalling the end of the meeting. Officer Harper went to his desk and sat down. Whoever had printed off the pictures had left a set for him, nestled beside a drawing Callie had done and a family photograph taken a few years before. Seeing the mutilated decaying corpses of the victims beside the happy faces of his family was uncomfortable, to say the least. He regarded the images for a moment, then carefully gathered the photograph, the drawing and the few other scattered decorations supplied by his children, and tucked them into a drawer.

Desk clear, save for the grisly reminders of what had happened, Officer Harper began the task of gathering and sifting through every missing child case the Sarum Vale Police Department had, searching for any that might be a match. The computer system was practically an antique and prone to frequent meltdowns so the chief insisted that everything should have an additional hard copy. They were kept stored in a small cupboard whose door bore the generous label of 'Records Room'.

It didn't take long for Officer Harper to search through the boxes and files for the relevant documents. There were remarkably few, just one slim folder wedged between two precarious stacks of boxes.

He took the file back to his desk and flicked through. There were only a handful of cases inside and most were at least a decade old. Officer Harper sighed, picked up the phone and dialled the number for the Redwood Police Department.

"Redwood P.D. Officer Hendrix speaking."

"Hey, Lewis, it's Michael Harper."

"Michael! It's been a long time. How you been? How's Ruth?"

"We're alright. Martha good?"

"She's great. But… I assume you're not calling at this time of night for a catch-up?"

"Unfortunately not. Actually, I need a favour."

"Is this about the Alexander case? Because I am already doing what I can with that."

"No, it's not that. We've got a bit of a situation up here and we need all the files for unsolved missing children case in Redwood."

"All of them?"

"Yes."

"That's… a lot."

"Well, we need them. Can you send them over?"

"I guess, it just might take a little while."

"As soon as you can Lewis, I'd really appreciate it. And… keep me updated on the Alexander case."

"Sure thing Michael. Talk soon."

"Thanks, Lewis."

Officer Harper hung up the phone and picked up his file, opening it to the first case. Maybe one of them would shine some light on things.

# DEPARTMENT OF HEALTH
## Certificate of Death

THIS IS TO CERTIFY, That out records show:

Name_____ Hope Julianne Knight

Died_____ May 11th_____ at 22:16 pm at _____ 12 Ash Street, Sarum Vale

Age at death_____ 6 months _____Sex_____ Female _____Ethnicity Caucasian___Marital Status___N/A

Immediate cause of death given was_____ SIDS

Certified by___John Grantham, MD___Address___Sarum Vale

Place of burial or removal___Sarum Vale Cemetery

Date of burial___May 21st___Funeral Director___William Carroll Address___Sarum Vale

Record was filed___May 24th

# XVIII

Despite Jamie's best efforts to remain awake, his body eventually succumbed to exhaustion and he fell into a haunted sleep.

He was in a cave. Black stone curving in a nearly perfect circle, small openings that gave way to narrow tunnels the only break in the surface. A girl in her early teens was sitting, almost hidden, in the entrance to one of the tunnels. A fractured beam of light from the ceiling lightly caressed her legs. She was naked and her body held the signs of the early stages of pregnancy.

Jamie took a step towards her, curious. The air felt strange, thick and almost liquid. The girl was humming softly to herself, running her fingers over the slight swell of her belly. She didn't seem happy, nor did she seem particularly sad. Her expression was clouded, as though deep in thought.

"Hello…?" he said softly. She didn't react, focused on something else. A shadow flitted across the wall

A terrible screaming ripped through the air, more animal than human. The girl doubled over, blood pouring from out between her legs. She was dragged backwards, vanishing into the darkness. Jamie tried to run after her but he stumbled, falling into the blackness.

The shadows consumed him, burying him in cold oblivion. He cast around desperately, searching for some source of light. The air around him had grown even thicker making it difficult to breathe and as he gulped it down, he realised that he was swallowing icy water. The endless void he found himself in had been replaced by swirling Cimmerian waters, impenetrable. He kicked out, hoping to swim towards the surface but everything looked the same and his sense of direction had fled, leaving him lost and alone, lungs screaming out for air.

In the murky depths, something moved and Jamie felt it brush against his leg. He jerked wildly, searching for the source of the contact. His eyes strained, trying to penetrate the gloom.

A face loomed out of the darkness, a rotten mask of flesh stretched over bone, pale fragile hair drifting. He recoiled, kicking out desperately. His body collided with something solid and, although he didn't want to, he found himself turning. Bodies floated around him, lifeless eyes staring at him, maggot-ridden limbs reaching for him. Amongst them, one face stood out. Callie's face, contorted in an expression of terror. Jamie screamed, water flooding down his throat and into his lungs.

From the bowels something reached up and entwined around his ankle, a slithering snake-like creature that crept up his leg, dragging him down.

Jamie woke with a start. His bed sheets were tangled around his legs, his clothes soaked with a cold sweat. The cat was sat beside his head, watching him. He sat up slowly, running his fingers through his hair. For a blissful moment, the previous night was a haze of incoherent memory but as he sat there it all began to return to him. He felt the sting of bile in his throat and had to fight the urge to vomit.

There was a light knock at the door. It opened before he had a chance to respond and Sammy came in, balancing a tray.

"Hey Jay," she said with a slight smile. It was an expression he recognised, the smile where people were trying not to upset someone. "Your mom let me in. I... heard about what happened."

"How?"

"Your dad told me. He figured I'd hear it from you anyway and that you could probably use a friendly face..."

She set the tray down and perched on the edge of his bed. The cat sniffed at her before jumping from the bed and disappearing underneath it.

"Do you want to talk about it?" she asked softly.

"No. I want to forget it ever happened. But I doubt that's going to happen somehow."

"Jay... I'm sorry you have to go through this... I don't really know what to say," she confessed, biting her lip.

"That's a first."

"You're not that traumatised then." Sammy sighed and shifted to sit beside him. "What were you doing out there?"

"I woke up there…" He paused, resting his head in his hand. His face held an expression Sammy had never seen before, a vacancy that frightened her. He looked like part of him had been removed, like he'd lost what made him who he was. "I think I'm losing my mind, Sammy… I keep seeing things, hearing things… everything is falling apart around me and now this…"

He closed his eyes and the exhaustion was clear on every line of his face.

"I can't keep doing this Sammy. I just want it to end."

"You'll get through this Jamie. You're stronger than you think." Sammy reached over and squeezed his hand lightly. "I have to get to school. I'll check in on you after okay?"

She kissed his cheek lightly before getting to her feet. Jamie watched her go and listened for the sound of her bike outside. When silence had returned to the room, he lay on the bed, staring up at the ceiling. The room seemed to be shrinking around him, the emptiness giving him nowhere to hide from his thoughts. He tried his music but for once even that wasn't enough to drown them out.

Jamie wasn't sure why he decided to go to the hospital. Maybe it was because of his dream or maybe it was because he knew she wouldn't care if he was losing his mind. He could be not okay for a bit and she wouldn't care. Whatever the reason, he left his room, intending to head to the hospital. He'd only gone a few steps when he realised how idiotic his plan was. His legs were already protesting the movement and by the time he reached the front door, he was exhausted, trembling from the pain. He paused to catch his breath, holding onto the sofa.

The front door opened and his mom entered, returning from dropping Callie at school.

"Jamie! What are you doing up? Let's get you back to bed."

She reached out to guide him back up the stairs but he shrugged her off.

"Mom, I want to go to the hospital. There's someone I need to visit there."

"You're not going anywhere in your condition."

"Please? It's important."

"What could be more important than your health?"

"Mom…" he sighed. "I want to see that girl… the one from the woods? Please, I feel responsible for her… and I promised her I'd visit."

"Maybe so but that was before all… this happened."

"Please, mom… she doesn't have anyone…" Jamie could see her resolve weakening. "Just give me half an hour. And you can check in on your patients while we're there. I know you're hating not being able to take care of them."

"You're the one I need to take care of," she murmured.

"Well if you give me a lift up there, you're preventing me from sustaining further damage by walking there," he pointed out.

His mom sighed and shook her head disapprovingly, but Jamie could tell from her expression that he'd won.

"Come on then. Just half an hour though. Then we come home and you stay in bed until I tell you otherwise."

The pair headed out to the car, Jamie leaning on his mom and trying not to show how much pain he was in. Once in the vehicle, he curled up in the passenger seat and put on a neutral expression that, over the years, he had perfected into an art form. His eyes stared vacantly out of the window, the scenery an inconsequential blur that barely registered to his frazzled mind.

When they pulled up at the hospital, his mom insisted on escorting him to the ward.

"Half an hour Jamie. No disappearing."

"Yes, I'm incredibly likely to run off. You know… with the leg I can hardly stand on," he said, rolling his eyes and letting himself into the ward.

Dr Cantrell was on duty, reading at the desk. He glanced up as Jamie hobbled passed him.

"Need a wheelchair?" he teased.

"No, I can manage."

Jamie made his way into the girl's room. He blinked in confusion as his eyes came to rest on the bed, empty and sheets pulled back. Had she been moved? But if she had, why would they still have a doctor here?

He was about to leave when he spotted an arm protruding from under the bed. He crouched down slowly, images of bodies tucked away in darkened crevices forming in his mind. Two green eyes met his and he sighed in relief.

"Hi," he said, smiling slightly.

The girl smiled back and reached out to grasp his wrist, gently drawing him under the bed to join her. Jamie wriggled into the narrow space and stretched out beside her. There was something immensely comforting about being tucked away in the dark, hidden from the rest of the world. The girl reached up and ran her fingers across his cheek, tracing the scratches he'd sustained the night before.

"I'm okay," he told her. "They don't hurt."

As she gazed up at him, Jamie felt strange feelings stirring inside him. Her expression, the wide trusting eyes made him think of Callie. There was something innately childlike about the girl, reminding him of how different they were. Despite their closeness in age, they were worlds apart. Maybe that was why he kept coming back? The same protectiveness he felt around Callie stirred by the girl's childish mind?

"Oh, I brought something for you." He fished his iPod from his pocket. "Everyone's assumed that some nasty stuff happened to you... I don't know if it's true, but I do know a lot about... well, some pretty nasty stuff myself. And music always helps me... to drown out some of it anyway."

He offered her one of the earbuds then, when she didn't react, reached over and carefully placed it in her ear for her.

"I didn't know what kind of stuff you'd like so I put together a list of my favourites."

He switched on the device and selected the first song, ensuring the volume was down low before he hit play. Gentle violin music and a soft soprano voice filtered from the earbuds. The girl stiffened momentarily, her forehead creasing as she took in the new sounds. Jamie gave her hand a reassuring squeeze, watching her face carefully for any sign that she was getting upset.

Slowly, her expression changed into a serene smile and her eyes closed. She inched closer, resting her head against his chest so that her other ear was filled with the thrum of his heartbeat. Jamie picked up the other earbud and popped it into his own ear, relaxing beside her as the music played. He gently toyed with the fragile strands of her pale hair, humming along softly.

Despite the peaceful surroundings, Jamie couldn't keep the darkness from seeping into his thoughts. What would happen to her? In truth, he knew but the reality of it wasn't something that he wanted to accept. Chances were, once her baby was born and the hospital deemed her fit for travel, he'd never see her again. Her child would be put into care, they'd never let her keep it. She'd get sent away to some facility, spend the rest of her days in a single room. Lifers. He'd seen two of them, up in the psych ward. The ones beyond fixing.

At the thought, his arms tightened reflexively around her. She felt so fragile, like a tiny porcelain doll and if he held her too tight he feared she would break. He felt her quiver slightly in his arms. There it was again, that feeling that he didn't really understand. Every soft touch made it grow even stronger, the brush of her fingers against his arms, the stir of her breath on his hair.

There was no time in their space, the only way that they could tell it was passing at all was by the change of music and after a while, even that merged into one. Neither of them made a sound or even moved, except for the rise and fall of their chests. Jamie knew it couldn't last, after all, he only had half an hour, but part of him wished he could just stay there, in that moment. He sighed to himself, the noise catching the attention of the girl who lifted her head slightly to look at him.

"I'm going to have to go soon..."

She looked at him, her expression saddening. Jamie struggled to come up with the right way to comfort her, words that she would be able to understand.

"I... I'm sorry... I..." As he floundered to find the right words, he noticed her eyes sliding away from him to rest on something over his shoulder. He trailed off and turned his head slightly, following her gaze. He expected to see feet, one of the doctors checking in on them or maybe his mom come to retrieve him, but at first glance, the space seemed to be empty. He frowned, feeling the girl start to tremble beside him, and squinted.

It took a moment but gradually he made out a faint distortion in the air. He sensed rather than saw it and once he'd focused on it, it became clearer. It was like looking through water, both sides seemed just a little out of line with one another. The girl whimpered, gripping hold of his shirt.

"It's okay," he said softly. He touched her cheek, forcing her eyes to him rather than to the presence across the room. "There's nothing there. It's just a trick of the light."

The words were meant to reassure her but they came out hollow and false. He took a deep breath, trying to calm his fluttering heart. Treat her like you would Callie, he told himself. When she called him to her room late at night, scared of monsters under the bed or creatures lurking in the shadows, he would make it all seem okay, tell her it wasn't real even when he saw them too.

"Don't be afraid," he told the girl. "It's not real and being scared will just make it seem worse than it is."

As he spoke, there was a burst of static and the music cut off. As his ears adjusted to the sudden silence, every tiny sound seemed amplified. The girl's ragged breathing, the pounding of blood in his ears and then, ringing clearly through the room, the sound of footsteps approaching the bed. Steadily, they approached the bed. There was a pause and then the creak of bedsprings above their heads.

"Focus on me. I'll look after you," he whispered, his voice dipping instinctively. He locked eyes with her, trying to keep her attention on him and away from… it.

Jamie felt an icy coldness run across the nape of his neck but he tried to ignore it. It wasn't real, none of it was real.

The girl let out a sharp cry of pain and released hold of him, doubling over. Jamie reached out, unsure exactly what he was going to do but desperate to do something, he felt something pull hard at his hair, wrenching his head back until his neck was straining. The girl wrapped her arms around her belly, letting out a string of incoherent noises.

Blood ran down her thighs and began to drip onto the ground around her.

Jamie's eyes widened in horror and he struggled against the unseen force keeping him in place. The girl was crying now, tears streaming down her cheeks as her lips formed unspoken words. Suddenly Jamie was hurled across the room, slamming into a wall. His head was spinning but he forced himself to his feet and staggered to the door.

"Help!" he shouted. "We need help!"

Dr Cantrell rushed in, a nurse close behind him. Jamie watched, breathing hard, as they carefully lifted the girl out from under the bed and began trying to stem the bleeding as she writhed in pain.

"Jamie!" His mom had appeared in the doorway, her face tense as she took in the scene. "Let's get you home."

"But…"

"You can't do anything to help her right now. Let them work."

Before he could protest, she steered him out of the room. He reluctantly allowed her to lead him out of the hospital and down to the car park.

# REPORT OF INVESTIGATION BY COUNTY MEDICAL EXAMINER

DECEDENT: Benjamin Steven Taylor

RACE: Caucasian          SEX: Male          AGE: Four

HOME ADDRESS: 24 Sycamore Avenue          OCCUPATION: N/A

TYPE OF DEATH: Found Dead

COMMENT: Police responded to an anonymous tip leading to the discovery of the body and two other children.

IF MOTOR VEHICLE ACCIDENT INDICATE
DRIVER/PASSENGER/PEDESTRIAN/UNKNOWN: N/A

NOTIFICATION BY: Unknown          ADDRESS: Unknown

INVESTIGATING AGENCY: Sarum Vale Police Department

**DESCRIPTION OF BODY**

CLOTHED/UNCLOTHED/PARTIAL: Clothed

EYES: Brown          HAIR: Ginger

MOUSTACHE: N/A     BEARD: N/A

WEIGHT: 35IBs          LENGTH: 3ft. 4in

BODY TEMP: 102 degrees Fahrenheit

DATE AND TIME: 06:12 am     June 19th

RIGOUR: Yes     LYSED: Yes

**MARKS AND WOUNDS**

Decedent was uninjured, appears to have died from abnormally high fever.

Decedent has no birthmarks or tattoos.

**ADDITIONAL NOTES**

Decedent was reported missing last month along with two other children. Slightly underfed but otherwise was in largely good condition when died. Was found with the other missing children who showed similar signs of fever and illness

## PROBABLE CAUSE OF DEATH

Most likely result of fever brought on by unsuitable living conditions and neglect.

## MANNER OF DEATH

No sign of foul play, death appears to have been accidental as a result of illness.

I hereby declare that the information contained herein regarding the death described is true and correct to the best of my knowledge.

Examination performed June 20th at Sarum Vale Hospital by K. Mortimer

# XIX

Almost a week had passed since Jamie's discovery in the woods. His mom had insisted he stay home since he'd visited the hospital and his ankle had largely recovered but his head was still a mess. Every night he'd see the skeletal faces of the buried children no matter how hard to block it out. He'd not been allowed to visit the girl again but his mom had returned home from work the day after his visit and had assured him that she was fine. Still, when his mind gave him a break from the horrors of the woods, he couldn't help but think about her.

On this particular night, the entire family was home. Officer Harper was seated at the dining room table, working through a stack of files from the Redwood P.D. Jamie, Callie and their mom were seated nearby watching a movie together, enjoying a rare night where they were all in the same place. Jamie was only half paying attention, more interested in what his dad was doing and shooting occasional glances in that direction whenever he thought his mom wasn't looking.

His dad let out a groan as he finished another file and yet again came up blank. Over the week, despite his best efforts he'd had very little success with connecting the missing children to the dead children. He'd managed to match up the most recent ones but he was overwhelmed by the sheer amount that he'd received from Redwood.

"You alright honey?" Ruth asked, twisting in her seat to look at her husband.

"Yeah… just… it's worse than we ever thought…"

"How can it be worse?" Jamie asked.

"We're up to about two hundred boxes. And these files are just a fraction of the ones I have to look through," Officer Harper explained. His wife cleared her throat and shot a pointed look at their daughter who had been watching the exchange with wide eyes.

"How about some popcorn Cal?" Ruth said, putting on a cheery voice. She paused the film and led the girl out to the kitchen. Jamie got up and wandered over to the table, peering over the shoulder of his father who shot him a look but didn't protest his presence.

"What are these?" Jamie asked, pointing at a sheet of paper that bore the list of initials and numbers found on the victim's necklaces.

"They were found with the bodies. Each of them had an ID tag with initials and a number... we think it's the year they were buried."

"Do you have a picture?" Jamie asked, frowning slightly as something stirred at the back of his brain.

"Err... yeah, somewhere..." His father sorted through the papers stacked on the table and pulled out a small photograph of one of the ID tags.

"They all had one of these?" he asked, taking hold of the picture and examining it.

"Well... Jamie, it's not healthy for you to be dwelling on all this," Officer Harper said, his tact changing abruptly as Ruth and Callie came back into the room with the bowl of popcorn.

"Dad, I'm not a child. And I already saw the bodies. The damage is done, me knowing more or less isn't going to change anything..."

His father glanced at his mother and shook his head. Jamie scowled and stalked off upstairs, photograph still in hand. He went to his bedside table and pulled out one of the drawers, retrieving the necklace he'd found. Holding it up to the light, he compared the object to the image. There was no denying the similarities. Feeling vindicated, he returned downstairs and dropped the necklace on top of the pile of papers.

Officer Harper blinked, a frown forming.

"Where did you get this Jamie?"

"I found it. In the river by the school. I didn't think much of it... but I mean, it looks like one of yours, right?"

"It does..." his father said slowly, turning the necklace over in his fingers. "And the year would match to the box with the missing body..."

Ruth let out an aggravated sigh. Officer Harper looked at her and then at his son, tucking the necklace underneath the files and giving Jamie a 'we'll talk later' look. The two of them went over to the sofa and joined the girls. They tried to watch the film but both of them were distracted.

If the necklace had belonged to one of the victims, how had it ended up in the river? And where was the body that went with it?

When the film came to an end, Ruth took Callie up to bed and Officer Harper gestured for Jamie to join him at the table.

"So you think that this might belong to one of the victims?" Jamie asked as soon as they were both seated.

"It seems likely. I would assume as well that since the one we found in the box was male, this one belonged to the female victim of that year. I'll have to see if there were any missing girls with the initials E.K from that year in Redwood. It's just a shame we don't know how old she was, that would narrow things down."

"What about locally?"

"It's unlikely. Sarum's only had about a dozen missing children in the past decade." His father nodded at the folder, dwarfed by the stack from Redwood. Despite his dismissal, Jamie picked up the folder and began to look through.

"There's an E.K in here," Jamie said.

"The Eden Knight case? It's doubtful, it doesn't fit the same pattern most of the other victims seem to fall into."

"Who's Eden Knight?"

"Eden Knight was a girl who disappeared eleven years ago. She was about four years old. Her parents went to bed one night, the next morning she was gone. No sign of forced entry, everything was locked up and the girl's sister, who she shared a room with, was still in her bed fast asleep. The only sign that things weren't right was the family dog. He'd been fed glass."

"Did they ever figure out what happened?"

"No. There were theories. A lot of people thought it might be one of the parents, but the police couldn't understand why they would only have taken one of the children. And by all accounts, they were a devoted loving couple, good parents, no reason that anyone could see that one of them would have wanted to run off with their daughter."

"So they never found her?"

"Nope. And then a few months later, her mom, Evelyn, killed herself. Or that's what it looked like anyway. They found her car abandoned and all her possessions left by the river. And then later that year, the dad Richard, hung himself."

"Shit... what happened to the sister?"

"She still lives in the same house, under the care of her uncle. She'd be thirteen now?"

Jamie looked down at the file in front of him and turned the pages slowly. It just detailed what his dad had already said, the initial report, the searches conducted without success, the veterinary report. With each page he turned, Jamie could feel the hopelessness in the writing get stronger. The last page was a crumpled missing person's poster, a picture of a small girl with light hair and green eyes staring out from the centre, surrounded by smudgy text.

Looking at the picture, the smiling child, Jamie was struck by an immediate sense of recognition. There was no way he could mistake those eyes.

"Dad, I don't think you're looking for a body."

"What do you mean?"

He held up the missing poster for his father's inspection, who stared at it blankly. Jamie sighed.

"Are you saying that this doesn't look remotely familiar? At all?" he asked, exasperated.

"Jamie, I'm exhausted. I've been working on this for days without a break. Please, just tell me whatever it is you're trying to get at."

"The girl. The girl from the woods. This is her. Just... eleven years younger."

"Are you serious?" his father asked, taking the poster from him. "I guess they have... a slight resemblance."

"It would make sense. She was taken as one of the victims, she escaped and-"

"And she's been living in the woods for eleven years?"

"Fine, don't listen to me. But I know that it's the same girl. I don't know how she survived out there but I'm positive it's her."

Jamie snatched up the necklace from the table and left the room. Officer Harper watched him go with a soft sigh and turned his focus back to the files in front of him. He put the poster down and tried to concentrate on his list of initials. No matter how hard he tried to concentrate, his eyes kept sliding over to the poster, the girl in the picture pleading with him.

"You better be right about this Jamie," he muttered, picking up his phone and dialling.

"Michael, what can I do for you?" said the police chief, picking up after one ring.

"Sorry to call you so late sir, I have a theory about the missing body that I wanted to run by you."

"Okay?"

"I think the missing victim is the girl in the hospital... and I think she's Eden Knight."

"Do you have any proof of this?"

"Well, the girl is the same age as the Knight girl would have been. They share a physical resemblance. She has scars on her wrists like the other victims, the box with the missing body was buried the year Eden disappeared. And I think we may have found the missing necklace too."

"You're sure?"

"Fairly confident. It's the same design as the others and the year matches up."

"And the initials? Let me guess, E.K?"

"Exactly."

For a minute there was silence on the other end of the phone. Officer Harper waited anxiously for a response, fiddling with his sleeve in a nervous gesture.

"It's a good theory... but we need concrete evidence before we move on this."

"It might be difficult to prove. Due to her age, any dental records we have will be useless and it's unlikely we'll have any fingerprints for her on file. We could approach the sister, do a DNA test?"

"Contact her guardian, get their consent. Keep the details to a minimum, no use getting hopes up."

"I'll drop by their house first thing tomorrow."

"Good man."

They finished up the call and Officer Harper began to tidy up. The more he thought about it, the more convinced he was by Jamie's theory. The evidence in support was stacking up too much to be a coincidence.


The next day Officer Harper was ready to leave bright and early. Jamie had therapy that day so, in order to make sure he went, his dad decided to take him along to the Knight house. He hoped that having someone closer in age around might set the Knight girl at ease.

After dragging his slumbering teenage son from the tangle of bedding, Officer Harper had explained the situation. Although reluctant, Jamie had agreed to come on the condition that he be allowed to visit the hospital that day.

The pair of them set off in the cruiser. Jamie kept his head down, his attention on his phone. Despite asking to go to the hospital, he was somewhat nervous about the prospect. His last visit still played on his mind and, although he tried to convince himself that it was a trick of the mind… somehow, he couldn't shake the peculiar feeling he had.

When they reached the Knight house, Officer Harper went ahead to knock as Jamie lagged behind. A thin balding man answered the door, a frown forming as he took in the uniform and police car.

"Mr Knight?"

"Yes…?"

"My name is Officer Michael Harper, this is my son Jamie. Don't worry, nothing's wrong, but I need to have a chat with you. It's about a matter concerning your ward."

"Faith? She's not got in trouble has she?"

"No, like I said everything is fine. I just need to talk to both of you. Can we come in?"

"Alright…"

He stepped aside to let them in. Jamie followed close behind, looking around curiously as they were led to the living room. The house felt cold almost museum-like. There were a handful of pictures dotted around, all faded and sporting a fine layer of dust. Looking from one to another, Jamie felt like he was reading a story that stopped abruptly without resolution. A young man in a graduation cap. A smiling couple on their wedding day, the woman already sporting the early signs of pregnancy. The same woman clutching a baby. A toddler with bright green eyes, clinging to the man. A formal staged photo; man, woman, two little girls a few years apart, one dark and one fair. Then nothing.

There was a creak on the stairs and Jamie looked up to see a teenage girl with muddy brown hair and grey eyes. Jamie glanced at the living room door where the two men were deep in conversation.

"Hi," he said softly. "Faith, right?"

Faith nodded, her eyes darting to the door, fingers tugging unconsciously at her cuff. Jamie frowned slightly. Looking closer at the girl, she seemed nervous. Her skin was washed out, her hair lanky and greasy. She looked… ill.

"Are you okay?" he asked quietly. Faith opened her mouth to speak but stopped abruptly as her uncle left the living room, followed by Officer Harper.

"Faith!" He seemed surprised to see her there. "This is Officer Harper, he needs to have a talk with you."

Officer Harper gave her a friendly smile and Jamie could almost see him shift from the reassuring but authoritative manner he used with adults to a more relaxed and friendly demeanour.

"Hello, Faith. Now don't worry, you're not in any trouble. I'm here because we need your help." When Faith didn't respond, Officer Harper pressed on. "We need a sample of your DNA. Your uncle has given his consent and said it's okay but obviously, we won't force you."

"Is this about Eden?" Faith said abruptly.

Officer Harper hesitated for a moment before nodding slowly.

"Due to the time that has passed since her disappearance, the likelihood of locating or identifying her has decreased. However, with a DNA sample from you, our chances increase greatly."

"If you find her, will she come live here?"

Jamie watched his father squirm uncomfortably, not wanting to upset Faith while avoiding giving her false hope.

"She might. That'll be up to social services though... she might need to go somewhere more... equipped to care for her. But even if that happens, you'll be able to see her, or you might even be moved with her."

"I'll do it. I'll do the test," Faith said abruptly, cutting in.

"Good... great in fact. Mr Knight, would you be able to take her up to the hospital for... two this afternoon? Or I can chaperone her there if you're busy?"

"No, I'll do it. But it'll have to be after three when classes have finished."

"Three-thirty then? I'll make sure they're expecting you." Officer Harper smiled at them both. "Thank you for your cooperation with this."

He headed to the door, ushering Jamie with him. The boy glanced back at Faith and her uncle. He was smiling, one arm around the teen, fingers gripping her upper arm. Her lips were pursed, her forehead wrinkled like she was wincing. The door swung shut, cutting off Jamie's view.

# REDWOOD CHRONICLE

*Monday, January 11th*

SEARCH FOR MISSING GIRLS GROWS DESPERATE

The search for the two local girls, Natasha and Alice Beaton (ages 14 and 6) has ground to a halt. The girls were reported missing on Christmas day having left their home the night before and not returned. Their mother, Olivia Beaton, told police the pair had gone to attend the Winter Fayre in the nearby town of Sarum Vale at midday on the 24th and she had grown concerned when they had not come home by early evening.

Officers involved in the case have searched the area and spoken to a number of the Fayre attendants, so far no witnesses to the disappearance have been located. The investigation has been hampered by the weather conditions as heavy snow and ice have made the town and the surrounding area difficult to navigate.

The police are appealing for anyone with any information to come forward.

# XX

"So Jamie, how are you today?"

The same people, the same room, the same questions. He felt like he was stuck in a never-ending loop, his world shrinking to the bland room and the uncomfortable chair.

Her eyes bored into him as Jamie mulled over possible answers in his head. *I saw a bunch of dead children... how am I supposed to feel?* he thought to himself.

"Fine, I guess."

"Can you elaborate on that?"

"There's not much else I can say. I'm... fine."

"Really?" Jamie shrugged in response. "And, speaking more generally now, how would you describe your emotions recently?"

Trick question... his mind whispered. You tell her anything specific and she'll pin it to you. Be vague. But don't use something that could have multiple meanings. Negative could mean anything from anger to loneliness to depression. Don't give her anything she can use against you.

Jamie blinked, confused by his own contradictory thoughts. He forced himself to focus on Dr Lilith.

"Neutral."

"Neutral?"

"Yes. As in, not excessively positive or negative."

"I'm aware of what neutral means." She toyed with her pen before scribbling something down. "Alright then... let's move on. How are you sleeping?"

"I'm not."

"At all?"

"Well, very little. And when I do... the nightmares are getting worse."

"Could you please elaborate?"

"Before it was just… it was being a kid again, in a dark space and hearing him coming down the stairs… these are… I'm in the forest, or in a cave… I can't breathe. Sometimes I'm drowning, sometimes I'm being buried alive. The bodies are everywhere and Callie's always there, sometimes other people I know. They're surrounding me, closing in on me. I almost miss the old nightmares, these are just…" he trailed off.

"That's hardly surprising given what you've experienced recently. You mentioned last time that, when you discovered the bodies, you were asleep?"

"I was awake when I found the bodies," he corrected. "But I was asleep when I went into the woods."

"Have there been any more occurrences of sleepwalking?"

"No."

Dr Lilith tapped the nib of her pen against her notebook, expression contemplative. Jamie couldn't tell if she thought he was lying. His answer about the sleepwalking was, in fact, one of the only things that was completely true. Of course, he didn't lie, he knew better than that. But, then lying and omitting were different things, weren't they?

"I know last time you were too upset to discuss what happened in much detail. Now that you've had a little time to get some distance and perspective on the events, can you think why you walked to that particular spot?"

"Why? Are you trying to suggest that I knew about the bodies?"

"Not at all. I'm merely interested in why you might have been drawn there. I'm sure you're aware that most people view dreams as your mind's way of processing the events of the day. Perhaps your subconscious was attempting to process something related to that spot, and that is why you walked there?"

"I can't think of anything."

Okay, maybe one outright lie wouldn't hurt. He could think of one thing that might have drawn him there, but it was a tenuous link at best. At least, if he hadn't known what he knew now it would have been. That scrap of fabric, that he'd found during his last camping trip, while seemingly a random object now began to take on new meaning. It hadn't been found on exactly that spot, but near enough that it might have triggered his nighttime walk.

"Your father told me you're returning to school soon. Do you feel ready?"

"I don't want to go back. I mean, I don't feel any better but that's not really the issue. I don't think I'm likely to change how I feel any time soon. But that's not why I don't want to go back."

"You're worried about your peers? Why?"

"Well, the police are trying to keep it under wraps. But one person hears one thing, someone else hears… its Chinese whispers. Eventually, everyone knows or thinks they do."

"And you're afraid they'll judge you?"

"They already judge me. I'm the weird kid who hallucinates dead birds talking to him and tried to kill himself. And now I'm the boy who found a bunch of rotting corpses… somehow. They're most likely going to think I'm even crazier… and probably that I murdered them."

"I highly doubt anyone could consider you capable of murder Jamie."

"Well, most people prefer to tell stories and sensationalise things. It's more interesting than reality."

"How are you at school? Do you feel isolated?"

"Yes. I didn't used to be… in fact I used to actually be… well not popular but, somewhere near that."

"What changed?"

Jamie looked down at his hands, neatly folded in his lap. He smiled bitterly to himself.

"Chinese whispers…"

Dr Lilith looked at him, waiting for him to elaborate. The boy said nothing. His fingers began to drum anxiously on his knee, his face unreadable.

"How would you change things?"

"Well, I wish that I didn't get the shit beaten out of me. That I didn't have people laughing at me and calling me names. Of course I do, I mean I'm not a masochist, I don't enjoy being treated like crap." He sighed and slumped back in the chair. "You know, high school movies really screw up kids like me."

"I don't follow," Dr Lilith said after a moment of confused silence.

"In movies with teenagers. I mean, ones that are specifically about them, it always shows the schools as having…erm… cliques. You know, different groups of people who have like one shared interest and they always hang out together and eat lunch together and things like that. You've got jocks, drama kids, cheerleaders, goths, nerds… do I need to keep going?"

"No, I get what you're saying. Where in this fictional school do you fit in? Out of curiosity?"

"I'd be one of the art kids. But that makes it even worse in a way. You expect the jocks and the cheerleaders to be dicks and bitches. But the weirdo misfit kids are supposed to stick together through thick and thin because they know what it feels like to be outcast. And if you grow up watching those films you go in expecting school to be like that and it's just not… it's more like psychological warfare."

Dr Lilith had been writing furiously as he spoke but now her pen stilled and she looked at him with one of her rare moments of genuine compassion.

"Jamie, there's a reason school isn't like the movies. Firstly you probably shouldn't base your life on movies, it's not healthy. But secondly and more importantly, you need to remember that the people in those cliques work because they're not different people. They're just one person copied and styled differently. All the art kids stick together because they are the same person. The same with the jocks and cheerleaders. And even if schools operated exactly like that in reality, you'd still feel isolated because you are different. No one has been through what you have, so there is no way they can understand or welcome the experience. And you know that often people view the unknown as a threat."

"Way to make me feel better," Jamie muttered. Dr Lilith smiled slightly.

"I wasn't finished. You need to remember that being unique is nothing to be ashamed of and that those who will welcome you for what you are, are worth a thousand times what those who shun you are." She paused, considering her notebook for a moment. "Now, how about things at home?"

By the time the session finished and Jamie arrived at the hospital with his father, the arrangements had already been made for the DNA test. When they reached the girl's room, the two of them were greeted by loud screeches. Dr Knott and Dr Matting were in the process of trying to collect a sample from the girl who was responding to their invasion with her usual hostility. They had decided against saliva for their sample, given her prediction for biting them and instead were attempting to collect her blood. She was bucking wildly, shrieking and attempting to claw or snap at anything that came within range.

"What the hell is going on?" Officer Harper blurted out, startled by the chaotic frenzy he'd walked into. The sound seemed to momentarily distract the girl whose head turned sharply and for a moment her body stopped vaulting.

The two doctors quickly grabbed her limbs and held them down, Dr Knott jabbing her arm with the syringe and pulling back the plunger. He straightened up and looked to the door.

"Good timing Michael."

"Was that really necessary?"

"Yes! You saw her the first night she woke up. She almost bit someone's nose off!"

"Yes, but I thought she'd improved… Jamie, has she been like that with you?" Officer Harper glanced at his son.

"No, she's fine with me."

As if to illustrate his point, he crossed the room and perched on the edge of the bed. The girl immediately relaxed, although her eyes remained wary, darting from man to man.

After a brief quiet discussion, the two doctors departed the room with Officer Harper in tow. Jamie felt the tension melt from his body as the room emptied and he shifted onto the bed more fully. He looked at the girl, her head resting on the pillow and green eyes fixed on his face.

"Eden...?" he said softly. Her head twitched slightly, the movement so small he would have missed it if he hadn't been looking for it. "Your name is Eden, isn't it?"

The girl closed her eyes, turning her head away from him. Jamie sighed softly. He was right, he knew it, but he could also understand her reluctance to acknowledge it. He doubted there were particularly pleasant memories attached to that name for anyone but especially her.

He stared up at the ceiling, deciding against pushing it any further. She didn't pressure him, unlike the rest of the world, he should return the favour. But he couldn't help but be a little curious, it was an itch at the back of his brain that wouldn't go away.

Quietly, he took hold of her hand, lifting it slightly. She didn't react as he turned it over, examining her palm. He'd not examined the bodies enough to see the symbol carved into their flesh but he'd seen the pictures amongst his dad's file. He almost hoped he was wrong and that there would be nothing there.

But there it was, an image made of thin silver scars. Jamie looked at the mark and felt nausea stirring in the pit of his stomach. In his mind, he could almost see the moment she received it. A young girl, arms bound, being led through the dark trees. Candles flickering, tall ominous figures, faces masked in darkness. A knife glimmering in the candlelight, brought down to meet flesh. A wail of pain, green eyes glistening with tears that made them shine like emeralds.

Jamie blinked, forcing the images out of his head. It wasn't real, his mind had probably just created it from bits of different horror films.

"Jamie," called a voice from the doorway. He looked over to see his father hovering there, an uncomfortable look on his face. Jamie hopped off the bed and went over to him.

"Hey dad, what's up?"

"Are you... sure it's a good idea for you to be sitting so close with her?"

229

"Yes… she's fine with me."

"I'm sure she behaves herself around you but you have to remember that she's still unpredictable. She could get upset and lash out. She wouldn't mean to hurt you but that doesn't mean she wouldn't."

"Dad, really, it's fine. Can I go now?"

"No. I'm not done." Jamie looked at his dad with a combination of expectation and impatience. His dad didn't speak, trying to come up with the right words. "Do you… Your friendship with the girl is a little… unusual. You're aware of that right?"

"I know it's not… that normal. But it's not super weird or anything. She just needs a friend."

"And… that's all you're interested in?"

"What else would I be interested in?"

His dad looked at him like he was missing something obvious. Jamie blinked, confused, trying to work out what exactly was being implied. Officer Harper groaned internally, pulling a face. He escorted Jamie over to some chairs positioned near the far wall. The two of them sat, Officer Harper turning his chair to face his son.

"Jamie, I understand that… now you're a certain age, you're going to be interested in… girls. And honestly, I was expecting it a little earlier but… I really think that trying to get involved with this girl is a terrible idea."

The penny dropped. Jamie let out a cry of disgust and bolted from his chair.

"You think I'm nice to her because I want to… that's horrible. She's like… like a child, I would never…!"

"Jamie I'm not saying you would do anything, I just don't think you should be spending so much time here with her."

Jamie shook his head and walked off. He didn't go back to the girl's room, he just wanted to get some distance from his dad. He found a small alcove and tucked himself away, sitting on the floor. He closed his eyes and rested his head against the wall.

Thinking about the girl as anything more than a friend just felt wrong. She was so… vulnerable. In his mind, making a move on her or viewing her sexually was practically the same as looking at Callie in that way. Really he'd never thought about any girl like that, not seriously. Maybe once or twice in passing but nothing more than that.

> **Yet another way you're not normal.**

"Shut up," he mumbled to himself, covering his ears. Jamie felt the first hint of tears at the corner of his eyes and wiped them away angrily.

*Admit it to yourself… you'll be happier. You're not normal. You're less than human.*

"You're wrong."

*You're disgusting. You're a monster*

> **Your fault. You'll hurt her like you hurt everyone else.**

*Not normal.*

*Disgusting. Even your dad thinks so.*

**Useless.**

Breathe. It's not real. The voices can't hurt you.

*We don't need to.*

        *not*      *hurting*
    *You're*    *worth*

        *not*      *anything*
    *You're*    *worth*

Jamie gritted his teeth and clenched his fists.

"I am… I am…" He covered his head with his arms and curled up in the corner, mumbling to himself.

*Stupid*                     *useless*
    *kill*                   *monster*

   *yourself*

   *your*          *fault*           *rotten*

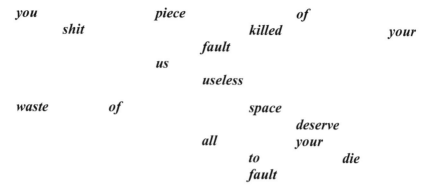

*you*        *piece*        *of*
    *shit*        *killed*        *your*
      *fault*
    *us*
     *useless*

*waste*     *of*        *space*
       *deserve*
     *all*     *your*
    *to*     *die*
    *fault*

He stayed there for an unknown amount of time, tucked away from view. The voices in his head didn't fade but gradually he was able to push them further back in his mind, ignoring them in the way he usually did. His breathing steadied and the familiar numbness settled back over him where the rest of the world seemed distant, like he was inside a glass box looking out.

Slowly he got to his feet and headed back down the corridor to where the girl and his dad were waiting.

# MEDICAL CERTIFICATE OF STILLBIRTH

## PERSONAL PARTICULARS OF DECEASED CHILD

### DETAILS OF CHILD

Surname: *Knight*                     Forename(s): *Arin Gideon*

Weight of Child: *6ibs*               Type of birth: *Single*

### DATE OF STILLBIRTH

Month (By name), day: *March 26th*     Name of Hospital: *Sarum Vale Hospital*

### PLACE OF STLLBIRTH

City, town or village (by name): *Sarum Vale*

### OTHER PARTICULARS

MOTHER     Surname: *Knight*     Forename: *Evelyn*

FATHER     Surname: *Knott*     Forename: *Adam*

## INFORMATION ABOUT DEATH

### WHEN DID DEATH OCCUR?

Prior to Labour        ~~During Labour~~              ~~Post Labour~~

### CAUSE OF STILLBIRTH

Disease or Condition directly leading to stillbirth (give details)
*N/A*

Antecedent factors (give details)
*Mother has history of failed pregnancies (numerous miscarriages) – Cause unknown*

### DETAILS OF LABOUR

Was there manipulative, instrumental or other operative procedures for delivery?

*No*
If so was foetus deceased before the procedure?
*N/A*
Was an autopsy performed?
*No*

---

CERTIFICATION

I certify that I was/~~was not~~ in attendance at the stillbirth and the statements herein are true and correct to the best of my knowledge and belief:

Name:  *Megan Norton*          Designation: *Attending physician*

# XXI

Jamie wasn't sure what woke him. He was on his bed, an empty space beside him where the cat had been sleeping. The room felt colder without the warm furry presence tucked against his arm. He blinked, sleep blurring his vision and clogging his senses. His eyes burned, cheeks stiff from dried tears.

"Is this how you want to spend your life? Cowering? Never living up to your worth?" The voice came seemingly from nowhere, an almost seductive whisper straight into his ear. Jamie tried to move but the night-time paralysis had taken a tight hold and refused to relinquish him.

"I can smell fear on you. You wear it like cologne. But you don't need to be afraid. Not of me anyway, at least not at this time. I have no intention of harming you, I am merely taking advantage of your temporary immobility to force you to listen to what I have to say. This seemed like the best time to ensure I had your full attention." The voice paused, seemingly thinking over how to phrase its words. "You have much greater potential than you realise and you will continue to fall short as long as you yield to those around you. I am going to offer you an opportunity. I will only do this once and after that, you will have until sunrise to accept. Do you comprehend what I am saying?"

Jamie didn't speak, tongue dull and heavy like the rest of him. He understood the words but to him, the sentence made no sense. His auditory hallucinations had never been so coherent and tangible before. He could practically feel the cool breath of the speaker on his cheek.

"I want to present you with a chance to reach a level of greatness. Allow me to help you shed your fear and embrace what lies beyond. You will be at nobody's mercy. Your world will become infinite. Anything you want will be within your grasp."

An image formed in front of Jamie's eyes. Sammy, stretched out on his bed in her underwear, hair splayed out around her. He grimaced, struggling against his frozen limbs.

"Not her? Someone else makes your blood run hot... someone you bury thoughts of deep at the back of your mind..."

A new image. A lazy summer afternoon, warm sun on bare skin, a hand in his, a whispered promise.

"Oh, Jamie... I might blush." The voice sounded almost amused. "Not what I'm used to but I can be adaptable." There was a low chuckle. "Think it over... let me know if you're tempted."

Jamie's limbs relaxed and he felt a flood of warmth as the feeling returned to them. He sat up slowly, eyes searching the room, apprehensive. He was sure that he was asleep, lost in some kind of confused dream state where fact and fiction were blurred into one.

He rolled onto his side and tucked his legs up, staring out of the window. The sky was stained a sickly orange by the street lights, the colour bleeding into the darkness of the night. His mind seemed to be stuck on a loop, playing the conversation over and over. He couldn't deny the words were tempting but of course, they would be. The voice was a product of his mind – it knew what he wanted to hear.

In the glass of the window, he could see the outline of his room, the bed. The shapes were distorted, blurring into a different room entirely. Something about the sight, no matter how much he tried to rationalise it as just the effect of the glass, disturbed him and he found himself drawn towards it. Jamie crossed the space between the bed and the window slowly, the floorboards seeming like an endless abyss stretching on into infinity.

He met his gaze in the glass and gently ran a finger across the glass.

"No fear... you promise?" No answer came but his reflection almost seemed to smile back at him. "Alright..."


It was a simple matter for him to slip out of the house and soon he was trudging through the trees that surrounded it. Mud clung to his trouser legs and with each step, he regretted agreeing more and more.

"Where am I supposed to be going?" he asked aloud. His voice sounded small and uncertain, swallowed up by the trees.

"Just walk. I'll tell you when to stop."

Jamie scowled to himself, trying to avoid the patches of nettles that seemed to materialise every few feet. The voice guided him around the back of the houses and into a deeper section of woodland where the trees grew closer together, making the path nearly inaccessible. Jamie had to stoop to make it through the tangle of branches above his head, muttering to himself as he went. Occasionally he thought he heard the sound of something moving nearby, footsteps on the carpet of leaves.

Eventually, he came to a spot where the trees thinned out once more to form a clearing. It took Jamie to realise exactly where he was, the shapes of structures warped by age momentarily confusing him. When clarity came, he felt almost excited. It was a place he'd heard about but never seen.

Years before a travelling carnival had set up in the woods, opting to keep themselves a little separated from the town residents. They'd left abruptly only a few days later, leaving most of their equipment behind. It had been a popular site for teenagers until the local wolves claimed it for themselves.

Jamie glanced around anxiously, expecting to be met with fangs and snarls but the area appeared empty. He could make out some signs of recent activity though. A paw print, some fur caught on a low branch, claw marks on a tree and, rather oddly, a red hoodie hanging neatly on the abandoned carousel.

"Sit."

"What about the wolves? This place isn't safe."

"No fear Jamie. They won't bother us, I promise." Jamie hesitated slightly, glancing around warily. "Trust me. I won't let you get hurt."

It almost sounded like the voice was mocking him. Jamie sat down on the ground, eyes still roaming the shadows.

"Close your eyes."

"Why? It's dark and there's no one around."

"Because I said so. And you asked for this, so stop arguing with me," it sniped back.

Muttering under his breath, Jamie closed his eyes. He felt like he was being messed with and that any moment the kids from school would appear, revealing it was all an elaborate prank. He almost preferred that idea if he was honest with himself, as the other option was that he really was crazy. After all, only a crazy person would wander into a forest at the whim of a voice in their head.

"You need to let go of your fear Jamie. It weakens you. You could be much more than this, instead, you let your emotions enslave you." The voice sounded different, no longer without direction. It seemed closer. "I wasn't lying when I said I would make you stronger. I can. And I will. But you need to let me in, let me see you."

"You're already in my head. How much more 'in' can you be?"

"You'll see." Jamie felt rather than saw the smirk in the voice and his eyelids flickered. "Not yet. Patience." He felt a cold pressure on his wrists, a sensation like dead flesh touching his skin. "Open your mind first. Tell me what you fear the most."

A hundred answers tripped over Jamie's tongue. That he was crazy, that every taunt from the school bullies was true. Those fears went deeper than others. They weren't the fears that gave him nightmares; they were the ones that left him lying awake, drenched in icy sweat and paralysed by the intensity of his thoughts.

"Snakes," he said finally.

"Liar."

Jamie's eyes opened sharply and he almost cried out. He was no longer alone. A man was sat opposite him, watching him intently. Jamie blinked, trying to dispel the hallucination. The man smiled, visibly enjoying the boy's confusion.

"I thought this would make conversation easier. What do you think?" the man asked, quirking his lip. Jamie stammered, managing only a string of incoherent words. The man laughed. "Oh come on Jamie, no need to be coy with me. You forget I've seen inside your mind. I know what makes you tick."

Jamie flushed, casting his eyes down. The man chuckled softly and reached over, placing a single finger beneath the boy's chin, raising his head until Jamie was forced to meet his eye.

"Don't hide Jamie. Not from me. I know you inside and out and trust me, you have no reason to be ashamed."

Jamie nodded slowly and looked the man over. He was tall and well-built with broad shoulders and an angular face that was both young and old all at once. His hair was cropped short, light brown, and had a rough look to it. His eyes were what startled Jamie most. A strange shade of bronze with long narrow pupils like those of a cats and possessing the same fixated intensity. Watching him, Jamie got the impression of a leopard or tiger, a restless predator coiled and ready to strike. He was posed, mirroring Jamie's body language in a way that couldn't be mistaken for anything but deliberate.

"Relax," the man drawled. "Tell me… what really keeps you up at night? What is it that makes your blood run cold?"

For a moment there was nothing but silence. Even the forest went quiet. Jamie didn't speak, he didn't need to. The moment the man said the word, the images came. They were dragged from every recess of his brain, forced upon him in excruciating detail that made his stomach twist.

"I see…" The man rested back on his heels and cocked his head to the side, studying the boy as he thought. There was a look in his eyes that made Jamie feel like he had been stripped completely bare, taken apart in a single gaze. The man smiled, or Jamie guessed that what he was doing. It looked wrong somehow like he didn't know exactly what he was doing. "Let's play a game shall we?"

"What kind of –" He was cut off before he could finish, the man moving forward and knocking him to the ground. "Hey!"

The man laughed but it seemed far away. The darkness reached out and engulfed Jamie, swallowing him whole. The forest around him fell away and he felt himself sinking into the ground, walls of dirt rising up around him until there was nothing else. His heart raced and his breathing spiked. He felt the pull on his lungs as they struggled to find air, a painful, rasping sensation.

"How does this feel Jamie? Dying slowly? No one caring enough to save you? Is this what it was like last time?" The narrow space seemed to be closing in, each breath becoming harder as he sucked in more of the precious oxygen. It was icy cold and as he clawed desperately at the dirt surrounding him, they hardened into rigid walls slick with ice crystals. The chill permeated his body, burrowing through his skin and deep into his bones.

"No!" Jamie yelled, knowing he was wasting the little air he had left. It wasn't true. People cared. His family cared about him… they had to… they had chosen to have him.

"Are you not enjoying our game, Jamie? Shall we up the stakes a little? Make it more exciting for you?"

He became aware of a low hissing from somewhere around his feet and the panic he felt rocketed up. He screamed, a terrified strangled cry more animal than human. The hissing grew louder and something cool brushed against his ankle. The scar burned at the touch and Jamie had to fight to hold onto reality as his mind threatened the catapult him into memories.

Reality… no, this wasn't reality, it couldn't be. No matter how much he screamed and yelled, it didn't get any harder to breathe. It was a struggle but no more than before.

Jamie took a long slow breath and closed his eyes. He counted in his head, did times tables, played the alphabet game. All the tricks he used to try and quell his panic. His heart rate began to slow and his breathing evened out.

He opened one eye, peaking at his surroundings. The trees loomed over him, a patch of starry sky visible between the branches. The man was crouched nearby, watching him and drumming his fingers against his knees.

"You managed that quicker than I expected… I may have underestimated you."

Jamie leapt to his feet and rounded on the man, face contorting in rage.

"What the hell? What was that?"

"Jamie… relax. You were never in any danger. I was just trying to help you."

"By making me think I'm dying?"

"I can't make you into something you're not Jamie, I can just amplify or reduce what you already feel. Tip the scales, so to speak. Fear is the emotion that controls you and I needed to get a sense of the balance. Do you still feel afraid?"

"No, I feel angry! You messed with my brain!"

"It was necessary. Stop whining like a baby," the man snapped. His voice had taken on a rough quality, almost a growl. "I needed to get a sense of you, beyond the superficial. If you want to spend the rest of your life being pushed around and stepped on, then, by all means, leave now and stop wasting my time."

Jamie looked at his feet, kicking at the ground.

"Trust my mind to come up with a hallucination who's basically a more psychotic version of my therapist..."

"I wouldn't go that far," murmured the man. "But whatever you need to rationalise this. Now, are you done with your little temper tantrum? Can we continue?"

Jamie was wary, but while his hallucinations terrified him he knew that they couldn't really hurt him.

"How is any of this going to help me?"

"Just trust me when I say it will. Maybe I'm lying and just want to mess with you... you'll have to wait and see."

\*\*\*\*\*

The DNA results came a few days after the test. Officer Harper was at his desk when an envelope was dropped in front of him. He opened it quickly, eyes scanning the paper. Most of the details he didn't understand but he didn't need to. All he needed was the answer.

"Well shit, Jamie was right..." he murmured. Officer Harper got up and went to the Chief's office, knocking lightly before letting himself in. "The results are back," he said, handing over the paper and waiting by the door for instructions.

The chief looked through the paper, expression grave.

"Alright. So she's Eden Knight. I'll be honest I wish I could have been given these results eleven years back... but this is good news," he said before handing the paper back.

"What's the next step?"

"Contact social services and let them know the situation, then call the family. Might be worth calling the hospital too, that way they can liaise with the social services and arrange a visit between her and the family in a more controlled environment."

"Yes, sir."

"How are you getting on with identifying the bodies against the missing person cases?"

"We think we've linked about a quarter of them based on the initials and we're checking against whatever physical records we can get hold of. It's slow work, we've managed to concretely identify three of the victims," Officer Harper explained.

"Well keep at it. I know you'll figure them out."

His tone was dismissive; Officer Harper took the hint and left the room. He sat at his desk and looked around the station. Everyone was busy, wearing identical expressions of grim exhaustion. Not only were they working on the bodies, which was taking up most of their time, they had their normal duties and a handful of new cases had sprung up. Everyone had been working longer hours and it felt like they weren't making any progress.

Officer Harper meant to call social services but his eyes fell on the stack of papers that had been delivered with the DNA result. There was a letter with them, torn open to show a collection of newspaper clippings tucked away inside. They were from the Redwood Chronicle, sent over by Officer Hendrix. Most of them were fairly old, from back when he'd lived in Redwood. His career had been on the rise. Perhaps if he'd stayed up there, his life would have ended up very different, who could say really? When he'd moved, the clippings had been lost... or so he thought.

Seeing them again didn't fill the officer with pride of what he had once achieved, it just made him feel like he'd lost something he once had. He wasn't even able to protect his son anymore. Since their... conversation at the hospital, Jamie had been even more withdrawn than normal. He'd retreated into himself and had barely said a word to anyone since then. He'd not returned to school yet but the fear lingered in Officer Harper's mind that it would push the boy over the edge. What kind of father couldn't protect his family? He felt like such a failure...

With a long sigh, he tucked the clippings away in his drawer and picked up the phone. Officer Harper had a handful of contacts, including one or two in city hall and at social services, so it didn't take him long to get through. He had briefed them on the situation previously, when the girl had first been taken to the hospital, so there was already a social worker attached to the case. They agreed to speak with both the hospital and the social worker assigned to Faith Knight and arrange a supervised visit between the two girls. There was no telling how the girl would react to meeting her sister, especially given how unpredictable she had been in the past.

After speaking to the social workers, Officer Harper decided that, although the social services had agreed to arrange the meeting, it would be a good idea to speak to Mr Knight himself, to at least forewarn him of the impending visit. He dialled the number Mr Knight had given him and rested the phone against his shoulder while it rang. Officer Harper picked up the DNA results and looked them over once again. Although the summary attached stated that the two girls were related, when he looked at the more detailed description on the second page, the numbers seemed off. He'd never been great at science, but he remembered enough from high school biology to know that a child's DNA would come from both sets of parents and that a pair of siblings wouldn't have the exact same combination of alleles but he had expected there to be more of a similarity between the two samples.

The third page contained additional information. They had a record of Evelyn Knight's DNA, from her disappearance and likely suicide, which had been compared to the girls. Looking at the paper, Officer Harper could see the numbers that reoccurred in the girls and in the mother, but none of the other numbers from the two girls matched up.

"Hello?"

"Oh! Mr Knight?"

"Yes?"

"It's Officer Harper. I just wanted to call you and let you know that we got the DNA results back."

"And…?"

"She is Eden."

There was silence on the end of the phone for a moment, Mr Knight shocked into silence. After a minute, he cleared his throat.

"Wow… that's great news…"

"The social services will be in touch with you very soon to discuss things and arrange a visit. I just wanted to let you know the good news."

"Thank you… I appreciate it. I… I have to go. But thank you."

He hung up before Officer Harper could say anything. He frowned as he set down the phone. Had it been his imagination or had he heard the faintest sound of someone crying in the background?

*****

There were six people gathered in the tiny meeting room, Officer Harper amongst them. Dr Knott was at the head of the table.

"Good afternoon everyone and thank you all for coming. I'm sure some of you know one another but just for the benefit of those who don't we'll do quick introductions. I'm Dr Adam Knott, I am the head of paediatrics and I've been leading the treatment in this case. We also have Dr Jade Ng, head of psychiatric. Officer Michael Harper from the Sarum Vale P.D. Mr Knight is here to represent the interests of the family and we have Tabitha Fields and Noah Robinson joining us from social services," Dr Knott explained.

The meeting had been arranged in record time and there hadn't been a lot of opportunity for introductions. It had been decided that it was in the best interest of both girls for a decision to be made about Eden's future before they were introduced to one another. After all, if they got along and were then separated, it would cause unnecessary upset to two already fragile young ladies.

"The greatest issue in this matter, as I see it, is Eden's mental state," began Dr Ng. "Physically speaking, her condition has already improved greatly, correct Dr Knott?"

Dr Knott glanced at her and Officer Harper noticed a look of irritation briefly cross his face. He wasn't sure if it was because Dr Ng had taken charge of the situation and he couldn't help but wonder if Dr Knott was slightly intimidated by her. The officer had met her before, following Jamie's attempted suicide and he'd always been struck by how remarkably young she was for someone in her position. In fact, the first time they'd met, he'd assumed she was a nurse until she'd introduced herself.

"Yes…" Dr Knott said slowly. "The injuries she sustained were largely superficial, at least her external ones. As long as we keep an eye on them, I don't foresee an issue there. The main concern that I have is her malnutrition. While it has improved since she was brought in, the progress has been far slower than we anticipated. It's crucial that we raise her weight, especially given the pregnancy."

"Could this be done out of the hospital?" asked one of the social workers.

"Yes, with regular supervision it could. Another pressing matter is the physical damage done to her vagina from the prolonged sexual abuse. When she was brought in, a brief examination was conducted but at the time the focus was stopping her blood loss, ensuring the child was alright. We do need to perform a proper examination to see if she's going to require a caesarean and whether, if she does give birth naturally, the damage will put her at risk."

"But again, that doesn't require her continued presence in one place. It could be performed anywhere that has a suitable OBGYN. Her mental condition is another matter entirely," said Dr Ng, once again steering the conversation. "She has been assessed and the central issue is her lack of socialisation. She is mentally competent, she seems to have some idea of where she is and a sensation of time. Her speech is limited, obviously, but she's able to express basic emotions and desires."

"What is the problem with her socialisation exactly?" asked Mr Knight.

"Well, as you're aware human beings learn most of their social lessons at a young age, through exposure to others in a natural environment. Since she was taken at such a young age and presumably kept away from people, her social development was stunted. She doesn't know how to act in certain situations because she's not used to them. That's why, when she feels uncomfortable or confused she lashes out because she doesn't know how else to resolve it." Dr Ng paused and shuffled through her notes. "We know that she's not completely adverse to people, she's able to demonstrate basic social skills and form some type of friendship or at the very least attachment to specific people. We will need to conduct further psychological assessments on her to understand her current level of executive functioning, her attachment to others and cognitive functioning. But the longer that she goes without socialisation, the harder life will be for her. With work and the right support, we could most likely get her to a level where she can integrate into society once more."

"That seems a little optimistic," cut in Dr Knott. "I think we might have to settle for her not biting people who get too close."

Dr Ng gave the smallest of noises in indication of her annoyance but pressed on, focusing on the social workers and Mr Knight.

"The key to this is consistency. She needs structure, a safe and stable environment to learn and grow. She's befriended a local boy I believe...?" She glanced at Dr Knott and Officer Harper.

"Umm... yes, my son, Jamie, has become very close with her..." Officer Harper replied, shifting awkwardly in his seat.

"I think that it would help her recovery to remain in the area. She's already begun to open up and develop. If you relocate her, it could severely delay her recovery process... but if you insist on moving her, I suggest doing it soon before she gets too settled," she explained.

"What kind of facilities does she need?" asked Noah. "To most effectively aid her mental health recovery?"

"I would say regular counselling, with someone who specialises in child development. She'll need one on one attention, regular interaction with a variety of age groups to get her comfortable with them."

"In terms of a home environment, will she be able to live with other children or do we need to find a home where the parents can focus their attention solely on her?"

"In my opinion, both options would be beneficial for her. It would be good for her to see a familial unit, allow her to interact with others in a relaxed unpressured environment that she would hopefully feel comfortable in. Of course, the risk remains that she might... lash out."

"It is a tricky situation," said Tabitha. "Will she be required further for the ongoing investigation?"

"We're hoping that when she's better she might be able to identify where she was held and that could provide us with a lead to pursue."

"So if we relocate her, it needs to be soon but it can't be too far away…"

"We also need to consider her unborn child. Obviously, she's not in a position to raise it…"

"We can deal with that when the child is born," said Dr Knott. "Right now, Eden is the concern. I believe that, for the time being at least, she should remain in Sarum Vale. By the time you manage to locate a suitable home for her outside of town, the snow will have come and she won't be able to travel anyway. I say we wait until the spring and then we can review if she needs relocation."

"That's all well and good Doctor, but where does she go in the meantime? Are the hospital in a position to maintain her for the next three, four months?" asked Tabitha, raising an eyebrow.

"If mental and physical treatment and check-ups can be arranged, that meet her needs and requirements, we could probably find a local family. We do have a few local foster families on our books and we can contact them… but, it may take a few weeks," said Noah.

"And most of them have multiple children already, which might overwhelm Eden too much," Tabitha added.

"Mr Knight, would you be able to take her in? I understand that you are Faith's legal guardian and that taking on another child would be a challenge, particularly one with Eden's… circumstances. But it would allow her to adjust to life outside of the hospital, with other people before she gets thrown into a larger family. Sort of… a halfway house to make the transition easier?" Dr Knott asked.

"I could… we don't have much space in the house, but if there's no other option, of course, I'll take her. She's my niece after all…"

Despite his words, he seemed reluctant and a little uncomfortable. Officer Harper watched him out of the corner of his eye, concerned although he wasn't entirely sure why.

"I really would advise against that. She needs round the clock care in a facility dedicated to her needs until we can be sure that she's not a danger to anyone," Dr Ng warned.

"Thank you for your opinion, Dr Ng, however as Eden's primary physician, I determine whether or not she is discharged. You said yourself she needs a stable and safe environment. The psychiatric unit might provide her with some of the care she needs but it cannot compare to a loving home and being around people with mental health issues is hardly going to aid her recovery," Dr Knott said. He didn't raise his voice but there was a sense of finality to what he said and Dr Ng reluctantly fell silent.

"Okay then, we can arrange for her to move in, set up some counselling, some basic education as well, hopefully get her talking again. In the meantime, if it's alright with you, Dr Knott, maybe she could take escorted leave into the town as soon as possible so she can get a sense of the area? Officer Harper, perhaps your son could accompany her as well?" Noah suggested.

There was a general murmur of agreement, followed by a brief discussion to iron out the details before the meeting was concluded. The group left and went their separate ways, Officer Harper heading to his car and setting off in the direction of home. He was sure Jamie would be happy to take Eden out, although he wasn't entirely comfortable with the idea…

As he was thinking about the prospect, a realisation struck him. Eden. He hadn't told Jamie that she'd been identified. The meeting had been set up so quickly, he'd had no time to talk to his son about it and he resolved to rectify that as soon as he reached home.

While he drove, Officer Harper couldn't help but think about the conversations that had just passed. Even though he knew that everyone had the best interest of the girl at heart, he couldn't help but feel… uneasy. He put it down to natural concern. He was a police officer and a father after all, he cared about people. It was completely natural for him to be concerned about Eden. After everything he'd seen, he could imagine Callie in her place and that thought terrified him.

He pulled into the drive. In the upstairs window, he could see Jamie, sitting at his desk with his head down. The boy looked up, as though sensing the eyes on him, and for a moment he met his father's gaze, before turning away once more. Officer Harper sighed softly to himself, running his fingers through his hair, before getting out of the car and trudging up to the house. Callie was still at school, Ruth at work. Now was the perfect time to talk to Jamie, not only about the confirmation of

Eden's identity but about everything else that had happened recently. Yet as he climbed the stairs to Jamie's room, he felt strangely nervous. Something about Jamie was just… different recently and he didn't know how to handle it. It unsettled him.

Jamie didn't look up as his dad entered the room. He was drawing, eyes fixed intently on his paper.

"Hi, Jamie… how are you feeling?"

"Fine."

"I… you were right. About Eden."

"That happens occasionally. Don't sound so surprised."

"Jamie that's not… I know that you're a smart kid, I just wanted to let you know and say thank you… if it weren't for you, we might never have identified her."

"No need to thank me for being better at your job than you are."

"Jamie!"

Jamie lifted his head and looked over at his father. Officer Harper had to strain not to flinch backwards. The look on the teenager's face was venomous, skin pale and drawn with the circles around his eyes ingrained so deeply that it looked like the flesh had been stripped from his skull, leaving nothing but a mask of bone.

"What? It's true. And you're only thanking me now because you feel guilty, not because you actually care about my feelings. They only matter as long as they're of some use to you, just like the rest of me." Jamie got up and he seemed to grow taller before his father's eyes. "I don't care. I'm used to it. After all, that's just how things are around here. It's great having a son who can look after the house, cook, take care of the other child you don't have time for but the moment you actually have to start giving a fuck, it's just an inconvenience you'd rather not have to deal with." One of Jamie's hands was gripping the desk, knuckles white from the exertion. "Now, if you don't mind, I'm very busy."

He turned away and sat back down. Officer Harper blinked, momentarily stumbling for words. Of course, he'd had arguments with Jamie, it was to be expected, but the boy had never acted like this.

249

Officer Harper opened his mouth, intending to reprimand Jamie but stopped abruptly. Something about the boy's demeanour caused him to rethink and he retreated from the room, deciding to discuss the matter later when Jamie had had a chance to calm down a little.

In his room, Jamie's eyes were locked on his paper. He'd started a new drawing, preliminary pencil marks forming the faintest shapes of creatures that were somewhere between people and animals. As he picked up his pencil once more, part of him wondered why he'd said what he had. He didn't want to upset his dad... of course he wished his parents had more free time but he didn't resent them for it... why had he said those things?

He rubbed the palm of his hand against the wood of the desk, fingers drumming lightly on the surface. His head hurt, a constant throbbing pain at the back of his skull, and there was a twisting sensation in his stomach. The hand that was holding the pencil clenched tightly, splintering the tool and causing shards of wood and graphite to cut into Jamie's skin, beads of blood bubbling up from the lacerations. His eyes didn't leave his paper. He registered the pain of the injury but it seemed distant, more like the echo of a wound.

Jamie released the shards of the pencil and selected a new one, continuing to sketch as rivulets of crimson ran across his fingers and dripped onto the paper.

# Police Report

**Case No**: 88-1-00024-4

**Reporting Officer:** Delacroix, Casper

**Incident:** Child Abduction

**Date:** June 19th

**Prepared by:** Fisher, Marisse

## Details of Event:

The station received a call from an anonymous source who stated where the missing children could be found. Upon investigating the tip, the children were located. One was deceased while the other two were suffering from an intense fever.

## Action Taken:

The children were removed and taken to the hospital. Officers are investigating the tip in an effort to locate the informant

## Summary:

Children to be interviewed when recovered. Further investigation required to discern if informant was abductor.

# XXII

The cat had been sleeping outside Jamie's window all day. His room overlooked the porch and the drive, the porch roof meeting the wall of the house just below his window, allowing the cat the perfect spot to doze. It had tucked its paws under its body so that it formed a shape reminiscent of a loaf of bread and, although its eyes were closed, its ears moved often as they picked up sounds from the surroundings.

As darkness fell and the street lights began to flicker on, the cat rose. It stretched lazily before jumping down from the porch. The cat's first stop was the fence that bordered the stretch of lawn beside the drive. It raked its claws along the wood, amber eyes resting on a symbol carved near the top of the post. The cat reached up and quickly shredded the symbol, obliterating any trace of it.

Satisfied, it slunk off in search of a quick meal. Weaving its way through the gardens, its ears twitched as it tried to discern a difference between the general cacophony of background noise and the more subtle sounds of its potential prey. The streets were painted in shades of grey, obliterated at moments by careless splashes of harsh orange. The cat relished it. This was its world, its kingdom.

The cat leapt onto a high wall, surveying the ground below. Its nostrils quivered slightly, picking through the texture of scents. Its superior senses allowed it an almost visual view, figures like ghosts that grew fainter the older the scent got. Each left behind a streak of coloured residue, visible only to the animal, adding new layers to the night time world.

From its vantage point, the cat picked up the trail of a mouse. The bitter acrid stench of animal urine left streaks of harsh white light on the blank canvas of the street, disappearing into a nearby bush. The cat stalked closer, its body lowering until the animal was flush with the brick. In the bush, the mouse was visible accompanied by a warm, rich smell. It seemed to pulse gently with the flutter of the mouse's heart. It knew the cat was there, body tensed and ready to flee. The cat crawled forward slowly, teasing the tiny creature. After all, what was a meal without a little seasoning? And fear made it all so much more delicious.

The cat pounced. It crashed into the bush, claws swiping at the mouse who stiffened and collapsed, heart giving out in terror. The cat prodded it with its paw, disappointed that the hunt was over so soon. Still, the night was young and there was hardly a shortage of rodents. The cat dug in, sharp teeth quickly tearing through coarse fur, fillings its mouth with the delicious taste of warm salty blood. It was hardly a delicacy but for a moment every other sense was overwhelmed.

The cat left the skull, stripped of the little meat it held so that the eyeballs bulged out obscenely. It disregarded the remains and continued on, following a new trail. It knew that even if it didn't find anything it wouldn't go hungry. Jamie was soft-hearted and if he didn't feed the animal, Callie usually would.

From nearby an unfamiliar smell emanated. It was earthy, like rotten leaves, but accompanied by both a bitterness and the unmistakable smell of something burning. The smell stung the cat's nose and it hissed softly, fur standing on end. But there was nothing to see so, after a moment of uncertainty, the cat moved on.

Its next stop was a garden, drawn by the aroma of rabbits. When it reached the hutch however, it found it empty, the animals moved into the house for warmth. If it was possible for a cat to scowl, at that moment it would have managed. Instead, it slunk off, sulking.

The cat emerged into an alley between the houses, overgrown with weeds. The cat paused, ears pricking up. Soft footsteps, drawing near. The animal crouched in the undergrowth and waited for them to pass. It was a girl, somewhere in her late teens. She moved quickly, head down and one hand fisted in her coat, drawing the fabric closer for warmth. Her eyes roamed the alleyway, nervous, inexplicably so.

The darkness was thick like the air had been replaced by the fur of some great black beast. But that was ridiculous…

From somewhere behind her came a low growl. She paused, registering the sound and her mind rapidly running through the possibilities.

There was another growl. In the bush, the cat stiffened. That smell was back, stronger now. The cat clawed at its nose, trying to tear the invasive stench from its nostrils, eyes watering.

The girl turned. It took a moment for her eyes to adjust and make out the creature in the darkness. It was the size and shape of a large dog but its body seemed… off. It moved forward into a pool of light cast by the streetlamp. The girl could see that it was a dog, a collie. It was slumped a little and its limbs seemed to be barely attached to its body. Its fur was matted with an oily sheen to it and the girl could see clumps were missing, revealing raw flesh underneath. Its muzzle was curled into a snarl, ropes of saliva hanging from yellowing fangs that appeared to be rotting in their sockets. Its eyes were filled with a terrifying madness, black veins standing out lividly. Around its neck was a collar, a red band with a bone-shaped tag that declared its name as Patch.

It twitched, limbs jerking like a puppet having its strings pulled. The girl's hands were shaking, her body paralysed in place. The dog snarled, drooling, its eyes darting around frantically. The slightest movement could set it off.

There was a terrible twisted choking sound and the dog doubled over retching. Black fluid oozed out of its mouth, staining the fur around its muzzle. The girl risked a step backwards. The dog's head shot up, eyes spearing the girl. Quick as a flash, it lunged forward and pounced on her, teeth snapping at her throat. The girl screamed and attempted to shield herself, arms flying up to cover her face and neck. Sharp claws sliced through her skin, the dog frantically biting at her arms until they were slick with blood. The girl, possessed by a burst of adrenaline as she fought for her survival, kicked at the dog and rolled, momentarily throwing the beast off.

She ran, but the animal was quick to right itself and lunge after her, teeth clamping around the girl's ankle. With a cry, she fell to the ground, head slamming against the paving slabs. Dazed, she began to struggle up but the beast was upon her before she could right herself. For a moment she felt hot breath on her skin, the drip of saliva. Then came the pain, fangs driving into her shoulder and throat, slicing through her flesh and tearing open her veins.

The cat watched, tucked away under the bushes, as the dog continued to destroy the girl, mutilating her. There was no hunger in the animal, not in the conventional sense. The canine wasn't feeding, it was simply driven by a need to consume, a fierce undeniable appetite for slaughter and carnage. The girl wasn't screaming anymore but the scene was far from silent. The crunch of bone and the sickening tearing sound, along with soft growls and whimpers from the pair.

After a while, the girl's mind succumbed, after minutes of torturous agony that seemed to stretch on for hours. She went limp, eyes staring blankly up at the sky. The dog continued to bite and scratch at her lifeless form for a moment before pulling back and shambling off.

The cat waited until the stench had faded, ensuring that the dog was gone, before slipping out from under the bushes. It crept towards the girl, circling her uncertainly. Her face was deformed, lacerated beyond recognition. One of her arms had been torn almost completely away, connected only by a few strings of tissue. Deep cuts marked her stomach, a glistening nest of intestines visible amongst the shredded skin.

It lapped lightly at the droplets of blood on the ground, the flavour tainted by whatever poison had taken hold of the dog's mind. The cat gagged and lifted its head. Its eyes came to rest on a man, stood at the far end of the alley. It wasn't like he had suddenly appeared or had stepped into view, it was almost like he had been there the whole time. He was dressed entirely in black, trousers, shirt, waistcoat and a long jacket. Leather gloves covered his hands, an ornate silver pocket watch clutched in one, a leather leash in the other that was attached to a large Rottweiler.

He approached the body and knelt down to examine the damage. His eyes flickered from the corpse to his pocket watch. He snapped it shut with a sigh.

"Such a waste… this is getting out of hand..."

The man gently closed the girl's eyes and straightened up. He glanced at the cat, who had seated itself nearby. Its amber eyes were bright and intelligent, communicating silently with the man.

"I suggest you run along little one. You need to be more vigilant than ever," he said, reaching down and softly petting the cat. It head-butted his hand lightly and scampered off.

*****

Faith Knight was seated in the hallway of the hospital, her uncle beside her. She wore a shapeless jumper and a pleated skirt, her hands were folded in her lap, fingers twitching occasionally to scratch at the remains of purple polish that decorated her nails.

255

It was understandable for her to be nervous. Faith had spent her entire life in the shadow of her sister's disappearance, but she barely remembered her. She'd been two when Eden had vanished, all she knew about her was what she'd gleaned from old news reports and things she'd been told.

Her uncle glanced at her and reached over, gently rubbing her knee. Faith looked down at her hands, shifting slightly in her seat. The meeting between her and Eden had been arranged incredibly quickly after the discussions between the social services and the doctors. Dr Cantrell was on duty and when Faith had arrived, he had instructed her to wait while he made sure Eden was ready. Thirty minutes had passed since then and Dr Cantrell still hadn't returned.

"I think we should come back another time…" suggested Mr Knight. "It doesn't look like it's going to happen today… and I have papers to grade. I can't spend all day here waiting."

"I don't mind staying if you want to go… I can walk home…" Faith mumbled, glancing over at her uncle before looking away anxiously.

"That's not going to happen," her uncle said firmly.

Before the conversation could continue, a nurse exited Eden's room and approached them, gesturing for them to follow her with a smile. Faith got to her feet, smoothing down her skirt before heading after the nurse. Her uncle trailed behind her.

Eden was sitting on her bed, dressed in clean clothes and her hair brushed out as much as the fragile strands would allow. Tidied up and without either mud or blood on her skin, she looked calm and almost normal, save for her stunted form and doll-like limbs. Faith approached the bed hesitantly, looking at her sister. Despite their difference in age, Faith was far taller than her older sibling. Eden looked at her curiously as her sister searched her face for… something familiar… something that would prove they were related.

Nothing.

Faith knew she took after her father physically, she'd seen pictures and the resemblance was clear. This girl didn't look particularly like either of the Knight parents. Evelyn Knight had been blonde, but it was more of a honey tone, while Eden's hair was paler. Her eyes too were different, matching neither Richard Knight's expressive grey eyes nor Evelyn's kind blue ones.

Eden moved onto all fours, leaning towards Faith and sniffing slightly. She looked her younger sister over, examining inch of her for signs of possible threat, before allowing herself to relax. Faith, a little unnerved by the animalistic behaviour glanced over at Dr Cantrell, who was lingering in the corner of the room.

"Don't worry… you have to remember that she's been through a lot… just respect her space and don't act in a way that could be seen as aggressive, alright?"

Faith nodded, a little wary. She took a deep breath before taking a seat next to the bed and putting on a smile.

"Hi… Eden. I'm Faith… I don't know if you… remember me in anyway… I get if you don't… but I'm your sister. And I'm here to help you… I want you to get better so you can finally come home," Faith said, her voice breaking slightly as she did. Her hand reached out and found Eden's, squeezing tentatively.

Eden looked at her and, after a moment, responded to the touch. Her lips moved, no sound coming out, but they seemed to shape the word 'Faith'. The younger girl smiled, tears forming in her eyes. She felt like a great weight had been lifted from her, replaced instead by a welcome sense of resolution. Her whole life her name had been associated with tragedy. Her sister disappearing, her mom and dad dying. She knew nothing could undo that but she felt like a little piece of her heart had been restored.

Dr Cantrell, feeling that it was safe to leave the girls together, went to the door, ushering Mr Knight out with him. It was important, in his mind at least, to give the siblings some time to get to know one another.

"She seems… not as bad as I expected," Mr Knight said.

"She's in a lot of pain. Inside. But it's amazing what a shower and a fresh set of clothes can do for a person."

"I thought she was… feral? That's what I was told."

"Feral is a little extreme. She's a young girl with deep traumatic scars and extreme mental health issues. But if people stop treating her like an animal, maybe she'll stop responding to them like one."

"Is it… true that she bites people?"

Dr Cantrell suppressed a laugh.

"Yes, she does have a tendency to snap. But it's pretty exclusively reserved for Dr Knott and Dr Matting. She really doesn't like them. She's wary around new people but she doesn't attack unless she's provoked. And with a little effort, she learns to trust. When she first came in, it was an effort to get her to change clothes and her having a bath or shower was out of the question. Now she's relatively content to let us clean her up. She doesn't seem to understand why we do it and she really doesn't seem to appreciate clothing but she doesn't fight us at least," Dr Cantrell explained. "I'm sure she'll be okay with you and Faith, just have to give it a little bit of time."

Mr Knight nodded slowly, contemplating the prospect of what was to come. He knew that he was taking on a lot by offering his home to Eden. He'd learned first-hand how it was to abruptly have responsibility thrust onto you. He'd been twenty-three when his brother had died and he'd been labelled Faith's legal guardian. It had all been very sudden and, while he thought he'd got the hang of it to an extent, now he was opening himself up to a whole new set of problems. But it was only temporary until she could be placed somewhere better suited… it would be difficult but he could make it through a few weeks.

From the room, Faith's soft voice could be heard, talking to Eden. Her words were too hushed to be made out but her tone was animated, something that was unnatural for her, ordinarily being fairly reserved and quiet. Dr Cantrell busied himself with a few tasks while Mr Knight stayed seated in the hallway, watching the clock. He disliked being unable to see Faith or hear what she was saying and, as time ticked by, he fidgeted in the uncomfortable chair, growing more and more stressed.

Eventually, it grew too much for him and he sprung from his chair, the force sending it skidding backwards, the legs scraping against the linoleum. He went to the room, the sudden burst of movement startling Dr Cantrell who immediately followed him, unwilling to let Eden be unduly distressed.

"Faith, time to go," Mr Knight said sharply. Faith looked up, her mouth opening to protest but no words came out. "Come on."

"Do I have to go so soon…?" Faith asked timidly. "Please? Can't I stay for a bit longer?"

"No. Now Faith, get up."

Faith looked from her uncle to her sister. Mr Knight grabbed hold of her wrist, forcibly pulling her to her feet. Eden let out a whimper of protest as Faith was tugged away from her. Dr Cantrell looked like he wanted to intervene but really there wasn't anything he could do but watch as the two of them left the room. Eden curled up in a foetal position, pulling the covers up over herself so that only her eyes and the very top of her head was visible.

Through the window, the first flakes of snow began to fall, tossed by the gentle breeze before coming to rest on the glass. Eden watched it settle and thicken, forming a light layer that turned the window into a distorted zigzag of crystal, blocking her view of the world outside.

Eden lay there for a while, the walls fading away around her as she stared at the snow. The ice settled over her body, numbing her from the outside in and forming an arctic coffin around her. She pulled the covers up even further, disappearing from view entirely.

My dearest B,

I have exhausted my options and my appeals go unheeded. I know now that I was a fool to think one person could make a difference in this world of monsters. You chided me in the past for my recklessness and now I am paying a heavy price.

These walls that once gave me comfort in the knowledge that I was doing godly work now fill me with cold terror. My own father turns away from me in disgust, friends that I once treasured view me as a parasite to be destroyed and you refuse to write back, not even allowing me one kind voice amongst the hundreds that scream in my head.

It is funny in a way. I always wished for more, to expand my horizons and know more of the world. Now I know every truth. And I have never been more contained.

Please, you know that I am not insane. Speak to father and make him see sense! You always were his favourite child... I am sure you will be able to convince him.

I cannot survive much longer. The walls are closing in and I feel him watching me.

Please.

Love

~A

# XXIII

Jamie lay in his bed staring up at the ceiling. The cat was curled up on the pillow beside his head, Echo stretched out across his feet. The room was illuminated with pale grey light, filtering in from the frosted window. He listened to the sounds of the house around him, his father leaving for work, his mother making breakfast for Callie before taking her off to school. Silence drifted through the rooms like a fog, settling over the house.

He got up and began to go through the motions of getting ready for the day. His actions were robotic, slow and methodical but with little emotion. As he dressed, the cat stretched and sat up, its amber eyes tracking his motions. Jamie looked over at the animal.

"Alright you, time to go," he said, walking over to the bed and scooping the cat into his arms. His accidental adoption of the cat only extended to the nights and during the day, he did his best to keep the animal out of the house. Jamie opened the bedroom window and dropped the feline onto the porch roof. It struggled for a moment to get its footing, giving Jamie a resentful look before clambering down from the roof and disappearing down the street.

Jamie closed the window and finished getting dressed. He took Echo for a walk while he contemplated what he should do that day. As much as he appreciated the break from school, being inside the house for prolonged periods of time was starting to get to him. He really wanted to see Sammy but she would be at school. He'd not seen her much recently, although she'd visited briefly once or twice she'd been somewhat distant since his discovery. It was probably just his paranoia, but he felt like she was avoiding him.

Eventually, he decided to go and visit Eden. At least then he'd have someone to talk to for a bit.

He dropped Echo off at home and headed up towards the hospital. The grass was frosty and bore a light dusting of snow like the town had been sprinkled with icing sugar. It was a pretty scene but Jamie knew that it was deceptive, a sign of worse to come. A chill wind bit at his cheeks and exposed hands, turning the skin an angry scarlet. He thrust his hands into his pockets and kept his head down, trying to minimise the damage as best he could, quickening his pace as he did so.

261

When he reached the hospital, he went straight to Eden's room. Dr Cantrell was working again and he smiled as Jamie entered the ward.

"Morning Jamie. Can I talk to you for a minute?"

"Erm… sure?" Jamie stopped by the desk and looked at the doctor, wary of what was to come. He half expected to be told he couldn't see Eden anymore.

"They're looking to release her soon but in the meantime, it's been decided that she should be allowed out into the town for some short visits. Would you be up for accompanying her?"

"Sure… when were you looking to do this?"

"Today? I can get her dressed up in some warm clothes and the two of you can go for a walk?"

"Wait… just me and her? Don't you need someone to supervise us?"

"Yes, I'm not going to send you two out alone. I'll be following nearby, but you can just pretend I'm not there," he explained.

Jamie nodded slowly and Dr Cantrell went to Eden's room to get her ready. Jamie perched on a nearby chair, waiting.

***You're going to hurt her. Just like you hurt everyone else.***

"Shut up…" he muttered under his breath. "It's not true…"

***All you do is hurt people…***

***You ruin everything…***

***You're just like him…***

"Jamie?"

He lifted his head to see Dr Cantrell stood nearby with Eden. She was wearing the dress that Jamie had given her, with a thick jumper over the top and a pair of snow boots, fidgeting uncomfortably, unused to being so constricted. Jamie smiled and came over, gently taking Eden's hand in his.

The trio left the hospital and began to make their way towards the town centre. Rather than follow the road, Dr Cantrell led them along the longer but quieter side path. It snaked across the vast stretches of crisp, frosted grass. Eden at first stayed close to Jamie, her hand clasped tightly in his, but as they walked her curiosity rose and she loosened her grip. Eventually, she released her hold entirely, straying away from the others to crunch merrily on the frozen grass, marvelling at the footprints she left behind.

Jamie paused and watched her, the expression on her face one of absolute serenity. She laughed, the sound so normal and yet completely unnatural all at once. Her excitement was contagious and Jamie couldn't help but smile. Eden spread her arms, closed her eyes and threw back her head. The wind toyed with her hair, the few stray rays of sunlight that managed to break through the clouds caressing her skin and bathing her in faint golden light.

"This was a good idea," Dr Cantrell said softly, smiling fondly.

Jamie nodded absently, his attention fixed on Eden.

"She looks like an angel…" he murmured, more to himself than the doctor.

"Pretty close…"

The shrill ringing of a phone cut through the calm. Dr Cantrell fumbled quickly at his pockets and stepped away to take the call. Jamie watched him go and then turned back to Eden. She had moved closer while he'd been distracted and was now only a few inches away. She glanced over at Dr Cantrell before taking Jamie's hand and gently tugging at him. He allowed her to lead him forward, expecting that she wanted to share the bliss she'd created. But rather than stop on the grass, she continued towards the treeline, drawing him with her. He knew that she wouldn't have the strength to force him to follow and he was incredibly reluctant to enter the forest again after last time, but something about Eden's expression told him she would go in with or without him. He couldn't let her go in alone…

The trees swallowed up the two of them and it wasn't long before Jamie couldn't see anything but the forest, the buildings and open spaces completely obliterated by dense woodland. Eden kept on, stumbling slightly as she moved over the rough ground. She scowled and stopped, leaning against a tree and pulling frantically at her boots. She picked at the knots on the laces and gave a sharp kick of each leg in turn, the boots flying off and crashing into the undergrowth.

"That's probably not a good idea Eden…"

Eden paid no attention to him and began to move again, picking up speed as she went to the point that she was almost running. Jamie took off after her, knowing that if he let her go she was likely to get lost.

"Eden!" Jamie called, struggling to keep up with the girl as she barrelled over the uneven terrain. His ankle hurt and the sight of the trees looming over him filled him with nausea. "Eden, please stop!"

Eden ignored him, moving with single-minded determination. She reached the mass grave, the remains of the police tape still clinging to trees, and stopped. She stood for a moment, head bowed. Her dress blew around her ankles, her hair masked her face and, as Jamie grew level with her, he thought he saw tears glistening on her cheeks.

"Eden…?" he said softly. "We really shouldn't be here… this is a crime scene…"

She lifted her head and looked at him, hands resting on the curve of her belly. Slowly, she raised her hand and held it out to him. Her eyes held a silent questioning and he realised that this was his chance to leave. He hesitated. He didn't want her to get hurt but he'd seen so many things recently… horrific things that would plague his mind for the rest of his life. Could he condemn himself with further horrors? Whatever had drawn her here, he had a sense that it wasn't going to be anything pleasant…

He took her hand, his fingers brushing lightly against the scars on her wrist. She smiled slightly and began to lead him around the open graves. There were so many now, more than Jamie would have ever thought possible.

They reached the thicket and Eden prised apart the outer branches to let Jamie through. Slightly confused, he pushed his way in, wincing as brambles whipped around his ankles.

In the centre of the thicket was a stack of rocks with a narrow hole at the base, forming a makeshift cave entrance. The rocks were covered in patches of moss and the air in the thicket felt cold and damp. Jamie had seen the pile before, from a distance. He'd assumed that the formation was coincidental. The space was too small to fit any actual animal inside.

As he watched, Eden dropped to her knees and slotted her legs into the opening. She wriggled around a little and Jamie noted a look of fear on her face. She closed her eyes, holding onto the rocks for leverage, and pushed herself into the darkness, disappearing from view in a second. Jamie's eyes widened and he darted forward, kneeling down and peering into the opening. He took his phone from his pocket and turned on the flashlight, shining it into the shadows. He realised that there was no ground inside the hole, instead, the rocks concealed a tunnel pointing downwards.

He bit his lip, pocketed his phone once more, and carefully pushed himself into the hole, feeling the emptiness below him. He closed his eyes, copying Eden's example, and pushed himself down into the tunnel.

He expected to fall, but the tunnel wasn't perfectly straight and it was too narrow to allow him to slip through with ease the way Eden had. He had to scrabble at the sides of the passage, forcing his way through the confined space. The walls were tight around him, the air was damp and every time he breathed in, he felt like he was inhaling dirt.

He pushed down, trying to worm his way through, hoping that he was nearly at the end. He didn't move. He frowned and tried to push further down but his body was wedged in the narrow passage and no matter how much he squirmed, nothing gave. He felt panic beginning to set in, his breathing spiking. Was he going to die in here? Suffocating slowly in the dirt? Rotting until he was just one of many bodies buried under the woods?

He clawed at the walls around him, trying to loosen himself. It crumbled a little, falling onto his face and down his throat. He coughed and spluttered, stilling. If he kept digging at it, he feared that the ground would collapse on top of him. It already felt like the walls were getting tighter, closing in.

Something grasped his foot and gave a sharp tug. He felt himself falling. The walls disappeared and there was nothing but empty air for a moment before he crashed in a heap on hard stone. He groaned softly, looking around. It was pointless. The cave was pitch black, no way of telling how big it was. Eden touched Jamie's hand, making him jump. He squinted, managing to make out her shape in the darkness. Her pale skin seemed almost to glow, a faint point of light in the black.

She helped him to his feet. He had to stoop to avoid banging his head on the low ceiling and now realised why Eden walked with a crouch. She took his hand in hers and guided it to the wall of the cave. The stone was cold and seemed almost to vibrate under his fingers, although there was no sound or detectable movement. Moisture collected on his fingertips. He brought them to his nose and sniffed, a faint metallic smell wafting up to his nostrils.

Eden began to move forward, her hand releasing Jamie's as she did so. He pulled his phone from his pocket and pressed a button to unlock it. Nothing happened. He felt for the power button but still, the phone stayed dark. He grimaced and tucked it away, resigning himself to feeling his way forward. He started after Eden, quickening his pace to keep up. He kept his fingers against the wall, feeling for turns or dead ends.

The wall curved and the ceiling sloped upwards. Relieved not to stoop, Jamie straightened up and looked around. The stone tunnel had widened out into a large cavern. Thin beams of light cut through the darkness from cracks in the roof. Huge stalactites hung down with razor-sharp points, puddles of still water were dotted around the cave. Tree roots, thick as a man's arm, snaked along the ceiling, reminding Jamie of the forest above.

It took him a moment to realise but when it dawned on him, he could see it as nothing else. This was the cave from his nightmares.

A steady dripping sound echoed around the cavern and, ever so faintly, the sound of a child crying. Jamie stiffened.

"Eden...? Do you hear that?" he whispered.

He looked around but couldn't see any sign of Eden. How had he managed to get separated from her? He was sure he'd been right behind her...

A flash of white in the depths of the cave drew his attention. He moved closer, both curious and fearful. Huddled in a nook was a child, a young girl. Her arms were wrapped around her knees, her chin resting atop them. She was crying, tears streaming down her cheeks.

As he neared, she lifted her head slightly, brilliant green eyes vibrant and distinctive. He froze, frowning. Those eyes, the eyes that had haunted his dreams since he'd first seen them. Eden's eyes. He reached out to touch her, to try and comfort her somehow, he wasn't really sure but his hand found nothing but air. He pulled back sharply. The girl was gone.

A ripple seemed to run through the cave. Jamie turned sharply. The world blurred and twisted around him, bending in strange ways.

The sound of laughter carried to him and he frowned. He couldn't imagine anyone in a place like this would ever have a reason to laugh. Shadows crossed the walls, the shape of two people danced around him. The laughter grew louder, passing by his ear, before fading away down one of the tunnels.

"Eden!" he called, hoping that she would hear him and return from wherever she had disappeared to. "We need to get out of here!"

He thought he heard a voice from down one of the tunnels so he set off in that direction. It only took a little distance from the cavern for the darkness to consume him.

*I can't do this anymore.*

He spun around, trying to pinpoint the source of the voice. It seemed to come from somewhere very close but at the same time far away.

*Please, Adam, I love him. I don't want to be part of this anymore.*

Shapes moved in the darkness, flickering pale grey forms that faded in and out of reality as quickly as they were recognised. Not quite shadows, not quite ghosts. He squinted, trying to make them out.

As he looked, they seemed to become more real, the outlines more solid but still not quite there. Like grainy images from an old movie, he saw them. A man. A woman.

*I can't do this anymore. I want to be free.*

        *You don't want to be free. You want to be normal.*

*Yes. I want to be normal.*

        *You want a normal life with that pathetic boy?*

*Don't call him that.*

        *You think he can make you happy?*

*I love him.*

                                                     *You love him.*

The woman turned away, her head down. The man grabbed hold of her wrist and pushed her roughly against the tunnel wall.

                                   *And what about me?*

*Adam…*

                         *What about everything I've done for you?*

"I don't want to see this," Jamie said. He wasn't sure who he was really talking to, the strange ghosts, Eden or the cave itself. It made no difference. The film continued to play before his eyes, fading in and out for a moment but never coming to a complete end.

*I never asked you to.*

                     *You didn't have to. You knew. You caused this.*

*That's not true.*

                   *I would do anything for you, to make you happy.*

*Anything… but not everything.*

The man pulled back sharply like he'd been slapped. The woman lifted her head to look at the man.

*Please, Adam. Let me have this… let me be a mother.*

The woman stood there for a moment before pulling away and turning to walk off. The man clenched his fists. Their expressions were faded and indistinct but at that moment, Jamie could see the rage cross his face.

The man moved quickly, grabbing hold of the woman and throwing her to the floor. The woman screamed, but it was cut off sharply as the man climbed on top of her and clamped his hand over her mouth.

           *You want to be a mother Evelyn? I always give you what you want.*

Jamie turned his head, unable to look anymore, but he could still hear. The fumble of fabric, the woman's cries, the man's grunts. From the corner of Jamie's eye, he saw a flash of silver and he half turned slightly.

The man, holding the woman down with the weight of his body, pulled a silver dagger from his belt. He took hold of the woman's hand and slashed it with the blade. She let out a scream and the images faded entirely.

Jamie stumbled back, shocked and confused by what he had seen. He retreated towards the cavern, deciding of the illusions he'd seen shadows and sounds were preferable to the twisted visions that lurked in the tunnels.

The tunnel twisted and split. He took the left fork, assuming it would lead him back to the cavern but found himself at a dead end. He ran his hand over the stones, feeling the surface. It wasn't a natural end, it seemed to be the result of a cave-in.

Something rustled as he moved his foot and he knelt down to investigate. Scraps of fabric were littered on the floor. One of the largest was pale yellow and dotted with a daisy pattern. He picked it up. The soft fabric made him think of his sister.

His searching fingers moved across the floor and came into contact with something hard and cold. He flinched back. His body collided with something solid and he let out a yell. Eden was stood behind him, looking down with sad eyes. He got to his feet, unsure if she was real or yet another trick. She had felt real enough but maybe this cave held more tricks than he knew.

"Eden, come on! We have to get out of here." Even without the phantom apparitions, the cavern made Jamie uncomfortable. There was an energy to the space, a dark electricity that flowed through the walls.

Eden ignored him and sat down, sliding backwards into a small alcove that Jamie had failed to notice. With a sigh, he crouched down and peered inside. A few rays of light came through the cracked ceiling, allowing him a limited view. The space was just big enough for Eden if she curled up. The floor was covered with a layer of scraps, fabric, feathers, moss, piled to form a makeshift nest. The walls were marked, crude finger paintings that Jamie saw were done with dried blood.

"Eden..." He knew what he wanted to say but couldn't bring himself to say the words. He didn't really need to, the answer was in front of him. He felt a wave of pity wash over as he looked at Eden. The true magnitude of what her life had been seemed to hit him for the first time.

"I'm sorry," he said finally. How long had she spent down in this terrible place?

Jamie inspected the walls, taking in the drawings. Despite the crude manner in which they'd been drawn, they were clear in meaning. It was the same image repeated across the walls; a house, three smiling stick figures, a dog. Longing seeped from the illustrations, a desperate loneliness and need to go home. Looking at them, Jamie had to fight not to cry. His eyes flickered over to Eden, sitting in the darkness with her head resting on her knees, tears were streaming down her cheeks. Jamie reached over and pulled her close, holding her tight against him and letting her cry into his top. There were no words to say, nothing he could do to take away the pain and fear she felt. All he could do was hold her and wait.

*This Book of Shadows is the property of Samyra Luis*

*August 9ᵗʰ*
*New Moon*

*While Practitioners worship many different gods, the tribe of Saruma were known to follow a particular set of twelve. Each ruled over a specific month and, much like the Greek and Roman Gods, each was linked to particular elements of their life.*

*January – Vineya – Goddess of shadows, fire and prophecy.*

*February – Tamaril – Goddess of water, healing and luck*

*March – Saruma – Mother Goddess. Goddess of Motherhood, childbirth, earth and summer. She also ruled over half the year although the exact period I have been unable to determine. She was one of the two primary deities that ruled over the tribe and is the namesake of the town. Cats are sacred to her.*

*April – Alaero – God of Air, Travel and Knowledge.*

*May – Malax – God of fertility, sex and pleasure.*

*June – Astal – God of Sun, Battle and Victory.*

*July – Lenova – Goddess of Hunting*

*August – Xavina – Goddess of Art and the Harvest*

*September – Calestea – Goddess of Night, the Moon and Music*

*October – Drak – God of blood, war and weather. Sacred to the Sky Tribe*

*November – Jakr – God of Ice and Mischief. I believe that this God was the origin of the Jack Frost character.*

*December – Ilon – God of Death, the underworld and winter. He ruled over the second half of the year. Snakes are sacred to him. A belief held by the tribe of Saruma was that if a child was bitten by a snake and survived, they were granted a level of protection by Ilon, keeping them safe from death.*

# XXIV

Why had she come back?

Eden felt the question in the air although she wasn't sure where, or who, exactly it had come from. It almost felt like the cave itself was questioning her, brought alive by years of blood and tears soaked into the dirt. In truth, she hadn't intended to leave. Jamie probably imagined her fleeing desperately, evading her captor and seeking out her exit but really it had been far more mundane.

During one of her periods of wandering, her attention had been captured by a tiny bird that had somehow strayed into the tunnels. She had followed the creature and it had led her to a hole, just big enough for her to fit through. She hadn't been trying to run, she was just curious… of course, things had been different when she'd first been thrown into the cave. She had been terrified and spent hours, weeks, months even, searching for a way out but after a while, her memories of home faded until there was nothing left but the cave.

Perhaps it was to say goodbye or perhaps it was because she just didn't know where else to go.

Eden wiped her eyes and got to her feet. This place didn't feel like home anymore, it felt wrong… she didn't belong here.

Jamie was watching her, half hopeful, half expectant. Everything about the cave made him uneasy. He felt like he was being watched intently by something angry and unpleasant and all he wanted was to go somewhere far away from the dreary space.

Eden didn't seem quite ready to leave however. Her attention had shifted and she had begun to feel her way along the wall, searching for something near the alcove. Jamie grimaced and followed reluctantly. The cave seemed to have grown even darker somehow and the air felt thick, almost tangible. The sensation of being watched had built, making the boy fidget and sending his eyes roaming across the darkness in search of the unseen presence.

Eden stopped suddenly, the act so abrupt that Jamie almost fell over her. He managed to catch himself and knelt to see what she was looking at.

The pale contorted face of a corpse leered out from the darkness. Jamie suppressed a startled cry and forced himself to remain calm and rational. It was just a body… he'd seen plenty of them now… it couldn't hurt him after all…

Despite his attempts to reassure himself, he couldn't bring himself to look at so he focused on Eden instead. She had a strange expression on her face, one he couldn't begin to interpret. She reached out and clasped the corpse's waxy hand. She looked so lost, a child torn from all things warm and familiar.

Eden looked down at the body. It had been there as long as she had but it had barely changed at all. Tangled dirty hair, once blonde was now a mixture of white and silver. Blue glassy eyes stared into space, the woman's head twisted to an unnatural degree and her limbs were splayed out in an awkward manner, giving her the appearance of a puppet with the strings cut. She was dressed in a tunic style top and jeans, both with strips of the material torn away, but her feet were bare. Her fingers were coated in a layer of dirt as though she'd been clawing at the ground. A tarnished locket hung around her throat, a wooden bracelet on her wrist. Someone had carefully arranged an assortment of objects around her: shiny pebbles, flowers long dead, a collection of animal bones, a feather, a tiny piece of frayed rope stained stiff. The objects were almost memorial like in the precision with which they were displayed.

Eden leaned over and kissed the woman's cheek lightly, before moving to get to her feet. Something caught her eye and she paused, bending slightly to scoop something from the line. It was a knife, handmade and clearly very old. The blade was made of polished stone, shaped to a wicked point. The handle was made from an antler, a mixture of leather and fur bound around it for grip. A word had been carved into the side of the handle, the lettering neat and clear.

ARIS.

Eden tucked away the blade and turned to Jamie.

"Can we go now?" he asked. His skin was crawling and he swore he could feel breathing on the back of his neck. Eden nodded and took his hand. She moved with complete confidence, although inside her heart was beating frantically in fear that the tunnels would twist and play tricks on her, that the exit would be gone, that she would be trapped once more at His mercy.

The path stretched out ahead of them and with each step that didn't reveal the way out, the pair grew steadily more afraid. Eden's hand grasped Jamie's tighter, fingers clasping his, greedy for contact and reassurance. Around them, the walls seemed to come alive the darkness shifting restlessly like many creatures moving amongst one another. Faint indistinct whispering started up. Jamie thought he could make out the occasional word but wasn't sure his ears weren't just interpreting the sound as words.

Eden, familiar with the games the shadows played and the poisonous thoughts they spewed forth, quickened her pace a little and tried to concentrate on something else, but even then the whispers continued to worm their way into his brain.

Mother... mother... mother...

Kill him... he'll hurt you... use the blade... use your hands... feed us... feel him die under you... feed on his flesh...

Take him...

Tear him apart...

Kill

Kill

Kill

Unconsciously, Eden released Jamie's hand. A deep-rooted pain had started in her stomach, a terrible hunger. She'd felt this only once before, and as it began to overwhelm her body, her mind found itself back in the moment.

Lost in the tunnels, blood caking her thighs, her calves, her hands. So much blood... Her body hurt, she was dizzy, barely able to stand. The blood flowed...

She had found it then. No idea what it was or how it had come to be there. The dim part of her brain that was still faintly human recognised it, took in the helpless pink limbs, the mewling cries it made, saw it, and knew it. Something inside her yearned to reach out and take hold of it.

But the hunger was stronger, driving her into a frenzy, bones snapping, flesh rent in two, the cries growing more frantic before cutting off

274

entirely. The whispers in her mind, the pain and need in her stomach were sated and driven away for a time.

"Eden!" Jamie's voice cut through the fog in her brain. She was on top of him, nails digging into his face. Seeing him, really seeing him for who he was and not just as a way to curb the whisper induced madness, snapped her out of her hallucination fully.

She hurried to her feet, retreating from Jamie as she did. He got up slowly, avoiding her gaze. He seemed like he wasn't really there, like part of him had slipped away into some far off place.

Hesitantly Eden took his hand once again and began to lead the way to the exit. The whispers still continued but less frantically and the pair were able to reach the hole without further incident.

After some struggle, they managed to clamber out of the tunnel and into the fresh air. Jamie blinked as he stood beneath the trees, disorientated. He felt like he'd woken from a deep sleep. The sky had darkened considerably during their time underground and it was snowing heavily, a thick blanket already spread across the land.

"We need to get back," Jamie said softly. There was a tinge of guilt to his voice as his own vision from the whispers played on a loop in his mind.

They started to walk, Eden shivering a little beside him. Jamie glanced at her feet and immediately felt like an idiot. He'd forgotten she'd abandoned her shoes earlier. She would be freezing…

"Hang on," he said, pausing by a tree. He could probably handle the cold for a while… but then she might just throw his shoes away as well. He settled on a compromise, keeping his shoes but giving her his sock to take off the worst of the chill before picking her up carefully. He'd carry her as far as he could, hopefully he'd get them both to the hospital.

They were about to resume their trudge when a sound caught Eden's ear. Her entire body went rigid in Jamie's arms, eyes darting around like a startled deer searching for a predator.

Amongst the trees, something moved. Jamie and Eden held their breath, watching silently and praying they wouldn't be seen. It was probably nothing, just an animal but there was no harm in being cautious. After a moment whatever it was moved on, heading towards the lake, silent as a ghost. As it moved, Jamie was able to make out that it was a person, dressed in a hooded cloak. Jamie glanced at Eden, his curiosity compelling him to follow the stranger. She inclined her head. Jamie took it as consent and turned to follow the hooded figure, balancing Eden in his arms.

They moved slowly, hampered by the growing snowdrifts and the uneven terrain beneath. The sound of voices wafted on the wind, a steady rhythmic noise that rose and fell. Jamie set Eden down and the pair of them crouched in the undergrowth, huddling together for warmth as they looked out at the lake. A group of people were gathered by the water, all dressed in hooded cloaks and wearing some form of mask, made to look like animals. Each clutched a flickering candle which turned their shadows into distorted demons on the snowy ground. Jamie felt his breath catch in his throat and his heart faltered. There were so many of them, at least fifty. More than he had ever thought.

Two of the assembly stood apart from the others and raised their hands. The group fell silent, looking to the pair.

"Greetings brethren, under the dark eye we gather," said one of the pair, a clear male voice ringing out through the clearing. "Let us walk in shadows as one, for we are brothers."

"Let the Master guide our hearts and know our devotion," the group intoned back.

"Thank you for gathering at such short notice, we have to discuss a matter of great importance. As you are aware, the police have discovered our... offerings. They have been removed from the sacred ground, so any who made a request of the master during our last gathering should assume they are not going to be granted. Ordinarily, I would suggest that we make a new offering, however, I feel that on this occasion our largest priority should be the girl."

Jamie fumbled in his pocket for his phone. He could call his dad, get the police down here and get them arrested. It was better than just sitting and doing nothing. He frantically stabbed at the buttons on the phone with nothing happening and cursed to himself.

"How do we know that the child is the Master's?"

"The signs are there. Her body is weakened by the darkness within her and she will likely succumb soon. If she had not been found when she did, she would likely be dead. The Scáthanna are growing in strength and the Master's reach has stretched further than ever before. The child is his," said the other member of the duo, this voice icy and female. "We shall monitor the girl until she gives birth. After that, she is of no consequence."

"Wouldn't it be easier to take her now and keep hold of her until the birth?"

"She's under too much scrutiny at the moment. And even if we found a way to get her away undetected, the risk that her body will succumb to the darkness. We need to keep her healthy or all this effort will have been for nothing."

Eden pressed herself closer to Jamie, her breath clouding in the air in front of them. The cold was eating into her body, a freezing burn that painted her skin bright red. She shivered, wrapping her arms around herself. She could barely feel her fingers and toes and with each moment that passed a little more of her turned numb. Her hand clutched at Jamie's sleeve, tugging as best she could with her stiff digits.

Jamie looked over at her, seeing the first signs of frostbite on her skin. He wanted to stay and try to hear more but he knew his friend's health was more important. Besides, the longer they spent there, the greater the chances of them being discovered. They wriggled out of their hiding place and crept away from the lake, keeping their bodies low to the ground in an effort to avoid being seen. The sound of their feet on the snow making Jamie wince, fearing the sound would draw the attention of the gathering.

The night was moonless and the falling snow turned the forest into a blank map, every landmark Jamie knew was obliterated by the powder. They could have been walking in circles and he wouldn't have been able to tell. Their clothes were soaked through and the bitter night air was affecting them both. Eden was flagging badly, stumbling with each step.

*Leave her. She's a liability.*

Jamie grimaced and shook his head, trying to dislodge the errant thoughts. He picked Eden up, balancing her small frame in his arms. She snuggled close to him, resting her head against his chest, and closed her eyes. Jamie continued on, his mind filled with a fierce resolution.

Get Eden to safety. Find someone who can help, tell them what you saw.

It took a while, but he was able to move quicker carrying Eden than walking at her pace. They made it to the hospital, Jamie's hands changing to a strange purple colour from the cold. He was muttering under his breath, repeating his objectives over and over. Eden was quiet and barely moving, the only sign of life was the slow rise and fall of her chest. Jamie snuck in and hurried up to the ward where Eden was kept. He expected to see frantic staff, police officers, concerned about her disappearance but there was only Dr Cantrell, sitting in the ward, waiting patiently. He looked up as Jamie entered.

"Is she hurt?" he asked.

"No. She's cold and damp but she's not hurt," Jamie said.

He went and set Eden down on her bed. Dr Cantrell followed him. He didn't seem angry, which surprised the teenager. He seemed like he'd expected the two of them to run off and had been waiting patiently for them to return. The doctor carefully removed Eden's wet clothes while Jamie turned away respectfully to give her some privacy. His head was spinning with everything he'd seen and heard, trying to make sense of things.

Jamie wasn't naïve enough to think that small towns were immune from horror. He knew enough to know that bad things happened wherever you went and that people could be monsters no matter what they looked like, where they came from or what they did. They could wear masks of respectability but underneath they were rotten. But even knowing all that, even after seeing the bodies, he couldn't quite make himself believe that it was real. Monsters came in all shapes and sizes but ghosts? Demons? They belonged in stories and movies. He knew that there weren't creatures lurking under the bed, but he couldn't keep denying that something... something was out there...

"Jamie," said Dr Cantrell. "Can I speak with you for a minute?"

Jamie looked around. Eden was curled up in her bed, dressed in dry clothes and sleeping soundly. He sighed and nodded, letting the doctor lead him out of the room, bracing himself automatically.

"Are you okay Jamie? You seem... shaken?"

Jamie was taken aback by the question. He hesitated, wanting to tell the doctor about what he had seen but something stopped him from saying the words.

"I'm fine," he lied. "Are you... mad? About us disappearing?"

"No. She probably would have run off with or without you. At least with you, she had a way of getting back safely. Just count yourself lucky that Dr Knott has the night off, I doubt he would have been as forgiving." Dr Cantrell paused, looking like he wanted to say something else. After a moment, he decided against it. "You best run home Jamie before it gets late."

Jamie nodded slowly and began to walk away, both of them leaving their unspoken words hanging in the air between them. Dr Cantrell returned to his vigil over Eden, like a faithful dog guarding her door.

MORNINGWOOD SANITORIUM PATIENT ROSTER

STRICTLY CONFIDENTIAL

| NAME | SEX | AGE | PATIENT NOTES |
|------|-----|-----|---------------|
| Abbott, Louis | M | 32 | Addict |
| Attwood, Cassandra | F | 17 | Claims to see 'visions'. |
| Boggs, Charlotte | F | 28 | Excessive Mental Labour |
| Brinley, Penelope (Masturbation) | F | 16 | Sexual Deviance |
| Compton, Joseph | M | 31 | Idiocy |
| Daniels, Oliver staff only | M | 42 | Extremely aggressive – Male |
| Danvers, Christian | M | 27 | Superstition |
| Dowers, Maggie | F | 20 | Epilepsy |
| Edwards, Victoria | F | 33 | Nymphomaniac |
| Eyre, Helen | F | 20 | Immorality |
| Geneva, Lulu Syphilis | F | 22 | Committed by husband – |
| Jackson, Nathan | M | 18 | Imprisonment |
| Prentice, Elizabeth | F | 15 | Murderer. Treat with caution. |
| Randall, Eric sexual deviance | M | 36 | Unnatural behaviour and |
| St John, Emilia | F | 27 | Indulgence of temper |
| Tarrant, Andrew | M | 26 | Shellshock |
| Vincent, Harriet | F | 23 | Hysteria |
| Wallace, Mary | F | 14 | Parental abuse |
| Williams, Nancy | F | 47 | Melancholia |

# XXV

Jamie left but he didn't go home. Instead, he made his way to the large apartment block in the centre of town, the one that housed exclusively the most affluent members of the community. That was where Sammy lived. The doorman refused to let Jamie, in his damp and muddy clothes, past the lobby and informed him that Sammy was out somewhere, so the teenager sat down to wait for her. His eyes roamed the beautifully decorated space, took in the rows of post boxes set in one of the walls. Each bore the name of a resident, most of them he knew. How many of them were part of what he'd seen? How many of them had blood on their hands?

"Jamie? What are you doing here… you're soaking wet!"

He looked up to see Sammy. She was dressed in warm clothes, lightly dusted with snow and had a pair of hiking boots on, her normal mess of hair tied up in a bun.

"Can we talk?" he asked softly. "Privately?"

"Sure. Come upstairs. I'll get you a towel."

They went to the lift and stepped inside, Sammy shrugging off her jacket as they went. The silence between them in the confining space felt suffocating. Jamie wasn't sure why he'd gone to her. Maybe it was because she never treated him like he was crazy? If anyone would believe him about what he saw it would be her, he was sure of it.

They exited the lift and headed down the hall to the Luis apartment. Jamie had been there a few times before but most of the time they chose to spend time at his, or somewhere in the neighbourhood. He felt out of place in the apartment. It was always neat and meticulously decorated. He felt like he made the place untidy just by sitting there. Sammy's room was a nice reprieve, a chaotic clash of themes and decorations that screamed against one another to be the centre of attention. Standing in her room, what he'd seen in the woods felt even more unrealistic. This space was warm and familiar, the dresser holding knickknacks that he had given her, the leather diary with the metal clasp that she'd kept since she was nine, the pentagram necklace she wore tucked under her clothes. How could what he'd seen be real?

281

Sammy fetched him a towel while Jamie struggled to undress himself, his fingers numb and unresponsive. His hands were trembling, whether from the cold or the anxiety he was experiencing he wasn't sure. Sammy sighed and came over, helping him strip off his damp clothes and hanging them on the radiator to dry. He perched on the edge of her bed in his underwear, towel wrapped around his shoulders.

"Jay? What's wrong?"

"I saw something tonight."

"Like… one of your… hallucinations?"

"No, this was real. I saw… I saw the cult. They were in the forest…"

Sammy's face paled slightly and she sat beside him.

"Are… are you sure?"

"Am I sure that the creepy group in the middle of the woods wearing masks and cloaks were a cult? Yeah, I'm pretty sure!"

"Calm down Jamie, I was just asking a question." She rubbed her hands together, deep in thought. "Have you told anyone?"

"No… just you… but I'm going to tell my dad… he needs to know what I saw… and about the tunnels… what they're going to do… they're going after her and I have to keep her safe…"

"Jamie, you're not making any sense!"

"Yes, I am! I've never made more sense in my life! Why are you just sitting there when I'm telling you I saw a cult plotting together! We have to tell someone!" He leapt to his feet, heading for the door.

"No. We don't. And we won't." Her voice was firm and Jamie stopped abruptly, turning to look at her. She had her head in her hands, the inky locks beginning to stray from her bun. "Jamie… I've known about the cult for a year…"

"Wh… what are you talking about?"

"About a year ago, my mom was acting really weird. I was worried about her so I followed her one night. She went to the forest… which was like an immediate red flag because she hates nature. And she went in and that's when I saw them…"

"And you've just kept it quiet? For a year? About your mom being a child murderer? Are you insane?"

"She's not a murderer!" Sammy snapped. "She didn't kill anyone."

"She may not have cut them open herself, but by being in that cult she was part of it! She didn't stop it! You have to tell the police!"

"Well forgive me for not wanting to lose the only parent I have! You have a family Jamie, it's easy for you to stand there and judge but I only have her and yeah, I may not like her all the time but she is my mom!" There were furious tears in her eyes as she spoke. "I'm not okay with it, but I don't have any other choice!"

"Sammy, I'm sorry but I have to tell them. Maybe if your mom is helpful, they won't lock her up. Like… a witness protection deal?"

"Jamie be real, that doesn't happen outside of TV shows. If they get caught, she'll be locked up with the rest of them. And I'll have no one."

"You could end up with a really nice family, social services will-"

"If social services are so fucking great and you have such a wonderful life cause of them, why do you still hate yourself?"

Jamie flinched back like she'd slapped him.

"I'm leaving."

"Jamie… wait, I'm sorry. I didn't mean it. I just… I know that I'm not likely to convince you because you are so stubborn, but will you just listen to me for five minutes so I can explain properly? Please?" Jamie looked at her and nodded slightly. He didn't return to the bed instead, he leant against her door, ready to leave at a second's notice. "Even if I told the police, the only person I could actually identify would be my mom. I have no idea who was under the masks. And if you decide to tell your dad what you saw, you won't be able to tell them anything new either. The police know that there is a cult, they know they kill children and they know they do it in the woods. The fact that you saw them doesn't tell them anything they don't already know. I mean, could you identify any of them?"

"No…" he admitted reluctantly.

"Exactly. So you running to the station and shouting that you've seen them will just put you in danger. Cause, I really doubt they're going to

283

want to risk you spilling their secrets, especially after you were the one to find the graves. You're probably already on their shit list."

The more she spoke, the more Jamie realised what she was saying was true. He thought about the figure he'd seen from his window, watching the house. Had that been someone from the cult? Watching him?

"So what do I do? I can't just sit back and do nothing when I know they're going to hurt people."

"I know. You're a little superhero," Sammy said, giving him a slight smile. "I'm not saying that you can't do anything, I'm just saying that you need to be smart about it. Take some time, act like normal and think. They're not going to do anything right now with the police on such high alert."

It made sense. Jamie couldn't deny that. He was exhausted, the events of the day had drained him greatly. Sammy came over and put a hand on his shoulder.

"Go home, Jamie. Get some rest. Play with Callie, walk your dog. Come over on Halloween like we planned and we'll hang out, watch films… discuss this some more if you really want. You need a few days of normality," she told him. He nodded and gathered up his clothes, still somewhat damp, dressed and left the apartment.

His head felt fuzzy. He hadn't even told Sammy about the tunnels and the things he'd seen down there but he didn't want to anymore. It would make him look crazy and unstable. Besides, he felt a little… hurt. Not by her comments, although those still stung, but by the secrets she'd kept. She knew everything about him, he told her all his secrets and she hadn't told him.

The snow had stopped falling and that made his journey home a little easier. The police cruiser wasn't in the drive but his mom's car was. He let himself in and trudged up the stairs, hoping his mom wouldn't try to talk to him. Despite his agreement with Sammy, he wasn't sure that he'd be able to keep what he'd seen quiet if prompted.

He made it to his room undisturbed and found Callie curled up in his bed, Echo on one side and the cat on the other. Jamie watched her fondly for a few minutes as she lay there, expression peaceful. He sighed quietly. It made it all much easier to understand when he looked at her. He couldn't put her in any danger, even if it meant putting someone else at risk. He didn't care what happened to him, but he cared what happened to her. If staying quiet and not doing anything, kept her safe he could do it. The choice was easy.

He changed into his pyjamas and climbed into bed beside her. She responded to his presence, automatically shifting closer and her eyes flickered open for a moment.

"Jay… the monster won't leave me alone…" she mumbled sleepily, her eyes sliding closed once more. Jamie lay beside her, staring up at the ceiling as her words sunk in. Maybe not doing anything wasn't going to be enough to keep her safe…

The next morning, Jamie was woken by his mom bustling into his room and pulling the curtains open wide. Jamie grimaced and pulled the covers up, recoiling from the light. He'd not slept well, his mind haunted by shadowy creatures, endless tunnels and cloaked figures.

"Up you get Jay, it's time for school," his mom said cheerily.

"School? But… I'm still traumatised…" Jamie mumbled, peeking out from under the covers.

"Well, your father says it's time to be traumatised at school. And I agree, it's not healthy for you to stay cooped up in the house by yourself. Now, if you get up quickly enough, I'll have time to drop you there. Your breakfast is downstairs," she told him firmly.

His mom left the room and Jamie reluctantly detached himself from his bedding. Callie had already got up and he could hear her clattering downstairs. He dressed quickly and ran his fingers through his hair in an effort to tame the bedraggled mess.

As he made his way down the hall, he paused by Callie's door, her words echoing in his mind. He reached out, his fingers lightly caressing the door handle. Monsters weren't real, no matter what a crazy cult thought. Whatever he'd seen in the tunnels was just… something else.

Jamie pushed open Callie's door and stepped inside. He wasn't sure what he expected to see but he felt instant relief when he took in the untouched room. It looked the same as it always did, with the exception of her unmade bed. No sign of any monsters.

He went over to her bed and pulled the duvet up, smoothing it out and tucking the sides in. His eyes noted a spot of reddish-brown on the edge of her baby blue cover. He frowned and lifted the covers, exposing the sheets beneath. There were more of the rust coloured stains splashed across the lower half of the sheets. Jamie felt his blood run cold and he stared at the bed.

Slowly, he lowered the covers once more. He wasn't sure what it meant and part of him was afraid to find out.

He left the room and went downstairs, hoping to ask Callie about it. His mom had set out a bowl of cereal for him and Callie was perched at the breakfast bar, munching a piece of toast. Jamie took a seat beside her and glanced over at his mom, who was washing dishes nearby. He tapped the table lightly, getting his sister's attention.

*Are you okay?*

As he signed, he kept one eye on his mom. He didn't want her to worry and he knew that Callie wouldn't tell him anything if she was watching. His sister set down her toast and brushed the crumbs off her fingers before signing back.

*Why?*

*You were scared last night? You said about a monster?*

*Bad dream*

*I saw the blood. What happened?*

Callie didn't reply and turned her head away. She moved to get up, her chair scraping against the tiles. Jamie reached over and grabbed hold of her arm.

*Please. I'm worried about you!*

*It was the monster…*

Before Jamie could ask her what she meant, their mom came over. She smiled at the two of them.

"You all ready to go? Jamie, you've not eaten much?"

"I'm not hungry…"

"Well okay… why don't you two head out to the car? I'll be right out."

She went to fetch her coat and handbag, while Jamie and Callie went out to the car. They both got into the back and the moment the doors were closed, Jamie turned to his sister.

*Show me.*

Callie looked down, clearly uncomfortable. Gradually, she reached out and rolled up her trouser leg, revealing five short scratches across her ankle. They were swollen and a livid red, crusted with dried blood. Seeing them, Jamie felt a burst of anger, fiery fury that flowed through his veins like lava. His sister was hurting and that was something he couldn't allow.

*I'll make this right*, he told her, reaching over to tug her trouser leg back down. They sat in silence as their mom returned to the car and got in. Callie stared out of the window and Jamie looked down at his lap. Their mom babbled about Halloween, suggesting costume ideas for Callie to wear. Jamie usually took her trick or treating before dropping her at the elementary school party. It was something they both loved, but neither of them could muster much enthusiasm.

Jamie was dropped off first, which he was glad for. It meant he didn't have to spend time sitting with just his mom trying to evade her concerned questioning. It felt strangely surreal being back at school. It hadn't been that long, barely even two weeks but stepping out on the parking lot it felt alien to him.

He watched his mom drive off before heading up the steps and into the hallway. As he walked down to his locker, he was aware of eyes watching him and people beginning to whisper. Despite the best efforts of the police, the discovery of the bodies in the forest had made the papers. It seemed almost inevitable and, while Jamie's name hadn't been included, rumours had spread and with his absence, it wasn't hard for people to figure out his part in things. He had expected some sort of response to his return and all he could do was hold his head up and keep going.

Reaching his locker, Jamie began to fiddle with the dial. He braced himself as he entered the combination, half expecting his locker to be stuffed with something horrible, but there was nothing inside except his books.

"Hey, Harper!" Tucker's voice cut through the noise of the hallway. "Thought they'd finally shipped your crazy ass off to the loony bin?"

Jamie closed his eyes, inhaling slowly through his nose. He counted inside his head, taking a moment to keep his composure. When he opened his eyes again, he took the books from the locker and slammed the door shut. Tucker had closed the gap between them and was a few feet away, his minions lurking behind him. Jamie ignored them, turning away and making his way down the crowded hall. His classroom was in the other direction but he couldn't help that. He knew that Tucker and his cronies wouldn't let him past them.

"Oi! Harper! I'm talking to you!"

Jamie turned off the main corridor into the hall that housed the English classrooms and library. It was fairly empty, still early enough that most of the students were chatting outside or by the lockers, and Jamie figured he would be able to duck into one of the classrooms until Tucker wandered off. Part of him hoped that the number of people in the hall he'd come from would have distracted them enough so that they hadn't seen where he'd gone.

"Harper, you know it's not nice to ignore people right?"

Okay, so they'd followed him. There was nowhere he could hide without them seeing him and the only other exit was a fire escape, but even if he reached it they'd just follow him out. He stopped in the hallway and turned to face them.

"What do you want Tucker?"

"I heard that you've been getting all cosy with that weirdo who likes to run around naked?"

"She's not a weirdo…"

"And you're a great judge of that," he said with a mean laugh. "Is it true that you found all those dead kids in the woods?"

"Yeah…"

"How'd you know they were there?" The group had formed a loose semi-circle around him, trapping him against a wall. "I think that's pretty fishy."

"I didn't know they were there. And I don't care what you think." That exhaustion was back, the feeling that he just couldn't make himself care about what was happening.

"They were all kids right?" said Tucker, leaning against the wall so his face was close to Jamie's. "That's really fucked up, you know. You're a proper sicko."

"I heard that he screws them before he kills them," cut in Scott, one of Tucker's sycophants.

"Is that right Harper? You like using little kids to get your dick wet?"

"No, I prefer to use your mom for that. She's had plenty of practice," Jamie snapped back venomously.

He could deal with a lot of insults, he could handle being called crazy and stand in relative silence, but he had reached his threshold. Tucker looked at his friends.

"Grab him," he said.

Before Jamie had a chance to react, each of Tucker's friends seized one of his limbs and lifted him from the ground. They carried him down the hall to the fire escape and outside to where the dumpsters were kept. Jamie struggled, kicking out at them. He heard the shriek of metal as the rusted lid to a dumpster was lifted a second before he was hurled inside it. Jamie's body collided with solid metal and landed in a reeking pile of garbage.

Tucker and his friends peered over the edge, sneering at him.

"This is where pieces of trash like you belong. You should just slit your wrists so we don't have to fucking look at you anymore. Maybe do it right this time?"

The lid came down, plunging Jamie into darkness. He struggled up, his hands sinking into the muck, and pushed at the lid. It was heavy but he was fuelled by the frustration that had been brewing inside him and he managed to push it open. Tucker was still nearby, walking away as he clearly didn't expect Jamie to make a move so soon. When he heard the sound of the dumpster, Tucker turned back to look at Jamie.

"You don't know when to take a hint…" he said, watching as Jamie climbed out of the dumpster.

"I'm not a paedophile. And if you say I am again, I will kill you," Jamie said. He wasn't sure where the words were coming from but that hot anger was flowing through his body again, controlling him like a puppet.

Tucker looked at his friends, clearly amused by Jamie's attempt to stand up to him. He advanced on the boy, flanked by the others like bodyguards.

"Did I hurt your feelings? Are you upset that you're just like your perve of a father?"

"Don't say that…" said Jamie softly.

"You may act like someone new but you'll always come from criminals and trash and that's all you'll ever be," Tucker said, his lip curling. "Maybe that's why you're not into that little psycho from the forest? She too old for you? You're more into girls… your sister's age yeah?"

Something snapped inside Jamie. All the anger, all the resentment that he'd been feeling and had been building for days broke through like water through a dam. He lunged at Tucker, tackling him and knocking the boy to the floor. He rained down his fists on Tucker's face, not caring where he hit, just wanting to make Tucker feel a fraction of the pain that he was feeling, that he felt every day.

"I. Am. Not. A. Paedophile!" Jamie roared.

His fists slammed repeatedly against Tucker, shattering his nose as the boy struggled against him. Blood was flowing and there was pain in his knuckles but he ignored it. He wanted to destroy, to cave in the other boy's head.

Tucker's face was a bloody pulp, his friends were trying to prise Jamie away but he forced them off, letting out an enraged sound that was somewhere between a snarl and a scream. They retreated. Although Tucker had always said Jamie was crazy and they'd gone along with that, they never thought he was capable of the intense rage they saw as he attacked the other boy.

Jamie felt like he had floated far away from his body. He was dimly aware of voices, panicked shouts calling for him to stop. One hand grabbed Tucker's hair, the other wrapped around his throat. He slammed Tucker's head into the cement repeatedly, hearing a sickening crunch as he did so.

People were rushing over. Tucker wasn't crying out anymore, but Jamie didn't stop. He felt the bones under his fingers, the coppery smell of blood hung in the air. Even as he was grabbed from behind and dragged off, he felt ecstatic, every part of his body was alive.

B

Why do you persist in ignoring me? You know that I desperately need your help yet still you do nothing? Of course, you must be glad to be rid of me. Now you can finally have everything you wished for. I hear that you are to be married. That was the one thing I could best you in. Is that why you leave me to rot in here? So he can be yours?

You always wanted to take what was mine.

I would not think so much of this betrayal had you not ensnared my child away from me at the first opportunity. Yes, I know about that as well. Of course, you would have been the first to tear him away from me. It is the perfect arrangement for you. The husband, the home, the son.

You sicken me.

I will be free again. And he will know me as his mother. And you as the imposter you are.

~Amelia

# XXVI

He expected to get expelled, or at the very least suspended. He was surprised when, after being taken to the principal's office and sitting outside it for the rest of the school to walk by and judge him until his mom arrived, he was only slapped with isolation. Privately Jamie wondered how many favours his parents had had to call in to get him off so easy. Then again, it was hardly a secret that Tucker was a bully and a lot of Jamie's classmates had probably wanted to punch him for a long time. Maybe they'd had something to do with it. He wasn't sure.

Needless to say, his mom wasn't happy, but she chalked the outburst up to his recent experiences and decided not to be too harsh with him. He had to stay in his room that night but he wasn't forbidden from going out to see Sammy on Halloween. The only downside was his confinement meant he couldn't talk to Callie and try to learn more about what had injured her. Instead, he spent the evening staring up at his ceiling, clenching and unclenching his fists, replaying his attack on Tucker with a smile on his face. No matter how hard he tried the images grew more vivid with every repetition.

"Stop it," he said quietly. "I just want to sleep."

"It felt good. Admit it." The voice was sudden, loud by his left ear. He could feel the shape of a person beside him but he refused to look. "Now now, don't be like that. You have wanted to destroy him for a long time. And today was just a taste of that!"

Jamie jerked to his feet and paced across the floor, shaking his head.

"I don't want this anymore. I'm not like this…"

"Liar."

"No, I don't start fights. I don't do things like this.

"Only because you're afraid to." Jamie turned, eyes locking on his. It had gone too far. Voices were one thing and they were bad enough but here he was talking to a figment of his imagination, arguing with a person who didn't exist.

"I'm done. I don't know what bit of my brain conjured you up but you're not real and I'm listening."

The man sighed, expression more disappointed than anything and he strolled over. Despite the casual action, the movement was unsettling and predatory. He stopped a foot away, eyes sweeping over the teen with a peculiar look of amusement forming across his face. Jamie felt pinpricks of ice running across his skin and he had to fight the urge to look away.

Suddenly he was slammed backwards, body colliding with the sink. A rough hand wrapped around his throat, strong digits pressing into the skin in a way that was too vivid to be anything but reality. The man's other hand reached up and brushed Jamie's cheek, cocking his head to one side as he did. His eyes never left Jamie's and when he spoke, his voice was soft, almost a whisper.

"Does this feel real Jamie?" The hand caressing his cheek gripped the boy's chin and turned sharply so that Jamie could see his reflection, the two of them locked together in the glass. "Does this look real?"

He leant down and bit at the flesh over Jamie's pulse point, eliciting a strangled cry.

"You're not the first. Eden had to learn this lesson too… and I took great delight in teaching her. Many others as well." His cheek was flush against the teenager's as he spoke. "I'm as real as you let me. I made you better. You think that I changed you into something else, something you're not but I told you before… I just amplify what's already there." He bit once more, this time on Jamie's earlobe. "If you let fear take root in your brain, it will grow, blossoming into something new. The fearful mind is a very powerful thing, it can transform men into monsters beyond recognition. It can strangle a person inside their own head. I took away your fear and gave everything else room to grow."

The man pulled back slightly and ran his fingers across Jamie's cheek, twisting them so his nails grazed the skin sharply leaving raised red lines.

"When the time comes, you'll welcome me back. But until then… I'll wait." His other tightened around Jamie's throat, cutting off the air with ease. "Sleep well, sweetheart. Try not to miss me too much."

Jamie's eyes were watering, the man blurring in and out of focus. His lungs burned, screaming for oxygen. Dark spots danced across his vision and he felt the blood pounding in his skull.

Then the pressure was gone. He was left, standing alone in his bathroom, gasping for breath. Only the dark purple bruise forming on his skin and the red marks on his cheek confirmed it had even happened.

*****

The next day of school was better than any he'd ever had. The rules of isolation meant he had to report to the reception and was escorted to the isolation block, to remain there for the rest of the day. He didn't have to put up with what the other students were inevitably saying about him, he could actually relax and get on with his work. His throat still burned but he ignored it.

By the time he arrived at Sammy's apartment that evening, he was feeling remarkably calm and the chaos in his head seemed to have disappeared. He'd not been the one to take Callie out trick or treating since his mom pointed out most of the neighbours (at least the ones with kids at Jamie's school) wouldn't be pleased to see him on their doorstep. While he was a little disappointed, it spared him the indignation of having to dress up which was always a relief, although he had put in a pair of plastic vampire fangs just for fun.

"Happy Halloween!" Sammy said as she opened the door. She was dressed in a tight black dress and had a pair of cat ears perched precariously on her head.

"Evening!" Jamie said, his voice distorted by the fangs. He spat them into his hand and smiled at her.

"Come on in. You seem… better?"

"I feel better."

They went into Sammy's room and he sprawled out on her bed. The lights were off but she'd set candles up around the room and the air was heavy with a mixture of strange perfumes. Jamie stretched, letting out a contented sound.

"Where's your mom tonight?"

"Out with Logan."

"Which one's Logan?'"

"The guy who owns that club, Fever."

"Ah. Right." Jamie pulled a face. "So… dare I ask what's been going around school about me?"

"Pretty standard stuff. One person said that you tore open Tucker's throat with your teeth… so maybe you should keep those vampire teeth handy when you're out of isolation. None of the others are really that interesting though," Sammy told him as she went to her cupboard and retrieved a large folder. She dumped it on the bed. "Shall we pick tonight's entertainment then?"

Jamie nodded, suppressing a yawn, and sat up to flick through the folder with her. She crouched beside him, her shoulder touching his as they looked. It was a familiar routine and one that comforted them both, the normality of the act making the weirdness of the past few weeks seem a far off dream

"How about… this one?" said Sammy, pausing with her fingers resting on one of the films.

"The birds…?" Jamie asked, raising an eyebrow at her. Although his injuries from the incident with the birds had largely healed, he still bore the scar and his nightly dreams often featured them.

"Too soon?" Sammy asked with a grin.

"Just a bit…"

"Okay, so we have to rule out anything with birds… snakes… rats…"

"Neither of us are afraid of rats," Jamie pointed out.

"No, but I think they're misrepresented in horror films."

"Right."

"So rats… spiders…"

"You think they're misrepresented too?"

"No. I just don't have any spider-based films. How about… clowns?"

"I never got the whole clown thing," Jamie said, reclining back on the bed.

"Me either. I know it's meant to be something to do with the way they look? Like, your brain registers features that are human but not quite and that unsettles them. Plus, you know, Stephen King really messed things up for clowns."

"There goes that career path for me. Damn you, Stephen!"

"Although… Pennywise wasn't actually a clown, was he?"

"No…. wasn't he a giant turtle or something?"

"How do you pass your exams with a memory that bad?"

"Sorry for not having an encyclopaedic knowledge of every horror movie ever," Jamie said with a roll of his eyes. "And while we're crossing films off you can take Rosemary's Baby, Suspiria, The Wicker Man and Children of the Corn out of there too."

"You really are no fun. Do you want me to take Hot Fuzz out as well since that's got a bloody cult in it?"

"Look normally I'm all for a night of horror movie madness and I will admit that pounding Tucker's face into the pavement did make me feel a bit better, but unfortunately I am still concerned about the cult that is currently active in our town and planning on doing something nasty with Eden and her baby."

"Who? Oh… right, the forest girl… why do you care about what happens to her?"

"Because I'm not completely heartless?"

"That's not what I meant and you know it. Your concern for her goes way beyond normal concern for a stranger. So what's your deal?"

She closed the folder and crossed her arm, fixing him with an intense stare. Jamie looked down at his lap, considering his words. He'd spent many hours thinking about the answer to that very question. And deep down he knew the answer.

"She reminds me of Lily."

"She's nothing like Lily. I mean, apart from the blonde hair."

"Did you know… Lily was pregnant when she died…?"

"No, I…" Realisation appeared on Sammy's face and she let out a long sigh as she connected the dots. "I get it. You see a young, vulnerable pregnant girl… and you think that if you can protect her, you're somehow making it up to Lily. Is that it?"

"Something like that…" he admitted.

"That girl is not Lily. She is not your responsibility. And if this cult is after her, then maybe leaving her alone is the best option for you!"

"I can't… I have to help her… it's my fault…" Jamie said, looking away from Sammy and gazing pensively at the flickering flame of a nearby candle.

"You don't have anything to make up or atone for. Lily's death was not your fault. I've told you that, your parents have told you that, your therapist has told you that. What do we have to say for it to sink in?"

"It is my fault though…" he muttered under her breath. No matter how many times people told him he wasn't to blame, he knew it was his fault and that nothing he could do would change that.

"I know I won't be able to change your mind… but I do have an idea that might help."

She put the DVD folder away and lay on her stomach to retrieve something from under the bed. She came out with a wooden box, sealed with a small padlock. Jamie watched curiously as Sammy unlocked the box and picked up something flat and rectangular from inside. It was only when she returned to the bed and placed the object between them that he saw what it was.

"A Ouija board? Are you fucking kidding me, Sammy?"

"Yeah I know it's weird and stupid but I thought that maybe if you could talk to Lily, you might be able to get some kind of… closure and maybe she could tell you that it's not your fault. Besides, it's Samhain, it's the perfect night for it."

"Is this more of your witchy nonsense?"

"Cults, possibly satanic creatures you're fine with, but witches? That's going too far?" Sammy said, tone dripping with sarcasm.

"Well if witches are too far, then ghosts definitely are. Besides, aren't you always saying that Ouija boards are dangerous and not to be messed with?"

"Yes… but that's because people are stupid. If anyone is going to mess with this stuff, I'm probably one of the best people to do it."

Jamie didn't say anything. He was conflicted, reluctant to receive actual acknowledgement of what he'd done but more afraid not to have the opportunity to talk to Lily again. And maybe, on the slim chance, they actually managed to talk to something, he might be able to get some answers about… whatever had been bothering Callie. He sighed and nodded.

"Fine. I'll do it. But if we don't hear anything, and we won't, then you let me decide what is best for me."

"Deal."

Sammy gestured for them to move off the bed, settling on the floor instead where the board could lie flat. She placed the planchette on the board before sprinkling a ring of salt around them. Jamie raised an eyebrow and tried not to roll his eyes. Sammy sat down opposite him, placing her fingers on the edge of the planchette, glaring at Jamie until he did the same.

She closed her eyes and took a few long slow breaths, clearing her mind.

"Hello… I am reaching out to any spirits that may be present. We wish to communicate with you"

"I can't believe you're actually doing this…" Jamie mumbled. Sammy ignored him.

"If there is anyone with us, please make your presence known."

They were both silent, eyes resting on the planchette. It didn't move. Jamie opened his mouth to say something but Sammy gave him a venomous look that made him close it again. She focused on the planchette.

"Please, if there are any spirits here, make yourself known."

Nothing.

"Can I say I told you so yet?" Jamie asked, removing his hands and getting up.

"No, because if you do, I will hit you. I knew it was a long shot... I just wanted to help," she said with a defeated sigh.

They decamped from the floor and returned to the bed. After a few minutes they settled on a film and the two of them curled up around one another. Sammy rested her head on his shoulder, the pair quietly content in each other's arms, limbs entwined. From the street below came the sound of laughter and playful shrieks, the younger residents of Sarum Vale tucked up in bed leaving the streets free for the high schoolers.

On the floor, the planchette twitched. It was the smallest of movements, one that would have gone unnoticed even if anyone had been watching the board. Jamie yawned, toying with Sammy's hair.

"Hey, Jay...?" Sammy said sleepily.

"Yeah?"

"Please don't do anything stupid..." She tilted her head to meet his eye. "I don't want anything to happen... don't want to lose you..."

As she spoke, her eyes slid over to the Ouija board, discarded on the floor. The planchette moved again, gliding across the wood in a slow movement. Sammy bit her lip before turning away once more, an intense feeling of guilt twisting her stomach into knots. She closed her eyes, moving her head to Jamie's chest so her ears were filled with the gentle thrum of his heartbeat.

In the streets of Sarum Vale, the houses were quiet, the world was sleeping peacefully. Candles shone from inside jack o'lanterns, casting distorted shadows across the ground. The cat watched from Jamie's window, trembling softly.

Far below, the darkness began to come alive. Slim tendrils of inky blackness inched from the shadows, creeping across the ground towards the houses. They moved with a squirming leechlike action, spreading out like a stain.

Reaching the nearest of the houses, the creatures began to clamber up the walls. If anyone had happened to pass by they would have been unable to distinguish them from the moss that clung to the bricks. Maybe someone might have stopped, confused by the motion but they would easily have disregarded it as something else.

The sound of footsteps resonated on the streets and the faded imprints of feet appeared on the snow, there for just a moment before disappearing once again. Up by the window of one of the houses, the creatures gathered, peering through the frosted glass. They moved on quickly enough, losing interest and passed onto the next house. Their movements were silent but on the street, a sound like water lapping against a shore could be heard, the many voices of the whispers speaking as one.

They continued along the street, spreading out, a hostile wave that left whatever living thing they encountered singed and dying slowly.

An excited noise, something akin to the squeal of a rodent, came from one of the windows and the creatures flocked to their brethren to see what had been found. Through the glass, the room of a young girl was visible. In the bed, she lay sleeping peacefully, about nine years old with light brown hair. One of the slithering shadows oozed through a crack between the glass and the frame, worming its way across the room to where the girl slept.

It inched along the covers, seeking out a place that was warm and dark. It crawled up across her cheek, feeling warm breath wafting from her slightly parted lips. The creature toyed with her lip for a moment before moving its focus to her nostril, probing the skin lightly. The girl let out a sleepy grumble, batting at the intrusive presence half-heartedly before relaxing once more. The creature paused for a moment, waiting for her to fall completely still before resuming its gentle investigation. When the girl showed no further sign of movement, it probed once again at her nostril then dived up the narrow passage, disappearing into the nasal cavity. The girl jerked upright, spluttering furiously as it wormed its way up inside her skull.

The girl stopped moving abruptly. The veins in her eyes darkened slowly and her pupils dilated. Her body stiffened and she rose from the bed. Silently the child crossed the room and opened the door. The house was dark and as the girl passed her parent's room she stopped, looking over at their bed where they lay sleeping. Then she continued down the stairs.

She prowled through the house, actions stiff and jerky. Her first target was the kitchen, ghosting across the tiles, pausing only to select a knife from the block on the counter before moving on. For a moment she stopped in the hall, eyes scanning the space in search of something. Evidently, she didn't find it or decided against conducting a full search, as she turned to the front door and left the house. Her feet were bare and she wore only a nightie but didn't react to the cold as she walked down the street, resolute in her path.

Across town, a similar scene was being played out as the shadows locked onto their prey. Five girls left their houses, walked through the snow and gathered obediently at the town square. The luxury apartments overlooked them, the town hall stood monolithic behind them. The girls lined up beneath a large tree that stood in the centre of the square, each clutching an object: the knife and five lengths of rope.

# REQUEST FOR DOMESTIC VIOLENCE RESTRAINING ORDER

## APPLICANTS DETAILS

Surname: Alexander

Forename: Helen

Address: 12 Robin Way, Redwood

Occupation: Music teacher (part-time)

Nature of relationship with person who committed act of domestic violence: Spouse

## RESPONDENTS DETAILS

Surname: Alexander

Forename: Russell

Address: 12 Robin Way, Redwood

Occupation: Mechanic

## EXTENSION OF ORDER TO ADDITIONAL PEOPLE

| Name | Age | Sex | Live with you? |
| --- | --- | --- | --- |
| Lily Isabelle Alexander *(Daughter)* | 15 | Female | Yes |
| Daniel Steven Alexander *(Son)* | 13 | Male | Yes |
| Jamie Anthony Alexander *(Son)* | 5 | Male | Yes |

# XXVII

The sound of shouting woke Jamie. He struggled into a sitting position, tangled in the covers and many silk scarves that Sammy kept draped across her bed. Sammy was asleep beside him, tucked under the covers and dressed in Jamie's shirt. He nudged her, ruffling his hair and rubbing his eyes as he tried to separate himself from the bed.

"Wha…?" Sammy mumbled. Despite the sound, she gave no other indication of waking, wrapping herself tighter in the duvet. "'s too early."

Jamie sighed and gave her a hard shove, catapulting her onto the bed with a thump. Before she could voice too much annoyance, Jamie freed himself from the bed and went over to the window. Down in the square, a crowd had gathered. Most were still in their nightclothes and their attention was fixed on something. It took a moment for Jamie to work out what they were looking at and once he did, he wished he hadn't.

"Sammy," he said, cutting into his friend's irate monologue.

"What is it?" she asked, getting up and coming to join him by the window. She let out a soft gasp as she registered the scene below.

Perched precariously in the branches of the tree in the centre of the square were five girls. Each had a noose around their neck, attached to a higher branch. Whenever anyone took a step towards them, they would move to jump from the branches, their actions perfectly synchronised. A small contingent of police officers were trying to control the frantic crowd and coax the girls down from a safe distance.

Jamie and Sammy watched from the window, horrified but unable to look away. Jamie grasped Sammy's hand, unsure if the act was designed to comfort her or himself. Below there was a sharp cry and a woman broke from the group, sprinting towards the girls. The officers made to restrain her but they were too late. As one, the girls stepped from the branches. Their bodies plummeted, the ropes went taut and silence fell.

The girls hung there. Two of them were lucky, their necks snapping instantly and sparing them a dragged out death while the others choked and kicked, one clawing at her throat in a momentary attempt to free herself.

For a moment, no one moved or spoke, paralysed as the five bodies hung from the tree. Then the screaming started. The assembled group erupted into chaos, rushing to free the girls and try to save them. By the time they reached the tree, the girls had fallen still, eyes staring blankly out at the snow. Sammy buried her face in Jamie's chest and he clutched her tight.

Over the next few hours, the town square and the area around it were placed in a state of lockdown. The residents of the apartment block were asked to remain inside while the bodies were removed from the tree and the area searched. Despite the best efforts of the officers, word spread very quickly. The town radio station began to broadcast the news, the online version of the local paper began posting and a video, crudely shot on someone's phone, began to circulate.

Kane, who lived in the block a few doors down from Sammy, went out to examine the bodies. They were laid out in the snow beneath the tree, cut down but still wearing the loop of rope around their necks. It hadn't been difficult to identify them and while the police interviewed the parents, Kane began his examination.

The first thing he noticed was the blood. Each girl had splatters, long dried, on one side of their body, clustered around their left hand. Turning their hands over, Kane found the reason. Each had something carved into their palm, crudely done and encrusted with blood. The first had a symbol, the same as the one found on the cult victims, almost like a signature to the crime. The other four girls possessed a letter each which spelt out the word S-T-O-P.

Kane grimaced. Most killers were content to taunt the police by mail.

He took a few quick pictures to refer to later before continuing. He was searching for injuries, defensive wounds, anything that would indicate the situation had been created by force. The bodies, with the exception of their palms, were largely unmarked. There were some mild cuts and bruises on the girls' feet but there was no sign of anything to suggest a struggle had taken place.

The police chief approached Kane, who straightened up to greet him.

"Morning Kane. Sorry to get you up so early."

"Hey, I'm used to it. You don't control when people die."

"What are we dealing with here?"

"Well, it doesn't look like they were forced up there. It's strange… they've got cuts on their hand that clearly seem to be intended as a message. And it implicates the same killer, or killers, as the bodies found in the woods but… everything else points to the girls acting of their own free will."

"You think five nine-year-olds decided to carve up their palms and hang themselves?" The police chief's expression was one of annoyed disbelief. Clearly, he had already made his mind up of what had actually happened.

"I'm not saying that. I'm just telling you what the condition of the bodies is indicating. Was there any sign of forced entry at the homes?" Kane asked pointedly.

"No," admitted the chief.

"Well then, that combined with the condition of their feet, the lack of injuries and the fact that half the town watched them jump out of the tree with a noose around their necks, rather than waiting to be helped down, I think suicide might just be a possibility." Kane's voice had grown louder as he spoke and people were craning their necks to look over at the two of them. "Unless you have a better suggestion? Sir?"

The chief stood there for a minute, unused to anger from the usually reserved and soft-spoken mortician.

"You can go home Kane," he said finally. "Thank you for your help."

Kane stalked off, irritated. The examination over, the bodies would be removed for the families to bury. Bagged up, no one was there to see the viscous black fluid that began to drip slowly from the nose, the eyes and the ears of the dead girls.

*****

306

A peculiar atmosphere settled over the town in the days that followed the hangings. Death, particularly that of a child, would always be difficult to handle but ordinarily, it would only really be seen to affect the family and close friends. After the hangings, it felt like the entire town was in mourning, trapped in limbo. No one knew what to do with themselves. Most of the businesses were closed, the schools had granted their students a few days leave. Only a handful of places in town were still open.

The bodies had been removed, the rope stripped from the tree and the knife found in the snow nearby. A toxicology report found the girls' blood clear of anything that may have aided their death or prompted the behaviour. The police had no choice but to officially rule it as a suicide, leaving the town perplexed. No one could imagine a nine-year-old committing suicide or even having a reason to want to, let alone five of them doing it at once.

The hangings were weighing heavily on Jamie's mind. Not only had the image of the girls dangling from the tree ingrained itself into his brain and joined the parade of nightmares he endured nightly, something else was niggling at the back of his head. It wasn't until the newspaper published the story that he realised what it was.

He was sat on the floor of his bedroom, looking at the paper. The front pages of the paper were devoted to a recounting of the incident and an extended obituary of the five girls. This included individual pictures of them, smiling happily, and a class photo. Seeing the girls clustered together in a picture that he recognised made it seem obvious. Brown hair, roughly the same shade and length. Hazel eyes. Nine years old. He knew a sixth girl who shared that description. Callie.

As that sank in, he knew with absolute certainty that the message had been meant for him.

Five more deaths to add to your list…

Might as well have tied the noose yourself…

"It's not my fault," Jamie said, crumpling the paper. "I'd already stopped. They did this, not me."

He repeated the words, trying to get rid of the guilt that had begun to churn in the pit of his stomach.

*You should listen…*

*Do what you're told…*

*Stay away from all of them…*

*You'll just end up hurting them like everyone else…*

*Better yet, you should leave.*

*Or kill yourself.*

*Then you know you won't get them hurt.*

*Your life is worthless.*

*Do the world a favour.*

The door to Jamie's room opened in time for Sammy to see Jamie hurling the crumpled newspaper at the wall.

"What did print journalism ever do to you?" she asked. Jamie frowned.

"How'd you get in here?"

He wasn't upset to see his friend, just perplexed as both his parents were at work and Callie was in bed meaning no one was around to let her in.

"You guys really need to lock your back door," she said. "Anyone could wander in."

"And then Echo would raise the alarm," Jamie said. Sammy swivelled her gaze to the dog in question, sprawled out on his back, fast asleep.

"I'm sure an intruder would quake in fear at the sight of him," she said with a roll of her eyes. "Hell, I think that mangy cat you picked up could do more damage than your dog."

As if to prove her point, the cat hissed at her and sprinted under the bed.

"No one knows that we don't lock it except you," Jamie pointed out, closing his eyes and leaning back to rest his head against the side of the bed.

Sammy shrugged and murmured something under her breath as she seated herself beside Jamie. She looked over at him expectantly and he could feel her gaze burning into him. He opened one eye.

"What?" he asked.

"You're in a mood. What's going on?"

"Nothing," he said, opening his eyes fully.

"Jamie, in all the time you've known me, when have I ever accepted that as an answer?"

Jamie let out a long sigh. He wanted to tell Sammy his fears but something stopped him. He shouldn't get her involved. And she'd only tell him more of the same – stay away from Eden, don't tell anyone what he saw, act normal.

"I had a fight with my dad, that's all," he lied.

"About what?" Sammy probed.

"My friendship was Eden." He was surprised how easy it was to lie to her. Normally she would have seen right through him. "I mean, I've not seen her since… well… anyway, I think he was just in a bad mood and looking for an easy target."

"That's really unfair… I mean, I get that he's going through stuff and I'm sure being a cop right now is far from pleasant… but he shouldn't take it out on you, no matter how tired or stressed he is."

"You're preaching to the choir, Sam."

"I heard she's getting released tomorrow. That's probably not helping matters," Sammy said.

"Who'd you hear that from?" Jamie asked, frowning. He'd not heard anything about Eden's release date.

"My mom. She went out with one of the doctors last night… Dr Matting I think she said," Sammy replied with a shrug of her shoulders, voice disinterested.

"Is there anyone in town she isn't dating?"

"You. And I know she wants to."

"Shut up!" Jamie said, giving her a playful shove.

"I'm serious! She's always asking when you're coming over and talking about how cute you are. Honestly, she's such a cougar!"

Jamie couldn't keep from laughing, blushing a little, but as it died he found himself feeling a little awkward. It felt like something had shifted between the two of them and he wasn't entirely sure what, but it felt incredibly uncomfortable.

"So are you going to… see her? Eden, I mean? Before she's release or when she gets let out?" There was a hint of judgement in Sammy's voice and Jamie fidgeted beside her.

"I don't know… I guess. I mean, it would probably be good for her to have a familiar face if she's going somewhere strange… I'm not sure…"

Sammy was watching him and the discomfort in the air was building. Jamie picked at his jeans, unwilling to look at her. Sensing something was wrong but for once deciding not to push the matter, Sammy gave Jamie a light hug and got to her feet.

"I have to get to the radio station for my shift. I just wanted to check in, make sure you were okay."

"I'm fine Sammy… I'm always fine…" he said, looking down at the floor. Sammy hesitated, on the verge of saying something, but decided against it and left the room. Jamie closed his eyes and listened, hearing the sound of the back door closing followed by the roar of a bike engine.

The cat poked its head out from under the bed and mewed softly, before clambering onto Jamie's lap. He stroked its head absently, eyes still closed. He wasn't sure about seeing Eden. Every time he saw her, something crazy seemed to happen and it was exhausting to deal with. Besides, the very clear threat to Callie was playing on his mind and if seeing Eden would provoke an attack on her, or even on some other innocent person, he wasn't prepared to take that chance.

Echo woke abruptly and barked, something catching his ears. Jamie opened his eyes in time to see the dog run over to the window, standing on his hind legs in an effort to see out. The cat mewed and leapt from its seat, streaking across the floor and jumping up onto the window ledge to peer down at the drive. Jamie rolled his eyes, assuming the animals were just being odd, but when they didn't leave the window he got up and went over to see what had drawn their attention.

At first, Jamie wasn't entirely sure that his eyes were working right. A strange misshapen creature was standing beneath his window and despite the darkness, he could see that it was looking up at him. The body was humanoid, hunched over but still taller than any person he'd ever seen, arms extended to exaggerated lengths and ended with three long fingers that curved into wicked claws. The head was that of a deer, a bare skull with antlers jutting out, its neck and shoulders were covered with thick black fur.

The cat hissed and scratched at the window angrily. The creature didn't move, just continued to stare up at Jamie. His heartbeat quickened and he stepped back, trying to keep his actions slow and steady like he would when faced with an angry animal. He pulled the curtains closed until only a slither of the street was visible.

He couldn't forget that it, whatever it was, was out there but he could pretend. In his head, he saw the house surrounded by the beasts, drawing closer. Echo barked and whimpered, retreating from the window. Jamie stood there for a moment, his mind racing and trying to figure out his next move. There was only one... and as long as it was out where he could see it, he wasn't in any danger.

*But what if there's more? They could be surrounding you...*

From downstairs, he thought he heard a floorboard creak. His entire body stiffened, straining his ears.

Another creak.

Jamie flew in action. There was no thought behind what he did, he moved solely on instinct, dashing out of the room and down the hall to Callie's room. He scooped her out of her bed, waking her in the process. She let out a sleepy groan, eyes flickering open. Jamie barely noticed, trying to determine his next move. He didn't want to move Callie and put at risk, but his room had a lock on it and hers didn't.

"Jay...?" she mumbled, still half asleep.

Jamie put a finger to his lips and carried her out of the room, moving as quickly as he could across the hall. He kicked the door firmly shut and balanced Callie awkwardly in one arm so that he could lock the door. Callie had woken up fully by this point and was struggling, scared by his erratic behaviour. Jamie set her down carefully, looking around anxiously as though expecting one of the horrific creatures to materialise in the room.

*What's going on?* she signed frantically.

*We need to stay quiet!*

Jamie's paranoia had kicked into overdrive, every groan or grumble in the house made him imagine some new horror coming to get them. The cat started to yowl and dashed to the bedroom door, scratching at the wood. He ignored the animal and went over to the window, tweaking the curtain to peer out.

The monster was gone.

For a moment, Jamie didn't know if he should feel relieved. Then he heard the steady thud-thud-creak of someone coming up the stairs. Jamie turned sharply. Callie was staring at the door, her hearing aid now in, the colour draining from her face as she registered the noise.

Making a split-second decision, Jamie took her hand and led Callie to his wardrobe. The pair of them climbed inside, Echo sprinting to join them, and Jamie pulled the door shut behind them with a light click. Sitting in the darkness, he was hyperaware of Callie's ragged breathing. Echo whimpered, nuzzling against the two of them nervously.

"Jamie… I'm scared…" whispered Callie. "What's going on?"

Jamie hesitated. He didn't want to make things worse for her or scare her further. His mind went to Lily, an image forming. Tucked away in a darkened space, clutching a young boy in her arms while shouts and screams came from outside. She covered his ears, trying to make him feel just a little bit safer.

Swallowing his fear, Jamie forced himself to keep his voice calm and steady.

"I promise Callie, you don't need to be scared. I won't let anyone hurt you. But, we need to stay here for a bit and keep very quiet. You trust me?"

"Yes…" Her voice was barely a squeak but there was no doubt in her tone.

"Take out your hearing aid, close your eyes and hold onto me."

Handshaking, Callie removed her hearing aid and handed it over to Jamie. She closed her eyes and lay down as best she could in the narrow space, her head on Jamie's leg. He stroked her hair gently, wishing he could block everything out as well. The thudding had stopped and instead, strains of grunting and growling were drifting from the other side of Jamie's door. A grating scraping scratching noise could be heard as whatever it was clawed at the wood, trying to find a way in.

Jamie screwed his eyes shut, feeling scared tears beginning to run down his cheek. He clutched Callie tightly, his lips forming words that no one could hear. The noises from the hall got louder and louder. The hand that wasn't stroking Callie's hair clenched, gripping the side of his leg, digging his fingers into the flesh.

There was a loud bang, a cracking sound followed by the splintering of wood. Heavy footfall echoed through the room and a scraping sound like something sharp was being dragged across the walls. The cat let out a piercing howl and then fell silent. The footsteps paused and then approached the wardrobe.

*I'm going to die...* Jamie thought. *I'm going to die.*

Agency Name: Redwood Police Department

Date Generated: November 15th

Domestic Population at time of report: 11,912

Report Generated by: Carlton, David

| Offense | Number Reported | Number Recorded previously |
|---|---|---|
| Homicide | 259 | 144 |
| Abduction | 1,339 | 1,001 |
| Sexual Assault | 218 | 276 |
| Physical Assault | 162 | 184 |
| Harassment | 91 | 73 |
| Burglary | 46 | 42 |
| Destruction | 26 | 47 |
| Vandalism | 182 | 159 |
| Possession | 33 | 75 |

# XXVIII

Eden was awake with the sunrise. Something was different and although she didn't know what, she could feel a change in the air. Dr Cantrell was on duty when she woke, something that relieved her. Dr Knott made her uncomfortable, but at least he was fairly distant during the majority of his shifts. Dr Matting seemed to take delight in pushing her and making her squirm.

When she padded out into the hallway where Dr Cantrell was seated, he gave her a bright smile.

"Good morning Eden. How are you this morning?"

No matter how silent or strange Eden was, Dr Cantrell always treated her like an actual person rather than a dangerous animal and the more time she spent with him and with Jamie, the more normal she began to feel.

Eden gave him a shy smile and sat beside him. He pulled a book from his bag and gestured to it.

"Shall we continue? We've got a little bit of time."

As Dr Cantrell had the morning shift quite often and Eden struggled to sleep once the sun had risen, having grown accustomed to the darkness, he had taken to reading to her. He was hoping it might encourage her efforts to communicate and, while he had no idea if she understood what he was saying or what was going on in the story, she seemed to enjoy listening to his voice.

"There seemed to be no end to this wood, and no beginning, and no difference in it, and, worse of all, no way out," Dr Cantrell began to read. Eden watched him intently, her lips twitching slightly as she shaped the words in an effort to make sense of them.

There was a dreamy atmosphere in the ward corridor, the two of them caught up in their own little bubble and for a time it felt like there was no one else in the world but them.

Then the door was pushed open so hard that it struck the walls and bounced back. Dr Knott came in, accompanied by Eden's social worker.

"Sorry, are we interrupting?" he asked, raising an eyebrow. "I was expecting her to be ready to go?"

"We lost track of time," Dr Cantrell said unapologetically. "I'll get her dressed. It will take a few minutes."

"Good. We want to make the best impression we can."

Dr Cantrell barely suppressed a roll of his eyes as he ushered Eden out of the hallway and back into her room to dress her. The handful of clothes she had had been donated by locals and hadn't taken long to pack the night before. As Dr Cantrell gathered the clothes for that day, Eden seated herself on the bed, looking around with sad eyes. The doctor paused and looked over at her.

"You know what's going on?" he asked.

She looked back at him and inclined her head before looking away. Dr Cantrell touched her shoulder and gave her what he hoped was a comforting smile.

"It'll be okay. This a good thing, I promise."

Eden chewed her lip but decided to trust him. She didn't have many people that she allowed herself to trust and she couldn't really afford to turn away the ones she had. Instead, she allowed the doctor to dress her and escort her out of the ward. He had intended to hand her over to the social worker but she clung to him so he ended up staying with her until the group reached the parking lot and Eden had been loaded into the car.

He watched the car head away and couldn't help shaking his head. Despite what he'd said to Eden, the entire situation felt wrong to him and he couldn't really believe that it had all been arranged quite so quickly. It just seemed rushed and... off.

As she was driven away, Eden craned her neck round to look at Dr Cantrell, watching as he faded from view. When he had completely disappeared from sight, she shrunk down in her seat. The feeling of the car vibrating underneath her was uncomfortable, everything about the machine turned her stomach. The social worker was babbling happily about her new home, how this was the start of something positive for her. With each cliché, Eden retreated further inside her head. Sometimes when things had gotten really bad, she would feel herself drift out of her own body into somewhere safer.

316

The car wound slowly through the snowy streets before pulling up outside the Knight house. The social worker left the car and knocked at the door. Eden peered out of the window, her mind automatically trying to link the building to the murky soup of memories in the back of her brain. She shivered, even though the heating was on, and pressed herself against the fabric of the seat, wishing it would absorb her into it.

Mr Knight had emerged from the house and was talking to the social worker, occasionally glancing over at the car. In an upstairs window, Faith peeked out from behind a curtain.

Finishing her conversation, the social worker returned to the car and opened the door.

"Eden, are you ready to see your new home?" she asked kindly.

Eden whimpered and tried to clamber further away from the open door, impossible in the confined space. The social worker took her hand and gently eased her out of the car, steering her up the path to the house. Mr Knight smiled at Eden.

"Hello, Eden. I'm your Uncle Nicholas. Come on inside and we'll get you settled in." He paused and looked over at the social worker. "Do you want to come with us?"

"No, I'll be on my way. But I'll be back in a few days to check that everything is going well. You have my number in the meantime."

Mr Knight nodded and put a hand on Eden's back, guiding her inside. She stiffened at the contact and let out a sound akin to a growl. Mr Knight either didn't hear or didn't care as he kept his hand firmly in place.

"Faith!" he called. "Come down here!"

There was a pause, the creak of a bedroom door being swung open and the patter of light feet before Faith appeared at the top of the stairs. She gave a tentative smile, tugging anxiously at her sleeve before giving a shy wave.

"Show Eden to her room," Mr Knight prompted, removing his hand from Eden's back. She immediately distanced herself, heading up the stairs to join Faith who led her to a small room at the end of the corridor, tucked away from the other rooms. She pushed the door opened to reveal a room with a small fold-out bed against one wall, a small set of drawers and no other furniture.

"Sorry, it's a bit small," Faith said quietly. "It used to be dad's office… but all the furniture got put into storage… I used some of my best bedding though to try and make it nice for you and you can borrow my books and things."

Eden smiled slightly and sat down on the bed. Her hands lightly caressed her stomach. There had been no aches or pains for a while now, no movement either. She welcomed the respite. Faith leant against the door frame, head bowed so that her messy brown hair hung down and obscured her eyes. A large bruise was visible on the curve of her throat.

"Umm… do you want me to show you around?" Faith asked, feeling a little awkward. Eden's eyes were fixed on her and the unblinking stare was intimidating.

Without waiting for any kind of response, Faith left the room and went to her own. Eden followed obediently. Upon entering the bedroom, the first thing she felt was an unmistakable aura of sadness throughout the space. Despite Faith being a teenager, the walls were decorated as they had been when she was a child, the paint peeling in places and the shelves on one side of the room clustered with battered stuffed animals. There were a few objects that were clearly new, a CD player, a laptop, a TV, some other scattered odds and ends, clearly expensive. They all seemed to be untouched, the condition pristine, and they looked awkward amongst everything else.

Eden went over to the shelves, running her fingers over the matted fur of the toys. The shelves, the ornaments dotted around had a layer of dust on them.

"That was your side of the room," said Faith. "All the furniture was left there for ages after you… went. A lot of that stuff was yours, they only really got rid of your bed… if you want some of that stuff, you can help yourself."

Eden picked up a small teddy bear, stroking it affectionately. The glassy eyes of the bear looked back at her earnestly and the painted irises seemed to hold secrets within them. Memories clung to its fur like a layer of dust. The things it had been witness too…

Clutching the teddy, Eden went to the bedroom window and looked out. The garden was overgrown, a rusted swing set erect in the centre, thick with cobwebs. As she looked down at it, for a moment Eden swore she could hear laughter, a child's happy voice, a dog barking.

Then silence.

*****

The silence was eating at him, driving him insane.

Jamie had spent the night curled up inside the wardrobe, ears straining for any sound that might indicate the monster was still on the other side. At times it had quietened and he'd almost dared to push open the door, only for it to let out a grunt, a growl. The wardrobe door hadn't opened, although the doorknob had rattled as the beast struggled to work its long-clawed fingers around it. Jamie had held his breath, covering Callie's mouth to stifle hers and prayed to whoever cared to listen that it wouldn't find a way in.

Eventually, it had stopped trying but had continued to shamble around the room. As the sun had risen, Jamie became aware that the room had been silent for a long stretch of time. He fidgeted in the confined space, reaching out to open the door just a little. Callie, who had somehow managed to fall asleep during one of the lulls in activity, woke with a start, looking around frantically for signs of attack. Jamie tapped her hand lightly, reaffirming his presence and her safety. He gestured for her to keep quiet before lightly pushing the door. It inched open.

No noise. No sign that the monster was there. Heart in his throat, he struggled to his feet, his muscles screaming after hours of confinement. Callie grasped at his trouser leg, unwilling to let him go or be left behind.

*It's okay.*

It wasn't okay. Nothing about the situation was remotely okay. But what else could he say to her?

Jamie pushed the door more firmly so that it swung wide, allowing him to see the room in its entirety. No monster. He stepped out of the wardrobe, eyes sweeping from one side of the space to another. The creature was gone, but there were signs of its presence. Deep gouges ran across the ceiling where its antlers had scraped, flakes of plaster were dotted across the floor. Large bloody marks were visible on the furniture, muddy prints showed its path, and dangling from the light fitting was the mangled corpse of a hare.

Callie let out a squeak, shadowing Jamie out of the wardrobe. He took her hand and the pair of them walked through the house. He wasn't sure what they were looking for, damage, further proof that the night's events were real, or signs that the monster might still be lurking. The downstairs was largely undamaged, just a few muddy footprints and some minor scratches to the walls and ceiling. The back door was open, swinging lightly in the breeze.

Jamie approached it warily and pulled it tight shut. Callie tugged at his sleeve to get his attention.

*Are we safe?*

He wanted to say yes and tell her the monster was gone and never coming back but… he just couldn't.

*For now.*

*Will it come back?*

*I don't know.*

*Should we tell mommy and daddy?*

Jamie paused. He imagined how that conversation would go and blanched slightly. They'd throw him in the looney bin for sure… even with the scrapes on the wall and ceiling, they'd never believe his version of the events. After all, monsters weren't real.

*No.*

*What do we do?*

*I'm going to protect us.*

Even though his heart was beating frantically, his hands were steady. He would protect her, protect their home.

They set about tidying the house as best they could. There was a lingering smell in the air, like damp leaves and wet fur that made Jamie want to gag every time he breathed in. It took him a while to get the hare down from the light fitting and as he held the rigid creature he had to fight the urge to vomit. He bagged the poor animal up and threw it in the garbage before washing his hands thoroughly. Callie watched him, her eyes wide and nervous. Looking at her broke his heart, seeing how terrified she was, the way she jumped at every tiny noise. It reminded him of how he used to be…

"Let's get you out of the house for a bit, yeah?" he suggested. He got her dressed and took her into town to the leisure centre. There was a crèche there and she'd be okay for an hour or so while he figured out what he was going to do. He had no way of knowing if the… thing was going to come back or if something worse would take its place. He needed to prepare.

Once he'd safely deposited Callie, he found himself stood in the town square, now reopened, staring into space. He had no idea where to start. How did you fight back against something that you didn't know what it was?

A nearby shop caught his eye and he felt his feet begin to carry him towards it. It was a store he'd been in many times before, usually with his dad. It sold hunting supplies, tents, fishing equipment, weapons…

Technically speaking, Jamie owned a gun already. However, it was kept at his uncle's house most of the time. If he was armed, he could protect Callie, but he knew there was no chance of him being able to buy one. His uncle worked there part-time and the owner was friends with his father so he couldn't bluff his age. Maybe he could swipe his one? He knew where his uncle kept them and he usually went on holiday for the winter… it was a possibility.

In the window of the store was a taxidermy deer, staring out with glass eyes. Jamie shuddered, looking at the sharp curve of its antlers. He had to do something.

A rich warm smell wafted to his nostrils, reminiscent of spiced apples. Jamie turned his head, nostrils twitching. His eyes fell on a ramshackle shop, half-tucked away down a side street. There was a small panelled window next to an old fashioned wooden door, a stained glass window set in the centre. A sign was fixed over the window, hand-painted with neat gold lettering, too small to read from a distance. He headed over, curiosity peaked, to see what the sign said.

Est Magickae.

He grimaced. There weren't many shops in Sarum Vale but he'd probably walked passed this one hundreds of times in his life without paying any attention to it. He knew it existed, Sammy occasionally shopped there when she'd used up one of her thousands of candles, but he'd always steadfastly refused to go with her.

Jamie pushed open the door, sending a little bell ringing merrily. The inside was small, full of wooden shelves crammed with bottles, jars and boxes. A narrow counter divided the space with an old fashioned register on it and a small altar with incense and candles at one end. A birdcage stood proudly in one corner, a rack of dried herbs and spices was tucked behind the counter with a young woman with dark hair was in the process of organising them. As he approached, she turned and smiled warmly.

"Good morning. What can I help you with today?"

"I'm not sure you can… I just sort of…"

"Wandered in? We get a lot of that. And you didn't look like our normal type of customer," she said with a smile. "Can I offer you a tea?"

"I guess…" The woman busied herself with cups and an old fashioned teapot as Jamie seated himself on an old stool positioned by the counter. He looked over at the birdcage where two birds were perched, one red and the other a vibrant blue. "That's a cardinal, right?"

"Yes," said the woman, placing a teacup in front of him. "And the other is a blue jay. They promote a good atmosphere." She seated herself opposite him and smiled. "My name is Iris."

"Jamie."

"And what is troubling you, Jamie?"

"Who says something is troubling me?"

"Well, ordinarily there are three reasons people come in here. Besides, the ones who are actually practitioners I mean. Curiosity is the most common. Teenagers come in for a joke or a dare. The second reason is to ask us to post flyers about missing pets."

"And the third?"

"Need. Those who need help find their way here. So tell me, what is it you need?"

Jamie was silent for a long time, stirring his tea, eyes fixed on the swirling liquid.

"I don't believe in this stuff... but I don't know if I have any other choice right now. Last night something attacked me and my sister. It broke into our home and terrorised us. And it's not the first time... I mean, it's the first time that anything's broken in but... my sister keeps saying there's a monster in the house and sometimes... I see things... hear whispers..."

"Can you tell me more?"

Jamie nodded slowly. He began to talk, explaining everything that he could think of that might be involved. The smell of the incense in the air and the warm tea before him was soothing and he found it surprisingly easy to tell Iris everything. As he spoke, she began to gather items and started working on something on the counter, but still listening intently. As Jamie finished his recount and lapsed into silence, he peered over to see what she was doing.

"It sounds like you are being targeted by something. I... cannot say what, but... I know that some practitioners in this town are not as inclined to the light as my sister and I. This will provide some protection, against dark magic... I cannot guarantee that it will keep every demon at bay but it should help." She continued, grinding herbs in a mortar.

"Thank you… I appreciate it."

"This is ague weed," she explained, seeing him looking. "Mixed with althea root, basil, cloves, spearmint and a tiny bit of belladonna…"

"Isn't belladonna poisonous?"

"Yes. I tend to avoid using it, except in extreme circumstances." She retrieved a bowl from under the counter, filled with a thick red liquid.

"Is that blood?" Jamie asked, shifting nervously.

"No. Blood magic is… dangerous. There are a few people who use it for good but it's a slippery slope and can lead to a very dark path. This is red wine that's had bloodroot steeped in it. It works in a pinch."

Iris mixed a little of the wine with the powdered mixture, forming a paste, before retrieving two leather cords, each with a small piece of wood and a small gemstone attached. She took the two pieces of wood and used the paste to paint a small symbol on them before setting it aside to dry.

"I'm making you three types of charm. One for your home, one for you and one for your sister." She bottled the rest of the paste and held her hands over the charms. She murmured under her breath and Jamie swore he felt a light breeze. "You put the paste over the doors and windows. The charms you need to wear."

She placed the charms in a small bag and handed them over with a smile.

"Thanks… umm… how much do I owe you?"

"This is on the house. Our community in this town is small and we are supposed to use our magic to grow and to help. I hate to think that someone has broken that rule. However, if you want to give thanks, you can leave an offering for ones of the gods. Maybe one of them will smile on you and help you."

She gestured at the altar where twelve small wooden figures had been placed, intricately designed.

"What do they mean?"

"We have twelve old gods. Each rule over a particular month, particular aspects of our world and our lives. Jakr, the mischief god is ruling currently but really any that speak to you is fine."

Jamie hesitated, eyeing the figures. One was carved to resemble a person with a snake wrapped around his body. The teenager let out a slight shudder but couldn't deny that the totem 'spoke to him', albeit not in the way Iris had intended. He opened his backpack and removed his sketchbook, carefully tearing out one of the drawings he prized the most. He folded it neatly and set it before the figure. Iris was watching him.

"Interesting choice…"

"Sorry, it's probably not what you meant by offering right?"

"The offering is fine. Anything that has value to a person works. But I meant your choice."

"Who is he?"

"His name is Ilon. The God of winter, of the underworld, of death. Most people gravitate towards the figurines linked with things they subconsciously want… luck, wealth, happiness, knowledge… you get the gist. It says a lot about you."

"Good things…?"

"That's for you to determine. Now, you should go. I'm sure you must be exhausted after the night you had."

Jamie nodded, said his goodbyes and left the shop, bag clutched in his hand.

# SARUM VALE GAZETTE

*Wednesday, 19th May*

SANATORIUM IN ASHES

Morningwood Sanatorium lies in ruin following a brutal fire. The fire is believed to have started in the early hours of the morning by a patient of the institute. Although there is no confirmation at this time, authorities believe the patient was notorious murderer Elizabeth Prentice. Prentice was committed to the institute December 26th following the murder of her parents, Isabelle and Stewart Prentice, and her sister Maria.

Authorities responded to the call in the early hours of the morning but were unable to contain the blaze. It is unknown how many staff casualties were sustained during the incident but it has been confirmed that only one patient escaped.

The owner of the building was unavailable for comment and has yet to confirm whether the institute will be rebuilt.

# XXIX

Eden had spent the rest of the day 'adjusting' to her new environment, which largely consisted of her lying on her bed staring into space. She could see faint outlines on the walls where pictures had once hung, indents in the carpet where furniture had stood. She felt out of place in the strange room, a piece of furniture nobody wanted, shoved away out of sight.

When Mr Knight called that it was dinnertime, she rose tentatively and, after hearing Faith leaving her room, she went downstairs. The dining room was the only room in the house that retained all of the original furniture but even though everything fitted into place, it just made Eden feel more at odds with her surroundings. It was like a stage awaiting its performers. She looked around, the ornaments placed with precision, the paint touched up unlike the rest of the house where it was faded and even peeling in places. This room was set up, a formal space that gave the illusion of warmth and functionality.

The three of them took their seats at the table, actors running through a scene without any energy or enthusiasm. Faith was silent, picking at her food while Mr Knight made stilted small talk no one responded to. Eden focused on her plate, consuming every morsel. She knew better than to be picky and in her mind, she still couldn't shake the paranoia that every meal might be her last for a long time, like back in the underground.

"The schools are opening up again tomorrow, you excited to go back Faith?" Mr Knight asked. Faith made a noncommittal noise. "Faith that is not an answer."

"It's school... I'm hardly going to cheerlead over the prospect..." she said quietly.

"Aren't you happy to see your friends?"

"I could have seen them while school was closed."

Mr Knight sighed softly and decided to change tactics. He pasted on a smile and turned his attention to Eden instead.

"We'll have to find something for you to do tomorrow Eden. I know they're arranging some private lessons for you but until that happens...

maybe we can find someone to keep an eye on you... or I guess I'll have to call social services for advice."

Eden made no attempt to even acknowledge Mr Knight, keep her eyes resolutely fixed on her plate. He continued anyway.

"I'm sorry your room is so drab, I'm sure we can furnish it a bit more, especially if you're going to be staying with us for a while. Maybe at the weekend we can go shopping, find some things... maybe get you some new clothes too... something pretty?"

Faith pushed away her plate, barely touched.

"May I be excused?" she asked, already getting to her feet.

"You've hardly eaten anything," her uncle protested.

"I don't feel good..." she mumbled, retreating rapidly from the dining room and into the kitchen. Mr Knight got up and followed her. Eden reached over and took Faith's plate, quickly devouring the contents before abandoning the table.

With the meal was finished, Eden returned to her room. She had grown so accustomed to being limited to one space that the idea of exploring further was alien. Instead, she lay on the bed once more, watching the light change through the window. She heard the buzz of the TV downstairs, running water as Faith got ready for bed, followed by the hum of music from her bedroom. Gradually the sounds were replaced with the creak of floorboards, doors opening and closing and then, as the light faded almost entirely outside her window, so did the sounds of the household until silence reigned. This was how she liked it, when it felt like she was the only person left. The new world she'd been pushed into was too loud, too busy. She treasured the peaceful moments.

The shadows danced across the ceiling, bisected by errant headlights before reforming once more. Eden's eyelids grew heavy as she watched them, the fluid movements soothing, and she found herself drifting off into the swirling grey of her mind.


She wasn't sure if she was in a dream or a memory. She was stood in a park, swings, a slide and a climbing frame visible. The sky was bleak, the trees bare. Children ran nearby, a jumble of brightly coloured coats and hats, cheeks painted scarlet by the breeze which nipped at them playfully. One group were playing with a ball, chasing it like excitable puppies.

She saw not as a participant but as an observer, cut off from everything like she was sealed behind glass and, despite the children's playful movements, all was quiet.

To one side of the park, a young woman was sat on a bench. She had a pushchair, a toddler safely strapped inside, and her eyes were following a young girl, about three years old, in a ladybird red coat and bright green boots.

A man approached the woman and sat beside her. His face was familiar but seemed almost blurry like the features had been crudely erased. The couple were talking… no, arguing. The woman tried to turn away but the man grabbed hold of her wrist.

A flash of red caught Eden's eye and she turned slightly. The girl was watching the couple, her expression mirroring Eden's. She took a step towards the woman, who gestured wildly at her to stay away. The girl's face saddened before she turned away, the ball careening past her and captivating her attention. She ran off to catch it and Eden looked back to the couple. Their argument had grown more animated, the woman gesticulating angrily while the man's body was rigid, tension written across every line.

The man took a deep breath and leaned over, saying something to the woman that made her stiffen. She stood up sharply, looking around frantically. The girl had disappeared from sight, the only sign she had even been there in the first place was a discarded red coat, hung on a tree branch. The man moved closer to the woman and murmured something in her ear before turning and walking away.

The park blurred and faded, glitching in and out. When it steadied, the children were gone. The woman had vanished. Eden looked around. The park was a barren wasteland, the swing moving slowly in the breeze, let out a pained creak as it did so. The soft sound of crying reached her and she turned. Seated against the small fence that enclosed the park was the young girl. She was wearing her green boots, arms wrapped around her legs, sobbing. The more she cried, the darker the sky seemed to grow and the fiercer the wind battering the tiny child became.

A figure emerged from the darkness, approaching the girl. She lifted her head and reached out, inviting the arrival to scoop her up. Warm arms embraced her and carried her away, the sound of her crying fading into the distance.

Eden stirred. Even as her dream faded, the sounds lingered. Her eyes fluttered open slowly. From down the hall, a noise drifted to Eden's ears and she sat up. It was a peculiar noise that at first she couldn't place, a sort of frantic breathing punctuated with a twisted high pitched gasp. Crying? Eden got up and padded silently down the corridor to Faith's door. It was closed tight but she pressed her ear against it, face flush with the wood, listening intently.

The light clatter of bedsprings.

The rustle of fabric.

Stifled sobs that turned to choked up whimpers.

Heavy pained breathing.

Eden's hand brushed the doorknob, considering. She wanted to open it but everything was new and confusing, she didn't know what the right thing to do was. Maybe this was just how the world was? She had no frame of reference... but something about the noises set her on edge.

A jangle, a creak and the sound of footsteps sent her scurrying back to her room, peeking around the door once she was safely sequestered inside. Faith came out of her room. It was too dark for Eden to see her face but her body language, hunched, head down, shambling gait, confirmed Eden's fears. Faith went to the bathroom, pausing at the door and looking back to her room, head cocked slightly as though listening to someone. She nodded and mumbled something indistinct before disappearing inside the bathroom.

After a moment, Mr Knight emerged from Faith's room, heading to his own. He paused, spotting Eden standing ghost-like in the gap of the doorway.

"Eden... you should be in bed..." he said, folding his arms. She didn't move, just stared at him. "Faith had a nightmare. I was just making sure she was okay."

When Eden continued to stand there, he reached over tentatively and shut her door, before shuffling into his own room. She glared resolutely at the door, her hands balling into fists as she felt a bitter seed sprouting in the pit of her stomach. The room felt suffocating, the entire house seemed to be pressing down onto her.

She let herself out of the room, not caring if anyone heard, moved through the hall and down the stairs to the front door. It only took a few moments for her to free herself from the confines of the house and she stepped out into the chill night. Her feet burned as they made contact with the icy ground but she relished in it. The frozen grass crunched as she left the house and wandered over to the main road.

Her movements were slow, almost trancelike, as she walked down the middle of the road. Overhead the streetlights flickered as she passed them by. Ahead the church loomed into view and she found herself drawn towards the great stone building. The iron fence around the graveyard was dappled with frost, making it sparkle in the moonlight. The snow inside was largely untouched, unlike the rest of the town which had already began to take on a grey hue.

She hesitated by the gate, a strange foreboding halting her movements. Something seemed to whisper that she didn't belong there, that this place was off-limits to her, but the call was too strong and she pushed through her uncertainties. She found herself moving amongst the gravestones with a purpose she didn't fully understand. Some of the stones were clustered together, rows of family members, some fenced off from the rest of the graveyard. One in particular caught her eye.

It was a single large tomb, surrounded by elegant iron fencing. A set of stone steps, small decorative flowerpots on each corner, led up to a long rectangle box, a full-length sculpture of a woman carved out of marble was stretched out on top. At one end, words had been carved into the stone box, not a name but two short lines of text.

*Deep in earth, my love is lying*
*And I must weep alone.*

The words didn't make sense to Eden so she focused her attention on the woman. Her arms were laid out beside her, palms facing the sky. A stone apple was clutched in one hand. Her eyes were closed, her expression making it seem almost like she was deep in thought. Eden wasn't sure what it was about the woman that fascinated her but she couldn't find it in herself to look away.

331

"I didn't expect to see you here."

She looked up sharply to see Dr Knott standing nearby. He'd managed to get within a few feet of her without her hearing. Eden immediately made to move away but he held up a hand, a gesture of peace.

"Don't worry, I'm not here because of you… although I see your new guardian isn't exactly keeping a close eye on you… but anyway, I digress." He came closer, standing beside her and looking over at the tomb. "My sister is memorialised here… I come at least once a week. It makes me feel close to her… even though she's not actually buried here."

He produced a key from his pocket and unlocked the gate to the tomb before heading inside the fenced area. Eden followed him, seating herself on the steps as Dr Knott busied himself, ensuring that the sculpture was clean and removing the dead plants from the flower pots. Eden watched absently, her fingers tracing the lettering.

"She was a unique woman," Dr Knott said as he finished his work. "When she was passionate about something, she would do anything to see it come to life." He sighed and sat beside Eden. "The one thing she wanted more than anything was a child… it drove her to the brink of insanity and pushed her to do things I never thought she was capable of… I'm not sure she ever recovered…" He closed his eyes, resting his head back against the tomb. "I would have done anything to see her happy, but it reached the point where I had to look at what she needed instead of what she wanted. Sometimes you have to make painful choices, do bad things even to take care of the ones you love." He opened his eyes, pale green colouring just visible in the moonlight. "You understand that?"

Eden nodded. The words themselves didn't matter to her, his tone spoke to her in a way language never code. He had rarely spoken but on the few occasions He had, she knew not to trust what was said. Words were snake-like, manipulative and deceptive. Tone was easier for her and Dr Knott spoke with a fierce energy, a powerful belief in what he said. Dr Knott smiled slightly and for once it seemed genuine.

"You remind me of her," he said. "I didn't realise it at first. You don't look like her, but you have the same… aura about you. You're beautiful, like she was, in your own strange way… maybe it's me. I can't help but be drawn to broken people. You're made all the more exquisite for your damage…"

He looked at her, his expression contemplative but his eyes held a dark predatory gaze that made her feel naked in front of him. He leaned forward and kissed her. It was a light touch, barely there and for a moment Eden wasn't sure it actually happened. He paused, face inches from hers, calculating his next move, and then moved in again. This time the action was more aggressive, abrupt and forceful, lips pressing firmly against hers. Eden reacted with the only weapon she had, sinking her teeth into his lower lip with as much force as she could manage.

Dr Knott let out a noise akin to a growl and pulled back, lips smeared with blood. He winced and pulled a handkerchief from his pocket, dabbing at the damaged skin. A slight smirk formed on his face as he looked at her.

"You really are like her..." he said, voice soft and almost tender.

For a moment neither of them moved, trapped in that split second which stretched on seemingly infinitely. Then Dr Knott got to his feet, breaking the spell.

"You should run home Eden. Bad things wait in the dark."

Eden got up slowly and retreated from the grave, her pace quickening the further she got. She glanced back once, the shape of the man still visible, standing in the darkness. It felt like the shadows were closing in on her, the night threatening to engulf her. She broke into a run, pushing herself as she felt a sudden need to be far away from that man, that place.

As she ran, something caught her nose, halting her abruptly. It was dull at first, a strange musty scent that suddenly seemed to sharpen. She cocked her head to the side, eyes searching for clues to its source. All she saw were endless identical fence panels, sealing her off from whatever lay beyond. Despite the similarities, she found herself moving towards one in particular, guided by some unseen force. A few of the slats were damaged, having been broken and crudely repaired. With very little effort, Eden was able to break in.

She didn't know exactly what she was searching for but she found herself driven on to keep looking. She became aware of a soft squeaking coming from a stout wooden structure propped against the fence. Through a metal grill at the front, she could make out the shape of two small furry animals huddled together. Something curled and twisted inside her stomach. The pain that never truly left her was stirring, awakening like a beast from slumber. She whimpered. Her body, long ago surrendered to the whims of others, was wrenched with a terrible desire. Not hunger, just pure need, like nothing she'd felt before.

Without being fully aware of what she was doing, Eden reached out and unlatched the hutch. The creatures watched her curiously, too used to being handled by their owners to fear her. She picked one up, her touch gentle as she held it, enjoying the feel of fur under the pads of her fingers. The animal squeaked at her and squirmed as she probed the softness of its belly, tiny paws scrabbling at her hand. Her stomach seemed to clench and the overwhelming need she felt clamped down on her brain like a vice. A low whine slipped from her lips. She couldn't take it.

She brought the animal closer to her face, rubbing her cheek lightly against it. Then she sank her teeth into the tiny creature, driving them through layers of fur, fat and muscle before twisting sharply to tear open a horrific gaping wound. The sounds the animal made were impossibly loud, desperate screeches as its guts tumbled from its fragile body. Eden bit down again and its cries faded.

She crouched by the hutch, gnawing at the carcass in a near frenzied state, spitting out scraps of fur and shards of bone. The meat was warm, the blood thick and as it slid down her throat, the pain faded away almost entirely and the weight on her brain lifted.

Eden returned to the house chin stained with blood and crept upstairs. Her clothes were damp from the snow and muddy in places. The bathroom was empty, Faith having long since returned to her bed. Her door was ajar and Eden paused as she passed, looking in on her sister. She was curled up under the covers, her face just about visible, brow furrowed, not peaceful even in sleep.

Eden felt that same bitterness inside of her and Dr Knott's words returned to her. Sometimes you had to do bad things for people you cared about. She hadn't known Faith very long but she felt an intense bond. She was her sister, they were kin.

She went back to her room and removed her wet clothes. Her skin was damp and the room was cold but she barely felt the chill as she stretched out on top of her bed, staring up at the ceiling.

When day broke Jamie breathed a sigh of relief. After visiting the magic shop, he'd spent the afternoon smearing the doorways with the paste he'd been given and then endured what felt like an endless night as he waited to see if it worked. Callie had slumbered fitfully beside him as he'd forced himself to stay awake, unwilling to let even a second pass by where he wasn't on guard.

But now, the sun had risen and there had been no incidents. His mom called for Callie to get ready for school and Jamie decided that after his classes had finished he'd stop by the Knight house and give Eden the rest of the paste. After all, it was better to be safe than sorry.

School was strained and the halls held a strange atmosphere of tension. Jamie wasn't entirely sure if he was meant to be in isolation still but none of the teachers commented on his presence. Still, it gave people a break from talking talk about was the recent deaths. Tucker was back at school, his face still sporting the bruises from Jamie's attack on him. The rumours had been flying but seeing the lingering impression showed just how much damage had been done, not just to Tucker's face but also to his throat which bore purple finger marks. Jamie made an effort to stay out of his way, a little worried that he might find himself on the receiving end of some retaliation.

When class ended, he shot out of the building. He picked up Callie from school, as both his parents had left word they'd be working late, and dropped her at home. He didn't want to take her with him to see Eden, in case that put her in danger. The Knight house wasn't too far away, it wouldn't take much time to get there and as long as he was back by sundown, he figured she'd be alright at the house alone.

He moved briskly, hands deep in his pockets and head down, hood pulled up in an attempt to conceal himself. No one answered when he knocked at the front door but the side gate to the back garden was open and a trail of footprints were visible in the snow. He ducked into the garden, following the tracks to the back door, which was partially open and swinging gently in the breeze.

Jamie paused. The white plastic of the door was smeared with a streak of red, a partial handprint. He frowned and reached out to pull it open fully, but hesitated. Instead, he peered through the narrow gap, into the kitchen. The tiles were coated in a layer of sticky vermilion, patchy in places and the shape of footprints visible. Splashes of claret marked the counters and walls, a deep puddle was slowly spreading across the floor, aided by steady drips from the ceiling which was splattered wildly like a Jackson Pollock painting.

Amongst the blood was a body or rather parts of one. An arm, wrenched off at the shoulder, was stretched out towards the door and there were small scratches in the tile as though the owner of the arm had tried to claw at the ground in an attempt to save himself.

The rest of the body was in ragged chunks, lacerated to almost beyond recognition, torn flesh strewn carelessly across the room. The victim's chest had been ripped open, intestines wrenched from the body and shredded in places. The room was already thick with flies and reeked, reminding Jamie of the shed where his dad used to hang his kills, rancid meat, piss and fear. The severed head was resting in the corner, mouth open in a permanent scream. One of the eyes had been cleaved from its socket, the tongue had been rent from the jaw and instead, a penis had been crammed into the mouth. It was only once Jamie spotted the man's lower half that he realised what it was, a jagged stump of skin and testicles all that remained.

B

There is no hope in this building. I do not know if there ever was.

God is dead, we are alone.

~Amelia

# XXX

Jamie fled the gruesome scene. He had shouted for Eden but heard nothing. After a brief moment of panic where he thought she might have been taken, he remembered the footprints. It looked like she'd left of her own accord and, although he really hoped he was wrong, he had a good idea where she would have gone.

He reached his house and let himself in, hands trembling so hard that it took him several attempts before he finally managed to get the door open.

"CALLIE!" he shouted. There was no sign of her in the living room or kitchen so he tore up the stairs, calling frantically for her. His heart was racing and icy terror began to take over his body. Had they taken Callie? He'd been so sure that she'd be safer in the house but now wild theories were rushing through his head about what might have happened. There was no sign of a struggle... maybe she'd just gone to sleep or taken out her hearing aids... maybe... maybe...

Jamie threw himself through her bedroom door and into her room. Callie was sitting on her bed, a handful of dolls strewn across the cover. Eden was perched opposite her. Her clothes were thick with blood, her arms, face and neck also stained.

*Hi Jamie!* Callie signed, smiling brightly. *Your friend came over!*

Eden smiled shyly at Jamie who could only stand and stare at the two girls. They both seemed completely at ease, neither caring about the gruesome evidence of what had happened at the Knight house. For a moment he didn't know what to do, how to react to the slightly bizarre scene before him. He blinked, shaking himself out of his daze, before crossing the room in two brisk strides, seizing hold of Eden's arm and pulling her up to her feet.

He all but dragged her out of the room, only realising what he was doing when Eden jerked back sharply, eyes turning fearful.

"I... sorry..." He looked down, glancing at his hands which bore smudges of the blood from her arm. He rubbed them fiercely against his jeans, trying to get the taint from his skin. "Look, I... I saw what happened... I know about... that..."

338

Jamie's words stuck in his throat and as he tried in vain to clear off the lingering tarnish.

*Pussy. Can't take a little blood. Man up or I'll give you something to cry about.*

He closed his eyes, taking a deep breath as he organised his thoughts. As soon as someone else found the... remains, the police would be after Eden. She'd be locked away, then she'd be somewhere safe... he should call his dad... no, no! He couldn't do that. He couldn't trust them. He didn't know which people were working against him. Eden wouldn't be safe there...

"We need to get you somewhere safe. And you can't stay here, not because I don't want you here, but because it's too obvious. They will find you here, they're already watching me. We need to get some distance between you and... people." He paused, pinching the bridge of his nose and running his fingers through his hair. "Alright... go shower. We can't go anywhere with you looking like that. I'll pack some clothes and food and things... we need to be quick. I figure you've got..." His eyes glanced at the hall clock. It was almost four. "An hour tops before Faith gets home from school and raises the alarm."

Eden looked at him blankly for a moment before nodding slowly. Jamie pointed to the bathroom and she quickly headed inside. Jamie waited until the door had closed behind her before returning to Callie.

"Cal, I need you to get your spare backpack. Go downstairs, get some water and dry food from the pantry. Nothing that needs cooking or a tin opener or anything, okay?"

Callie nodded and got up. There was no hesitation, no doubt that what her brother was telling her was the right thing to do. She grabbed her backpack from the wardrobe and left the room, scampering down the stairs.

Jamie paced the room, fingers tugging at his hair. His brain felt like it was on fire, his thoughts conflicting against one another. Was he doing the right thing? He had no idea... a man was dead... and he'd just left him there!

"Fuck... shit... what am I doing... what am I doing..."

Before he could stop himself, his legs carried him to the bathroom. He didn't knock. Eden was stood under the showerhead, pink-tinted water running down her body. She turned her head when he entered but made no attempt to cover herself.

"Eden... I... I have to know... did you kill him...?"

She looked down at her hands for a moment, before raising her head once more and meeting his eyes. Her eyes were like stone and even though she made no move to answer his question, he felt like he already knew. He crossed the space and came to stand directly in front of the shower, a thin pane of glass the only thing that separated them.

Eyes still locked, Eden slid the glass door open, water streaming around her.

"Why did you do it?" he asked softly.

She reached out and took his hand in hers, damp fingers brushing against his knuckles. She guided his hand to her chest, placing it in the gap between her breasts. Slowly she moved his fingers down, over the curve of her stomach to the top of her thighs. His fingers were inches away from the soft mound of her vagina, and still, she kept moving them, across the skin. There were rough welts and scars marring the otherwise smooth area. He allowed her to hold him there for just a moment before pulling back.

He had his answer, at least in part. He knew that he was doing the right thing.

Cheeks colouring, he left the bathroom abruptly, suddenly embarrassed by his forwardness. There was no time for hesitation or distraction of any type. He had to finish packing up and get Eden out of the house.

Jamie flew around the upstairs in a frenzy of activity, gathering anything he thought might be remotely useful to her. Clothes, a torch, a towel, a blanket and, after a moment's pause, his iPod. Not useful but he remembered how calm she'd seemed when he'd played it for her. Callie came in, clutching the bag which now bulged with the contents of their pantry.

"Thanks, Cal," he said taking it from her and adding his own contributions.

He handed Callie a small pile of clean dry clothes, too large for Eden but suitable while he got her out. Callie left the room without instruction, heading to the bathroom to deliver the bundle. Jamie seated himself on the edge of the bed, trying to work out what was missing. After a moment's hesitation, he removed the pendant the witch had given him from around his neck. She needed it more than he did.

The three of them gathered downstairs, Eden clean except for a few faded traces of blood that lingered on her skin. They were faint enough that Jamie decided they'd go unnoticed and that they couldn't afford to waste any more time. He took hold of Callie's hand, uncomfortable with the prospect of leaving her at home after the scare he'd had, and guided Eden out of the house.

After raking his brains, he'd come up with one place that Eden could stay and potentially remain safe. His initial instinct had been to hide her somewhere in the woods but given the weather, he'd realised it wasn't a feasible option. Instead, he'd settled on somewhere a little closer to town, which would provide her with a somewhat safer environment, at least until he could find a more permanent solution.

They took a slightly longer route than Jamie would have liked, attempting to avoid anyone who might notice them or any cameras that might record their paths. His uncle rented a storage building on a piece of land owned by a dog trainer. It was a little way out of town, close enough that Jamie could bring her supplies but not so close that she was likely to be found.

As they neared the fence that marked the boundary of the land, Jamie paused, eyes scanning the surroundings to make sure there was no one nearby. Once he was satisfied, he led them to the little brick outbuilding, skirting around the large barn where the dogs were housed. Eden whimpered softly at the loud barking coming from in and she clutched Jamie's arm. He paused, giving her a reassuring smile.

"Don't worry, they won't hurt you. I'm going to make sure you're safe."

The words resonated with Eden. She'd heard them all before and every time nothing but pain followed… she thought Jamie was someone she could trust but her fear was clouding her mind, everything was overwhelming her and she couldn't organise her thoughts into anything coherent. Without him though…

She had no choice. She let Jamie lead her to the outbuilding, Callie close beside them. The door to the building was closed with a sliding latch rather than anything that required a key, yet another reason Jamie had settled on it as a hiding place. The space was small, most of it taken up by stacked boxes of equipment and tools. The floor was cold flagstone, but a worn rug had been draped across it.

"I know it's not great…" Jamie said, apologetically. It had seemed like a better option in his mind, now seeing it he wasn't entirely sure. It was dark and the air held an intense chill, both of the girls were already shivering. "I can't think of anywhere else…"

Eden squeezed his hand lightly and seated herself on the ground, arms wrapped around her knees. Jamie got what she was trying to say. It's okay.

Jamie and Callie set about trying to turn the space into something that was workable. They built a makeshift bed, piled high with everything warm they'd gathered, and put the supplies to one side. Callie found a wind-up camping lamp in one of the boxes which gave the room a pale blue glow.

As they worked, Jamie felt his phone buzzing in his pocket. He leaned against the wall and pulled it out, grimacing when he saw his dad's name flashing on the screen.

"Shit…" he muttered under his breath. It looked like time was up. "Callie we need to get going."

Callie gave Eden a quick hug and pulled her teddy from her pocket, tucking it into the pile of blankets before returning to Jamie's side. The two siblings turned to leave, Jamie hesitating when he saw the sad expression on Eden's face.

"We'll come back as soon as we can," he promised. "You won't have to stay here for long."

He closed the door, sealing Eden inside, and took firm hold of Callie's hand. They began to make their way home, Jamie's phone ringing repeatedly. The first few times were his dad, then after a pause, Sammy's name popped up on the screen. Jamie sighed and answered the call.

"Jamie! What the fuck? Your dad has been calling me incessantly trying to find you. I thought you might have died! What's happening?"

"It's a long story, I can't get into it right now, okay? Just… if he calls again… I don't know."

He hung up and switched the phone off before it had a chance to ring once more. The pair of them quickened their pace, cutting through side streets to get home quicker. As they passed by Ash Street, where the Knight house was, he spotted a police car turning into the street, confirming his fears. He stopped, tucked out of sight, and turned to Callie.

*You can't tell anyone where she is, okay?* He signed. *Promise me.*

Jamie held out his hand, pinkie finger raised. Callie bit her lip but nodded and linked her finger around his.

*I promise.*

Satisfied, Jamie nodded and the two of them hurried on, not stopping until they reached the house. His dad was standing in the doorway as they walked up the drive, arms folded.

"Where is she, Jamie?"

"Where's who? Callie? She's here," he said.

"You know who I mean. Where is Eden?"

"Is she not at her home…?" he asked innocently. He was aware of the stain on his palm and pressed his hand against his jeans, hoping his dad wouldn't notice.

"No. And you are the only person I can think of that she'd go to."

"I've not seen her. I've been out with Callie," he lied.

His father looked him dead in the eye. Jamie kept his expression carefully cultivated in a mask of neutrality until his dad turned his gaze to Callie instead.

"Callie, I need you to tell me… have you seen this girl?" he asked, pulling a photograph of Eden from his pocket. Jamie felt his heart skip a beat.

No, it's fine, she promised, he told himself.

Callie shook her head, expression deliberately confused. Their father nodded slowly, unwilling to believe that his daughter was lying to him, and sighed.

"Okay… I have to go out but if you see her I need you to call me immediately. Do you understand?"

"Of course," Jamie said, trying to keep the relief out of his voice.

The two of them watched as their father headed down the drive and got into his car, speeding off down the road. For a moment, neither of them spoke, just stared down the empty road. Then Jamie turned to Callie.

"Get anything in your room that Eden touched and put it in a bin bag."

They spent the rest of the evening cleaning the house with the precision of someone hiding a crime. Even after Callie had gone to bed, still Jamie worked. He scrubbed every trace of Eden's presence from the bathroom, removing any lingering residue from her shower and brushing up any stray hairs. He took Callie's bedding, which had been stripped off and inspected for any marks left by Eden's attack on Mr Knight. When he determined there weren't any, he put it in the wash with every type of fabric soap he could find. Lastly, he took Eden's bloodstained clothes, lit a fire in the fireplace and threw them in. He sat down on the wooden floor, gazing into the flames as they hungrily lapped at the cloth, watching it singe and then catch. He felt numb and, not for the first time, wondered what had he gotten himself into?

*****

The next morning, after a sleepless night, Jamie turned his phone back on. He was immediately bombarded by texts and voicemails from Sammy, demanding to know what was going on. Reluctantly, he dialled her number and balanced the phone against his shoulder as he brushed his teeth.

"Jamie. About bloody time!" Sammy said as she picked up.

"Sammy, always a pleasure."

"Why didn't you call me back?"

"I was… busy," he said with a mouthful of toothpaste.

"Hiding your little criminal girlfriend?"

Her words took Jamie by surprise and he choked, stumbling for a response.

"Wh…what? No? Of course not… what are you talking about?"

"Oh, you don't know about that? I heard that Mr Knight got ground up into dog food and your girlfriend has done a runner. I assumed that since you disappeared last night and since you're her BFF you'd be involved."

"I… I don't know anything about that," he lied.

"Jamie, you are a terrible liar. I know you're involved. And I'm guessing she is too, no matter what everyone else says."

"What's everyone saying?" Jamie asked, trying to change the subject and deflect the attention away from himself.

"Well, there are a few theories floating around now since the news broke. A couple of people are blaming the feral… but there's also talks of it being an animal attack… which I think is unlikely given that animals aren't usually known for dramatics or for shoving genitals in a person's mouth."

"How do you know about that?" Jamie asked. He realised what he'd said the moment the words left his mouth and quickly backpedalled. "Umm… I mean, that sounds like the kind of information that wouldn't be advertised to the public."

"Nice try… and no, it's not. I have a friend who works in the morgue. He thinks maybe Mr Knight was messing around with someone's wife and that's why he got killed. And I think the police are planning on blaming it on the cult… given that Eden was one of their victims. So tell me… what have you done with her?"

"I told you, I'm not involved."

"Uh huh. And yet I still don't believe you…" she said with a soft sigh. "You're going to get yourself killed Jamie if you keep this up. You're messing with things that are dangerous!"

Jamie grimaced. He knew that he was putting himself at risk, he knew that every time he got involved he was making himself a target but he felt compelled to help. Sammy sighed again.

"I have to go Jamie. Please stop this…"

She hung up. Jamie stood stock still, the silence hanging in their air. Slowly, he set the phone down, eyes fixed on his reflection. Everything seemed to be crashing down around him and the weight of everything that had happened felt like it was pressing on his skull.

He grabbed some paracetamol, swallowing them dry, before leaving the bathroom. He pulled on his jeans and hoodie, grabbed his bag and left the house. For once he was actually glad to go to school. It was a piece of normality, a mercy after everything else that was going on. Of course, everyone was already talking about the body but he kept his head down and ignored the chatter. He wished he had his iPod so he could block out everything else, but had to make do.

His mind wandered frequently and he wondered how Eden was doing, tucked away in that dark shed. He felt sorry for her, she had gone through just as much as he had. Maybe that was why he helped her, she was a kindred soul and he felt she, more than anyone else, could understand his feelings.

As the day drew to a close, Jamie dragged his feet, reluctant to return home. Callie had after school clubs so he couldn't even attempt to slip into their normal routine. The thought of having nothing to do but sit at home and think about everything else made him feel nauseous. He tried to dawdle around the town centre, taking the longest routes he could and pausing regularly to look in shop windows, but he couldn't shake the feeling that people were staring at him. The sensation of lingering eyes on the back of his neck made him intensely uncomfortable and his mind began to whisper to him.

*They know.*

No, they don't.

*They do. They all know. They know what you've done.*

*You're a bad person. They all know.*

Jamie clenched his fists, resisting the urge to cover his ears. As much as he didn't want to go home, he knew it was the best place for him.

Sometimes, the darkness that overwhelmed his mind came out of nowhere but there were times when he could see it coming. He could feel it now, the gnawing sensation of an impending shadow that threatened to take over his mind. The only thing he could do was go home, hide himself away and wait for it to pass.

His mom had an evening shift that day and he hoped she'd still be home when he got there. She couldn't make the situation any better but it made things a little easier if he knew that the rest of the family were aware he was feeling vulnerable. That had been one of the agreements they'd made after he got released from the hospital after his suicide attempt, he was supposed to share his feelings.

Unfortunately, the house was empty. His mom had left a note, directing him to the slow cooker where dinner was waiting for him. Jamie got a bowl and poured himself a drink before heading upstairs. He'd attempt to distract himself as best he could until he felt somewhat human again.

Settling on the bed with his food, he ate slowly, relaxing against his pillows. The thoughts were still there, the toxic whispers scratching at the inside of his brain. He plugged in his laptop and switched on something mindless and colourful that would occupy him and was easy to focus on.

As he sat there, Jamie felt a strange dizziness settle over him. He frowned, trying to concentrate. His brain felt like it was filling with swirling fog. He pushed the laptop aside, sliding off the bed to get a glass of water in the hope that would help. Getting to his feet, the world twisted sharply. He stumbled, grabbing at the nearest object in an attempt to steady himself. Clutching the bedframe, he stilled, closing his eyes, waiting for the world to settle once more.

Slowly, it did and once he felt confident enough to let go of the bed, he began to move for the door again. He'd gone no more than three steps when the room tilted sickeningly once more and his legs crumpled underneath him, sending him crashing to the floor. He groaned, head ringing and room spinning around him, and tried to get back up. His legs felt like spaghetti and refused to cooperate. The more he fought to get up, the harder it was and the less responsive his limbs became.

Jamie tried to break the hold that was over him but his muscles seemed to stiffen, every part of his body had turned into a rigid block that felt incredibly heavy and no matter how hard he tried he was unable to move them at all. The only thing still working were his eyes, which roamed the room, searching for a clue to what was going on or, better yet, a way out.

His vision blurred in and out of focus, spots dancing across his line of sight. The room seemed to tremble and tilt back and forth like a carnival ride.

Through the ringing in his ears, Jamie became aware of footsteps. A door opened and closed. He strained, trying to see what was happening. Three figures stepped into his field of vision. They were dressed in hooded cloaks, tied shut so that their body was hidden, and their faces were covered with masks... no, not masks he realised. Skulls. Animal skulls. A goat, a deer, a mountain lion. They stared down at him, the image distorted and twisting sickeningly before his eyes.

Without words, they retreated, leaving Jamie trapped there, helpless. Although he couldn't see them, he was aware of faint noises that signalled they were still present. They moved purposefully, gathering items from around the room before returning to where Jamie lay.

He was lifted from the floor and set on the bed. A moment later, he felt multiple hands moving across his chest, pulling at his t-shirt. He tried to yell but his tongue was heavy and useless, only managing to produce a groan. The person in the deer mask reached out and gently stroked his hair, the hands delicate and feminine.

"This will be easier if you relax," she said softly, her tone almost motherly. "Do you want me to cover your eyes?"

Jamie groaned again, struggling as best he could. As much as he hated seeing them, feeling weak and defenceless, the idea of surrendering any of his senses was far more terrifying to him. They finished stripping off his top half, leaving him exposed and even more vulnerable. Jamie half feared that they'd move onto his trousers.

I don't want to die in my pants, he found himself thinking. Idiotic to think that, he told himself. Far worse to die at all.

"Who wants to go first?" asked the goat, this voice rough and male.

"I will," replied the lion. His voice was also male and despite Jamie's terror, he tried to commit the tiny details to memory. Anything that could help him identify them later... if he survived that long.

He held up a knife in a gloved hand. It was from the kitchen, the blade serrated. Jamie whimpered, trying to muster the strength to kick out. The man grabbed hold of the boy's arm, pressing the sharp edge of the knife into his skin. Jamie stiffened. The man sliced the knife across his flesh, the metal tearing through the boy's arm with minimal resistance. Jamie wanted to howl in pain but all that came out was a pained sob. Blood welled up in the wound and began to spill down his arm, dripping onto his duvet.

"Not too deep," the woman warned.

"It has to look real," one of the men snapped back.

The words seemed distant like they were being said from somewhere far away. Whatever had put Jamie at their mercy was growing stronger, pumping through his body and seeping into every part of him. He was aware enough to see the lion hand the knife over to the goat man, who mimicked his comrade's action, cutting into Jamie's arm, a little further down.

One by one, each of them took turns to cut into the teenager until each of his arms bore six horizontal cuts and his skin was slick with blood. It stretched into an eternity, the minutes transformed into hours by the agony as his skin was severed like a slab of meat on a butcher's block. Tears were running down his cheeks, falling onto his pillows. The pain was intense, a deep burning that roared into life with each new cut. Jamie was fading in and out of consciousness, but he clung to his awareness, fearing that if he let go for even a moment he might not wake up again.

"Think that's enough?"

"Should be."

"What if they don't come home in time?"

"Well, that's what he gets for interfering."

Around him the strangers seemed to change, human to animal and back again, faces distorting as the drugs sunk their claws deeper into his addled mind. There was a flash of silver over Jamie's head and he caught a glimpse of his pocket knife.

How did they get that...? A distant part of his brain asked. I hid it...

"Where?"

"There,"

He felt a light prod at his hip.

"Please…" he slurred.

"Shhh love," said the woman. "We'll be done soon. You should sleep."

"I don't want to die," he mumbled.

A new pain had started up, this time at his hip, as one of them cut into the soft skin there. These marks were smaller, more intricate and precise compared to the fierce gashes that marred his arms, but no less painful.

The darkness was closing in on him and he couldn't tell if it was from the drugs in his system or the blood loss.

"I don't wanna die…" he managed once more.

The last thing he saw before he was consumed entirely were the three ghoulish animals looming over him and the knife, silver transformed into ruby by his lifeblood. He wasn't awake to feel one of the men pressing the knife into his hand, or the woman gently covering up the mark on his hip as the blood from his arms pooled around him, turning the bedsheets stiff at it dried beneath him. He didn't hear them leave the room or when they threw away the jug of lemonade laced with Rohypnol. By the time they had closed the back door and disappeared to their own homes, to live their normal lives, care for their own children, their partners, their pets, he was too far gone to know anything at all.

**Name:** *Faith Knight*

**Period**: *5th*    **Subject**: *English*    **Assignment**: *Poetry*

**Task:** *Write a poem on the theme of 'Masks'*

Through the halls walks a girl
with skin of bone
and hair of raven wing.
Her body is stitched together
from painful memories
and broken promises.
She wears a mask of sweet pretence
to hide the rotten soul
that festers beneath.

Cruel eyes watch her pageantry
and play their hateful tunes
to make her dance.
She performs her role
without complaint
or adulation.
An artist who paints
a picture of normality
on a canvas of bitter tears.

As days go by cracks start to show
as words bite deep and
scratch with deadly malice.
Nightmares map her path
from day to day
and lie to lie.
And each scar remains unhealed
each wound left open
going deeper than the last.

Until
one night she takes away the mask
and looks upon herself
a face she does not know.

She writes the truth
upon the pages of herself

in crimson ink more
precious than gold.

She says her goodbye
in lethal clarity
and leaves behind
a doll
with hair of raven
and skin of bone.
A broken mask
upon an unfamiliar face.

# XXXI

The house was completely empty. Jamie found himself stood in the middle of a small attic bedroom, the roof sloping sharply down and providing little headroom. The room was familiar but at the same time, he couldn't place it. A large clock was set against one wall, ticking softly, and a candle, half-burned out, was on the small bedside table. A bed and an armchair were the only other pieces of furniture. Across from the bed were a row of wooden doors, each with a stained glass window styled to look like a flower. He was dressed the same as he'd been when the attack had happened, topless and wearing only his jeans.

Jamie moved slowly towards one of the doors, gently touching the handle before trying to open it. It didn't move, locked up tight. He tried the next door and got the same result.

"You're early. Again," said a voice. Jamie turned to see a man, pale with dark hair. He was dressed smartly and was inspecting the clock. Just like the room, the man was oddly familiar in a way he didn't understand. The man turned to fix Jamie with a hard stare. "Once is unlucky, twice is just being careless."

"Wh… what? Who are you? Where am I?"

"I have to go through this again?" The man sighed and seated himself in the armchair. "This is… it has many names but I suppose you could call it a waiting room?"

"Waiting for what?"

"For what comes after. For what is behind the doors."

"They're locked," Jamie pointed out.

"Yes but there are still things behind them. You're just not ready to go through them yet. As I said, you're not meant to be here yet."

"Am I… dead?" Jamie guessed.

"Not quite. You have until the candle goes out."

"What happens then…?"

"I unlock the doors and you choose your path."

"To... heaven? Hell?"

The man smiled and laughed softly.

"It's not quite that simplistic."

Jamie looked at him expectantly, waiting for more information. The man raised an eyebrow, looking back at him, clearly not intending to say anything further on the matter. Jamie decided to switch tactics. He turned his gaze to the doors.

"So... do you tell me what doors lead where?" Jamie asked, eyeing the doors warily.

"No, I prefer to let people make their own mistakes," the man said. "But I tell you what they represent and after that, it really depends on what you want from your afterlife. Vengeance, judgement, peace, etc. All good options."

Jamie couldn't help but notice he sounded incredibly bored and he shifted awkwardly on his spot.

"Do you stay here the entire time?"

"No. I'm far too busy cleaning up after your nightmare of a town. But you're not stable enough yet to leave alone. Which means I get the delight of babysitting you until you settle down a bit."

"Oh..." Jamie, still feeling awkward and somewhat uncomfortable under the man's intense stare. His lack of clothing didn't help matters and he covered his chest with his arms as best he could.

"Don't flatter yourself," the man said. "You're not my type."

The teen couldn't tell if he was joking but it helped a little, making him feel a little more at ease. He smiled slightly.

"What? Too young? Or is it the scars?"

"I'm not technically human so the age thing isn't really an issue. Or the scars," he chuckled softly. "But we're not here to discuss my dating preferences."

Jamie nodded slowly and wandered over to a small window, peering out. There was nothing but grey like the bedroom was surrounded by

354

thick fog. He turned to face the man once more. "There's nothing out there?"

"Of course not. You think limbo actually looks like this?" The man gestured at the room. "Do you read science fiction?"

"Umm… occasionally…?" Jamie said, confused by the question.

"Have you ever read one where something takes a human form to stop people from panicking?"

"I think so…"

"Well, this place is a little like that. If you saw what it was actually like, your tiny mind wouldn't be able to handle it. So we decorated it a bit."

"Are you like that?" Jamie asked, curious. "I mean, taking a human form so we don't freak out?"

"No!" The man scowled, offended. "Are you trying to say there's something wrong with how I look?"

"No… not at all… I was just… you're not exactly what I pictured death as looking like."

"Technically my title is 'Reaper' but either way, it's just a job. There's more than just me. One of the others probably goes in for the whole robes and scythe look but I am less dramatic… most of the time."

Jamie seated himself on the bed, chewing his lip and lapsing into silence. His eyes fell on his arms which were still stained with his blood.

"Does this go away…?" he asked. "Does the pain stop?"

"The pain of living? Sometimes. But the scars never leave you. They might fade a little, depending on where you end up but you'll always have them." The man's voice had softened a little and his expression became a little warmer. "But if you're here hoping that death contains all the answers, you're going to be disappointed."

"I wasn't hoping for that… I honestly didn't expect any afterlife." He smiled sadly. "I bet Lily was disappointed. She always loved the whole pearly gates clouds and angels thing."

"Angels are real," the man said absently. "They're not super pleasant though."

"Is... never mind, it's stupid."

"Is what?"

"Is... God real?"

"Yes. In fact, pretty much every God imagined exists in some form. Zeus, Jupiter, Horus, Freya, Thor... they're all there. Or... do you mean an all-powerful ruling god? There's one of those too."

"There is?"

"Yes."

"What's he like?"

"Honestly? Rather dull. And a bit of a womanizer."

"Oh."

"Not what you expected?" the man asked, smiling slightly.

"Not exactly," Jamie replied, giving a shy grin.

For a few minutes, both of them were quiet. Jamie tried to wrap his head around the prospect of afterlives, angels, gods, things he'd never bought into. If those things were real then... maybe...

The man cleared his throat.

"So... are you going to ask?"

"Ask what?"

"About your family? I can see your brain whirring away, putting the pieces together. If there's a God and a heaven, what else could be real? Am I right?" Jamie nodded slowly. "You want to know if you'll see them again."

"Yes. Or are you going to tell me that it depends on where I go?"

"Well, of course, it does. It's like asking if you'll see your friend from Canada when you're in Germany. You have to be where they are to see them. But... well, there's a chance. I'm not going to guarantee it but there is a chance you'll get to see at least one of them." The man got up and stretched. "But that's not something for you to worry about today."

"Why not?"

"Because, as I said, you are too early. I wasn't sure you'd pull through but life is full of surprises."

The man shrugged and pulled a ring of keys from his pocket. He went over to one of the doors and unlocked it, pulling it open. Beyond Jamie could see only darkness and he got up slowly, hesitating.

Jamie!

The voice rang clear around him and he jumped, searching the room for the source. The man smiled.

"They're calling you home Jamie... of course, you don't have to go... it's up to you..."

Jamie!

He moved slowly towards the door, the voices growing louder. He glanced at the man who nodded reassuringly. Jamie's feet faltered on the threshold. Did he really want to go back? He thought of the pain, the fear, the tears he'd shed and the blood that had fallen. Could he go back to that?

"I don't want to feel like that again..." he said quietly. "It hurt. Everything hurt..."

"Life is pain, Jamie. Life is a fight. There's no shame in giving up... but you have to ask yourself, do you have something worth fighting for?"

Jamie...

This voice was fainter but unmistakable. Callie. He couldn't leave her.

He stepped through the door. Darkness swallowed him up and a vicious wind swirled around him, battering him from all sides. The voices called, loud and insistent.

*Jamie*  *Jamie*  *Jamie*  *Jamie*

*Jamie*  *Jamie*  *Jamie*

*Jamie*　　　*Jamie*

*Jamie*　　　*Jamie*

*Jamie...*

"Jamie?"

*Ritual for Pregnancy*

*Consecrate the ground in the blood of the young. Prepare the male specimen with a solution of Damiana, Cinnamon, Juniper Berries and Gingko. Wash them inside and outside. The female should bathe in purified water and rose petals.*

*Form a circle of red candles and merge the male and female as one.*

*Ensure the male specimen is completely drained at completion.*

*When the merging is complete, slit the throat of the male and offer their life for that of the unborn. Consume the blood with a mixture of raw eggs for the next seven days.*

# XXXII

Psychiatric ward. Jamie looked at the sign, looming over the door like a vulture, as he was marched down the hallway towards it. Silently he prayed that the hall would stretch on endlessly and he'd never reach the door. The words immediately conjured images in his mind of creepy old buildings, inmates in foul conditions, flickering lights in dark corridors where echoing silence was broken by abrupt screams. He shook his head, trying to dislodge the images. He'd been here before, he knew what it was like, but still, the horror movies visions stayed rigidly lodged in his brain.

The group paused at the door and one of the orderlies who was escorting him swiped a key card against the lock. There was a beep, a click and a loud metallic buzz, three sounds that he knew well, that made every muscle in his body tense up automatically.

The door was opened and he was ushered inside. Dr Ng was stood in a small office nearby and she looked over as he entered, her expression saddening.

"Jamie," she said, stepping out of the office. "How are you?"

"Insane. Apparently."

His mind was fuzzy and despite how much he tried to remember what had happened, his brain refused to cooperate. He'd woken in the hospital, having been found by Callie unconscious and close to death on his bedroom floor. He knew that he hadn't tried to kill himself again. Last time, the memory had stayed crystal clear, burned into his brain… if he'd done this, he would remember, he was sure.

But no matter what he said, once the doctors determined he was fit to leave, his parents had told him that, upon recommendation by Dr Lilith, they were going to have him committed again. And now, the time had come and his stomach was twisted into knots.

"I wish I could help you out, personally I don't think you should be back here."

"Then tell someone that? I swear I didn't try to kill myself, just please send me home."

"I would if I could but… you're not actually staying here. You're not my patient."

"What?" Jamie blinked, taken aback.

"It's been decided that your case is more… severe than our facilities can meet. You're being taken to Morningwood."

Jamie frowned. He knew the name, who didn't in the town? Morningwood was a mental hospital on the outskirts of town, but it had been burned down in the 20s. The remains of the building, a scattering of ashen bricks and the old metal gate, now rusted and thick with ivy, still lingered in the woods, but no one dared go near them.

Dr Ng noted his expression.

"It was rebuilt a few years ago. They planned to use it as a historical site but the town couldn't afford it. It's a private hospital now," she explained. "I just got the call that you've been referred to them. I'm sorry for the short notice."

"When am I going?" he asked.

"They're sending someone to pick you up. And… I have to take this." She gestured to the suitcase his mom had brought in for him but made no move to take it.

"I'm not allowed my stuff?"

"I'm afraid not. They'll provide you with everything you'll need. I'll make sure your parents collect your bag."

Jamie felt like all the energy had been drained from his body and he slumped into a nearby chair. He looked out at the dayroom, the room he'd never wanted to see again and found himself longing to stay there. He closed his eyes and rested his head in his hands. Dr Ng stepped back into the office, giving him a moment with his thoughts. She didn't understand what was going on. She hadn't even known that Morningwood was up and running again, although she'd heard about the rebuild a while back. And why Jamie of all people? He wasn't dangerous, at least not to anyone else (and she didn't really think that he was a danger to himself anymore). His case wasn't even that severe, certainly not in comparison to some of the patients she cared for. So why were they so keen to take him?

361

Jamie sat in the chair for ten minutes before the escorts from Morningwood arrived. He followed them down to the carpark in silence. He wasn't going to resist. He wasn't going to run. Anything he did would just provide further evidence against him. The escorts, two large burly men in matching uniforms, took him to a black unmarked car and almost shoved him into the backseat. Jamie belted himself in and curled up as small as he could on the seat. The two men didn't speak as they got in the front and set off. The silence made it worse, Jamie so used to the constant hum of his music. At the back of his mind, the whispering that he worked so hard to suppress was rising up, taking root once more.

He rested his head against the window. They were blacked out, but a slither of light remained, allowing Jamie to peek through. The Halloween decorations had long been stripped away and a few houses already sported the first signs of Christmas. A scattered few remained morbidly blank, bouquets of flowers resting on the doorsteps. He looked away again quickly, ducking his head.

The car turned onto the main road out of town, the trees rising up either side like great walls, the watery sunlight cut off almost entirely. Originally, a road to Morningwood had been accessible through the town, but as the years had passed and the ruins had been left untouched, new buildings had been erected, leaving the path inaccessible. When the building had been repaired, a new road was formed, circling around the town and snaking through the trees to eventually merge with the main road. As they drove, turning onto the smaller side road, Jamie couldn't help but feel that the time and distance, the constant bending and twisting of the track, was all intentionally designed. The longer they journeyed, the less sense he had of where he was and how long he'd been in the car. One by one, the things that grounded him in reality – time, space, sight – were cut off from him.

The trees thinned out slightly as the track widened once more. Up ahead, the old gates of the hospital rose up proudly. The ivy had been cleaned away, the high walls that enclosed the building replaced, but the gates lingered, a snapshot of an unpleasant history that the town had tried to forget. Beside the gate was a plaque, the lettering worn down so that it was almost unreadable. Jamie squinted to make it out.

*Morningwood Sanatorium for the Mentally Disturbed*
*Founded 1810 by Dr E. Morningwood.*

The car grumbled up the uneven track and came to a stop outside the building. Jamie tried to twist his head in such a way as to see the hospital, but the position of the car and his slither of vision left him unable to see anything but a set of stone steps. The car door was opened and he was pulled out roughly, wincing as the fingers bit into his skin. The structure loomed over him, built of grey stone, moss clinging to the crevices. Jamie was struck by the impression of two separate buildings from different times merged into one. It was clear that it had been built using the remains of the original asylum, keeping to the original blueprints as much as possible. Looking up at it, barred windows and decrepit stone, he felt a chill settle over him.

The inside, however, was fairly neutral, white plaster concealing the decaying brick walls. The centre of the entrance hall was dominated by a desk. It was positioned in front of a metal grille that cut off the makeshift reception area from the corridor behind it. There was a wooden door set in the wall as well, which lead into a glass bubble that could oversee the corridor area.

Jamie shifted uncomfortably. It didn't feel right. The lights were too bright, the desk too neatly arranged. It felt false, like a set in a play.

As Jamie waited in the reception area, he saw movement behind the grille. At the furthest end of the corridor was another metal fence, a young woman was stood behind it, fingers entwined with the metal lattice. Her hair was short and a vivid pink, which stood out vividly against the bleak background. She was wearing an oversized t-shirt that may once have been white but had turned to a muted grey and a pair of brightly striped tights.

"Jamie Alexander?"

Jamie turned his head sharply. A bored-looking orderly had emerged from behind the door, holding a folder in their arms.

"It's Harper. Jamie Harper," he corrected, his voice taking on an unnatural sharpness and defensiveness.

"Oh, yes, that's right," the orderly said, looking at a page of the file. By her tone, Jamie could tell that she couldn't care less what he chose to call himself. "Come along, let's get you orientated."

She produced a key card from her belt and unlocked the metal gate, gesturing impatiently for him to follow. Once he was behind the gate with her, she secured it once again and led him halfway down the corridor to a door marked 'INDUCTION' in large letters.

"Go inside and undress. Place your clothes in the box along with any items you might have on you. You'll be given a shower, followed by your physical assessment. After that, you'll receive your patient uniform and be taken for your mental evaluation. Once you have been assessed, you'll be placed on a course of treatment and taken to your room," she intoned in a robotic voice. "Any questions?"

"What happens to my clothes?" he asked.

"They'll be stored until you leave us." She opened the door and nodded for him to enter, not bothering to wait and see if he had any more questions. Jamie reluctantly shuffled into the room. It was a strange amalgamation of a doctor's office and locker room. A crude shower space had been constructed in the furthest corner, just a collection of tiles and a drain in the floor but no curtain or anything that might provide a semblance of privacy. A shelf with a box was set near the door, a label bearing the words 'Patient M16JA-13'. He bit his lip and began to slowly undress. He found himself longing for the psychiatric ward at the hospital. This wasn't exactly the horror movie asylum of his nightmares but it was a million miles away from a place he'd actually want to stay in.

He folded his clothes and placed them in the box before approaching the shower, moving warily as one does when naked and vulnerable in a strange environment. There were no taps, just a push-button set halfway up the wall. He noticed a metal railing fixed onto one of the walls. It was badly scratched, which stood out amongst the otherwise pristinely identical surroundings. He wondered what it was for.

The cold air in the room was beginning to get to him, so he pressed the shower button, hoping that the water would warm him up. The pipes gurgled and an ear-splitting claxon sound reverberated around the room. Water crashed down on him, icy cold. The breath was knocked out of him by the force of it and he let out a yell as it spread through his bones, numbing every inch of him.

A moment later the claxon sounded again and the water cut off. He stood, frozen to the spot, trembling. His eyes searched the room for a towel or something to warm himself with. The only thing was the clothes he'd come in.

Before he could move towards them, the door opened and a man in a lab coat entered the room.

"Hello Jamie," he said with a smile, as though the site of a naked shivering boy was completely normal to him. "I'm Doctor Guildhard, I'll be conducting your physical examination. This will require me taking some readings, a few samples and asking a couple of questions. It's all very basic stuff."

"Can I have some clothes first?" Jamie asked, wrapping his arms around himself.

"In a moment." The doctor came over and began to examine the boy, measuring and probing at him with peculiar instruments Jamie had never seen before. As he did, he began his questioning and Jamie tried hard to ignore the intrusion of the doctor's hands and focus on what was being asked of him.

"How old are you?"

"Sixteen."

"Do you drink?"

"Never."

"Smoke?"

"No."

"Do you take any drugs?"

"Only the ones I'm prescribed."

"Which are?"

"Lurasidone, Clozapine, Quetiapine, Sertraline, Zopiclone, Rozerem, Triazolam, Trazodone and Doxepine."

The doctor blinked.

"All at once?"

"No. I lose track of which ones I'm on." In truth, he'd stopped taking any of the medication he was prescribed weeks before. His parents

365

trusted him enough to take them himself and as long as he presented an empty bottle for a refill when they expected it, they remained unaware that he was flushing them one by one.

"Allergies?"

"None."

"Vaccinations?"

"I don't know."

"Any major operations recently?"

"No."

"Pre-existing medical conditions?"

"Anaemia. Mild asthma." He stared resolutely at a spot on the far wall, trying to leave his body behind him and ignore what was happening to him.

"When did you first try to kill yourself?" the doctor asked, examining his arm. Jamie pulled back sharply and looked at the ground.

"If I've been referred here shouldn't you have my medical history?" he muttered angrily.

"Oh, we do, but medical history is only as good as the doctor. Some patients tend to withhold information."

He retreated and went to a cabinet, returning with a pile of grey clothing and a tray of slim vials.

"We're almost done here, Jamie. I just have to take those samples I mentioned. You're not afraid of needles, are you?"

No, Jamie wasn't afraid of needles. But then again, he wasn't particularly fond of a stranger sticking them into his arms. The doctor smiled slightly to himself and began his collecting, taking Jamie's silence as consent. One by one, he gathered samples of the teenager's hair, skin, saliva and finally his blood. Only when he was finished did he finally hand Jamie the clothing he had gathered.

"I'll leave you to get changed. Nice meeting you Jamie."

Doctor Guildhard left the room. Jamie looked down at the clothing in his hands. One pair of grey canvas slip-on shoes with soft soles, grey t-shirt with a small red logo over the left breast and a pair of soft flannel trousers, also grey. No zips, no buckles, no laces. He thought of the girl in the stripy tights and wondered how she had found such colourful items in this sea of grey.

He began to dress, taking his time. With each item he put on, he felt like he'd lost a part of himself.

When he was finished, he stood there, uncertain of what to do next. He'd found a pair of underpants tucked in the pile but no socks. His feet, damp and clammy from the shower, were beginning to go numb.

After standing there for a few minutes growing steadily colder and feeling moisture from his hair soak into his collar, Jamie went to the door and peeked out. The orderly was stood, leaning against a nearby wall, with an expression of annoyance on her face as though irritated that Jamie had made her wait. She gestured impatiently for him to follow before striding off down the corridor. Jamie hurried after her, more out of reluctance to be left alone in the endless grey void of the hallway than anything else.

The orderly led him to a large rectangular hall. There were several tables forming a neat row along one side of the room, each bolted to the ground and with chairs built-in. There was a door with a sign declaring it as the kitchen and a serving hatch in the wall nearby. There was another metal gate to the right of the kitchen, sealing off another corridor. Two sets of stairs were positioned at either end of the kitchen, both fenced off.

To the right of the hall was a corridor, not closed off, with a sign that said 'Dormitories'. Jamie noticed a similar hallway had been built to the left but unlike the first, it didn't seem to lead anywhere. A wall, hastily constructed sealed it off a few feet in.

"You're allowed in the hall and the dorms," the orderly droned. "Anywhere else and you need permission and an escort."

She marched off in the direction of the dorm, Jamie following behind. The dorm was made up of four rooms and three bathrooms, as well as a small space that Jamie initially assumed was a cupboard until he saw it was neatly labelled saying 'Reflection Room'. Images of padded cells and straitjackets formed in his head.

"Someone will be along shortly to take you for your psychological assessment. This is your bunk," the orderly said, pointing to a bed with a shelf beside it, containing a small pile of folded clothes. "And you have a locker over there for toiletries. You're listed as a potential risk to yourself so if you need something from the locker you'll have to request it and be supervised."

Jamie couldn't stay silent anymore, his irritation finally pushing through.

"You think I'm going to kill myself with soap?" he asked, sarcasm leaking into his voice. The orderly gave him a cold look.

"It's happened before."

"But sheets are okay?"

The orderly seemed to decide he wasn't worth arguing with and walked off. Jamie sat down on the bed, scratching at his wrists unconsciously. The skin itched and burned under his bandages. There was a strange pain at his hip, which he assumed was irritation from the coarse fabric of his trousers. He squirmed, rubbing his side to try and stifle the sensation.

He stretched out on the bed, looking up at the ceiling. Dark wooden beams crisscrossed the roof, cobwebs clinging to them, swaying gently in the draft from the roof. Jamie grimaced and went to pick up his pillow so he could attempt to block out his surroundings. It was stitched onto the mattress. He sighed, thinking of his home, his bed, his family. This was everything he had feared. It felt like a prison and every second that passed, he felt like a little part of himself was being drained away.

A young woman entered the dorm, feet bare and wearing a ragged grey dress, a tangle of deep auburn hair descending down her back.

"Hi..." Jamie said softly, half sitting up.

She ignored him and settled herself on a nearby bed. Jamie watched her for a moment, before closing his eyes. Maybe if wished hard enough, it would turn out just to be another nightmare.

# REQUEST FOR RESTRAINING ORDER

## APPLICANTS DETAILS

Surname: Knight

Forename: Evelyn

Address: 12 Ash Street, Sarum Vale

Occupation: Head of Social Services

## RESPONDENTS DETAILS

Surname: Knott

Forename: Adam

Address: Apartment 415, Larkrise Apartments, Sarum Vale

Occupation: Doctor – Head of Paediatric Department

## PLEASE DETAIL REASON FOR REQUEST

Excessive harassment by respondent.

## EXTENSION OF ORDER TO ADDITIONAL PEOPLE

| Name | Age | Sex | Live with you? |
|------|-----|-----|----------------|
| Eden Knight *(Daughter)* | Nine months | Female | Yes |

# XXXIII

Ruth lay in her husband's arms, cheek pressed against his bare chest. It had been a while since they'd indulged in such a soft, intimate moment, longer than she cared to admit. Oh, they had sex, during the brief times when their hectic shifts aligned and allowed for it but too often it was of the hurried demanding variety. Two bodies working like machines for individual goals, a far cry from the long tender time where she almost felt like they were a singular entity. Now, clutched in his embrace, warm and sated, she almost felt like crying.

It was wrong… not the act itself, that couldn't have felt more right. And that was exactly what disturbed her.

She kissed his cheek lightly and slipped free, wrapping her bathrobe around her. She wanted nothing more than to lie there but the guilt was gnawing at her insides and she knew that if she remained the tears she kept hidden would be seen. Padding down the hall to the bathroom, her eyes lingered on Jamie's door. It had been shut tight since… since… she couldn't complete the thought.

It had been Echo who'd found him. She'd always thought that when something bad happened to her children she'd feel it, some maternal instinct that would lead her to them, like how she always woke a few minutes before they started crying. But no. When she'd come home that night, she'd found Echo shut in the laundry room, barking like crazy. And even after she'd let him out and he continued barking, she'd ignored him. She did the ironing. She sorted Callie's socks in pairs and thought about her patients.

*And the dog had known.*

Now, stood in the darkened hall, the animal watched her with judgemental eyes. She was his mother. She had made a promise to protect him. Instead, she'd been unable to keep him safe from the monsters in his own head. She'd left him, alone and bleeding. And now she'd abandoned him. It didn't matter what anyone else said or even that she knew it was for his own benefit to stay in hospital, she felt like she had failed.

"Ruth?" Michael had come into the hall. Without his uniform to hide behind, she could see every line of worry and exhaustion written on his body. He looked older almost and vulnerable.

They closed the space between them and hugged each other. Ruth opened her mouth to say something, she didn't know what exactly, but was cut off by twin shrill cries from their cell phones.

"Work," she said softly.

"Work," he responded, nodding sadly.

They parted and went to their phones, no longer a unit joined in sadness but two strangers with separate lives that merely coincided occasionally. And perhaps it was better like that.

The ER was in chaos when Ruth arrived, she slipped into the locker room where one of the nurses was changing.

"What's going on?" she asked, retrieving her scrubs.

"There's been a series of animal attacks."

"We're up to six different dog bite victims in the last half hour," another nurse chimed in. "Plus two rangers who got gored by a deer, a mountain lion attack in someone's garden and a bear mauling on the main road."

"Don't forget the guy who claimed his girlfriend's cat tried to claw his eyes out."

Ruth frowned as she finished pulling on her scrubs, her thoughts turning to Callie asleep at home with Echo around. Was she safe? Was Echo a danger?

No, that was ridiculous… she was just being paranoid.

She headed out into the ER to see where she was needed. As she approached the desk, the automatic door slid open letting in a blast of frigid air. A woman rushed in, a bloody bundle in her arms. She yelled, calling for someone to help her before collapsing to the floor, cradling the object to her chest. Ruth and another doctor ran to her side to assess the situation.

It became quickly apparent that the woman herself was not injured, distressed and hysterical only. The bundle was what she directed their attention to but despite her repeated pleas she seemed reluctant to actually hand it over.

The other doctor worked to calm the woman while Ruth carefully took hold of the object. She tugged lightly at the wrapping, fumbling with the cloth until her fingers brushed skin. Hand trembling, she pulled the object free. Someone screamed and it took a moment for Ruth to realise that it was her.

In her arms was a baby, a few months old at a guess. Soft blonde hair covered its head and two serene blue eyes looked up at her but beneath that was mutilated mess of ragged skin and exposed bone.

*****

The dogs were howling, anguished cries that mingled with the screams of the wind. In his bed, Lorenzo Adams stirred, the sound drawing him out of his sleep. His eyes opened and he automatically shifted into a sitting position, legs hanging over the side of the bed and sliding into his boots. The location of his ranch, where he housed and trained his dogs, meant it was usually fairly quiet as it was far enough from town that there was no traffic noise. However, it also meant that wild animals sometimes came out from the forest and scared the dogs.

Lorenzo trudged down the stairs, grabbed his coat from by the door and stepped out into the bitter night air. He picked up his flashlight and pole, the one he used to wrangle unruly canines, and headed towards the barn where the dogs were kept, ducking his head to avoid the worst of the chill. It wouldn't be the first time a cougar had got too close to the property and spooked them.

Casting the flashlight around, he searched for any sign of what could be upsetting them. He couldn't see any indication of animals or intruders; no tracks, no scraps of fur. He frowned and changed direction, going over to the barn and letting himself in. In their stalls, the dogs were going crazy, foaming and yowling as they threw themselves at the walls to their enclosures, seemingly unconcerned with any injury they might cause themselves.

He checked the thermostat first, wondering if the strange behaviour was a result of the weather. He knew that animals were sensitive to the environment, but he'd never seen them act in this way before. The thermostat was at its usual level so Lorenzo decided to switch tactics. He pulled his dog whistle from his pocket and blew hard. The sharp noise cut through the air, momentarily halting the dogs' frantic bays.

"Alright, let's see what's going on…" he said, his voice soft and gentle so as to not spook them further. He approached the first of the pens, entering it, sweeping the surroundings before checking the animals over one by one for any sign of injury.

Fortunately, they all seemed to be unharmed, save for a few superficial scrapes sustained from battering themselves against the wooden panels. There was no sign of anything that Lorenzo thought might be causing them distress. He leant against the wall, contemplating the strange situation. The dogs had quietened down in his presence but they still seemed skittish, twisting and turning anxiously, whimpering occasionally.

Lorenzo grabbed a leash and attached it to the collar of his dog, Phantom. Only a handful of the dogs were actually his, the rest only there for training, and he wasn't sure how they'd react if they found… whatever it was that was distressing them. Phantom was his eldest, having immigrated with him when he moved to open his training ground, and the most well trained.

"Right boy," he said, giving the dog an affectionate pat as he led him out of the barn. "What's got your fur in a twist? Go on, find it."

The dog immediately began to snuffle at the ground and set off, racing as fast as he could across the grass towards the small cluster of outbuildings on the edge of Lorenzo's property.

*What the hell have you smelled?* Lorenzo thought to himself as he followed the dog. He didn't tend to pry into what his renters kept in their sheds… maybe rats had got into one of them? But would the dogs really have been able to smell that from their barn?

He let go of Phantom's leash, the dog sprinting off to one of the sheds. The animal began to scratch at the door, barking insistently.

"What have we got boy?" Lorenzo asked, taking hold of his pet's leash once more. If there was something dangerous inside, he wasn't going to let Phantom get hurt by it. Once the dog was safely restrained, he reached up and unbolted the door, pulling it open. His torch pierced the darkness, skewering a small figure. She was doubled over, groaning in clear pain. When the light hit her, the girl whimpered and flinched away, pressing herself against the wall of the shed, looking at Lorenzo in terror.

Phantom barked, the sound making the girl quiver and cringe in fear. Lorenzo hushed him and approached her slowly. He knelt beside her, moving slowly and keeping his actions gentle.

"Hello there…"

The girl let out a strangled sob, clutching her stomach. Lorenzo acted instinctively, carefully scooping the girl up into his arms and carrying her away from the shed, to his house. Everything else could wait, right now she needed his help and that was more important.

\*\*\*\*\*

Jamie didn't realise he'd fallen asleep but he woke with a start as someone shook him roughly. A man in scrubs was standing beside him, arms folded.

"Jamie Alexander?"

"Harper…" mumbled Jamie, sitting up sleepily. There was a strange buzzing sensation in his head, making it difficult to concentrate, and an ache centred on his temples.

"Whatever. It's time for your psychological assessment."

He beckoned to Jamie before setting off. The teen sighed and followed, still half asleep. His eyes flickered to the other bed, where the girl had been, but it was empty.

"How many patients are there?" Jamie asked as they navigated the maze of corridors.

"Fifteen, I think? I lose count…"

374

"Shouldn't you know how many patients you're supposed to be watching over?" Jamie asked, raising an eyebrow.

"They multiply, they disappear. There's fifteen on file but sometimes there's more," the man said with a shrug.

Jamie made a face behind the man's back. They reached an office and the man opened the door for him, waiting until the boy had entered before closing it firmly. There were two chairs set opposite one another, a bespectacled older woman seated in one. She smiled as Jamie approached the empty chair.

"Hello, Jamie. I'm Dr Gardner. I'm going to ask you some questions so we can get a sense of your mental state and choose the best course of treatment for you. Do you need anything? Water?"

"No, I'm fine..." He tapped his fingers on his knee, awaiting the standard questions he'd been asked multiple times before.

"Okay. Well firstly I've been reviewing your file, I just want to get a greater understanding of some of the events detailed in it. You were admitted to hospital when you were seven, correct?"

"Yes."

"And following that you received counselling for bereavement?"

"Yes."

"Can you elaborate on that?"

"My mom, brother and sister were killed. And I was understandably upset about that." He leaned back in his seat, grimacing. He hated saying those words aloud. Ten years had gone by and still, whenever he said it, his stomach would twist sharply.

"What happened after that?"

"Is it not in my file?" Jamie let out a long sigh. "I was adopted. But that was a long time ago and none of that has anything to do with now or what's currently happening."

"You don't think anything from your past might have been responsible for your present situation?"

"No. My present situation is that I'm in this hospital for no good reason. Which is nothing to do with anything from my past."

The doctor looked at him over her glasses, setting her pen down on her notebook.

"No good reason? Do you really believe that Jamie?"

"Yes."

"So you didn't attempt to take your own life?"

"I… yes, I did but that was over a year ago and I've been… mostly fine since," Jamie said, stumbling over his words. The doctor didn't speak but looked pointedly at the bandages that still covered his arms. "That's not what it looks like."

"It also says in your record that you once beat one of your peers to the point that he had to go to hospital."

"That was… complicated."

"Do you often find yourself in 'complicated' situations?"

"No!"

Dr Gardner tapped the tip of her pen against her notebook. Jamie focused his eyes on the clock as the doctor continued to question him, taking notes as she did. When a sharp bell cut through the building, he jerked upright, looking around in startled confusion. Dr Gardner smiled.

"That's the bell for meals and that seems like a good time to end this evaluation. I'm going to recommend a course of medication and regular counselling sessions, as well as close supervision during your stay here. We'll reassess you in six months' time."

"Six months? I can't stay here for six months! For one thing, there's nothing wrong with me!"

"The matter is closed, Jamie. I suggest you run along to the main hall to get something to eat," she said, getting up and pointing to the door. He considered staying and arguing with the doctor but he was fairly sure that wouldn't achieve anything. No one listened to children after all…

He left the room and made his way to the main hall. A line of grey-clad figures had formed at the serving hatch, other patients collecting their meal. Reluctantly, he joined the back of the queue and waited to approach the hatch.

"Name?" asked the server.

"Umm… Jamie. Harper."

The server checked her list before retrieving a tray and handing it to him. Jamie took it and found an empty table to sit at. The meal itself didn't look too bad, which he found mildly surprising, and although he couldn't summon up much gusto for the food, he was happy that at least it wasn't as dreary as everything else.

There was a thump as another tray was placed across the table from Jamie. He lifted his head. The girl he'd seen when he first arrived, the one with the pink hair, was sitting opposite him.

"Hey there!" she said brightly. "I'm Tasha!"

"Hi… I'm Jamie…"

"Nice to meet you, Jamie! We've not had a new person in a while… I'd ask what you're in for but I'm guessing that it was either an unsuccessful arson or you tried to take a vacation from life?"

"Neither. I was framed."

"That's a new one… but no judgement either way," she said with a shrug before turning her focus to her plate. She speared a chunk of meat of her fork. "Do you think this is chicken or pork?"

"I'm honestly not sure. It just tastes like…"

"Sadness?"

"Something like that, yeah," Jamie chuckled. He glanced around the room, looking at the collection of orderlies whose expressions ranged from boredom to outright disgust. "What's the deal with these guys? Given the level of training, I'm sure you need to work with mentally ill people… you'd think they'd be… interested. Or show any sign of actually caring about their work?"

"Nah, they're zombies."

Jamie blinked, momentarily confused, unsure if the strange girl was being serious.

"That… was a joke," Tasha clarified.

"Sorry, the things I've seen lately I honestly wouldn't be surprised if they really were."

"Nothing that interesting. They just… don't care. They're not paid to care, they're literally just paid to make sure we don't die. And so that management can prove they've got a staff on site."

"So it's not actually a hospital?"

"Oh, technically it is. And some of the staff are even real doctors. But people aren't brought here to get better. They're put here to be kept out of the way and forgotten about." Her voice was neutral as she spoke, with the detached air of someone who had long ago accepted that nothing they did would changes thing.

"How long have you been here Tasha…?" he asked hesitantly.

"Umm… I'm not sure. It's hard to tell time in here. What month is it?"

"November."

"Almost a year then. At least. It was Christmas when I first came here."

For a moment Jamie wanted to ask what year it had been when she'd been brought in, but at the same time, he was afraid of the answer. He couldn't really make himself believe what Tasha had said. He had a family who cared about him, they wouldn't leave him there. He wouldn't be forgotten.

Instead, he continued eating in silence. The ache at his temples had gotten worse and he massaged the side of his head with his free hand while he shovelled food into his mouth with the other.

"You okay?" Tasha asked.

"Just got a headache."

"Oh yeah, that… you'll get used to it."

"What?"

"It happens to everyone who comes here. But after a while, you just get used to it and stop noticing."

"What do you mean it happens to everyone? Why?"

Tasha shrugged, finishing up her food and skipping over to the hatch to return her plate and cutlery, before disappearing in the direction of the dorms. Jamie sat there, watching as she went, feeling immensely confused. He poked at his food a little more before giving up. His appetite had deserted him.

He slumped in his seat, resting his head against the table. His eyes flickered from patient to patient, noting their hollow eyes, drawn sallow faces and lifeless gestures. None of them were speaking, their actions were lacklustre and bordering on robotic. There was something unsettling about watching them, he couldn't quite put his finger on it but he found it difficult to look at them for too long.

Jamie got up and handed in his tray, then looked around for something to do. He didn't want to go back to his dorm but there was nowhere else he could really go. There was nothing to keep him occupied in the main hall, no books or paper he could use to draw. Instead, he seated himself in the slight alcove formed by the blocked up corridor. The wall that prevented him from going any further was a different colour to the rest of the walls, clearly not part of the original structure. He rested his head against the bricks, feeling the pitted surface.

Through the stone, he could make out a strange rushing sound like water was flowing through bricks. He frowned, pressing his ear, straining to determine what exactly it was. The noise was faint but at times it was almost like he could hear words being said. At first, they were indistinct, giving Jamie more a sense that a word had been spoken than allowing him to actually hear what was being whispered but the longer he sat that, the clearer they became as he grew to understand the pattern of the sounds and interpret them.

It was easy to see how a person could lose themselves in the hospital. There were no windows, no clocks, no change in the surroundings, just the constant dull glow of the lights overhead. No time, it was like being stuck in limbo.

Something tugged at his memory at the thought, a sense of being out of place. Lost.

The buzzing in his head, the pain persisted and the peculiar sounds from the wall disorientated him somewhat. He didn't move, just sat there leaning against the brick with the soft voices beyond the wall murmuring their secrets.

*This Book of Shadows is the property of Samyra Luis*

*June 16th*
*Waning Gibbous*

*Blood Magic*

*Blood Magic is one of the most taboo types of the craft. It is also the oldest, being based in sacrifice and the exchange of one thing for another. Blood is known to be one of the most powerful tools for the craft and is employed in a number of spells, but only ever in small amounts. Instead, blood magic calls for large quantities and frequently, death. It provides incredibly powerful but also extremely volatile results.*

*Because of the volatile nature of this strain of craft, it can only be used by those who are extremely experienced or have a natural affinity, allowing them to know exactly the right amount to use.*

# XXXIV

Damp. Mould. The drip of a broken pipe and the scratching of rats in the walls. The room was small, made of cold stone and rotten wood. Crammed into the confined space were children, packed like cuts of meat they tried to find a little space to call their own, fitting themselves around the assorted boxes that had been left there. They ranged in size and age. Hungry, cold, their bodies were emaciated and filthy, dressed in the ragged remains of clothes, their eyes were wide and fearful. The rats nipped at their toes until they were marred with bites and their skin was stained with blood as well as dirt.

Footsteps echoed through the darkness. Breathing spiked and bodies attempted to conceal themselves in the corners of the room. A bright light swept across the space, sending the occupants scurrying back like rats. The man strode forward, the light casting a circle around him that no one dared approach.

Dark eyes scanned the room, resting lightly on each of the inhabitants. He strode forward and seized a young girl, by the arm. She screamed and struggled, beseeching her comrades to help her. The other girls turned their head away, reluctant to put themselves in danger when they had been spared. She was dragged from the cellar, her cries cutting out abruptly.

Jamie jerked upright, the sound of screams ringing in his ears. He looked around, taking a minute to ground himself and get a sense of his surroundings. He was in bed in the hospital, the lights burning dimly above him. A few of the beds were occupied but most were empty. He had no idea what time it was or how long he'd been asleep for.

Time had passed slowly in Morningwood, an endless procession of sleeping, eating, medication and counselling. With no set routine, the only way Jamie could monitor how long he'd been there was by counting meals, but even that was far from accurate. He thought that he'd been there at least a week, maybe a little longer. He spent most of the time between meals in bed. The more he slept, the quicker the time went and the less he had to endure the monotony of the hospital. His appetite had dipped and he ate less and less each mealtime. It was already starting to show on him, although it was nowhere near as progressed as the shambling corpselike figures of the other patients.

He had tried to talk with the others but most were largely unresponsive. Tasha was talkative but made very little sense to him. Another issue with attempting to befriend the other patients is, despite the limited area they had to move around in, it was oddly hard to keep track of people. Patients seemed to disappear and reappear sporadically and he was beginning to understand what the orderly had meant about not knowing how many there actually were.

Sliding out of bed, he padded silently out of the dorm to the shared bathroom. The bathroom was one of the few places that actually allowed him to catch a glimpse of the outside world, through the ventilation system imbedded in the wall. Only one of the bathrooms was against the outside wall and this was the one that Jamie liked to frequent. If it was empty, he could hoist himself onto the sink and peek out of the narrow gap to catch a glimpse of sky, sometimes trees or grass.

The bathroom, at first glance, appeared to be empty, but as he crossed the tiles he noticed a woman stood in front of one of the mirrors. It was the redhead he'd seen his first day. There'd been no sign of her since and he had wondered if he'd imagined her.

As he approached, she turned her head slightly, acknowledging his presence.

"Hi," he said softly.

"Hello," she replied, stiffly.

"I'm Jamie."

"Amelia."

"Can I ask why you're here...?"

He wasn't sure why but she seemed slightly different from the other patients. Her dress looked a little older, her expression was nowhere near as vacant and despite her cold, distant tone, her eyes sparkled with a fiery intelligence.

"What business is it of yours?" she asked, looking him dead in the eye.

"Ummm it's not, I was just curious... sorry..."

Feeling somewhat uncomfortable, Jamie moved away busied himself at a sink, washing his face for lack of anything better to do. Amelia began to brush her hair and hum softly, forgetting about the boy as soon as he was out of sight. The lilting sound floated to his ears, a wistful tune that spoke of heartbreak and loneliness without saying a word.

Jamie glanced over at the vent, feeling a familiar pang of longing for the outside world, for home. He wondered how Callie was and Eden… did she have enough food to last? Had she already been found or was she still out there, waiting for him? The thought made him feel sick.

He rubbed his hip unconsciously. It was itching again, that burning prickling sensation that had plagued him since he'd woken up in bandages. Since the hospital rules required him to be supervised when showering, due to the apparent risk of him injuring himself with soap, he hadn't showered since his initial assessment which meant he also hadn't investigated the cause of the itching. Mostly he ignored it, as he did with the persistent ache at the back of his head. Now, however, his attempts to either ignore or assuage the feeling were failing.

Grimacing, he tugged at the waistband of his trousers, exposing his waist. In the mirror, he could see a large white square of gauze taped over his hip. He frowned, twisting and turning to get a better look. How had he not noticed that? He mentally ran through the times he'd undressed since he'd come to Morningwood. His initial assessment he'd been distracted by the cold water and the doctor… the other times he'd changed though… had he really been that much on autopilot?

His confusion wasn't just because of how he'd failed to notice the bandaging. The hospital hadn't said anything about an injury on his waist when they'd been treating his wrists. He probed the bandage gently, hissing in pain as a sharp sting emanated from the contact. With nimble fingers, he worked his nails under the edge of the gauze, ripping it away from his skin.

Underneath were several neat cuts, spelling out words in livid red. It was hard for him to read them clearly in the limited light but as he traced them slowly, he managed to decipher the crude message.

"Dead men… don't talk…" he murmured.

Things were beginning to make sense. His mind had begun to whir at the sight of the letters and connect the dots. He knew he hadn't tried to kill himself and this confirmed it in his mind. Someone else had done it, somehow. They'd wanted him here.

*People aren't brought here to get better. They're put here to be kept out of the way and forgotten about.*

Tasha's words resonated with him and he felt with a sense of dread certainty that they weren't going to let him out. They'd find a way to keep him here until he withered away like the rest of the patients. He would never see the sun again, never see his family again if they had their way.

Another day, brought another session. Jamie had had a few of them in Morningwood and they had mainly consisted of him sitting silently, evading the questions fired at him. Today was different though. When the orderly had found him in the bathroom, he'd been instructed to go to the office where the counselling sessions took place and he had no energy to argue. The realisation that he was imprisoned in the depressing surrounding had sapped him of any fight that might have lingered.

Ordinarily, the doctor would already be in the room, but on this occasion it was empty. He seated himself in the lumpy chair, allowing his eyes to wander the rooms. There were framed pictures, mostly old black and white images which he guessed were from the original asylum, along with some newspaper clippings. Most of them showed the progress of the construction, three men standing in front of the building site that would eventually become the hospital and moving on from there. The final pictures seemed to be staff photographs over the years, gathered in front of the finished building.

Mildly curious and with time to kill, Jamie wandered over to the pictures. He didn't know much about the history of the town and Morningwood had always been something of a mystery to even the most knowledgeable of local historians. Most people knew that it existed and had burned down but everything else around it had seemingly been lost to the ages.

It was quite interesting seeing how the land had been transformed, watching the men involved grow older to mark the passage of time. A few of the pictures had small bronze labels attached to the frames, badly tarnished but still readable. Jamie traced the words with his finger as he read.

Dr Elijah Morningwood (Founder) with colleagues Samuel and Adam at start of construction – 1810

Opening of Morningwood Sanatorium – 1812

Staff Photograph (1814): Dr E. Morningwood, Dr S. Attwood, Dr A. Knott and Dr M. Barton
Nurses: A. Morningwood, E. Knott, L. Knott, P. Simon and B. Lucan

Jamie registered the familiar surnames and he squinted at the photographs, trying to make out a family resemblance. It wasn't out of the question that the families had been there since 1814. A lot of the local families did go back multiple generations but given what he'd learned about his presence at the hospital, he couldn't help but wonder if the building held more significance than he'd realised.

Behind him, the office door opened and closed. Jamie turned to see Dr Gardner watching him with a small smile, a large box balanced in her arms. She set it down on the small table in between the chairs and seated herself, gesturing for him to join her.

"Good morning Jamie. How are you today?" she asked.

"Fine…" he replied as he returned to his seat.

"I see you were having a look at some of the building's history?"

"Yes…"

"Do you like history?"

"Sometimes. Depends on what particular bit I'm looking at."

"History was always my favourite subject and it's a very important one. After all, if we don't know what happened in the past, how can we know we're moving forward?" Jamie didn't respond, unimpressed by her attempt to engage him. "Anyway, I would like to try something a little different in today's session. Is that alright with you?"

"I guess?"

"Excellent. Now, I know that you show some sensitivity towards events of your childhood and while I do want you to be comfortable, I feel like these events may be a significant cause of your current issues. If you allow me to explore them, it's likely to aid your recovery and you may even be able to return home a little earlier."

"Okay…"

The doctor retrieved a photograph from Jamie's file and handed it over to him. It was a shot he knew well, it was the one that the papers had used. He sighed and ran his fingers across the smooth surface.

"Can you close your eyes for me?"

Reluctantly Jamie did so, his other senses pricking up immediately. He heard faint rustling which he assumed was the doctor getting her notebook.

"Tell me about your parents. Your biological parents."

"My mom was a music teacher. She had her first child at seventeen, got married a year later. My dad did odd jobs. He got fired a lot. Most of the time he found work as a mechanic. My grandparents always thought he was a waste of space and couldn't understand why she had married him. They never had much money, our house was pretty much falling apart although mom always tried her best… she'd go hungry to make sure we had enough."

Ten years of resentment that had been bubbling under the surface in silence was finally spilling free and although each word caused Jamie pain to say, he felt like they needed to be said.

"How would you describe your father? In a word?"

"Angry."

"How did he treat your mother?"

Jamie clenched his fists. Even years later the sound of his mother screaming and crying at night would haunt him.

"He took out his anger on her. She tried to make sure we didn't see but she didn't always manage… and we could always hear them."

"How about your siblings? You were the youngest?"

"Yes. My sister was the oldest, she was ten years older than me. And my brother was eight years older."

"You were close to them?"

"To Lily. Not so much to Daniel. She looked after me when I was younger. I told her everything."

"How did your father treat them?"

"My brother was usually okay. He was the son my dad wanted… athletic, brave, and good with his hands. Sometimes if my dad was really drunk, he might lash out but mostly my brother was left alone."

He was aware of the sound of the doctor moving around, the floorboards creaking as she did so. He frowned but tried to ignore the sound and keep his body relaxed.

"And your sister?"

Her voice was nearby and he felt a slight pressure on his shoulders, something warm and heavy being placed around him.

"Lily was… too close to me. She tried to protect me and put herself in harm's way to do it." Images burned into his mind that he would never be rid of began to stir once more. Lily had been brave, she'd tried to keep him safe from the nightmare that had invaded their house but she couldn't always hide her tears in time.

"He was physically abusive to her?"

"Sometimes… sometimes he was worse…"

There were some words he couldn't bring himself to say. The cuts were too deep and the hurt too great.

"Was he the same with you?" Her voice had softened a little. Jamie cringed into his seat. Even his parents didn't know the amount of damage he'd endured.

"Yes."

"Why do you think that was?"

"I wasn't what he wanted from a son. He wanted a man, whatever that means. He wanted me to be strong, to be brave. He would always push me into things he knew I hated… like, handle the snakes when he knew they terrified me. He told me if I acted like a girl, he'd treat me like a girl…"

"How did that make you feel?"

"Scared."

"Just scared?"

*Tell the truth. Tell her what you did. Tell her it was your fault.*

"Just scared."

The heaviness around his shoulders had slipped a little and it felt like it was moving. A soft hiss came from somewhere near his ear. Jamie's eyes flew open and he turned his head to investigate. A snake was resting on his shoulders, coiled around his neck. He felt every muscle in his body go rigid and his body turned to ice. The snake stared back at him, tongue flicking out to taste the air.

*It's just a little snake. Don't be a wuss Jamie! Are you a man or not?*

His father's voice roared in his ears and as he looked at the snake, he felt like he was a child again, stood in that cold basement with the tanks around him. The hum of the lights, the squeak of a mouse in his father's hand as he held it over the tank of his favourite snake. The smell of damp, of stale beer.

*Feed the damn snake or I'll throw you in there!*

Not just a memory. The memory, the last night.

*You listen to me you little bastard, do as I say!*

Lily had been there too. Always his protector. She was at the door, banging, wanting to reach her brother but unable.

*Fucking wimp! Need a girl to fight your battles for you?*

Heavy footsteps, shouting, a door locking behind him. Nimble fingers on a latch, unlocking the lid of a tank. Footsteps coming back, crying, Lily struggling and screaming.

*DO WHAT I SAY!*

"No!" Reality and memory converged into one around Jamie, his cry breaking through from the past. He struggled to his feet, throwing the snake as he tore from the room. Still, the sounds raged around him as he ran.

He sought out a space that was dark and quiet as the two worlds collided around him, the present and the past in conflict.

Screaming.

Hair pulling.

His arm yanked roughly, a stab of pain as it dislocated.

His sister was crying, screaming.

There was a shout and she was knocked down, stumbling back and knocking the tanks.

The open one tipped.

Then cold, darkness. Silence…

No, not silence. That was wrong. He was a child, trapped in the chest freezer where his father kept the frozen mice. He could hear him but not her anymore. Somewhere upstairs came the shrill scream of a phone. Then his footsteps faded away as he left, his daughter unconscious on the floor, his son trapped in his frozen tomb.

*It was your fault.*

Huddled in the darkness, that was the thought that came to him, whispered by a voice as smooth and dark as chocolate. Around him, the words echoed in the shadows, a chorus of guilt that repeated his worst fear over and over again.

*Your fault.*                                    *Your fault.*
                        *Your fault.*

*Adam*

*I detest your efforts to keep me from what I need. Why did you interfere? I was finally happy! I had the child I always wanted.*

*I hate you. You always ruin things for me.*

*Evelyn*

# XXXV

He wasn't sure where he'd tucked himself or how long he stayed there. The darkness was oddly comforting, surrounded by nothing but the smell of musty wood. The voices swirling around his head continued, blaming him until that was all he could hear. Jamie covered his head with his arms in an effort to block them out and pressed his cheek against the floorboards.

He'd spent so long trying to block it all out, to move on and be the son that the Harpers' wanted but he'd failed. He was a failure. It was all his fault and he deserved to die in this bleak prison.

"Don't say that Jamie," said a soft female voice.

He lifted his head, not realising that he'd been speaking aloud. A slim figure, clutching a lit candle approached him and as it neared, he realised that it was Amelia.

"None of this is your fault," she said, seating herself beside him.

"What do you know about it?" he asked, a little coldly.

"I know that this place was once built to help people and it has been transformed into somewhere that only cause's pain. And I know that no one comes here if they can help it."

"You… know about them…?" Jamie said hesitantly, sitting up. Amelia smiled sadly and nodded.

"They destroyed my world as much as they are destroying yours."

"What happened?"

"I'm afraid it's a rather long and bleak tale…"

"Well, I'm not going anywhere…"

Amelia sighed softly and rested her back against the wall.

"My full name is Amelia Margaret Morningwood. My father founded this place."

"But… that would make you… at least two hundred years old?"

She gave him a wane smile and inclined her head slightly, gesturing that she would explain.

"When my father first had this place built, he truly intended to help people. He was a good man, he believed that we had a duty to help those in need, particularly if they could not help themselves. Of course, building a place like this was an enormous undertaking and he could not do it alone. He had two close friends, a businessman who was responsible for the financial aspects and another doctor named Adam. The hospital opened when I was twelve and the first few years seemed to be successful. I wanted nothing more than to be like my father and help people, so when I turned sixteen I started working at the hospital as a nurse. I befriended another nurse, named Evelyn. She was Adam's sister but seemed nice enough. And I even found myself falling in love with a young man…"

"So far this is sounding a lot more positive than how I came to be here."

"That was just the beginning. I noticed things… it started when one of the female patients had a child. And the doctor claimed it had died but I knew that it hadn't. Sometimes late at night, I would hear the sound of an infant crying. Things just got worse from there. I decided to investigate and I discovered that in a room under the building, they were keeping children in terrible conditions and performing ungodly rituals… I told Evelyn about what I'd seen… I never imagined that she was part of it. She told her brother and he ensured that my father discovered my love affair. After that anything that I said only served to drive him further away. I ended up as a patient instead of a nurse. And after that, I discovered that the things I had seen, were just the tip of the iceberg and that was far worse underneath. I was kept here for two years before I was finally allowed to die. By that point so much of my blood had been spilt, I was part of the building. Passing on was impossible."

Jamie sat silently for a moment. Ghosts now? His head was spinning and he couldn't shake the idea that it was another trick designed to push him over the edge. But with everything else he'd seen, why couldn't ghosts exist?

He thought about the shape he saw sometimes late at night, the dark presence that felt like someone was watching him. Had that been a ghost as well?

"Does everyone become a ghost…?" Jamie asked hesitantly.

"I am not really a ghost Jamie. I am not that lucky. A ghost is a lost soul. By the time I died, I had no soul left." She looked down at her hands sadly before glancing at Jamie. "You lost someone didn't you?"

"More than one..."

"You should not wish this life on anyone. I believe that the only reason I am here is that Adam wanted me to suffer even after death." Her eyes moved to his arms and the bandages. "You attempted to take your own life?"

"Yeah..."

"Did you... see anything?"

"I saw a man... and... doors... but it's all hazy and I don't remember much. I don't think it's something the living is supposed to know. But... I guess I'll know soon enough... I think I'm going to die here..." Jamie mumbled.

"No," said Amelia firmly. "I will not allow that. I couldn't help the children or even myself but I can help you now."

"How?"

"I can tell what I know about them. It may be of some use to you. Follow me."

She rose and beckoned him. Jamie considered for a moment before getting to his feet and following close behind. After all, what choice did he have? Give up and die a broken husk of a person in an asylum or try to find a way out and fight back? Really there was only one option.

Amelia led him deeper into the darkness, the floorboards creaking underfoot.

"Where are we?" Jamie asked.

"This is a side hall that leads to the male wing. You heard about the fire I assume?"

"Yeah... a patient set the building on fire?"

"There was a little more to it than that but yes. The fire started in the records room, which was next to the male wing. Most of the exterior walls were relatively undamaged so when they reopened, they kept most of the original layout and blocked up the areas that were the most badly damaged," Amelia explained. "However there are a few holes big enough for a person to slip through. Be careful where you step, the floor is quite rotten."

Jamie hurried after her, trying to navigate in the limited lighting. The darkened hall had no windows and the only source of illumination came from Amelia's small candle. As he walked, the walls seemed to rustle around him, the shadows rippled and stretched.

*Just the candlelight*, he told himself.

"Stay close… they feed on your fear…" Amelia said, so softly that at first, Jamie wasn't entirely sure she'd spoken. He faltered.

"What did you say?"

Amelia paused and looked back at him.

"The shadows. You must have noticed."

"I… thought it was a trick of the light…"

"Unfortunately not. I would advise you to not let them get too close."

Jamie moved nearer to Amelia, feeling a little safer in the ring of candlelight. The two of them continued on, Jamie glancing around nervously as the walls continued to murmur around him.

"What are they exactly?"

"I call them Whispers. Adam called them Scáthanna…" She smiled sadly. "During my time here, he talked to me a lot. He was rather fond of the sound of his voice and he knew I was in no position to tell anyone. They exist all over the world but ordinarily, they are quite weak. They whisper into your ears and worm their way into your brain. Once they are in, they poison your thoughts, consuming your doubts and fears and pain to grow stronger. Mostly they are too weak to do much more than cause some mild negativity. Some are strong enough to blight the mind more permanently. And a few are strong enough to drive people to cruel acts to others… or themselves. But the ones in this town are more numerous and far more powerful than most. Particularly lately. They can do more than just whisper, they are able to manipulate the living, although they are far too toxic to maintain control for very long without killing the host."

"Where do they come from?"

"Ordinarily they are created by cruelty and evil. But these new ones were born not made. They do not flee the light, it is part of them. They are the result of an unholy union and the only comfort I can take is that they were not able to fully form and take on life."

Jamie bit his lip, something stirring at the back of his mind.

"I think I know where they're coming from… I have a friend, she's pregnant… I remember hearing the cult saying that there was a risk of her body rejecting it… being poisoned from the inside…"

"That is very grave news…"

They reached the remains of a doorway, charred lettering visible beside the frame. Ahead, Jamie could see a soot-blackened room, the floor almost entirely destroyed with only a few narrow strips of wood remaining in place.

"The stairs to the basement rooms are watched," Amelia explained. "This is the only other way down I have located."

"Do you know if there's a way out around here?" Jamie asked as he warily perched on the edge of the gaping hole and began to lower himself into the abyss below.

"Not down here. I know of a few broken windows and loose bricks if you could reach the upper levels. You might be able to use that as a route out?"

That didn't seem very likely to Jamie but he filed the comment away for further explanation at a later date. He released his hold on the wood and let himself drop the rest of the way, landing in a heap on the ground. His leg burned, limbs protesting angrily. He groaned and righted himself. A moment later and Amelia was beside him, having descended seemingly without actually moving.

They continued on, navigating the labyrinth of identical halls. The walls were faintly damp, the air musty and humid. The creatures on the walls were more numerous but quieter, sluggish almost, making no movement as Jamie passed by them.

"The warmth keeps them docile," Amelia explained.

"You know a lot about them."

"Like I said, Adam liked people to know how clever he was. And I was witness to some of his... experiments."

"Experiments?"

"Yes, he fancied himself something of a scientist."

"You said these ones are different. Do you think this Adam guy is behind that?"

"No. They're far too recent. Adam was capable of monstrous acts but he was, for the most part, human. He would be long dead by now."

They crossed through a room which contained nothing but bathtubs, rusted and stained, before reaching a door. It was undamaged and remarkably clean beside the grim encrusted walls.

"This is where he held them," Amelia said, voice soft. "This room has seen so much death..."

Jamie hesitated, then reached over. He slid back the bolt that held it in place. It moved smoothly, no trace of rust, and Jamie was able to push the door open with ease. The room was long, divided in tow by a slim wall and an archway, fitted with a barred gate. The first part contained a surgeon's table and two large empty cages. As Jamie entered the room, he was hit by a blast of cold stale air and his breath caught in his throat.

The floor was swept clean and tiled in an intricate pattern, forming shapes and symbols beneath their feet. Jamie focused on that, unwilling to examine the more sinister items in the room. The shapes, at first glance, seemed random but gradually he could make out a larger picture. A great tree with snakes entwined around the trunk. The base of the tree was festooned with skulls, more snakes sliding amongst them. Words in gold declared 'Death will not be our end, it is just a moment in eternity.'

Jamie turned away and went over to the table. It was old fashioned and had thick straps built-in, a tray of tools resting nearby.

"They're new," he said, frowning. "Everything else is old but these tools, the bolts on the door, it's all new."

His eyes flickered across the room and came to rest on a large book nestled inside a small hollow in the wall. He approached it warily, hoping it would help make some sense of everything. The book was heavy, thick with yellowing pages, and handmade with crude stitching to keep it together. As Jamie began to turn the pages, he felt a cold prickle at the back of his neck.

The first part of the book was set up like a scrapbook, filled with newspaper clippings, blurry photographs, medical and police reports. Some were old but the further Jamie went, the more recent they became. Interspersed were detailed handwritten notes, pages filled with cramped handwriting. He flicked through without really reading, just getting a general impression of what was written. The work stopped abruptly halfway through, leaving a collection of empty pages before the writing started up again, neater this time. Names in a neat list, each with a number beside, spanning multiple pages.

Jamie caught sight of Amelia's name a few pages in, then further on Eden's name. It had a thick line through it, an angry slash that almost severed the page.

"Do you recognise any of these?" Jamie asked. Amelia came over and peered at the pages.

"Yes… some of these were patients with me. But they…"

"Died?" finished Jamie.

"Yes."

"That's what this is…" he murmured. "It's a list of the dead, of their victims."

"But the writing is the same throughout. If you know some of them, that wouldn't be possible."

Jamie's eyes flickered to the tiled floor, the words burning into his retinas.

"Death will not be our end…" he murmured to himself.

"What?"

"You said they were performing rituals. Maybe they were trying to find a way to escape death?"

"That's ridiculous."

"Says the dead girl," he snapped, beginning to pace. "There were bodies found in the woods, always a boy and a girl, always children. Death for life... but why two?" He paused, mid-ramble. "You said Adam had a sister. She was involved, right? Could the second body be for her?"

"I suppose... he had a wife as well. She worked with us. And she was most definitely active in their blasphemy."

"What was her name? It's a long shot, but she might be on the list. At least then we can rule her out."

"Her name was Lilith. She was a vile woman."

Jamie froze.

"Lilith? That was Adam's wife?"

"Yes. She was horrible, cold and heartless."

"Blonde, grey eyes? Face like it's carved out of ice?"

"Yes..."

He stumbled back a little, physically startled. He'd had no idea if his theory was even close to accurate, he'd been clutching at straws in an attempt to form something coherent. Part of him had just been hoping all the signs were bizarre coincidences but there was really no way he could continue to deny the evidence.

"I know who our immortals are... I saw a photograph in the office... I thought the surname was from an ancestor but... no..."

He thought of Dr Knott in the paediatric ward, Dr Lilith working as a child psychologist. Predators, the both of them. Using their positions of trust to get close to vulnerable youngsters...

He wanted to throw up.

"I have to get out of here..."

In his mind it was clear. He could take the book, the photos, go to the police, tell them what was going on and they... would laugh in his face. No one would believe some nonsense about immortality. And the Knotts were well respected, they'd be almost impossible to implicate successfully without evidence. And even if he did manage, he had no idea who was working with them. There were confidential records in the book that they could only have gotten access to with help.

He sank down onto the floor, resting his head against the stone. The true hopelessness of the situation finally hit him. He'd been clinging to the vain hope that if he got out, got evidence, he'd be able to fix things somehow. The bad people would be caught and punished, that was how it was supposed to work!

*Who were you trying to kid? You know better.*

"I'm fucked. There's no way to make this go away."

"But this room... the book...?"

"They don't prove anything, except that there's a very morbid overzealous scrapbooker in the world. The evidence is circumstantial at best and it would cancel itself out. The police might believe that someone is crazy enough to think human sacrifice can bring immortality. But they'd never buy into it being a real thing. And I mean, who would you believe? The kid or the adult? It's always the same... no one ever believes the child."

He got to his feet and stalked towards the door, eyes on the ground.

"You can't leave Jamie, you're a part of this! You have to make him, make them all, account for what they have done!"

"Too bad. I'm out. Over. The end."

# XXXVI

Sleep.

Eat.

Pills.

Silence.

Cry.

Bleed.

Sleep. Eat. Pills. Silence. Cry. Bleed.

Those became Jamie's clock, and with each rotation that passed, he found himself becoming emptier. Any thoughts he might have had about finding a way out or trying to put a stop to what was happening had all but deserted him. The pills helped, turning down his senses and leaving him closed off. It was better that way. He welcomed the numbness, he could forget and pretend it was all okay like he used to. Eventually, he wouldn't need to try so hard to convince himself. He could finally understand why the other patients acted the way they did, shambling around like zombies.

His therapy sessions were filled with stilted silence where he would burrow deeper into his mind. He had accepted that he wouldn't be going home so really there was no point even trying to act differently.

After one session, he returned to his bed and lay down on top of the covers. Despite the rigid apathy, he maintained the majority of the time, it began to slip after each and every session. He hoped it would get easier but for the time being, he found his own ways to shed the bitter feelings.

*Shed the feelings, the sadness and the pain.*

*Shed the tears until there are none left.*

*Shed the tainted blood that makes you weak.*

*Shed it all, like an old skin until you are left empty once more.*

Jamie reached under the mattress where he kept his hidden things. His hand brushed something papery, unfamiliar and out of place. Carefully he slid the object loose.

The book. He'd not seen Amelia since he'd left her in the basement although he was sure she was nearby. Seeing the book he felt anger stirring in the pit of his stomach. She was judging him for giving up but it was easy to do that from the outside. It wasn't her at risk, it wasn't her family in danger.

If they realise the book is gone, they'll think you're trying to interfere.

As the thought filtered through his brain, he felt the cuts on his waist burning, a reminder of the price of interference. Although he'd tried to keep them clean, they weren't healing the way they should have been. He knew he should have been concerned but it was hard to conjure the energy in his doped state.

Put the book back before anyone notices.

Jamie slipped the book under his t-shirt, disguising it as best he could, before taking the route that would lead him to the male ward and the hole in the floor. He could feel the warm cocoon of drugs that usually enveloped him was slipping and as it did, he became more aware of the ache at his hip.

He made his way through the shadow infested rooms, ignoring their cruel whispers as best he could. As he neared the room, the sound of voices reached his ears. At first, he thought it was merely the whispers but quickly realised that they were coming from somewhere else.

"I can't believe you lost it! Why did you leave it down here? Why did you need to make it in the first place?"

"It's important to preserve and remember the past."

"Not with things like this! If you want to memorialise the past, just put a bloody plaque on a bench or something! If that book gets into the wrong hands, all our hard work will have been wasted!"

Jamie approached the door hesitantly and peeked round. Dr Lilith was pacing angrily, Dr Knott perched on a ledge nearby, looking rather bored with the conversation. Jamie bit his lip and cleared his throat. Both of them turned. Dr Lilith's eyes widened and behind her, Dr Knott got to his feet, the candlelight casting sharp lines across his face.

403

"Jamie!"

"Is this what you're missing?" he asked, producing the book. Dr Knott stepped towards him, automatically reaching for it.

"Where did you get that?" he demanded.

"Found it... don't worry... I haven't told anyone... I know when I've been beaten."

He handed the book over to the doctor, wincing as another stab of pain emanated from his hip. Dr Knott's quick eyes picked up on the movement and he frowned.

"You're in pain Show me?"

Jamie grimaced and hesitantly tugged at his clothing to reveal the cuts. The skin around the wound was an angry red, swollen and hot to the touch with pus oozing from the jagged letters.

"That looks unpleasant. Sit down, I'll see what I can do."

"Why are you helping me?" Jamie asked warily. He sat down, his leg hurting too much to stand much longer.

"You interest me. Lilith, can you get my bag?"

Lilith rolled her eyes but retrieved the bag, from which Dr Knott produced bandages and antiseptic. Jamie watched in confusion, trying to make sense of what was happening.

"But you tried to have me killed... isn't this a bit counter to that?"

"I didn't try to have you killed. Believe me, if I had we would not be having this discussion."

"You drugged me and sliced my arms open... that indicates a desire to kill me."

"No... while I may have been involved, I never wanted you dead. Just... out of the way."

"You're a very special young man, Jamie. In time you could be quite useful to use. We wouldn't want you dead, but of course, we couldn't have you interfering," said Lilith, coming over and gently brushing Jamie's hair from his face. The boy shifted, uncomfortable at the contact.

"I won't help you, ever."

"It's not as bad as you think… it comes with great perks," she smiled. "What do you want most Jamie? I'm sure we can arrange it."

Her voice was almost a purr, her eyes fixed on him with a predatory smile on her lips. Jamie shook his head fiercely, refusing to meet his gaze. Her smile faltered for a moment before she firmly plastered it back across her features.

"We'll see… time is a great motivator."

"Lilith, my sweet, my angel, you're being somewhat of a distraction for me and my patient. Could you please go…?" Dr Knott said suddenly, gesturing loosely across the room.

"Go where darling?"

"I don't actually care where you go as long as it's somewhere far away where your frankly grating voice can't reach my ears," he replied, his tone still carefully neutral.

Lilith scowled and stalked angrily out of the room. Dr Knott let out a sigh of relief.

"Never marry an immortal…" he muttered to himself, focusing on his work.

"I won't change my mind. I'll die in here first."

Dr Knott shrugged.

"That's up to you. I don't really care if I'm honest. I take in those who want to join, I don't force them into it."

"No, you just kill people instead."

"I do what I need to do."

"Nothing justifies what you do…"

"I am not trying to justify my actions. I take no joy in it but then I also have no regrets about what I do. It's just something I do to ensure my continued survival. You of all people cannot condemn me for that…" his voice trailed away and he locked eyes with Jamie, a clash of green against brown.

"I didn't kill anyone," Jamie said softly.

"Three graves in the churchyard say different."

"Those were accidents, not murder. They weren't my fault."

"No, the victims were accidents. The intention wasn't. Your part in it wasn't an accident." Jamie pulled away from the doctor roughly and got to his feet, wincing. Dr Knott sighed and straightened up, folding his arm. "Now you're being stupid. However much I've hurt your pride, your leg will hurt considerably more if you don't let me treat it."

Jamie stubbornly took a few stumbling steps towards the door before being forced to concede, sitting back down with a scowl on his face.

"I'm not judging what you did Jamie. What your father did was truly despicable. I abhor men like him. I will admit that your actions were somewhat misguided but only because you didn't plan things more carefully. Your reasoning and intentions were admirable, especially given your youth."

Jamie looked away, unconvinced. The doctor paused in his work.

"Tell me something, do you condemn Eden for killing her uncle?"

"No…"

"If you could go back and end your father's life, no casualties but him… would you do it?"

Even though it was only a theoretical question, Jamie hesitated, ashamed of his own thoughts. Eventually, he gave a slow nod. If he had the chance, he would take it. Some people didn't deserve the life they had.

"In a heartbeat…"

"Well then… you're happy to kill to protect your loved ones. That's all I'm doing, really I want to keep my family safe, at any cost." He finished working on Jamie's leg. "Imagine being able to ensure the safety of your sister, her children, countless descendants… doesn't that sound appealing…? Never needing to be afraid again?" His voice was soft and calm, full of promise, with an almost affectionate quality to it. "Just… think on it. I'm not unreasonable, I won't make you decide straight away. I'll return in a few days and we can talk further."

Jamie nodded slowly and got to his feet, the doctor steadying him as he did. The boy was trembling, mind at war with itself. He made his way from the room, lost in an almost trancelike state.

It sounded too good to be true and buried at the back of his mind, a tiny voice was hissing at him that he was treading on dangerous ground. It was drowned out by the fog that clouded his mind, which whispered sweet promises. No more fear... no pain... after living a half-life for so long, going through the motions of life more than really experiencing it... he couldn't deny that he was tempted.

You're not like them... you're not a killer... don't let them make you into a monster.

Eternity... he could make sure Callie grew up happy and healthy. He could help make the world better.

Eternity alone. Eternity haunted by your ghosts with only the voices in your head for company? Is that really what you want?

"Shut up," he muttered to himself.

Immortality won't solve your problems. It won't save you from your nightmares or ease your guilt. It will just make your suffering infinite.

He reached the dorms and lay down on his bed, staring up at the ceiling. Above his head, flakes of plaster were breaking away, drifting down to land on his face and neck. He sighed and brushed it away, closing his eyes.

"Jamie! Look! Cake!" Tasha skipped into the room, holding a plate bearing a piece of cake.

"Not now Tasha..." Jamie muttered. "Please, leave me alone."

His head was too foggy to focus on conversation and all his concentration was devoted to the offer he'd received. He needed clarity to think about things but it was difficult. If he turned his thoughts to what had been said in the basement, he felt a strange pain at the back of his skull.

"But... cake..."

"Fine. Leave the cake."

He stayed resolutely silent as Tasha babbled away for a few minutes before setting the plate down and heading off. Jamie tentatively opened his eyes. On the floor beside his bed was the plate with a block of dubious-looking sponge, decorated with watery icing and obnoxiously bright sprinkles. Just seeing it made Jamie feel nauseous.

A larger chunk of plaster fell down from the ceiling and he turned his attention upwards once again. A patch of floorboard was visible with a hole gnawed in it. If he strained his eyes, Jamie could make out the shape of a rat, nibbling at the wood.

As he watched, the rodent squirmed its way through the gap and began to scurry down the pitted surface of the wall. It leapt onto the bed frame and then down to the floor. Jamie stirred on the bed, following the motion curiously. His movement made the bed springs jangle and the rat froze, eyes landing on the boy. The two of them regarded each other carefully, waiting to see who would make the first move.

When Jamie didn't do anything, the rat scurried over to the cake, nibbling at the edge. As the boy watched, a second, larger rat poked its head out of a crack in the wall. It sized up the competitor before sprinting out of the hole to tackle the smaller rodent.

A terrible series of squeaky shrieks filled the room as the two animals clawed and bit at one another, battling over the cake. Jamie watched them numbly. The large rat sank its teeth into the smaller one, ripping open its throat. It let out one final cry before its body succumbed, blood puddling around the animal. The large rat ignored the cake and began to feast on the carcass instead, consuming the flesh with gusto.

Just doing what it had to in order to survive...

Kill or be killed...

Jamie looked at the shredded corpse of the small rodent, its entrails strewn across the floor.

Survive at any cost.

*This Book of Shadows is the property of Samyra Luis*

*September 15th*
*Waxing Crescent*

*Empathic Magic*

*Empathic magic is one of the least understood forms of magic and also one of the most dangerous. Many practitioners will ignore this particular branch, viewing it as lesser.*

*However, once mastered it can be incredibly effective. Unlike most strains of magic, empathic magic is far more like science. It involves the manipulation of chemicals in the brain which can have a result on more than just the emotions of the subject; it can also manipulate them into extreme behaviour.*

*True masters of this type of magic are rare, however, the original tribe of Saruma was said to have an exceptionally powerful empathic practitioner amongst them, although records from this time are scarce making it difficult to learn much about them.*

# XXXVII

"Okay Callie, time for bed now!"

Her mom's voice was rigidly cheery, the perkiness strained slightly. Callie stayed silent as her storybook was put away and the covers tucked tight around her. As her mom turned towards the door, the young girl reached out and grabbed her arm.

"Mommy, when is Jamie coming back?" she asked. The question had been building inside her for days and each time it had almost broken free, she'd bitten her tongue.

Her mother sighed and perched on the edge of the bed.

"Callie, Jamie may not be home for a long time. He's not very well at the moment... you remember last year when he went away? It's like that... he can't come back till he's better..."

"Can we go see him?"

"I don't think so, sweetie. He's gone to a special hospital to get well..."

Callie chewed her lip and cuddled her teddy bear close, not entirely convinced by her mom's words. Still, she let the subject drop and stayed quiet as the light was switched off and the door closed. She knew Jamie wasn't like most people, she'd always known. She knew when her mom said Jamie was sick, she was lying. Jamie had never got sick, not the type of sick that she sometimes got where she lay on the sofa in her pyjamas eating soup and watching Danger Mouse on repeat. He had something in his brain, like a weed that poisoned his thoughts.

She wanted to believe he'd come back like last time. She wanted to close her eyes, go to sleep and play pretend that everything would be okay. But instead, she got out of bed and tiptoed from the room, down the hall to the stairs. Both her parents were home and she could hear their voices drifting up from the living room.

"She asked about Jamie..."

"That's only to be expected. She misses him. We all do."

"Did we do the right thing sending him away?"

"The doctors all said it was the best. If it was just the suicide attempt, maybe it would have been better to keep him at the hospital, but you heard him… he didn't even remember doing it. He needs help, more than we realised."

"I just… I feel like it's our fault…"

"It's not. We did what we could. How could we know how bad he was getting?"

The two parents embraced. Callie could see tears glistening on her mom's cheek as she buried her face in the crook of her dad's neck.

"I remember the day we first saw him… he was so small… with all those cuts and bruises…"

"He's just as vulnerable now as he was then…"

"When we bought him home and his face lit up every time he got a hug or a nice word… I'd give anything to have that little boy back…"

Her voice trailed off as she broke down in tears. Callie crept off the stairs and went back up to her room. She lay in her bed, watching the shapes of the shadows her nightlight cast on the ceiling. She stayed there, lying awake, eyes beginning to burn with exhaustion, until she heard her parents come upstairs and go to their room.

When silence took hold of the house, she rose once more. Callie picked up her small mirror that was perched on her dresser and set it on the floor, before retrieving her nightlight and placing it in the centre of the mirror. The light bounced off the glass, dancing dizzyingly across the walls. She wasn't entirely sure what she was doing and could only hope that it worked out.

She sat in front of the mirror and waited. And waited. And waited.

*Come on…* Callie thought to herself. *I know you're there.*

Although the strange sightings in her bedroom had lessened, she was aware of eyes on her almost every night. It was always there. Sometimes she could see him… it… other times it was just a sense that he was there. And on yet other occasions he was all too present, tearing around her room in a hurricane of fury.

No sound. No movement.

411

Her body was cramped from sitting in one position too long and her eyelids kept sliding shut. The clock in the hall struck three am.

"Please…" she said softly. "Can you help me? My brother is stuck in hospital, I'm not allowed to see him and I'm really worried… we all are… I was wondering if you could find out what's going on… Please come now! I know you can help!"

The curtains stirred and the shadows faltered for a moment, obscured by something unseen.

"Please…" Callie repeated. A dark shape moved across the surface of the mirror and the nightlight went out. The young girl stiffened sharply as something cold brushed against her bare skin. "You're here…"

The nightlight turned back on and now as the lamp revolved, she could see the silhouette of a man sitting across from her. Occasionally, the light would catch on something and Callie got the impression of a face, two steely onyx eyes boring into her. What had seemed like a good idea was quickly beginning to sour but she pressed on.

"I need your help… I don't know if you can… but please try…"

The shape moved and as Callie looked at the reflection in the mirror, she saw an arm reaching over a moment before something touched her cheek. She tried not to flinch at the sensation of fingers against flesh, those fingers that had clawed open her legs and arms with ease when angered.

"What do I need to do?" Her voice cracked as she fought back tears. She needed Jamie. They were more than brother and sister, she was closer to him than she was anyone else and without him it felt like part of her been cut out. "Please, I will do anything to bring him home"

Callie's hearing aids let out a high pitched whine and she winced. The hand retreated and then something tapped clearly against the mirror. One short tap. Three long.

The nightlight flickered out for a second and this time when it reignited, Callie knew he was gone. She didn't know whether the knocking meant yes or no. All she could do was hope, pray and wait for a miracle.

*****

"Do you really think prayer will help you now? Surely by this point, you should admit that there is no God to help you. My very presence can attest to that."

"You have taken my family, my love, my life… but you will not rob me of my faith."

"Well now, that sounds like a challenge… I would hate to disappoint."

Two people. A man, prowling like a caged animal. A young woman in rags, knelt on the floor with her arms tethered to the ground nearby. She was frail, dark circles around her eyes and matted red hair forming a grimy curtain around her face. As the man circled the girl, a cruel smile formed on his lips.

"Of the things you have lost, I cannot help but wonder which loss hurts the most. Your father? Your lover?" He paused, his smirk growing. "Your child?"

The woman stiffened, her head rising sharply and locking on him.

"What have you done?"

"Nothing… yet… but children are rather costly and it appears your sister has fallen on hard times." A shrill cry came from the doorway and the woman turned to see a figure clutching a squalling infant. A choking sob caught in her throat and she strained at her tether in an effort to get to the child. "Of course, being a close friend of the family I was only too happy to help and take the child off her hands."

"Please… do not hurt my son!"

"What type of monster do you take me for? Do you think that I could be so heartless as to harm a child in front of his mother?"

His smile removed any doubt in the woman's mind. As she watched, he crossed over to the figure and lifted the child into his arms. The man cooed to the baby, calming its cries before carefully settling it on the ground in front of the woman. She pulled at her rope, reaching out as much as she could.

"I have conducted a number of experiments during my time here. I am sure you have noticed the fascinating creatures that inhabit your new home?" The man went over to a shelf set in the wall and lifted a glass jar, containing what looked like black ink. "They are wonderfully adept little things. They can thrive in almost any environment and require little food. They can also manipulate their surroundings to suit their needs better."

He took a set of metal tongs and opened the jar, extracting a slimy leechlike animal that squirmed and seemed to be both solid and liquid all at once. The woman hardly dared to breathe, her eyes flicking between the man and the child.

"They can even manipulate people in the same way… admittedly it is not always successful as their presence can have a rather… toxic effect."

He advanced on the boy, kneeling down in front of him. The man plastered a friendly smile across his features and offered the peculiar creature to the child, whispering soft words of encouragement and enticement until the boy reached out and grasped it in his chubby hand.

At first, nothing happened. Then the creature went rigid, letting out a high-pitched squeal of excitement. It bulged, viscous fluid visible beneath the translucent skin and there came a sharp pop. At first, the woman thought it had burst but after a moment she realised it had instead altered itself somehow, taking on a more liquid form in order to slip free.

It oozed up the boy's arm, leaving tiny cuts in its wake, until it reached the child's face. It seemed to nuzzle against his cheek before solidifying once more and roughly thrusting itself into the child's ear canal.

The boy let out a wail as the insidious creature worked its way into his skull and the woman flailed helplessly as every instinct screamed at her to comfort her child. The boy's cry faded to a whimper and he went limp.

As the mother watched, her son began to tremble. His veins darkened as the toxic influence entered his bloodstream and spread through his body. His skin took on a greyish hue and as he shook it began to split, peeling away from the muscle and releasing a foul odour into the air. The trembling became violent, the small boy thrashing wildly in place. His eyes rolled back in his skull and with the little control he had over his limbs, he clawed at his face, nails gouging into the soft rotting skin. He let out a terrible choking gurgling sound and black bile spewed from his mouth, running down his chin and onto his chest. More came from his nose and ears. It smelt like petrol and mud, the acrid stench clawing its way up the nostrils of everyone in the room.

"Please! Please stop this!" The woman begged. Her son was soaked in bile and blood, fingers ragged stumps, body failing before her eyes.

The man smiled.

"It is interesting. The effects of their influence can vary greatly depending on species. If the body accepts it, often it will allow for a relatively harmless symbiotic relationship. However, when it rejects the presence, like your dear son, the results can vary from necrosis, haemorrhage, rabies. It truly is fascinating," he said as he approached the gate that divided the room. "Their acceptance rate in humans seems to be on the lower side, but I have found great success with animals... although of course eventually, the body deteriorates under their influence."

"No..."

The man's smile never faltered as he slid back the gate which let out a grating screech as the rusted metal protested.

From the darkness on the other side came a long snarl that sent shudders through the woman's veins. Two great beasts emerged. They might have once been dogs but those days were long gone. Their fur was matted with saliva and had begun to fall out, exposing greying skin beneath, scarred with deep wounds that leaked inky pus. Their movements were awkward, limbs stiff and gangly. The left eye of one of them had been torn out and the gaping hole was already showing signs of infection. One was far larger than the other, a former guard dog at the asylum, scrabbling at the ground with its bloody paws as it cast its gaze around the room, trying to make sense of the images. The smaller of the two had once been a beloved pet, a sweet corgi who the woman knew well. Now there was no trace of the animal it had once been.

Without direction, the dogs leapt at the boy. Their fangs found flesh, savaging him furiously, stopping only to take the occasional swipe at their rival. The two of them seized the child's limbs, tugging mercilessly. The boy let out one brief scream, the sound piercing his mother's heart, telling her that her son was still in there, before his decaying body was completely torn in two.

Jamie vaulted upright in bed, breathing heavily. Amelia was perched at the foot of his bed, looking at him with clear contempt. He frowned, his mind putting two and two together.

"Was that… did you…?"

"Yes. You needed to see it."

"Do not do that! I don't want to see that shit and I definitely don't want you messing around inside my head!"

"Given that you decided to side with those monsters against all reason, I felt that it was important for you to know exactly what you have agreed to be part of."

"I haven't agreed to anything. And if I do, not only is it none of your business, but I am doing what I need in order to survive! Maybe if you'd focused more on your own survival and doing what you needed to, your son might still be alive!"

Amelia's expression turned to one of absolute fury and when she spoke there was pure venom in her voice.

"Do not dare blame me for that. I loved my son and I would have done anything to save him. But one evil act in place of another does nothing! And if you ever speak those words again, I will ensure that you not only rot in here for the rest of your miserable life, but I guarantee that you will remain here long after you have been forgotten!"

"Amelia, it's easy to take the high ground when you have nothing to lose. You're dead, your family are gone. I'm sorry about that but I am still alive and so is my family. And I intend to keep it that way. And if siding with Dr Knott is what I need to do, I'll do it. Now go away and stop bothering me before I find a way to bust you."

"You are making a mistake Jamie… I hope you see that before it costs you dearly…" Amelia said softly, before turning away and retreating from the bed.

Jamie watched her go and then slumped in the bed. He didn't feel nearly as confident as he had acted and that niggling doubt wouldn't go away. But he had made a promise to himself. Do what needed to be done. Survive. Now he just had to hope Dr Knott reappeared before he changed his mind again.

Too anxious to go back to sleep and with his dream still very present in his mind, he got up and headed to the main hall. He was slightly concerned Amelia might pop up again to harass him some more. He could see why she was angry but then she had tried to use him too, in her own way, to get revenge on the people who had hurt her. And her plan was much more likely to get him killed. If anything, he should be angry at her. But he just felt rather sad.

The hall was empty except for one sleepy-looking orderly. Jamie seated himself at a table and drummed his fingers on the smooth surface. He wondered what time it was. He wondered what Callie was doing. He wondered if Eden had been found or if she had managed to find food.

*Or maybe she's still stuck in the shed, slowly starving to death…*

"Oh will you just shut up…" he muttered to himself.

"Who are you talking to?" the orderly said, making the boy jump and turn sharply.

"I… myself."

"Yourself?"

"Yes. It's the only way I get any intelligent conversation around here."

The orderly opened his mouth to speak but before he could, all the lights went out.

"What the…?"

After the constant dull glow of the lamps, actual darkness was a startling change and it took Jamie a moment to realise what was going on. A loud siren began to blare, a flashing red light illuminating the room in fragments. The orderly seemed just as confused and, after a brief hesitation, gestured at Jamie to stay where he was before heading to the hall to investigate.

Some of the other patients had begun to gather, stirred from sleep by the obnoxious noise, and were adding to the chaos, letting out frenzied shouts, careening around the room. Jamie couldn't tell if their actions were prompted by excitement or fear but as orderlies began to emerge from the halls, the atmosphere quickly developed to terror.

The brief snatches of crimson light let him see in stills as the staff began to corral the patients, using whatever methods were easiest. Jamie saw

Tasha knocked to the ground, a hulking figure pinning her and restraining her arms.

Jamie retreated quickly, pressing himself into the darkest corner he could find, hoping he could go unnoticed. The room was painted in shades, white walls turned rose, grey uniforms stained scarlet and across the floor splashes of deep claret that could only be blood. He thought about fleeing to somewhere safer but the noise, the light, it was overwhelming after days of silence and perma-twilight, making the room spin about him and his head hurt.

Strong hands grasped hold of him and his face was smashed against the bricks. He managed one brief cry before he was silenced and enveloped in complete blackness.

SCHOOL NURSE INCIDENT REPORT

| | |
|---|---|
| Student: Jamie Harper | Grade: Freshman |
| Parent: Ruth Harper | Date: May 6th |
| Teacher: Mr A. Hart | Time: 9:02am |

**Description of the Incident:**

Jamie was found tied to the school flagpole with a bloody nose and a black eye

**Action taken:**

Taken to nurse. Parents contacted. Provided with ice pack.

# XXXVIII

There was nothing. No sound. No light. No time. Just endless floating space.

For a long while, there was just that, stretching on without end. Then a thin sliver of light appeared, the faintest crack between objects but enough to allow a view of what was.

The room was a small square, too narrow to stretch out in any direction. Three of the walls were padded, the fourth was taken up by a metal door with a sliding grate in the centre, to allow a person a view inside. As the light grew and spread, the padding on the walls became clearer, not smooth like first thought but pitted with deep lacerations where someone had carved rough letters over and over and over again. Some were old, others were new.

He had been there for a long time. Not long enough to make the first marks but long enough that he had already forgotten which were his. There was a toilet in one corner, the odour rising from it replacing every memory of smell he had known.

The first few segments of time where he occupied the world, he spent in silence. Gradually as his ears became more accustomed to the vast emptiness of his imprisonment, he became aware of other sounds. Voices from somewhere outside, although exactly where he couldn't tell. Then came the scratching, a persistent scrabbling within the walls, pausing occasionally only to start up again somewhere else. Once he was aware of it, no matter how hard he tried it was impossible to tune out.

*Scratch, Scratch, Scratch*

After a while, he began talking to himself.

*Scratch, Scratch, Scratch*

As a little more time passed, the walls began talking back.

*Scratch, Scratch, Scratch*

And still, the scratching continued.

420

It carved a hole in his brain, some small creature clawing its way into his soul.

*Scratch*

*Scratch*

*Scratch*

*Scratch*

*Scratch*

*Scratch*

*Scratch*

He lay there, hunched and miserable, losing himself little by little. His name was the first to go. Then everything else started to fade with it. The world disappeared, replaced with walls. Were there other people? He had heard voices, there had to be. Someone was out there, someone left him water during the floating times.

But slowly he became less and less sure. It was just how things worked in the room. Everything warm and familiar turned to scattered fragments in his brain. All he knew was the room. It provided him with what he needed.

All there was. The room. The words on the walls. The scratching.

At first, he slept, like the light that came from under the door, he rose and fell. On. Off. On. Off. On.

On.

*SCRATCH*

On.

Soon his eyes wouldn't close, parched they stared at the walls accusingly, fictional rodents scampering across the padded surface, mocking him. If he slept, he would be vulnerable. They would claw their way inside of him. He had to stay awake.

Then the tapping started. He thought it came from them. The monsters in the walls but realised it was his own fingers drumming on the floor. He stared up at the roof. He tapped.

*Tap. Tap. Tap*

*Scratch Scratch Scratch*

The walls were immeasurably high, the roof thick with spider webs and skittering creatures.

Couldn't sleep, they'd get him

Couldn't run, they'd chase him

Couldn't hide, they'd find him

*Tap. Tap. Tap.*

*Scratch.*
      *SCRATCH.*
      *Scratch*

The noise grew louder and seemed to come from all around him. His skin prickled like a thousand tiny insects were crawling over his body and although he tried to ignore it, the sensation persisted. He rubbed his arms against the floor, hoping the rough wood would alleviate it a little.

*Scratch*

*Scratch*

*Scratch*

He pressed his hands against his ears, blocking them as best he could. It got louder, building. Not from the walls. Not from the floor or ceiling.

It was in his head, in his ears. Something was scratching away at his brain, burrowing deeper, clawing at him.

*ScratchScratchScratchScratch*

It stirred away inside his skull. The itching burned at his skin. And inside his throat, something took root, digging in, making him cough.


*Tap.*


*Cough.*


*Scratch.*

He raked his nails against his limbs, digging them in until the itching subsided, only for it to spring up elsewhere. The niggling, gnawing pain in his throat grew. Every breath was strained like something was blocking his airways. He rubbed his neck, feeling something hard and swollen beneath the skin. He pressed down and it gave way, rising above the influence of his hand.

*Cough.*

*ScratchScratchScratchScratchScratchScratchScratch.*

Burning, choking, body rebelling against the elements, mind-destroying itself.

He gagged, the something rising further, blocking his airways entirely. Gasping, eyes streaming, clawing at his skin in the hope of dislodging the thing. At the back of his mouth, he felt something long and thin tickling the soft skin. The scratching in his head grew.

Cough. Retch.

He rolled onto his front, doubling over and spluttering, spitting. Something moved across his tongue. Fingers trembling, he parted his lips and reached into his mouth. Hard papering shell. Long skinny tendrils.

From his mouth he pulled a squirming insect, a cockroach coated in saliva. He dropped it to the ground and it scuttled off.

And still, the scratching continued.

*Dear Adam*

*Please stop writing to me. I have made my decision and I will not change my mind. My heart lies elsewhere now and I know you will say that it has done so in the past, but I have only felt like this one time in my life. And I'm sure you know who I refer to.*

*I am going to get married and have the life I always dreamed of. I will forgive you for what you did to me but only to the extent that I will keep your child. I do not want to ever see you again.*

*I am sorry but this is how things are going to be.*


*Evelyn*

# XXXIX

With a rusty creak, the door to the cell swung open. Jamie, huddled in the corner, lifted his head. His clothes were filthy, stained with sweat and dust, and hung loosely on his body. He winced as the light burned his eyes, cringing against the padding.

Dr Knott stood in the doorway, looking down at the boy with a combination of sympathy and amusement that conflicted wildly on his face.

"What's going on?" Jamie croaked, voice weak from neglect. His throat felt like it had been rubbed with sandpaper.

"There was a rather nasty riot downstairs and you were injured. We placed you in here for your own safety while you recovered. Not the nicest of accommodations I know, but needs must."

"I... I don't remember..."

"Yes, we had to administer some rather heavy medications. They can cause some temporary memory loss, but things should start to return to you soon."

Jamie looked his body, bruised and scarred, small scuffs of dried blood dotted across his skin, deep grooves around his wrists and ankles like something had been tied too tightly.

"But..."

"You experienced some hallucinations and acted rather violently. We tried to keep the damage to a minimum but you did sustain a few minor injuries."

"Dr Knott..."

"You can call me Adam." He approached Jamie and knelt down, touching his cheek lightly to turn his head for a better look. "I'm just going to ask you a few questions and then I'll be able to let you out. Now, can you tell me your name?"

"Jamie."

"How old are you?"

"Sixteen."

"What's the last thing you remember?"

Jamie hesitated, images dancing through his mind that he tried to organise and make sense of.

"Lights… flashing lights… and shouting…"

"Alright… it doesn't look like you've suffered any long term damage. With luck, all your memories will return over the next few days."

He straightened up and beckoned Jamie to follow, heading out of the cell. Jamie struggled to his feet and went after him, wobbling like a foal taking its first steps.

The cell was in a narrow hall, lined with doors that seemed to lead to more of the same. Adam led the way to an open space with a single large window and two sets of stairs which disappeared downwards. The paint on the walls was badly damaged and peeling, the floorboards were broken in places and rotted away.

"Where are we?"

"This is Morningwood's upper level. It's only used for storage these days but it used to house the medical and violent offenders wing. The room you were in was last used to hold the very young lady who set this place on fire." He continued towards an unmarked door, pausing beside it to let Jamie catch up. "Have you given any thought to my offer?"

"A bit. I really want to be able to go home… if helping you gets me there… but I still don't think I'd be able to kill a child…"

"What if I told you we may have found a way around that part? Would that convince you?"

"Is it actually true or are you just making it up so I'll agree?" Jamie asked warily. Adam laughed.

"Very astute. But it is true."

"Then… I guess… I'll help…"

"Excellent," said Adam, giving him a bright smile. Jamie wasn't sure why but the action made him uncomfortable.

Adam opened the door and stepped aside to let the boy pass. Jamie glanced around him once more before entering the room. It was clear even at a single glance that it had once been an operating room, but unlike the equipment in the basement which looked new and was well cared for, what was left lying around the upstairs room was old, rusted and dirty. In the centre was an operating table, modified with multiple straps to hold a patient down.

Behind him, the door clicked shut.

Jamie turned slowly. Nothing had changed about the doctor's demeanour but there was a darkness in his eyes that he hadn't seen before. A hunger, the way a fox might look at a rabbit before it strikes.

"So..." Jamie said, nervously. "What's this new way you've figured out...?"

"It's a little complicated."

"I'm sure I can keep up..."

He moved slowly across the ground, the two of them mirroring one another as Jamie attempted to distance himself without making it too obvious.

"It is a rather long story... I'd hate to bore you with the details."

"I'm sure I wouldn't be bored..."

"Well essentially the cause of our immortality isn't actually linked to the sacrifices and you're going to run aren't you?"

Jamie's eyes flickered from Adam to the door and back again. He made a split-second decision and sprinted for the exit. Adam darted forward and grabbed the teen by the hair, throwing him down on the floor, but made no further move to restrain him.

"I really wouldn't recommend trying that again. The drugs are probably still pumping through your system and you've not eaten in a while; if you exert yourself too much it will only end up with you hurting yourself." He leaned casually against the doorframe, watching the boy. Jamie forced himself up and lunged forward once again, Adam easily knocking him back. "Of course, feel free to ignore me."

Seizing hold of Jamie, the man dragged him over to the table and pushed him down onto it. He moved swiftly, fastening one of the straps

427

to hold the boy down before relaxing and taking his time with the rest. Both ankles, wrists, torso, throat and finally one across his forehead.

"There. All nice and secure. Don't want you wandering off... I'd sedate you but I'd like you to be conscious for this." Adam retrieved a metal tray of tools and returned to the table. "When I said it was a long story, I wasn't exaggerating. It started thousands of years ago. There were more of us then, but gradually the number dwindled to just the three of us. But our target never changed. We wanted to live forever... by any means."

He picked up two small objects, examining them under the light.

"We were successful. As you can see, but it wasn't by sacrificing children... well... one child... during our searches, we came across a tribe of witches. They lived in this very area as it happens. And they supposedly knew how to grant immortality. They weren't very keen to share, however."

Adam's voice remained calm and steady, as though he was discussing the weather. He reached down and prised Jamie's eyelid up, sliding something cold and metallic into place. The boy tried to blink but his eyelid was held rigidly in place. Adam repeated the process, ensuring that both eyes were kept wide, staring up at the ruined ceiling.

"We befriended a young man. He wanted to explore his potential. He pushed every limit he could... some too far. He was putting us all at risk..."

Jamie heard a sharp snap, rubber hitting skin. The doctor moved out of his line of sight and no matter how much he tried to find him, the restraints made it impossible.

"There's a particular spell, it can link people together. It's not widely used because it can have unexpected side effects... and it is part of a strain of magic that most are afraid to use... blood magic." There was a clatter of metal on metal. "It was blood magic that caused our young friend to get caught. He was found with the body of a newborn baby... his newborn baby. His punishment was exactly what he wanted... immortality. Under some restrictions. Are the restraints too tight?"

"What?"

"I want you to be comfortable."

"I'm strapped to a table…"

"Fair point. Would it help if I told you I wasn't going to kill you?"

"Not really."

"Hmm… anyway, where was I? Oh yes… the restrictions. He was sealed underground, to live forever imprisoned. Even if his body rotted, his mind would live on. We took advantage of that. I linked myself, my sister and my wife to him."

"Well done. You're immortal. Let me go!" Jamie's eyes were burning and he pulled at the restraints as much as he could.

"Restrictions Jamie… as long as he's imprisoned, so are we. We're stuck in this pathetic backwater town forever." For the first time, a hint of emotion leaked into his voice. Bitterness, anger. Adam let out a long sigh, moving back into Jamie's line of sight. "Do you know what a lobotomy is Jamie? You're smart, I'm sure you do. They're not used very often these days. It's a fairly antiquated technique but… we make do with what we have."

He produced a long thin spike and a small hammer, the kind that would be used to crack a nut. Jamie's heart was pounding, blood crashing in his ears, deafening him to everything else.

"This will hurt. But afterwards, you'll have exactly what you wanted… no more fear, no more pain, no more voices. I promise." Adam gave Jamie a friendly smile as he positioned the point of the needle over the boy's eye. "I know this will be difficult for you but I recommend that you do not struggle. If you move, it will throw off my aim and I could end up killing you."

"Please… please don't do this… there's got to be another way…" Jamie begged. The straps were biting into his skin and every movement made the pain worse.

"You asked me for another way before… and I found this. Are you going to choose yourself over the lives of potentially hundreds of children? I didn't think you were like that."

*Fight back! Be a man!*

Jamie didn't respond, he just glared. His mind was whirring as he tried to come up with some kind of solution.

*You're going to die. You're not a fighter, not even to save yourself. Pathetic.*

He tried each of the restraints, testing for any sign of weakness, any tiny amount of give in the unforgiving leather. The spike was resting just above his eyeball, almost close enough for Jamie to feel the sharpened point.

*Need to delay him… the longer you have, the more chance there is to escape.*

No arms, no legs, no movement. Jamie did the only thing he was able to. He gathered up the saliva in his mouth and spat hard at the doctor, striking him in the eye. He grimaced and set the tools aside.

"I've had far worse bodily fluids on me over the years," Adam said coldly, pulling a handkerchief from his pocket and dabbing at his eye.

Pull, twist. Pull, twist. The strap on his wrist had a tiny bit of stretch. Not enough to get free but enough to give him just a little bit of hope. Pull, twist. He could feel the skin on his wrists giving way to the brutal straps, blood lubricating the movement.

Jamie jerked sharply, wrenching his arm upwards. He wasn't sure if it was the withered leather or his actions that caused it, but something gave and his arm came free. He slammed his fist into Adam's face with as much force as he could muster, his knuckles colliding with the man's nose. There was a crunch and Adam recoiled sharply with a yell. Jamie fumbled for the other straps, not knowing if the man was actually hurt or if he was just startled by the attack.

He managed to free his other arm and remove the strap on his torso, then began to tear at the one on his head, pulling at chunks of his hair in the process. Adam's nose was streaming with blood and his eyes were full of fury as he turned his focus back on Jamie. He grabbed at the boy's arms, pushing them down and trying to secure them with the straps once more. Jamie twisted his wrist against Adam's thumb, breaking his hold. He moved wildly, acting without thought, just with the desperate need to break free. His nails raked across Adam's face, scratching at his eyes. He lashed out, using one hand to strike while the other reached up and struggled with the buckle of the strap.

Finally, it came loose and Jamie was able to lift his head. The strap on his throat was cutting in badly and it was getting hard to hold Adam off.

Jamie let out a yell and slammed his skull against his attacker's. He regretted it instantly, pain spreading rapidly. He just hoped he'd hurt Adam as much as he'd hurt himself.

Adam stepped back and grabbed a rusty scalpel from the tray of equipment. Jamie used the opportunity to pull the strap on his neck free and sit up, reaching to his ankles to undo his last restraints. Adam darted forward, whether his intention was to kill or just injure Jamie couldn't tell but he didn't care. He twisted sideways, the leather giving out just in time and allowing him to roll off the table and onto the floor.

The boy wasted no time. He scrambled to his feet and fled through the nearest door. He shut it firmly and dragged as much heavy furniture as he could manage in front of it.

*Now what? You're not a fighter, there's nowhere for you to run...*

It was true. In his haste to escape, he'd run through the wrong door and ended up not in the hallway but in the medical ward. Rows of empty metal beds, rotten stained mattresses, dirty jars of thick fluid, pigeon feathers scattered on the floor. No exit. He looked back at the door. There was no movement, no attempt to open it from the other side.

*He knows you're trapped.*

Jamie slumped against the wall, reaching up to his head where the locks on his eyes still remained. One had been dislodged slightly in the scuffle and was cutting into the side of his eye. Wincing, he removed the contraption, blinking repeatedly, before turning his attention to the second. It was harder to remove and as he did so, a sharp stab of pain sparked. He let out a sharp exhale, the jagged metal scratching his cornea as the device came away.

Sight clouded and growing worse by the second, he stumbled away from the wall. There had to be a way out.

*You don't fight, you don't run, you hide. That's all you're good at. And there's nowhere to hide here. You're helpless.*

"That's not all I'm good at..." Jamie mumbled to himself. He went over to one of the beds and tried to manoeuvre it into an upright position. The frame was heavy and Jamie's body rebelled against the movements. After a struggle, he managed to set it up and pulled the mattress down to expose the rungs of the frame. He clambered up to the top of the bed and reached up, his fingers brushing the wooden roof beams.

431

Three... two... one...

Jamie jumped, grabbing hold of the beam. He clasped the wood, the splinters digging into his fingers, dust and cobwebs raining down on him like confetti. He pulled himself up onto the beam, his instinct taking over and overriding the pain. When in doubt, get high. Height meant safety.

Balancing on the beam, he crawled to a spot where the roof was patchy. The pigeon feathers had given him the idea. No windows, the roof seemed to be the only possible point of entry for a bird. One hole could mean more.

The blood from his neck and shredded wrists was still flowing, his eye burned and his vision was getting worse. His head was spinning with every movement and he wasn't sure how much longer he'd be able to continue.

He picked his spot and slowly got to his feet, swaying precariously. He wasn't entirely sure that the beam would be able to hold his weight. Jamie pushed up at the roof where the hole was, shoving hard until it began to crumble.

Plaster, tile, grime, bird droppings, moss. Jamie pushed through it all until the hole was big enough. When he could finally fit through and pull himself out onto the roof, brilliant blinding sunlight striking him, he felt victorious. He was bruised, bloody, exhausted. But he was free.

PATIENT DETAILS

Patient Name: J. Alexander

Gender: Male                          P.o.B: Redwood Memorial

Birth Weight: 6 pounds 9 ounces       Birth Height: 19 inches

Blood Type: B

Mother: Helen Alexander               Father: Russell Alexander

Legal Guardian: Michael Harper

Current Residence: Sarum Vale

Hair Colour: Black                    Eye Colour: Brown

| Date of Admission | Age | Symptoms |
|---|---|---|
| June 6th | 2 | Fever |
| November 11th | 2 | Malnourishment |
| July 28th | 4 | Bruises to throat |
| October 12th | 4 | Broken wrist |
| August 14th | 5 | Difficulty breathing |
| September 1st | 6 | Bleeding from anal cavity |
| January 9th | 6 | Dislocated shoulder, frostbite |
| January 19th | 15 | Lacerations to wrist |

# XXXX

Jamie's jubilation didn't last long. The sun, the fresh air, it was intoxicating but reality quickly came crashing down. He'd got out of the building but now he was trapped on a crumbling roof with no way to get down and very little energy. Not quite out of the fire…

Balancing on the edge of the roof, he looked down. Two floors. High ceilings. If he jumped, he'd most likely break something, maybe even die. He'd have to find a way to climb down.

*Jump.*

The impulse came out of nowhere and it took everything not to obey the bizarre thought.

*Jump. Either way, it will make you free.*

His eyes roamed the side of the building. There were ornaments, ledges around the windows, ivy clinging to patches of brick. His mind began to put them together, forming the safest route. Still risky but safer than jumping. He just hoped that he'd be able to make it down and a safe distance from the building before his body gave out. He had no idea how long he'd been in isolation, how long it had been since he'd eaten anything, or what kind of drugs had been pumped into him.

Jamie began to make his way down, using anything he could as a foothold or hand rest. The world tilted sickeningly with each movement and his limbs threatened to give out. A little further, a little further and he'd be safe.

*What next? You have nowhere to go.*

One problem at a time. If he got down and away from the building, then he'd work out the next step and where to go.

A quick glance down showed that he was near the ground. Safe enough to let gravity do the work without worry at least. He released his grip on the brick and let himself fall the last few feet, landing awkwardly and falling backwards. He stared up at the sky for a moment, dazed. His sight had got worse, now barely able to see anything through his injured eye.

Lying in the snow, all Jamie wanted to do was stay there. Rest. Shut down. But he couldn't, not yet.

It took every ounce of his remaining strength to force himself to his feet. He glanced around to make sure there was no sign of anyone who might get in the way of his escape and then bolted. He ran at full speed across the grass to the treeline. Every inhale burned his throat, the blood pounded in his head but he didn't stop. He wouldn't, couldn't, not until he was safe.

Jamie only slowed once he had been swallowed up by the trees, but even then he wouldn't let himself pause for more than a few minutes at a time. It was hard work. The snow was packed firm, making it difficult to move, particularly through the trees where the ground was uneven and hidden roots tried to snare his feet. He knew he needed medical attention, shelter, food, rest. His clothing was useless against the cold, his soft shoes allowing the moisture from the snow to soak into his socks. He needed help but if anyone saw him in his state, they'd send him straight to hospital where Doctor Knott would be able to find him and finish what he'd started. He had to keep going.

*I've not done anything wrong… they're the monsters, why must I hide and flee like an animal?*

He wanted to throw up, collapse, scream, fight, all at once. But mostly, he just wanted to be safe. He wasn't even sure he could remember what that felt like. So many bad things were happening, one after the other… it almost felt like he was on the receiving end of some divine punishment, although for what he didn't know. Surely it wasn't normal to have this much bad luck, it couldn't just be random, could it? It had to be his fault, he was the only common factor… he just didn't know what he was doing wrong.

His legs ached and the thoughts weighed him down even more. Dying cold and alone in the darkness. He'd faced that fate once before and survived. Was it really just so that he could face it again and fail?

*Come on Jamie… you can do it. You are stronger than this. Just a little further, a little more and you'll be safe.*

*****

A dog barked. Lorenzo lifted his head and looked to the door. One of his dogs was pawing at the door, whining insistently and as he watched, more of them gathered. Lorenzo frowned and pushed his dinner to one side before getting to his feet. Tweaking the curtains to one side, he peered out. The world was grey, fat flakes of snow careening wildly through the air. Who'd be out on a night like that?

The dogs had begun to bay in frustration, rearing onto their hind legs as they scrabbled at the wood. Lorenzo glanced at the door to his guest bedroom, suspicion rising.

"About time…" he muttered to himself. He tugged on his boots, grabbed his coat, flashlight and opened the door. The dogs sprinted into the darkness, unconcerned by the fierce wind that buffeted them. Lorenzo clicked on the light and followed them. He had an idea where they'd go.

Sure enough, the dogs headed straight towards the outbuildings, barking loudly at whatever intruder they'd detected. Lorenzo followed, taking his time. He had a fair idea of who he'd find and didn't anticipate any threat to his dogs. By the time he reached the shed, the hounds had circled and one of the younger ones had taken hold of the intruder's arm.

"Baskerville, drop," Lorenzo said firmly. The dog whined but released the limb and stepped back. Lorenzo turned his torchlight to the huddled figure. "Jamie…"

The boy lifted his head and Lorenzo had to force himself not to show the shock he felt. He knew Jamie fairly well. He'd bred and trained the boy's dog and since he was thirteen, Jamie would help out during the summer break. The boy in front of him was barely recognisable as the same person. Matted hair, with chunks pulled out at the roots, a gaunt hollow face, body showing signs of emaciation and neglect. He was holding his fingers in an awkward angle, frost damage already visible and every part of his exposed skin seemed to be bruised or bloody.

"You look like shit."

Jamie lifted his head but didn't speak. His heart was beating so rapidly he was sure it would give out. He'd been so careful. He'd steered clear of town despite wanting nothing more than to go home and curl up in his bed. Now he was cornered. He wasn't afraid of Lorenzo, with his easy smile and boy next door features most people weren't. He wasn't even afraid of the dogs really, though they were certainly more intimidating. What sent his heart racing was the knowledge that after everything he'd endured, it might be all for nothing, that all it would take was a single word from Lorenzo for the dogs to strike, bite, hold, even kill if he wanted them to. He'd hoped he could trust him… but what if he was involved?

The two of them regarded one another, then Lorenzo slowly lowered his flashlight.

"Come on. Let's get you inside before we all freeze."

He pulled the boy up and ushered him towards the house, half-carrying him in places. The dogs followed them, barking joyously.

"I was wondering when you'd show up. What took so long?" Lorenzo asked as they reached the house and went into the kitchen.

"I was in hospital…" Jamie mumbled as he sank into a chair.

"And it looks like you should still be there… you've got some explaining to do Jay. Starting with why you left a pregnant girl in my shed."

"You found her?" Jamie said, bolting upright, wincing immediately after.

"Yes. And next time you should make sure you leave them food so they don't starve to death."

"She's dead?" Lorenzo was startled by the panic in the boy's voice and immediately backpedalled trying to reassure him.

"No! She's fine… now. But when I found her she was not…" he sighed. "This can wait till later. You need food, rest and some dry clothes. After that's done, then you can explain."

Lorenzo busied himself, stoking up the fire and fetching Jamie some food before disappearing upstairs to retrieve a towel and some dry clothes. Jamie yawned and picked at his food, his exhaustion crashing down on him.

"Here," said Lorenzo, returning to the room. He handed Jamie a towel and a small pile of clothing. "You left those here last time."

"And you kept them?" Jamie's lip quirked in a very slight smile.

437

"Of course I did. Get changed and I'll patch you up as best I can. At least you won't bite me like most of my patients."

Jamie struggled to his feet and began to shed his wet clothes, swaying as he did. Lorenzo reached over and steadied him, his hand resting on the young man's upper arm. They looked at one another, Jamie's eyes flickering away and refusing to rest for a moment. Lorenzo wanted to draw his friend close and hold him tight, the look in the teenager's eyes one of complete and utter hopelessness that saddened him. What could have happened to have him to shatter him so entirely?

Fingers trembling, Jamie attempted to remove his top, the frostbitten digits struggling to respond. With his free hand, Lorenzo guided his movements, helping him to lift the sodden cloth and toss it to the floor. Jamie opened his mouth to speak but instead pulled away, turning his back and continuing to change his clothes, working through the pain.

Once dry, Jamie seated himself and Lorenzo took care of his injuries. Most of the cuts were superficial and just required some antiseptic and a bandage. The damage to his eye was a little more severe and all Lorenzo could do was improvise, cleaning it and fashioning a makeshift eye patch so that it could heal without risk of dirt getting in.

"I've done what I can. You have to remember I only have basic first aid and rudimentary veterinary training. I'm not experienced with human patients. I don't suppose I can convince you to see an actual doctor?"

"No."

"Well, then this will have to do. Now, do I need to stick a cone on your head to keep you from chewing your stitches?"

"I think I can restrain myself."

Jamie smiled slightly and finished up his food. He tried to pretend that the recent events were just a bad dream and act like everything was alright, just for a little bit. He still didn't know if he was actually safe but for the time being, he didn't have the strength to make himself care. Lorenzo kept busy and didn't say anything while he ate, but it was comforting having him there. Even once he was done eating, Jamie didn't want to move and instead watched as Lorenzo set up a makeshift bed on the sofa, resting his head on the table and trying to suppress his yawns.

"Time for you to get some sleep," Lorenzo said, in a gentle but firm voice. Jamie nodded and got to his feet, heading towards the sofa. "No, you can take my bed. I'll take the sofa."

"You sure...?"

"Yes. You know where it is right?"

Jamie nodded, allowing a shy smile to show for just a moment before making his way out of the room and up the stairs. Lorenzo watched him go and glanced at his dogs, who had made themselves comfortable in their beds. He made a noise and one of the dogs got up, following the boy to the bedroom. Satisfied that the boy was safe, he finished his evening's tasks and got his beloved pets settled. He was about to head to the sofa but instead, he stopped by the spare bedroom, pushing the door open a little to peek inside.

Curled up under the covers, Eden looked to be asleep. She was peaceful and her face innocent, but something about her unsettled him. What had Jamie got himself mixed up in?

She let out a soft groan and rolled over, shifting restlessly under the covers. Even though her eyes were closed, Lorenzo felt like the girl was watching him. He pulled back, concealing himself behind the door for a moment as she settled down once more. Once she was still, he carefully and silently closed the door. He paused and, after a brief hesitation, slid the latch across.

In Loving Memory

Evelyn. A lover, sister, mother, friend.

You will never be forgotten

# XXXXI

Jamie was woken from a peaceful sleep by the smell of bacon frying. He didn't move at first, just lay in the bed, relishing in the sensation of warmth and safety. He stretched, his limbs obeying him completely for what felt the first time in an age. The pain had almost entirely gone, just some discomfort in his eye remaining.

He got up, testing his legs to make sure they could take him, before making his way to the door. A large dog was stretched out in front of it, head resting on its paws. Jamie paused to give the animal an affectionate pat, then headed out into the hall. Two more dogs were snoozing nearby and despite their relaxed demeanour, he got the impression they were on guard. Protecting him? Or making sure he couldn't run off?

He went downstairs. Lorenzo was cooking, back to the door, and didn't seem to notice Jamie's presence. The teen seated himself at the table, watching in silence as his friend worked.

"Sleep well?" Lorenzo asked after a few minutes had passed.

"Amazing. How long was I out for?"

"Little over two days. You must be starving by now."

He plated up two large cooked breakfasts and handed one to Jamie, who fell enthusiastically on the food. Lorenzo sat opposite him and began his own meal, moving slowly and methodically. Neither of them acknowledged the inevitable conversation to come, Lorenzo unwilling to push the boy too soon and Jamie reluctant to discuss the matter and lose his sense of safety.

"How are you feeling?" Lorenzo asked as they finished up.

"Better. My eye hurts but otherwise, I feel pretty good."

"Good... so... we need to have a talk..."

"Please..." Jamie said softly. "Please don't make me."

"I don't want to Jay, but I need to know. I'm sorry."

Jamie rested his head on the table and let out a long, low groan. He'd hoped that if he kept quiet, Lorenzo might forget or just let it go. No such luck, he should have known better.

"Start with the girl. Who is she? I tried asking but she won't talk to me."

"She doesn't talk to anyone. Her name's Eden Knight... she needed a place to hide for a little bit... I didn't mean to leave her here so long... it was meant to be a temporary measure."

"Okay, that's the who. Now the why."

"She... was in trouble."

"Jamie, I can't help you if you don't tell me the truth. The whole truth."

"She might... have been responsible... for someone dying. But I'm fairly sure it was self-defence!"

"And you were afraid of her getting arrested? So you put her in a shed? Pretty extreme reaction..."

"No... you heard about the bodies in the woods right?"

"The cult killings? Yeah...?"

"Well, the people involved in that seem to want Eden for... something. I think they think she's carrying their messiah or something. I couldn't let them hurt her... and I don't know who's involved. I'm fairly sure someone in the police force is, and if I took her to them for safety she'd just be in even more danger!" Jamie's voice had risen in pitch and the words rushed from his mouth in a garbled mess. Lorenzo reached over and touched his hand, the simple action calming the teenager. His breathing slowed and he closed his eyes, taking a moment.

"Are they after you as well?"

"Yes..." he sighed softly and began to explain everything that had happened to him since Eden had come into his life. When he had finished, Jamie felt like a large weight had been lifted from him. He stared down at the table, following the swirls and knots of the wood, waiting for Lorenzo to speak. When he didn't, Jamie lifted his head slightly. "Do you think I'm crazy?"

"No… and I don't think you're lying either. If you were, you'd probably come up with something more believable." Lorenzo squeezed Jamie's hand. "What are we going to do with you?"

"Are you going to make me go home?"

"I wouldn't put you in danger Jay. But I don't think you can stay here." Jamie eyes went wide in panic and he opened his mouth to protest, but Lorenzo continued before he had a chance. "It's not me being selfish. I'm thinking about your safety. By now, these people know you're free. They're going to be looking for you. Did you tell anyone about our… friendship?"

"No, of course not."

"Not even your friend… that girl… Sammy?"

"No. She'd make a big deal out of it and I didn't want to deal with that."

"Okay… that gives us a bit of extra time. Most likely they'll check the obvious places first. Your house, your friend's, anywhere else you're known to hang out. Then they'll broaden their search. This will probably be one of the last places they check but they will come here. How many of them are there?"

"I saw about fifty at the gathering. There might be more."

"Okay, the more of them are, the quicker they can search. You probably have a day or so… I think the safest thing would be to get you out of town entirely… but the damn snow has blocked the road… alright, you could stay at one of the old hunting cabins for a little bit, just until they've stopped searching, or at least have ruled me out as a hiding place. I can bring you food, blankets and then when the road thaws out, we'll get you far away."

"Eden too?"

"I… Jamie, she'll slow you down… you know that right?"

"Yes. But I'm not going to leave her."

"Well, that's your decision. I won't stop you from doing what you think is right… but she's going to have her kid any day now and that'll be something you'll have to deal with…"

"I'll... make it work. Somehow."

Lorenzo nodded and got up from the table, collecting their plates. The conversation was over and Jamie couldn't help the relief he felt. He had someone on his side. Not just that, but someone who wouldn't brush him off and would actually help him. It was more than he could have dared to hope for.

"How did you know I wouldn't be part of it?" Lorenzo asked as he started the washing up.

"Cause Enzo, that would require you to talk to people," Jamie replied, coming over to help.

Lorenzo laughed and flicked water at him. Jamie smiled a genuine smile that felt strange on his face after so long. They talked as they worked, not about anything big, but just the comfortable minutiae that filled the time and allowed Jamie to pretend once more.

As they were finishing up, Lorenzo went to a cupboard and retrieved a small package wrapped in brightly coloured paper. Jamie frowned.

"What's that?"

"It was your birthday last week."

"It was?"

"You don't know when your birthday was?"

"I don't know what day it is... how long was I gone for?"

"I don't know the exact time... but I was looking after your girl for almost a month before you arrived."

"A month?" Jamie leant against the wall, unable to really believe it. He knew time had passed but not that much. "Bloody hell..."

Lorenzo gently touched his wrist and pressed the package into Jamie's hands. The boy looked down at the package and smiled slightly.

"You didn't need to get me anything."

"I wanted to. Besides, I don't get many chances to celebrate."

"Spending your birthday in an insane asylum is hardly a celebration."

"Hmm... fair point... alright then." He snatched the package back.

"Hey!"

"You can open it tonight. Now, you need to go and get some rest while I run some errands."

"And why should I do that?"

"Because I'm telling you too."

"On what authority?"

"My authority as your temporary doctor."

"Hmm... well, I do know how much you love to play doctor..."

"Bed," Lorenzo said with a grin. "Now Jay."

Jamie rolled his eyes but trotted off upstairs. He lay on the bed, balling the covers between his fingers. He'd spent his last birthday in the hospital and Christmas. He wondered if he'd get to celebrate at home with his family again. If he managed to get out of the town, would he ever be able to come back? It wasn't just a case of hiding and waiting it out. As long as the cult were active and wanted to use him, he wasn't safe. He might never see Callie again... or Sammy or his parents... the last real conversation he'd had with his dad had been a fight. He wouldn't be able to say sorry...

Would they look for him? Would Morningwood tell them he was gone? Or would they find a way to fake his death? Make his very existence disappear?

He wished there was something he could do. Someway he could stay and still be safe... someway to win. But how could you win against someone who couldn't die?

Jamie closed his eyes. A sense of restlessness settled over him. After being trapped for so long, the last thing he wanted was to be inside. He knew that really he should stay in, stay hidden, but...

He got to his feet and gathered some of Lorenzo's clothing. The prospect of going out, not to run or hide but just to be, sparked an unexpected amount of excitement in him and he struggled to pull on the extra layers.

Once suitably clothed, he went down to the kitchen and out the back door. He didn't go any further than the porch but it was enough, just feeling the breeze on his skin, the weak sunlight. It was blissful. He sat down on the frosted wood and stared out at the trees, watching his breath cloud in front of him. Letting his eyes slide shut, he sat there quietly. His mind felt clearer than usual, the voices that so often whispered from the recesses of his brain silent allowing him a sense of peace and clarity that was unfamiliar to him.

In his mind, he saw himself as he had been. A child, dressed in hand-me-down pyjamas, feet bare, pale, thin, bleeding, crying. The memory hurt but not as much as it usually did. It was like he was observing from a great distance, seeing things clearly. His father was drunk, holding a mouse, its paw mangled from a trap, and shouting but he heard none of it. He grabbed hold of Jamie, trying to force the squirming animal down his son's throat. There was a bang from the door, his father went to investigate. Jamie's hand went to the tank, fiddled with the catch but didn't open the lid. He hesitated, about to lock it again when the door to the basement opened. Lily came in, trying to protect him as always. His father grabbed her and half threw her to the ground. Her head collided with the metal stand the tank was balanced on, it swayed but didn't fall.

Jamie rushed to his sister but his father grabbed his arm, pulling it sharply, dislocating it. As Jamie struggled, his father's flailing fists knocked the tank. This time it fell. Glass shattered and two slim black snakes slithered free. One slid out of sight, angry and fearful at the unfamiliar environment and loud sounds. The other struck out. First Lily. Then Jamie. It latched onto his ankle as he was lifted from his feet by his father and dumped in the chest freezer. The lid closed.

Finally, he could think straight. Finally, he didn't have those insidious demons telling him he was useless. He'd always thought of them as the voices of his family. His father, berating him as always, his mother and sister blaming him. They weren't real. His mother and sister were dead. His father was in jail. His memories of that night, always so fuzzy with only the worst parts standing out, were his and he could think clearly. He wasn't to blame for what had happened. He had unlocked the tank, yes, but not opened it. His father had knocked it over. He'd thrown the snake in with his child and left the other to roam the house. He'd let Lily die, letting her bleed on the basement floor.

"It wasn't my fault..." Jamie mumbled. He'd been told that countless times, by doctors, family, and friends. This was the first time he felt that it was true.

Jamie stayed on the porch until Lorenzo came home. When the car parked and his friend got out, he rose to his feet.

"I thought I told you to go to bed?"

"You did. I didn't listen."

Lorenzo examined the teenager's face, noting something different in his expression.

"You alright?"

"I think so."

"Do you want to go in?"

"Not yet."

"I'll put some wood in the burner and get us some drinks then."

Jamie nodded and settled back down. Lorenzo loaded some wood into the heater and disappeared into the kitchen, returning with a bottle of wine, a birthday cake, utensils and Eden in tow. When she saw Jamie, her face split into an exuberant smile and she rushed over, wrapping her arms tight around him. Jamie squeezed her lightly, pleased to see that despite what Lorenzo had said she seemed to be okay. He didn't say anything, he didn't need to.

Eden sat near the burner, watching the sparks flicker out into the evening sky with fascination, and Lorenzo sat beside Jamie, offering him the wine bottle.

"I'm only seventeen," Jamie pointed out.

"It's a special occasion. Besides, with your luck, you may not make it to twenty-one."

"Haha..." Jamie rolled his eyes but took the bottle. Lorenzo began to slice the cake. "You bought me a cake?"

"I did. You only turn seventeen once after all."

"Technically that's true for any age."

447

"Oh shut up."

Jamie laughed and passed the bottle of wine back. The two of them sat in a companionable silence, staring out as the sun disappeared behind the trees and painted the snow in twilight. Eden, growing bored of the fire, came over and rested her head on Jamie's leg. Lorenzo glanced at her, frowning slightly.

"What's the deal with little miss silent but deadly?"

"Don't call her that… she can understand you, even if she doesn't talk," Jamie said more sharply than he intended.

"Sorry… no offence intended. But I am curious as to how you and she got so close in such a short amount of time."

"I don't know… it just kind of happened. We met by accident and… we just get along. I feel like she understands me. Which I don't even feel with my best friend most of the time"

"Must be nice…" Lorenzo passed him the bottle and picked up a piece of cake. He prodded the icing with his fork. "I made you a promise in the summer, do you remember?"

Jamie looked down at his hand and took a gulp of the wine so he wouldn't have to answer straight away. He nodded slightly, not meeting Lorenzo's eye.

"I'm not… I'm not saying that I'm going to fulfil it now. But I wanted to ask if… you still wanted me to?"

"I do… not tonight but I've not changed my mind."

"I'm glad…" Feeling awkward, Lorenzo pushed a plate of cake over to Jamie. "Now, eat your cake."

*****

Despite their intentions, Jamie and Eden continued staying with Lorenzo for another two weeks. They all knew the inevitable departure would come soon but no one wanted to mention it. Lorenzo could see that it was doing Jamie good to be there; he was gaining back the weight he'd lost, sleeping properly for the first time in years and his face no longer held its usual haunted look. He didn't want to jeopardise that… even though he knew that not sending the two of them away was putting them at an even greater risk.

They fell into a comfortable routine. Lorenzo only took local clients during the winter season which meant his workload was low. Instead, they spent their days muddling around the ranch and during the evening they'd cook together. Jamie started to draw again, using the sketchbook and pencils Lorenzo had gifted him. Eden, during the times she wasn't confined to bed, spent her days playing with the dogs or just sitting near Jamie. They were all happy. No one wanted it to end.

As the second week came to an end, Lorenzo finally broke the stand-off. He approached Jamie in the kitchen, hovering nearby.

"I think I've stockpiled enough food for you guys to last a few weeks…"

"We're having that conversation then?" Jamie asked quietly.

"I guess so. I'd love to pretend that they've given up looking for you and we can just carry on like this but the longer we wait, the harder it'll be. I'll take the food up tomorrow and then bring the pair of you up the day after that."

"Okay."

Jamie turned and walked out of the room. Lorenzo watched him go, almost wishing he'd argued.

Once the conversation had happened, the atmosphere changed immediately. That night there was no talk and the air felt heavy with the silence, unlike previous evenings where there had simply been no need to speak because the silence was enough. The only person unaffected was Eden, who seemed oddly distracted and skittish, unable to sit still for longer than a few minutes at a time.

After they'd spent enough time outside to not seem rude, Jamie excused himself and went up to bed. He lay awake, listening to Lorenzo's soft noises from downstairs, the sounds of life. As they faded away, a new sound replaced them. Whispers.

Jamie sat upright sharply and went to the window. Looking down, he saw dark shapes moving through the snow. People. Downstairs, the dogs started to bark, first one and then gradually all of them joined in. Jamie's eyes widened and he raced down the stairs.

"Enzo, wake up!" he yelled, shaking him fiercely. Lorenzo blinked sleepily and sat up. It took him less than a minute to realise what was going on.

"Shit, they found you… get Eden, I'll release the dogs and you'll just have to run for it."

Jamie nodded and ran to Eden's room. She was awake, standing in the middle of the room. Jamie grabbed her hand, locking eyes with her. They communicated silently, his eyes telling her everything she needed. The two of them went to the back door and peeked out. The ranch had erupted in chaos, Lorenzo's dogs running wild, chasing after the intruders. Jamie caught Lorenzo's eye and he nodded to him. Jamie bit his lip, clasped Eden's hand tightly in his and ran from the house.

**Name:** *Faith Knight*

**Period**: *5th*    **Subject**: *English*    **Assignment**: *Poetry*

**Task:** *Write a poem about betrayal*


## The Consequences of Betrayal

Time tiptoes past like a wounded animal
leaving behind a bloody trail of a tortured past.

My body is stitched together
like Frankenstein's monster
made of painful memories
and bruises.

Each cut on my skin
maps my path from
one nightmare to another
and back.

Although time passes, each scar is unhealed
each wound bites as deep as the last.

# XXXXII

The sound of voices ebbed. Huddled in a tiny hollow, Jamie dared lift his head. They'd made it to the trees, unnoticed in the chaos as Lorenzo managed to drive the intruders back. That was the last thing Jamie had seen before the forest had swallowed them up. The pair had run for as long as they could but it became clear quickly that Eden was struggling. Rather than risk making her continue, Jamie had directed them to the earth alcove they now lay in.

It was cold, the ground, although relatively free of snow, was frozen solid and coated in frost. Eden buried her face in Jamie's chest, gripping his top. Every few minutes she would tense, her hand tightening around the fabric before relaxing once more, and stifled groans would slip from her lips. Jamie held her close, doing what he could to alleviate the pain she was in. His mind was whirring, trying to work out their next step. It didn't sound like they'd been followed but he wasn't sure. Either way, he knew they couldn't stay where they were.

Jamie considered trying to get them to the cabin. It wouldn't be stocked like they'd originally planned but at least it would provide some shelter. And maybe Lorenzo would think to check there and bring them what they needed.

But… its miles away and most of the journey is uphill, Jamie reminded himself. Eden wouldn't manage that.

He called up every bit of information he had about the forest, any place that might provide a viable hideout for them, even just for a few hours. Eden groaned and her fingers dug into his skin. Jamie felt a dampness on his leg and something concerning occurred to him. Was Eden…?

"Eden we need to move," he said softly. "Do you think you can walk for a little while?"

Eden nodded and tried to get up, but the movement sent another burst of pain and she was forced to sit down. Jamie considered for a moment and then picked her up. He wasn't as strong as he had once been and Eden wasn't as light, but he would manage.

They set off, Eden whimpering in Jamie's arms as the pain continued, coming in waves that washed over her before receding once more.

Jamie tried to comfort her, spewing soft nothings, trying to reassure her that everything would be okay when really he had no idea what was going to happen to them. Eden looked up at Jamie with a peculiar expression on her face, a kind of awe like she was looking at some kind of great hero. She smiled slightly, touching his cheek lightly with a trembling hand.

The pair of them reached a patch where the trees thinned and the ground began to slope. Jamie knew that they were straying dangerously close to the cult's hunting ground and he could hear the sound of the nearby river that snaked around it. He'd have to be careful. He didn't know if there would be anyone in the area but even if there wasn't, he didn't want to risk getting too close to the entrance to the underground and having his mind stolen by the whispers that lurked there.

He paused, getting a sense of the direction and adjusted accordingly. It would take longer but he wasn't prepared to put either of them in danger. Eden let out a weak cry, trying to cover her mouth as the noise escaped her. Jamie froze, eyes darting around for any disturbance that might indicate they'd been heard.

"You really need to stay quiet..." he whispered. "I know you're in pain but if they find us, it'll be much worse."

Eden nodded and bit into her knuckle, using her fist as a barrier against any errant sounds that might try to flee.

Satisfied that they hadn't been noticed, Jamie continued, slowly and carefully as the terrain grew more unsteady. He remembered how much he'd struggled when he'd escaped from Morningwood. Compared to that, this should be easy. He had shoes, proper sturdy ones that he'd shoved on before bolting. He was in a better condition, he should be able to manage, even with the added weight of Eden in his arms.

Out of the corner of his eye, he spotted a patch of brown among the blanket of white. Ground, uncovered. No rocks, no roots, just even ground with a layer of frosted leaves laying on top. He sighed in relief and headed towards it. It would make things a little easier, at least for a short time.

As Jamie walked, his eyes took in the surroundings. The snow was piled high either side of the blank patch, higher than it went anywhere else in the forest and the irregular hillocks almost looked like someone had shovelled it out of the way.

No sooner had the thought occurred to him, then the ground beneath his feet gave way and he fell through empty space. The two of them landed in a heap at the base of a large square hole. Dazed, Jamie lay there, staring up at the sky obscured by skeletal branches. His back hurt, his legs hurt, his head hurt. Eden, however, was unharmed, having landed on top of him rather than on the ground. She clambered off of him, running her gaze over him to see if he was badly hurt.

"I'm fine…" Jamie mumbled, disorientated.

God, I'm stupid… I've seen these traps before… I should have realised!

Although the Sarum woods had strict rules when hunting that forbade the use of traps that might result in injury to other hunters or hikers, his uncle had shown him a few of his favourites. The pit was one of them. It always seemed like a lot of effort to Jamie, until his uncle had explained that he would only use it for the most important quarry. The ones who were worth putting in the effort for.

Head still spinning, Jamie got up. Eden had retreated to a corner of the pit and was breathing heavily, emitting agonised moans. No way out. Even if he could climb up, he wouldn't be able to get Eden up there in her condition. And they knew that.

"I messed it all up…" he whispered, sinking back down. "If I hadn't gone to Lorenzo, you would have been safe. They wouldn't have known where to find you… if I'd just looked around we wouldn't be in this fucking… nightmare."

Jamie grabbed a small stone and hurled it at the wall, sending chunks of dirt raining down on them. He dropped his head to his hands, closing his eyes.

Maybe Lorenzo had been right. Maybe he should have left Eden behind. She'd have been safe at the house, he'd have been safer in the woods. But no, he had to try and play hero…

Snap out of it! Yes, maybe you messed up but right now Eden needs your help. She looks up to you, you got her into this mess, you need to take care of her. You can't back out when things get tough, that's not how life works.

Jamie took a deep breath and opened his eyes, looking over at Eden. Her face was screwed up in pain and she was wailing intermittently. He needed to help her. Even if he didn't know what to do, he had to try and do something.

He thought of what he'd seen on TV, what they'd told them about birth in health class. None of it seemed helpful.

"Fuck… okay, Eden, you're having your baby and I have no idea what to do… but I'm not going to leave you and we'll get through this," he told her, coming over to her.

Eden gave him an irritated look, clearly disinterested in his epiphany. Jamie took her hand and tried to help regulate her breathing. She squeezed his hand so tightly he was sure the bones would break and let out an animalistic scream. Birds fled from the trees and Jamie heard the familiar chorus of whispers start up. As Eden wailed, they emerged, sliding forward to gather around the pit. There were more than Jamie had seen before, even in the depths of Morningwood. They grouped together, giving the impression that the ground was coated in tar, but came no further than the edge.

Jamie eyed them warily, uncomfortable having them so close but knowing he had to focus on Eden for the time being. He felt like they were watching him, watching them both. He tried to concentrate on Eden as she groaned and sobbed, racked with pain, but he couldn't help the tentative glances he shot in the direction of the creatures.

Time ticked by and every moment felt like an eternity. The moon moved across the sky and disappeared behind the horizon, replaced with the rising sun. The shadows didn't move, Eden continued to pant as her contractions grew harder to deal with, Jamie felt more and more useless with every passing minute.

He was almost relieved when he heard footsteps approaching, the crunch of shoes on snow. The shadows fled, to be replaced by six figures in hooded cloaks, each wearing masks made of animal skulls. A few were carrying rifles which they trained on Jamie.

"Well now, look at what we have here…" said a familiar voice from behind one of the masks. Adam. Of course.

"You realise you could have killed both of us with this?" Jamie asked, glaring up at them.

"Yes. But it was a risk we had to take since you refused to cooperate."

He nodded to his companions and one of them dropped a knotted rope into the pit for Jamie to use to climb out. Jamie glanced at Eden who was cowering in fear in the corner and reluctantly climbed from the pit. After all, what choice did he have? They'd make him if he refused and even if they didn't, he'd just be stuck in the hole which wasn't any better.

Once Jamie had made it out of the pit, one of the figures levelled their gun at his forehead while another secured his hand. With Jamie restrained, the rest worked together to lift Eden from the hole. Jamie stayed quiet, focusing on the people. Maybe if he got away, he could use what he'd seen and heard to identify some of them.

"She's in labour, we'll need to move fast."

"You two carry the girl. I'll deal with our little runaway," Adam instructed. Two of the figures picked Eden up and began to carry her away from the hole. Adam took the end of the rope tied around Jamie's wrists and tugged, pulling him like a disobedient dog. The rest of the group followed, one close behind with the barrel of his gun pressed into Jamie's back.

They moved through the trees, an odd little procession that Jamie would have laughed at had he seen it anywhere else. It reminded him of a parade, the robes, the masks, it was so bizarre and theatrical. The eight of them marched across the snow, the forest oddly silent around them. Even the birds were quiet, perched in the trees looking down at them with sombre faces.

The group reached the rock pile that marked the entrance of the underground caverns. There were more cloaked figures gathered and a small contingent of them moved to help with Eden. She was set down on the ground nearby and they flocked around her, kneeling down. Jamie briefly caught the sound of a voice encouraging Eden to push, telling her what to do but he was quickly escorted away from them and up onto the rocks. Someone had set up four wooden stakes in the ground, with ropes lashed to them. Jamie was pushed to the ground, his arms roughly lifted above his head and quickly tethered to the stakes. His legs received the same treatment, leaving him strung up like an animal for slaughter. The cloaked figure he'd identified as Adam looked down at him and even with the mask on, Jamie knew he was smiling.

"Brethren, today is a joyous occasion. All our ambitions come to fruition and tonight the Master will be freed from his unjust prison. Behold our vessel!"

The gathering each raised their left hand.

"Hail to the vessel!"

"Prepare him."

Two of the gathering stepped forward and took hold of Jamie, stripping him of his clothes and leaving him in just his underwear.

From nearby, he heard a piercing scream from Eden. He tried to twist so to see her but his restraints made it impossible.

"Please don't hurt her!"

"Relax, we won't. As soon as she's given birth she'll be free to go. We only need the child," Adam told him.

Eden struggled against the hands holding her still. Her legs had been pulled apart by rough hands, exposing her most intimate areas. Slim fingers probed and grasped, a moment later a broken cry filled the air. One of the cultists produced a small knife and separated the baby from its mother. Eden lay there whimpering and reached for the squirming, squalling infant. She went ignored, the cultist carrying the child over to Adam.

"It's a boy. We have our final element. The vessel, the bride and the blood."

Adam took a knife from inside his cloak and lowered the point to the baby's skin. Jamie grimaced and closed his eyes, expecting the child's cries to fall silent but they seemed to increase. He dared to open one eye and saw that Adam had simply made a tiny cut on the baby's hand. Adam carefully daubed symbols on Jamie's forehead, chest, stomach and the soles of his feet, using the blood as crude ink.

There was another sharp wail that briefly drew the attention of the crowd in time to see a second child being placed in Eden's arms.

"Twins?" a female voice asked, surprised. Lilith.

"It would appear so."

"Hmm… always handy to have a spare I suppose."

"Should we secure her?"

"No, she won't be a problem in her current state."

Eden slumped, clutching her second born, breathing heavily, the inside of her legs slick, clothing dirty and damp. She looked over at Jamie, helpless, surrounded, at the mercy of monsters.

Adam handed the first child to Lilith and focused his attention on Jamie. He raised both hands, palms facing the sky.

"We offer this boy as vessel, in the hopes that the Master will find his soul worthy and free him from the mortal realm. We offer the blood of the Master, his sacrifice made us strong and with it, we shall be led into a new dawn. We offer the bride, the innocent whose spirit will bow and whose body will break as our Master walks amongst us once more."

"Blessed be the vessel. Blessed be the blood. Blessed be the bride."

"Let the blood seep into the soil as seed to egg and let the Master break from the earth as the child emerges from the womb."

Adam moved sharply and sliced the blade across Jamie's hand. He cried out in pain. Blood bubbled up and flowed down the boy's fingers, dripping onto the earth.

The air went still, no one even dared to breathe. At first, there was silence. Above them, the sky seemed to darken and the sound of flapping wings filled the air. Birds erupted from the trees, soaring upwards. More and more gathered, flocking together until they blocked out the sun entirely. Jamie's body contorted in pain and he twisted against the restraints. His body jerked sharply, skin rippling and bones snapping. He let out an agonised roar, a sound that was barely human. His breathing was rapid, sweat poured from his skin. Shadows coated his skin, his veins blackened and his eyes clouded.

Jamie fell still once more, glassy eyes staring up at the sky vacantly. He blinked once, twice, eyes darting around as though registering his surroundings.

"Untie me," he said. His voice was unchanged but something about the tone made it seem deeper almost. Lilith made the first move, reaching over and untying the boy. He got to his feet, eyes narrowed, examining the assembly. "Bring the girl to me. And the children."

One of the cultists helped Eden up and ushered her over, where Lilith handed her the other child. She clutched them both to her, looking at Jamie with terrified eyes. He smiled at her and gently touched her cheek, his fingers caressing the soft skin.

"My love, I have missed you."

He pulled back, closed his eyes and stretched, rolling his neck. His lip curled slightly, a wicked smirk forming. The beating of wings overhead grew louder, joined by the voices of the whispers. The cultists shifted uncomfortably, looking at one another in confusion.

Then the gun went off.

HR COMPLAINT FORM

**Date of Complaint:** 29th October

**Full Name of Person Filing Complaint:** Dr Jade Ng

**Nature of Complaint**: Inappropriate behaviour

**Name of Person the complaint is against:** Dr Adam Knott.

**Details of Complaint:** Frequently aggressive and ignores consultation from other staff.

**The effect on the person filing the complaint:** Unable to take full care of patients due to interference.

# XXXXIII

The shot rang through the trees and for a moment, the world seemed to slow down. The cultists turned, confused and trying to work out what had happened. Their attention was drawn to a member of the congregation, spread-eagled on the floor. Their weapon was clutched in their limp hand, their mask had been removed but there was no face to expose. Instead, it revealed a bloody mess of flesh surrounding a hole where the bullet had made impact.

There was barely any time to react. Another gunshot went off. And then another. Panic and confusion spread through the masses. First came the fear that they were under attack but that was quickly replaced as one by one they were seized by a fierce urge, an unquenchable hunger to destroy themselves. Those who were armed turned their guns on themselves. Those without began to grab rocks to beat themselves with, began to claw at their faces, anything they could to try to injure themselves.

Across town, the whispering began. It started quietly but grew into a crescendo that spread like a wildfire from house to house, each new place, new person that it caught making it burn stronger. The whispering was followed by a terrible pain, radiating through the brains of its victims and then came the desire.

At the school, Callie was sat at her desk. Her hearing aids let out a high pitched whistle, piercingly sharp. She winced and pulled them from her ears, momentarily disorientated by the noise. The teacher paused at the board, in the middle of writing something for the class. She stood there, swaying slightly on the spot. Her eyes rolled back in her head and she turned away from the board. Moving slowly, she went over to her desk. The actions weren't robotic or unnatural in any way, they seemed perfectly relaxed in fact. The teacher picked up a pair of scissors from her desk, spread the blades wide and calmly stabbed them into her eyes.

Callie leapt to her feet. No one else reacted. They got up as one. Some of the children took objects, pencils, scissors, anything sharp. Some left the room, heading for the roof of the building. Callie panicked and bolted from the room. The halls were full of students, teachers, and other staff. They were all involved in the same tasks, taking their lives by any means they could. As Callie ran, searching for someone to help, she saw kitchen staff with knives embedded deep into any part of their body they could reach, a janitor with a thick extension cord tied around his neck, a teacher dangling from the gym equipment, two children shovelling bits of tissue down their throat in an effort to choke themselves. Each of them acted with a smile frozen on their faces.

The hospital had erupted into chaos. Patients and doctors alike were in the grip of a terrible frenzy. Carts lay overturned in the halls, scalpels and syringes were scattered across the floor. IV lines had been ripped from veins and fistfuls of pills crammed into mouths. An ambulance swerved and crashed into the front entrance, the paramedic's head slamming against the steering wheel.

In the ER, Ruth Harper had been on the phone with her husband when her entire body seemed to freeze. The phone slipped from her hand and hit the floor, breaking apart. With a steady hand, she picked up a syringe and filled it with fluid from a nearby bottle. She jabbed the needle into the crook of her arm and pushed down on the plunger, letting the liquid flow into her veins.

A similar scene had begun at the police station. One by one the officers left their desk and went to the gun locker, retrieving a firearm each. However, instead of taking fire at themselves, they filed out of the station and headed into the town square, moving in a rigid line. They took position in the centre of the square, each facing a different direction. The locals, those unable to find their own way out, began to gather in front of the makeshift firing squad.

Aim, fire, and reload. Aim, fire, and reload.


Trapped inside his own head, Jamie saw it all through the eyes of the shadows. He screamed, trying to break free from the dark influence that had taken control of his body. Eden was stood beside him, seemingly unaffected and clutching the babies to her chest as the horror unfolded before them.

*Stop this!* He tried to yell, but no words came.

***Ahh… hello, again Jamie. I told you that I wasn't finished with you. Things are a bit different this time… but I do like having you around so be a good boy and I won't erase you entirely.***

Slowly, the sounds faded. The ground was littered with bodies, robes torn, masks scattered. Not all were dead, some were only injured, bleeding slowly. One, shorter than the others, lay face down in the dirt, groaning weakly. Coils of black hair peeked out from under the folds of scarlet cloth that made up her robes, streaks of red and blue interspersed throughout.

Adam was cowering by a tree, mask lost in the chaos and Jamie saw him clearly for the first time. A coward, a bully who had no real power when faced with someone stronger.

The creature operating Jamie's body advanced on the man, crouching so their faces were level.

"Hello, Adam. It has been a long time."

"Why are you doing this? I gave you your freedom! You should be grateful!" Adam snapped.

"Grateful!" The word flew aggressively from his mouth like venom. He paused, took a deep breath and when he next spoke, his voice was smooth and quiet but completely deadly. "I am grateful Adam. You brought me back to the world. You also stole my life from me. You murdered my child and condemned me to rot in the dirt for eternity."

He seized Adam by the throat, lifting him clear off his feet.

"Yes, and I'm sorry! I didn't mean for any of that to happen, that's why I worked so hard to bring you back!"

"I am no fool, Adam. I watched, I listened. I know you only brought me back to fulfil your needs. You tried to lobotomise the boy so I would be helpless in this form. And now I intend to show you just how grateful I am and give you everything that you deserve."

He tightened his grip, face blank and expressionless. Adam gasped and struggled, flailing helplessly. No longer a threat, he was more like a bug to be squashed. Nearby, Lilith, knocked down in the chaos, got to her feet. She saw what was happening to her husband, her followers and turned to flee.

"Stop right there Lilith. Do not think you will be unpunished for your part in this. If you run, you will not get far." He didn't look at her the entire time he spoke, his eyes fixed on Adam. Even so, she fell still instantly, head bowed like a chastised child.

"Are you going to kill me, Aris?" Adam wheezed, letting out a raspy laugh as he scratched at the hands-on his throat.

"I have spent centuries trapped, longing for death. Do you really think I would let your life end that quickly?"

He clenched his fist, cutting off Adam's ability to talk. Locked away, Jamie couldn't help but feel the smallest amount of satisfaction. But still… he couldn't let himself become a killer. The hand at Adam's throat faltered for a moment. Something flickered behind the eyes, the smallest trace of humanity.

*Please stop this.*

**You want this as much as I do… I have been with you for far longer than they know. I know how much you covet his destruction.**

*I am not a killer. I will not let you use my body for this.*

**I gave you a warning. If you argue, I will silence you. If you fight me, I will tear out your heart.**

*That would just kill you…*

**A heart can be made of many things.**

Images danced across Jamie's eyes. Callie, reading in her bed. Callie, cowering against her wall. Callie, stood in the bathroom, shivering. Callie, sleeping peacefully, a hand brushing her cheek.

**She really is quite a fetching little thing. They always are at that age. Trusting eyes, sweet innocent smiles. I have always had rather a taste for… soft things. There is something deliciously exquisite about breaking them.**

A new image. Callie pinned to her bed, sobbing, claw-like hands raking her skin to shreds.

**I may have my Eden back but, sometimes you hunger for something different. You of all people know that.**

"Don't you dare!"

He said the words aloud, the force of Jamie's anger allowing him to leak through for just a moment. Adam blinked, confused. The internal conversation had taken barely a second and the outburst seemed out of place to the onlookers.

*It's an easy decision. Be a good boy, let me play with this man who would see you dead or I will force you to watch as I destroy the one you love the most. Choose.*

There was no choice. Jamie let himself slip back into the darkness, falling silent. Shame washed over him, unable to believe what he was allowing to happen. But there was no other way.

*That's better. It's so much easier when you play nice.*

He released Adam, letting him drop to the floor. A look of relief appeared on the man's face, which quickly vanished as dark eyes were trained on his legs. With a sickening snap, they twisted, bending until the bones broke. One jutted out, piercing the skin.

"Just to ensure you do not run off while I speak to your jezebel." He stalked towards Lilith, who kept her eyes fixed on the ground.

"Please, my lord, I had no part in this deception. I sought only to free you."

"I know sweet child. You just wanted to help your husband. There is no shame in that."

"Yes, I just... I just did what he said! I didn't know why he was doing it!"

He reached up and touched Lilith's cheek. He sighed softly.

"Oh, what a vicious creature is a prideful woman. I may not have lived through the last years but I have listened. I know the stories. A man may destroy. They are hunters, animals at heart. But a woman has a power that is far greater. They can bring empires to ruin and cause men to obey their every command. They wrote stories about you, Lilith. The woman who refuses to obey. Salome. The one who dances and ensnares men to do her bidding. Lamia. Consumer of flesh. These are all you." He smiled kindly at Lilith. "Which is why I know that you were the true leader of this. You orchestrated everything. All Adam would have wanted was to be with his dear Evelyn. He would not have cared where. Which is why you got rid of her. To take back the control you had lost."

465

His hand fisted in her hair, pulling roughly at the blonde locks. Lilith's eyes went wide and her face paled. The veins on her body bulged and darkened. Her skin began to wither, dry and crack, growing tight around her bones. Her eyes became misty, her body seemed to shrink as the years piled onto her, leaving her shrivelled and decaying.

Releasing Lilith, he stepped back, smiling as he examined his handiwork.

"You are free to go Lilith. You wanted the world, it is yours. Let us see how far you get without your beauty."

He turned away, intending to return his focus to Adam. Instead, his eyes were caught by Eden. She was crying silently, clutching the babies in her arms.

"My love, do you feel sorry for these people?" He asked, approaching her. "They are monsters who prey on the weak and whose lives mean less than nothing. I am doing the world a favour by ensuring they do not pollute it further."

He offered Eden his hand. When she didn't move to take it, he wrapped his arms around her instead and placed a soft kiss on her forehead.

"I will be finished soon. And then the four of us can be together like we were always meant to."

Eden nodded slightly and stepped back. As he approached Adam, she silently sidled away, distancing herself slightly from him and the massacre site.

Adam was letting out soft groans, head resting against the trunk of the tree. He looked at the boy with hooded eyes, seeing the mannerisms of a man he had not seen in a long time. No trace of Jamie. No chance to appeal to the naïve teenager who might grant him mercy.

"You will spend the next thousand years in the dirt. And since you miss your dear Evelyn so much... so much that you never cared to search for her... you will get to spend that time with her. Maybe after that, I will look upon you with kindness and allow you the reprieve of death."

He placed a hand on either side of Adam's head, filling his brain with memories of Evelyn. But not as he had known her. No smile, no laughter. Every sign of happiness was stripped away from her. He saw her suffering, alone in darkness and when he reached out to her, she would look at him with sad eyes and tell him that he was to blame.

"I will tell you one last thing before I leave you to rot..." The monster said in Jamie's soft voice. "She never loved you back. You were her worst fear. She wanted nothing more than to be free of you. That is why I let Lilith off easy... her actions were cruel but she did Evelyn a kindness in the end."

He went to lift Adam up, intending to dump him in the hole that led to the underground, but something stopped him. His ears picked up the sound of a baby crying but it was distant.

"Eden?" He turned sharply. Eden was gone, leaving a trail of footprints in the blood-splattered snow. Jamie, sulking sullenly, stirred once more as his puppeteer abandoned Adam and began to follow the tracks.

*Where is she taking us?*

*You. There's no us.*

**She cares for you. It's one of the reasons I chose you initially.**

*Yippee...*

Eden's path led them up a slight incline to a rocky gorge overlooking the river. Jamie was startled by how quickly she had been able to move in such a short space of time. She must have known where she was going... there was no hesitation in her footsteps, it didn't seem like a random choice.

She was waiting for them at the top of the gorge, babies in her arms, looking down at the river. A thin layer of ice had formed over it but underneath the water still flowed, wild and angry.

"Eden my love, why have you come here?"

*What is she doing...?*

Eden turned and smiled. She beckoned, the action awkward with her arms full. They approached, both watching through their shared eyes. Eden kissed each of the children on their head, clutching them to her chest. She smiled once more, a sad faraway smile and her eyes showed an unusual peace for her.

*Oh no... Eden... No...*

Balancing the children, she wrapped one arm around Jamie's body and kissed him lightly. A silent message to the boy still lingering inside.

Then, still holding onto them, Eden stepped back off the edge of the cliff.

Eden knew pain, she knew well about the different types a person could endure and keep breathing. There was the pain that came with hunger and the burning pain that came from thirst. There was the twisting pain that came when the blood flowed between her legs. The pain when her body turned in on itself and ripped out the bitter seeds that took root inside her belly. The pain of being torn open by creatures that had never drawn breath.

But those passed. There was also the one that never went away. The pain that started when He came for her the first time. The same pain she saw in Jamie's eyes and in Faith's.

But as she fell, the pain disappeared. There was nothing. Even as they hit the ice, shattering it and sinking into the depths of the freezing water, there was nothing. She was free.

Jamie, screaming inside his head, tried to hold onto her but it was no good. The current pulled them apart and washed her away.

The trees were still, branches entangled with one another. It was almost like they were holding hands. A thin layer of frost clung to every surface, but the snow had almost completely melted away. Only a few small patches of grey sludge still lingered. The sun was disappearing behind the horizon, a narrow strip of washed-out blue sky still visible. Perched up high, a nightingale began to trill a soft song, clear and strong.

A crowd had gathered in the town square which was illuminated by candles and small lanterns. A podium had been erected and on it the mayor stood, watching the assembly as they fell silent.

"Good evening everyone. Thank you for joining me tonight. A year ago, our town was rocked by tragedy. We lost many good people in a disaster that left no one untouched. Tonight we remember those we have lost, not in sadness but in celebration of their lives. The time for mourning is at an end and now we can look forward to a positive future. Tonight we eat, we drink, and we honour the fallen. If anyone wishes to come up and speak, please feel free."

A quiet ripple of applause ran through the crowd. A year had passed but the memories were still fresh, the pain still raw. What made it worse was the uncertainty. No one really knew what had caused the events of that night. Theories ranged from terrorists releasing hallucinatory drugs into the air to alien abductions. All anyone actually knew was the aftermath. Over a hundred dead. Many more gravely wounded. Men, women, children, no one had been spared.

Stood in the crowd, Lorenzo looked around. His scar itched, a long thin line across his shoulder where he'd stabbed in a kitchen knife, but he knew that he'd got off lightly compared to some. He'd passed out shortly after he'd pulled the knife out, preventing him from doing anything worse.

Lorenzo spotted Sammy standing by the memorial that had been set up next to the podium, a board of pictures of the deceased, with a few absences. There had been a lot of arguments over whether or not to include the fallen cultists on the board, some arguing that they had still been members of the community with families who would miss them while others pointed out that their actions removed any goodwill they may have built up. Twenty-seven bodies had been found in the woods. Sixteen more had been found injured and were awaiting trial now they had recovered. The rest had vanished.

470

Lorenzo slipped away from the gathering and headed to the cemetery. He paused at the fence, looking across the grounds to where a lone figure knelt. As though sensing his presence, the figure rose and turned.

Jamie had changed in the year. He wore the expression of a battle-hardened soldier, rather than the teenager he was and his eyes showed exhaustion deeply ingrained into his soul. Bloody, broken, he'd been found sitting amongst the dead in the forest. No one knew how he'd ended up there or what had happened to him. He refused to discuss it with anyone.

"You're missing the celebration," said Jamie, approaching the fence.

"I don't feel like celebrating... I thought we were coming up here tomorrow, with the kids?"

"I needed some time by myself..." Jamie replied, looking away. Lorenzo grasped his hand.

"You know you can talk to me, right?"

"Of course." He manufactured a cheery smile. "Where are the kids? Don't tell me you lost them again?"

"No, I left them with your friend Ashlyn. She's keeping them out of trouble. Now... are you coming back to the memorial? Or... do you need more time?"

"I'm fine. We should head back."

Jamie looked back at the graves he'd been standing by. Three old, two new. He sighed and went to join Lorenzo on the other side of the fence. The two of them made their way back towards the gathering. Candles had been lit and the whole place had a warm, festive look to it. Ashlyn was sat on a bench, Callie and Faith sat next to her, a double pushchair in front of her. Inside were two young boys, each a year old. Their birth certificates listed them as Mark and Sean Harper. Jamie had opted to distance them from their mother's family, fearing it might put them in danger.

After a year, most of the staring had stopped, but people still wondered just where the twins had come from. They'd been in Jamie's arms when he'd been found and although most people had a hunch about their parentage, no one knew the truth.

Some people still stared and, although he had no way of knowing for certain, he felt sure they were the survivors of the cult wondering if he was still a threat. And well they might...

Jamie felt eyes burning into his back and he half turned. Adam was stood a short distance away, leaning on his walking stick. Jamie hadn't seen him since the night in the woods although he knew that he was still around, cooped up in the hospital recovering from his injuries.

"I'll be right back," he muttered to Lorenzo who followed his gaze.

"Need a hand?"

"No... he doesn't scare me anymore."

Jamie headed towards the doctor, who slipped away into a secluded spot. He couldn't suppress a sadistic glee at seeing his tormenter wince as they moved.

"How's the leg?"

"Fine," Adam said through gritted teeth.

"Shame... so what do you want? Are you going to threaten me? Or just spew a bunch of clichés about vengeance being yours?"

"Neither.... I want to know what happened to Eden."

Jamie froze, taken by surprise.

"She... she fell..."

"Fell?"

"Jumped. Into the river. Took us down with her but..."

"You survived and she didn't," Adam said bitterly, cutting him off.

"I guess someone out there wants me to stick around for a bit longer."

"Is that so..." Adam's voice had turned icy and his expression was one of intense loathing.

"Problem?" Jamie asked with an amused smile.

"No. But you should remember Jamie that we are still here. We know who you are and you know nothing about us. We could be your neighbour, your teacher, anyone on the street. And you would never know. You live by our grace. Bear that in mind before you start causing trouble for us."

Jamie's expression didn't change. He stepped closer to Adam and his smile grew. When he spoke, his voice seemed deeper, his words clipped and deadly.

"And you should bear in mind Adam that your pathetic life exists because I grant you clemency. Do not push me or I will change my mind. And you have seen just what I can do when enraged..."

A flicker of fear passed across Adam's eyes.

"You're bluffing. If he was still in your body, I'd be able to walk out of this town."

"Maybe... but after our last conversation... do you want to risk it?" Adam looked away. "I thought not."

Jamie turned away and walked back to the memorial, smiling to himself. The sound of nightingales in the trees reached his ears. Sometimes when he heard them singing, he imagined Eden as one of them, flying free and for a little while, things weren't so bleak.

Printed in Great
Britain
by Amazon